praise for the mark of the faerie series

"A magical tale of "what if." This story drew me in & cannot wait to interview Patricia for the podcast."
—Vikki Carter, *Authors of the Pacific Northwest* podcast, interview available for listening at: MarkOfTheFaerie.com

"This series of fairy tales is one of the best that I have read. It's exciting, romantic and fun to read. Can't wait for the rest of the series, books 4 & 5, to be available."
—Pamela, Amazon Review

"The second book in this series is as good as the first. Both are fast paced and make you want to turn the page. Patricia Rae knows how to keep the reader interested. I recommend it to those that like adventure stories."
—Susan, Goodreads Review

"I was drawn to this book because of my family's Scottish roots and the fact that this was going to be a series. Knowing that the story would continue with the same people meant that I would be able to enjoy the story over a period of time. Patricia's character development in this first book painted a colorful picture of each one and I was able to make a visual connection with her detailed descriptions. Great read, Patricia, for your first book. And so the journey begins…I'm hooked"
—Bobi, Goodreads Review

"Excited to read the next book in the series! The story line is fun & adventurous, set in Scotland. The characters are colorful, spunky, and the author does a great job developing them throughout the first 2 books. The story line is fun fantasy, but with some reality weaved throughout. These are fun easy reads!"
—River Girl, Amazon Review

"I finished book one and I loved it! You pull us right into the story and I could see the story come to life as I read it. On to book 2."
—Carolyn, Facebook comment

"Love the story line, I can easily visualize it as I read them."
—Terry, Facebook comment

"So well written it ties you into the story and to the characters! And different realms of existence! You never know! I'm excited to add these to my library without a doubt!"
—Erica, Amazon Review

"I purchased all three of your books today at the Renaissance fair in Moscow. Please keep me updated when any new works come out and I will gladly purchase it. I haven't been able to put the 1st book down!"
—Alexandria, Facebook comment

OF LACE AND LIONS

MARK OF THE FAERIE SERIES

Of Lace and Lions

Book IV of *Mark of the Faerie*

Patricia Rae

RaeDiance Productions

Books may be ordered through booksellers or from the publisher's website:

www.MarkoftheFaerie.com

Paperback ISBN: 978-1-7345528-9-8
E-book ISBN: 979-8-218-21047-2
Library of Congress Control Number: 2023909102

Cover and book design by Longfeather Book Design
All book cover artwork assigned to and owned by
RaeDiance Productions

I dedicate this book to my six beautiful grandchildren:
Stella, Mia, Tristan, Landon, Delilah and Bennett.
Seeing the world through their eyes keeps me young at heart
and fills my imagination with wonderment.

THE FLOATING ISLAND OF LUMINARA

THE LANDS OF THE UNDERLINGS
SILVERLEAF
ROGAURGH
SASHTONIA
TEREMENIA
EUPHORIA
NACMORID

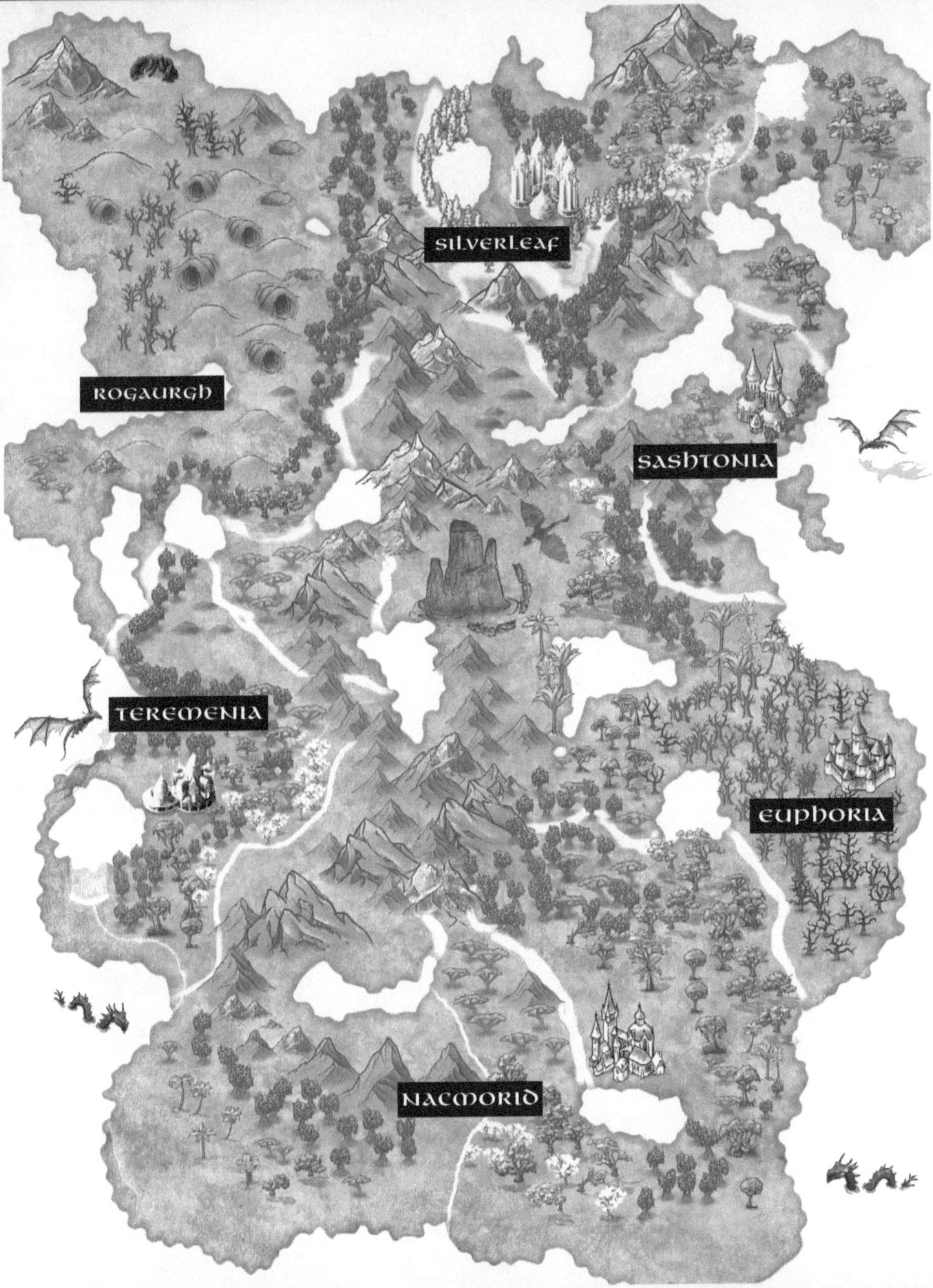

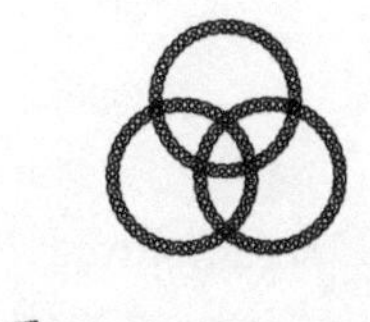

chapters

☙

SUMMARY OF
MARK OF THE FAERIE
BOOKS ONE THROUGH THREE

Isaboe McKinnon's incredible story begins on a late summer afternoon in 1746 in the Highlands of Scotland when she unwittingly passes through a portal in the forest behind her home and crosses over into the Realm of the Fey, changing her life forever.

After returning from a place of which she has no memory, Isaboe is shocked to discover that twenty years have passed, her family has been destroyed, and she is now pregnant. Learning that her husband has died of a broken heart, Isaboe is determined to discover what has become of her now grown children.

Accompanied by her faithful friend, Margaret McDougal, Isaboe sets out on a long journey across Scotland, hoping to find information on the location of her children. Along the way, they encounter Connor Grant, a former Jacobite rebel who reluctantly agrees to escort the ladies on the first leg of their journey. As Connor grows increasingly attracted to the beautiful Isaboe, he becomes a permanent part of their little band of travelers.

Assisted by Demetrick, a powerful wizard, Connor had also been transported to the land of the Underlings, where he participated in a sexual encounter with a beautiful mortal woman. After returning with no memory of his experience, twenty years have passed for him as well. He discovers a message from Demetrick that leads him to a mountaintop home where he meets Rosalyn, an intriguing sorceress who helps him realize that he is the father of Isaboe's unborn child.

Lorien, the demented Fey Queen, had manipulated them both for the sole purpose of creating their very gifted daughter, and with the intent to raise their child in Euphoria for her own evil purposes. Though Isaboe and Connor had faced many struggles to prevent that from happening, on one horrific night, Lorien makes a desperate attempt to take possession of the gifted child, even if it means taking Isaboe's life. Fortunately, the Fey Queen fails to acquire her prize when Rosalyn arrives just in time to bring Isaboe back from the edge of death. After Rosalyn helps to deliver baby Kaitlyn safely into the mortal world, Isaboe discovers that the sorceress is also her birth mother.

As a frightened runaway and too young to be a mother, Rosalyn had given Isaboe up at birth. Over a campfire one night on the route to the coastal village of Kirkwall, she shares her painful life story with her daughter and Connor. Though Isaboe was raised by the wealthy Cameron family of Edinburgh, she had never known love from her adopted mother, Marta Cameron. Now reunited, Isaboe finally has the loving relationship with a mother that she has always longed for.

Six months after the baby's birth, they are joined by friends, Margaret and Will Buchanan, who have learned of the location of Isaboe's older daughter, Anna. She is happily married to Jared McKnight, and they have a baby boy named Gabriel.

With this good news received, Connor and Isaboe want to believe that the worst is now behind them. Following the exchange of vows in marriage, they prepare to settle down in Kirkwall to raise their gifted baby daughter. However, when they learn of a possible threat to Anna, Isaboe convinces her family and friends to join her on a two-week trip across Scotland. But once they arrive at Anna and Jared's home, Isaboe discovers that it was a trap. Queen Lorien has sent her henchwoman, Lilabeth, into the mortal world to kidnap the young couple's son and bring him to Euphoria. When they learn that the queen intends to use the boy's life as ransom in exchange for Kaitlyn, Isaboe realizes that the fight is not yet over.

Determined to find a way to enter Euphoria and rescue Gabriel, they return to Rosalyn's home, a rock cave-dwelling at the top of a desolate ridge where the sorceress has kept esoteric manuals delivered to her by the great wizard, Demetrick. However, Rosalyn needs help in translating the Latin instructions, so she sends Connor and Will to the University of Edinburgh, where they recruit assistance from Hamish Cambridge, a cocky young science prodigy. After joining the rescue mission, Hamish helps to decipher the wizard's instructions and then supervises the construction of an astral portal they hope will provide an entrance into the realm of the Underlings.

Although clouded with doubt and uncertainty, Isaboe and Connor leave Kaitlyn in the protection of their friends and family to join Rosalyn on the incredible rescue mission. When they step into the swirling energy of the portal, the three astral travelers have no idea what to expect when they arrive on the other side.

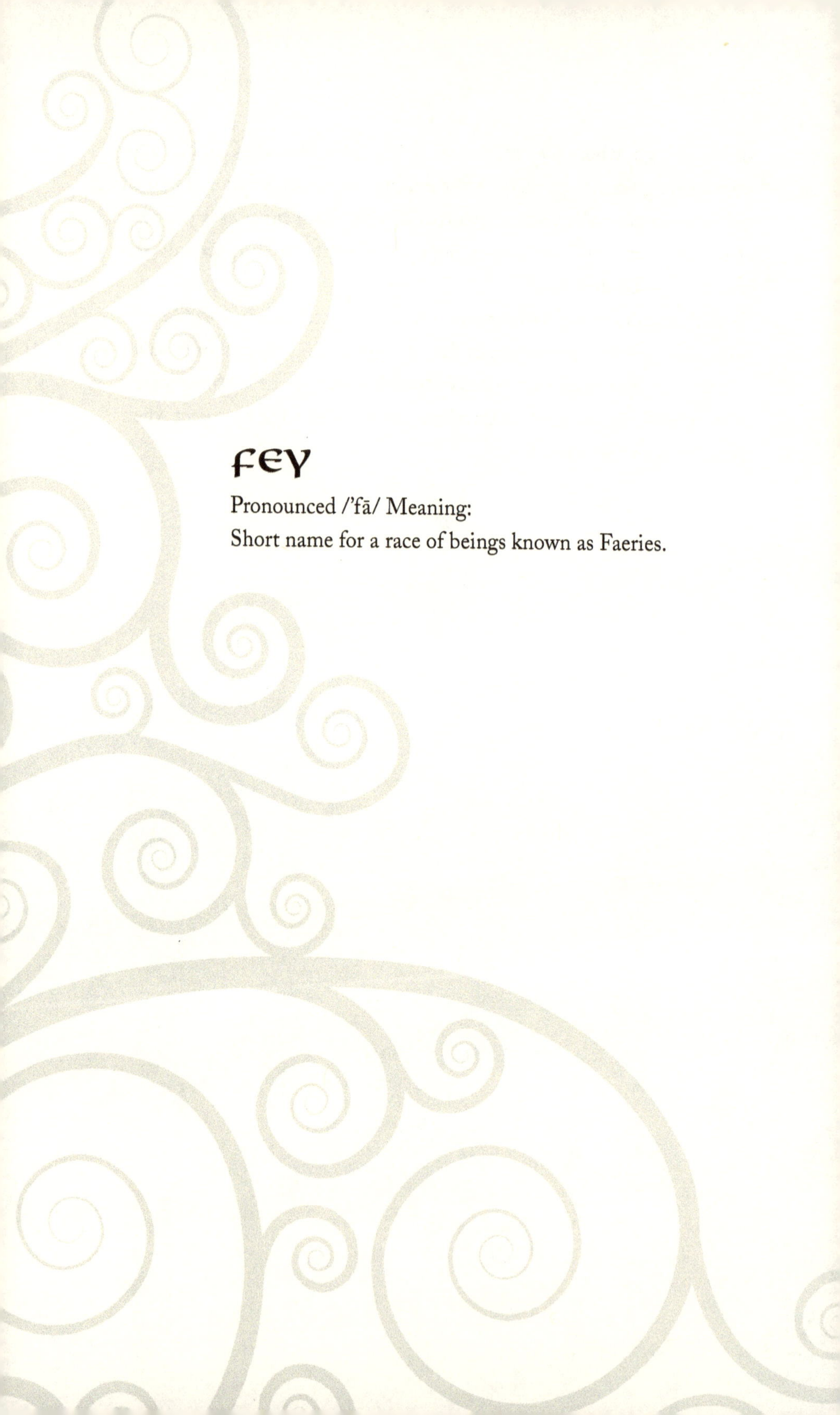

FEY

Pronounced /'fā/ Meaning:
Short name for a race of beings known as Faeries.

CHAPTER 1

AN UNWELCOMED ARRIVAL

Moving at unfathomable speeds, Connor Grant struggled with a plethora of broken thoughts that raced through his mind as he rocketed forward through a tunnel pulsating with mystical energy. *What in the hell are we doing!?* was the loudest of those thoughts. The only thing he knew for certain was that he still held onto his two astral traveling companions—his wife, Isaboe, and her mother, Rosalyn. As he squeezed their hands tightly, the three realm-travelers were caught in a vortex of magic that had been created to transport them into another world: the realm of the Underlings.

But none of them had control in this phantasmagoric projection they had volunteered for, and as Connor tried to focus on the swirling forms and images, the flashing lights that zipped by them, he fought the urge to vomit. The continuous roar in his ears only escalated the pressure growing inside his head, and Connor felt his heartbeat pounding in his bones. As the visions sped past, he squeezed his eyes shut, letting the freefall take him. With his eyes closed, he could have been floating or even flying, yet Connor was very cognizant of his separation from Earth.

Though the portal held no measure of time or distance, as fast as their journey had started, it was now over. On legs still weak and wobbly, the three realm voyagers took their first steps onto etheric soil.

"Are ye alright?" Connor asked, first glancing at his wife, then at her mother. After receiving their confirmation with only head nods, he looked back at the spinning column of energy they had just stepped out of, feeling grateful they had all come through the astral projection in one piece. Though his own legs still felt weak, the women were struggling to stand on their own—their balance somehow impacted by their slingshot-journey—so he supported them both as they struggled to regain their equilibrium.

Now assured that they had all survived the catapult through space, Connor's new concern *was: Where are we?* Their entrance into the world of the Underlings was blanketed in a gray haze, and as he squinted through the thick fog, all he could see was a barren and desolate landscape. Ash and dust particles floated around them, and the air smelled hot, like a scorched mist burning its way down their throats.

"There must be a fire nearby, Isaboe said between coughs.

"It dinnae really smell like smoke," Connor said, still struggling to see through the haze. "But the air's so thick that we've got to move." Clutching tighter to their still-linked hands, Connor took the lead.

"Wait!" Pulling free, Rosalyn stepped back toward the portal they had just passed through and inserted her hand into the whirling vortex. Instantly, the spiral of energy condensed into a slender thread and then disappeared into the ring she wore on her first finger. "We will need this to get back home," she said before falling into step.

They could see only a few paces in front of themselves, and the ground was covered with rocks, tumbleweeds, and gaping holes in the earth that forced their path to curve erratically. When Connor occasionally looked up, he found it odd to see small patches of sunlight breaking through the haze. Only moments before they had left their world under the cover of darkness, but now sunlight cast down between the thick, hazy layers—a sure indication that time moved differently here. Connor couldn't help but wonder what other oddities they would discover before this adventure was over.

"Of all the introductions into this world," Rosalyn mumbled through her cloak, "our first encounter feels like we've landed in hell!" she coughed. "I pray that's not a bad omen."

Connor heard the hint of humor in his mother-in-law's voice, though he knew it was just a disguise to cover her fears for them all. None of them had known what to expect when they decided to attempt this journey, or where they would enter after crossing over. But they hadn't really had a choice, and it was Rosalyn who had made the journey possible. In addition to being Isaboe's mother, she was called a sorceress by some, while others called her a witch, but she was neither. She was the first Feymora —a human woman born with fey blood flowing through her veins. The blood of the fey not only helped Rosalyn maintain her youthful countenance, looking years younger than a woman entering her sixth decade of life, it also gave her unique abilities; the gift of faerie magic.

It was this gift that had allowed them to journey into this strange unknown land under the guidance of Hamish: a brilliant, yet sometimes challenging, young science prodigy. Combining their strengths, they had created something deemed impossible: a portal into another world—the World of the Fey.

As they maneuvered around the large rocks and pitted earth, Connor squinted to see through the haze. At first, he could see nothing but the dry barren landscape dotted with a few sparse and broken trees. Finally spotting an area in the distance where the haze was thinner, he could make out a blanket of green trees on a rolling hillside. As he led them in that direction, the ground became even more treacherous, covered with potholes and broken rocks, requiring everyone to watch their footing even more carefully.

Continuing his course toward the tree line with his charges in tow, Connor had no idea what might be lurking ahead or behind them. Frequently turning to look over his shoulder, he did his best to shorten his stride, while trying to hurry the women along. Connor felt they were too exposed, and the safety of the trees seemed their best defense.

However, his focus quickly shifted and he stumbled to a halt when a large shadow passed overhead, blocking the hazy sunlight. *"Choq acar! Choq acar!"* A deep male voice sliced through the tainted air, and it was echoed by an inhuman screech. Looking up though the haze, Connor squinted, trying to make out who or what the threat was, when a huge form materialized through the dust cloud.

Circling above them was a giant eagle, so large that he could hear the roar of air passing over the bird's enormous wings. Upon its back was an equally impressive figure.

"Hao shacrua! Choq acar!" As the magnificent bird's rider shouted down at them, Connor realized he had heard correctly the first time; the stranger was speaking in an unknown language.

With the instinctual reaction of a warrior, Connor drew his sword from its scabbard and surveyed the area. Helping the women to get out of the open and find cover was now his top priority. He had no idea if the rider or the giant bird intended them harm, but Connor was heavily armed and prepared to fight, if it came to that.

The tree line was now only a short distance away, but when he urged Isaboe and Rosalyn toward cover, the eagle abruptly landed on the ground between them and the forest. Their path was blocked.

Leaping from the bird before it even touched down, the rider raced toward them, shouting the same odd words. His body shape and movements were those of a human, but he was covered in thick golden fur, even his man-like face. From ear to ear, a shaggy mane, much like a lion's, encircled his masculine features. Strapped around his forehead was a silver band that came down to a point just above his nose. Embedded at the bridge of his headgear was a red stone that gave him the appearance of having three eyes, one glowing red and angry. A bandolier filled with weapons rattled against his silver armor as he ran in their direction.

So, it was to be a fight. After corralling the women behind him, Connor raised his sword defensively. Though he had known that his talents would be called upon at some point on this adventure, he hadn't expected it to be so soon.

When his opponent saw Connor's defensive stance, he stopped abruptly. Although the imposing figure had come to a halt, he didn't look even slightly intimidated. Connor could see now that the stranger appeared as surprised to see them as they were to see him. As the two men sized each other up, waiting for the other to make the first move, Connor held his stance, wondering if he could take the larger man. Suddenly, a sound in the distance drew all their attention back to the sky.

"*Ulidrak ono horbacha! Horbacha!*" When the strange, fur-covered man spoke again, though his words were unrecognizable, his gesticulation was clear—*follow me!* Showing a noticeably urgent expression on his face, it seemed clear that the stranger wanted them to follow him, and quickly.

Connor very much disliked all of their options. Without letting down his guard, he glanced back at Isaboe and Rosalyn, silently seeking their guidance. Rosalyn's sharp eyes showed that she had caught the warrior's gesticulations as well. And when Connor met his wife's eyes, he could read her fright, but Isaboe nodded bravely, agreeing to go forward with the stranger.

With the sound in the sky growing louder, Connor lowered his sword, and the three dashed quickly across the ground toward the stranger, following him as he ran back toward the incredibly large eagle.

When the furry warrior called out to the bird, it screeched its response through a beak that could snap a man in two, and then spread its massive wings. Across the top of each long muscular wing was equally formidable armor that ran from the length of its backbone out to the end of each wingtip, covering the bird in a protective shield. The wings' shields folded in and out like a fan, and the bird's underbelly was covered with similar armor. After running under the bird's breastplate, their guide turned and waved for the travelers to join him.

Being so close to the giant eagle stopped them in their tracks, but only for a moment. As the rumble in the sky grew louder, the strange man's gestures grew more urgent. Realizing that he intended to use the bird's armor to defend against whatever was closing in on them, and having no other options, Connor hurried Isaboe and Rosalyn under the giant eagle's wing.

At the exact moment the bird dropped its wing, enclosing them in a protective shell, something extremely large hit the ground, shaking the earth as a rain of stones bounced off the bird's protective armor. Connor wrapped an arm around each woman as they all crouched down and looked across their temporary shelter at the man who may have just saved their lives, wondering who and what he was.

Nobody moved until the noise finally stopped and the bird unfurled its wings. Returning to the light of day, they discovered that the air was littered with renewed ash and falling debris. Isaboe and Rosalyn raised their cloaks over their faces as they followed the men through the haze.

After making their way up to the tree line and out of the dusty fog, the large, furry and heavily-armed man stopped to examine the three unusual beings whose lives he had just spared. The strange being was taller than Connor and all muscle. With eyes as dark as the night sky, he stared back, and Connor knew that he would indeed be a challenging foe, but the odd fellow didn't appear to be a threat, at least not for the moment.

"*Popa currcha murdrack?*" The words came in the form of a question, but the sound was as unfamiliar to Connor as the man who spoke them.

"What do you think he's trying to say?" Isaboe asked. Standing at her side, Connor could hear the anxiety in her words.

"I dinnae ken," he answered before looking down, first at Isaboe, and then at her mother. "Are ye two alright?" When Rosalyn and Isaboe both nodded, he turned back toward the armed man and offered his own question. "Do ye speak English? Can ye tell us what land this is?"

As the stoic fellow cocked his head to one side, his brows furrowed even more. "*Lugter fresen roquck!*" he responded, clearly frustrated.

"We're not getting anywhere this way," Connor grumbled before trying a different approach. "*A bheil tuig Gaidhlig?*"

Instantly, the other man scrutinized Connor with renewed interest and responded in like tongue. "*Bheil bruidhinn a cainnt a sinnsear.*"

Connor nodded in reply.

"Did you understand him?" Isaboe asked, surprised at Connor's gesture.

"Aye. It's old Scots Gaelic. He said I speak the language of the Old Ones. At least now we can communicate." Speaking in his ancestors' ancient tongue, a language he knew well, but hadn't used for some time, Connor initiated a conversation with the Underling.

"*My name is Connor. What are ye called?*" he asked in the ancient language.

"*I am Klute, a Jarcadian Warrior. You are strangers here. Where did you come from?*"

"*We've come from the mortal world.*"

Klute's eyes widened, and he took a moment to silently examine his new acquaintances before continuing. "*Humans,*" he grumbled as if the word left a bad taste in his mouth. "*Why are you here? What is your purpose?*"

"*Those are good questions that deserve answers, but since someone is launching huge stones in this direction, I need to get the women to safety.*"

Klute glanced at Rosalyn and Isaboe with the same scrutiny. "*You are right. It is not safe here. A pack of trolls is headed this way, and they are a nasty group. You can cross through the forest and reach the land of Silverleaf, the home* of the elves. But I warn you not to stay long; your kind is not welcome there."

"*We need to go to Euphoria. Do ye ken which direction that lies?*"

Klute shot Connor a steely glare at the mention of Queen Lorien's stronghold. "*No one enters Euphoria without an invitation! Why do you wish to go there?*"

"*A mortal child has been stolen and is being held there by the Fey Queen. We've come to take him back. How far is Euphoria from here?*" Connor demanded.

Klute went silent, and his intense stare turned cold before he stepped forward to confront Connor. "*By whatever means you used to enter this world, you should use it now and return. There is nothing but danger for you here.*"

Connor returned the cold stare as he spoke. "*We will not leave without the child, no matter what we're up against. So, I ask ye again; how far is it to Euphoria?*"

Klute's mouth pulled into a tight line as his dark eyes stared back intently, and for a moment Connor thought he would get no more from the stoic warrior. "*That depends. How do you intend to travel?*" Klute grumbled.

"*Well, unless ye have a pair of horses ye can lend us, we're traveling by foot.*"

Giving him a puzzled look, Klute glanced over Connor's shoulder at the two women. "*You will be crossing through some very unwelcoming territory, and it would take at least one thousand sunrises, if you make it there at all.*"

"What did he say?" Isaboe asked.

Turning to look at his wife, Connor saw the worry on her face, and he couldn't bring himself to dash her hopes so soon. Everything about this place was foreign, but there had to be another way. He just hadn't thought of it yet. With no map to go by, they were up against so many unknowns. All he knew for sure was that staying put was not an option. Trolls were heading in their direction, and he had to get the women away from harm. *Trolls? Really?* It was a hard concept to wrap his brain around, but the fact that they had just passed through a portal and were standing on the soil of another world could not be denied.

"It may take a while to get to Euphoria," he finally told her. "It appears we've entered on the wrong side of the realm." With renewed angst, he watched Klute walk back down the hillside toward the eagle that anxiously awaited its rider.

CHAPTER 2

WARRIORS
AND BATTLE EAGLES

Connor had little time to determine his next move when he again heard the sound of soaring wings overhead and another enormous eagle appeared out of the haze. It landed on the ground next to the first bird and stirred up more dust, but the rider that jumped down looked nothing like the lion-man on the ground.

The female warrior was almost as tall as Klute and wore similar armor, but that's where their similarities ended. Her skin was not covered with hair, but was dark and smooth, the color of Maplewood. As she ran toward the man, her lithe chiseled muscles flexed beneath her armor, but it was the tail that lashed through the air behind her that caught Connor's attention. Across her back, the female warrior's bow and quiver of arrows clanged off her armor. She stomped over to Klute, already shouting angry words in their native tongue as she gestured in the direction from which she had just come.

After a heated debate, Klute nodded toward the three mortals who stood at the tree line. The woman scrutinized them carefully before advancing in their direction. Her long dark hair was pulled back and braided, and around her head she wore a silver band. A red stone, similar to Klute's, glimmered in the center of the band just above her eyes. As she strode up the debris-littered hillside, her focus remained on the mortals. Maneuvering around the rocks and potholes, it was as if she had a sixth sense of exactly where to place her footing. When she was within good viewing distance, she finally came to a halt.

Staring at them with eyes that seemed to dance from iridescent blue to crystal clear, and then back to blue again, she looked every bit the warrior that Klute did, but she was breathtakingly beautiful. Decorating each arm from shoulder to wrist were distinctive red markings that Connor thought resembled etchings of ancient runes that were symbols of the pagan druids. Her defined jaw was tightly clenched, and her dark lips were pressed into a thin line of disapproval as she examined the three realm travelers. Mingled with her irritation, a hint of curiosity showed in her steely glare. Having apparently seen enough, she emitted a low grumble before turning and retreating down the hill.

Connor unconsciously let out a low whistle as he watched the female warrior's brown tail twitching behind her like a vexed cat above her well-shaped derriere. When he finally tore his eyes away from the woman's backside, he met his wife's disapproving glare and could immediately see that Isaboe was not as impressed. Making a poor attempt to defend himself, Connor whispered, "Ye havta admit, *Breagha,*; a tail on a woman's buttocks isn't somethin' ye see every day!"

"And I'm sure that won't be the last of the *interesting* things you'll see here," Isaboe scoffed. "We are, after all, in the land of the fey, my dear husband, and I'd appreciate it if you could refrain from making a fool of yourself."

Ignoring his wife's scowl, he silently returned to his observations. The two warriors were in a serious discussion, and the female's anger was clear. Whatever conclusion they came to, she turned and stalked back to her eagle as it extended one of its giant armored wings. Running up the wing, she climbed into the saddle that was securely strapped onto the impressive bird's back. With a hard jerk on the reins, the bird opened its magnificent wings and stepped forward on its huge feet. With talons as long as a man's arm, it dug into the earth and spread its massive wings. Each time the powerful tips of its wings touched the soil and its talons grabbed at the ground, dirt and rocks were thrown up until it finally lifted. Despite their anxiety, this was a truly impressive sight for the beleaguered travelers.

Klute ran back up the hill in strides that were long, even for a man his size. *"The Trolls are upon us! You have to move! Now!"* he shouted upon reaching the mound.

"And go where? I have no idea how to reach Euphoria from here!" Connor shouted back.

"That is not our problem! My job is to protect the realm, and right now that means preventing the trolls from advancing on Silverleaf—not helping foolish mortals who should not be here in the first place!"

Connor felt dread bubbling up in his stomach. They had only just arrived in this foreign land, and things were starting out so poorly. But they hadn't come this far to give up at the first sign of trouble.

"Ye have to help us, man! I have no idea where to go, and we can't go back. Not yet!"

"Connor, what's wrong?" He could hear the fear in Isaboe's voice as he looked over his shoulder. He wanted to offer words of comfort but had nothing positive to tell her.

"What is it?" she asked again with more urgency.

But before he could answer, another shriek came from above, and all eyes went skyward. The female warrior's giant eagle was still ascending when a huge rock caught both rider and eagle by surprise. When the jagged rock hit the bird in the breast plate, it shrieked loudly at the impact. Jolted backward, it flapped its wings rapidly, but could not prevent the rider from being thrown out of the saddle into a freefall toward the ground.

"Nyia!" Klute shouted as he helplessly watched the female warrior tumble through the air before dropping out of sight into the smoky haze. He ran down the hill toward his own giant eagle, which stomped anxiously, shrieking for its rider and eager to take flight. But before Klute could make it to his bird, the sound of thunder drew everyone's attention to the ridge top only a few hundred yards from where they stood.

Charging through the rolling cloud of haze and debris were the ugliest creatures Connor had ever seen. Four gruesome-looking beings—part man and part beast—charged toward Klute, wielding clubs and axes with deafening war cries.

Connor spun on his heels. "Run up into the trees and keep yerselves hidden! RUN!" he shouted to his two charges before sprinting down the hill to take his place at Klute's side, who had already retrieved a large lethal-looking spear.

With his sword in one hand and an axe in the other, Connor was ready for battle by the time he skidded to a halt next to the Jarcadian warrior. Klute only had a moment to glance in his direction before the trolls were upon them. The sound of clashing metal filled the air as the beasts charged, swinging clubs, swords, and fists at the two warriors and the battle eagle.

The large, hairy creatures fought upright, similar to a man, but their torsos resembled those of a bison. Jagged horns jutted out the sides of their enormous fur-covered heads, and out of the sides of their hideous mouths curled razor-sharp tusks that could rip a man to pieces. Thick muscular arms and legs completed the stocky build of the trolls as they lunged like ferocious bulls at the out-numbered warriors.

However, sharp horns and tusks were not enough. Swinging stone clubs and poorly made swords, the four lumbering beasts could not keep up with the quick-footed warriors or defend against the slashing talons and ripping beak of the angry battle eagle. Connor and Klute danced and dodged around the trolls as if it had been a choreographed performance. Blood, flesh, and fur littered the ground as the battle raged on and one troll after another dropped to the ground. With only two left, Connor focused on the beast in front of him but missed seeing two more trolls running down the hillside in their direction. Fortunately, the other battle eagle was still missing its rider and in a very bad mood.

Suddenly appearing out of the sky, the lone bird swooped down upon the two beasts running toward the skirmish. Snatching up a troll in each crushing talon, she flapped her massive wings across the soil, stirring up the earth before she gained altitude and climbed back into the sky.

The trolls roared and thrashed furiously in the grip of her talons, until she lowered her mighty beak and ripped the head off one troll, then the other. Tossing the heads to the ground she shook the lifeless torsos and screeched her battle cry. Blood sprayed from the limp, headless carcasses as the bird circled overhead before dropping them to the ground.

By the time the bird had landed, the last two trolls had also become corpses, and both warriors and eagles were covered in the gore of battle. Connor watched with admiration as the giant bird stomped toward them, her lethal head swinging low between her folded wings. She was making deep guttural growls, and her piercing amber eyes were wild and angry. Her rider was gone and she wasn't handling it well.

Klute attempted to approach her, but the eagle screeched in protest, backing away from his outstretched hand. Speaking softly, he continued forward slowly until the giant bird started to calm down. Once more he reached out, and this time she conceded. Placing a hand on each side of the bird's massive head, Klute dropped his forehead against the eagle's. Touching the red stone to the bird's forehead, Klute held her still as he closed his eyes. But the calm only lasted a moment before the eagle pulled away, shrieking a pitiful cry.

Connor watched Klute cast a quick look around at the carnage before meeting his gaze. He recognized a look washing over the other warrior's face that resembled something like respect.

"You did well, as well as any Jarcadian warrior," Klute declared as he stepped up to Connor. "Hopefully your skills will keep you and your women alive. Head up through the trees. You will find Silverleaf on the other side of the forest. But don't stay long in Elf territory. If you keep moving, you might survive." The warrior studied him for a second before turning to walk away, but Connor reached out and grabbed his arm, stopping him mid-stride. The lion-man jerked away and threw up his gore-covered spear, pointing it at Connor as he growled, "If you want to keep that hand, mortal, you best keep it to yourself!"

Holding up his hands in surrender, Connor stepped back but held Klute's stern glare. "Ye canna leave us here! We need yer help. I have no idea where to go, or what we're up against!"

"Then go home!" the warrior shouted. "Go back from whence you came. You should not be here in the first place!"

"We can't go back, not without the child. I also ken that we can't make it without yer help. Please, Klute. Dinnae abandon us." Connor knew he sounded pathetic, but he wasn't too proud to admit that he was in over his head and needed help.

"I must go rescue Nyia! If you had not come here, she would never have landed to check on me, and she would not have been captured!"

"She's been captured? How do you know that?"

"Loca showed me."

Connor gave him a curious look before Klute nodded toward the giant eagle. "Nyia and I are Jarcadian warriors. Loca and Rohan are our

Shekars—our battle eagles. They are linked to us. Loca knows exactly what happened and where Nyia was taken. I am going after her, and I do not have time to help you. You are on your own."

"Wait!" Connor shouted as he looked up the hill to where Rosalyn and Isaboe were huddled together behind a tree, watching and waiting. He had to make a decision, and he had to do it now. "Ye're right. If we hadn't shown up here, neither of ye would have been on the ground in the first place. So let me go after her. You take my wife and her mother on toward Euphoria, and after I rescue Nyia, we'll catch up to ye, somehow." Connor blurted out the suggestion before thinking it through, but nothing else came to mind, and his only hope was threatening to leave.

Klute's expression revealed his shock at Connor's suggestion. "Are you crazy, mortal, as well as stupid?"

"Perhaps, but I dinnae see any other option. We must go to Euphoria, and I have no idea how to get there. But you do. Nyia needs to be rescued, and I can do that. Ye saw me take on these beasts. I can handle this, Klute." Connor watched as rejection grew on the other man's face. "That bird knows where she is, aye? It can take me there, right?"

"What you propose is absurd! Even if Loca lets you ride her, which is doubtful, you don't know what you could be walking into, or the terrain you would have to travel through. Aye, you may take down a few more trolls on your own, but they've most likely taken Nyia underground into a maze of tunnels. Even Loca cannot take you where the trolls have gone. You are just one mortal against a pack of those beasts. You would not stand a chance!"

"Not against all of them at once but if that bird will take me as far as it can, I can find a way to sneak my way in. I've been in worse positions before and am still alive to talk about it. Come on, Klute. There's no other way."

"Nyia is not just another Jarcadian warrior," Klute shouted. "She is my mate!" The warrior's mane shook with an intensity that matched his words. "Why should I trust you?" he growled.

"I'm trusting ye with my mate. Trust me with yers."

Connor looked up the hill, as did Klute, to see Isaboe and Rosalyn appearing frightened and completely out of place. He understood that

Klute's doubts were real, and he shared the same sense of obligation to those he was sworn to protect. Looking back at the strange lion-man from a world they had just invaded, he knew that time was of the essence. "Klute!" he urgently shouted, pressing the warrior into action.

"Fine! We will do it your way. I will take your females as far as Sashtonia, on the other side of Silverleaf. They will be safe there. Then I will come back for Nyia, and I had best not find her dead, or you will be!" Klute snarled his warning under a fierce and deadly glare.

Connor nodded quickly and then ran up the hill to convey his plan to Isaboe and Rosalyn.

"No, Connor! No, you can't do this!" Isaboe shouted. "You can't leave us with him and go off to fight trolls. That's insane!" Holding a white-knuckled grip on the cuff of his jacket, Isaboe dug her fingers into the cloth. "We can't be separated in this strange place. We have to go to Euphoria together!"

"There is no other way, Isaboe," he said, gently pealing her fingers from his jacket and holding her hands in his. "We dinnae ken how to get to Euphoria, but Klute does. And that other warrior, she is his mate. Now that she's been captured, he's about to go after her and leave us on our own unless I go in his stead."

"I'm sorry she's been taken captive, but it's not your responsibility to save her!" Isaboe said frantically.

"If we hadn't been here, neither of them would've been on the ground in the first place. It's our fault she's been captured, and now I havta make it right. Klute will take ye to a place called Sashtonia where ye'll be safe. I'll meet up with ye as soon as I can."

"Connor, are you sure this is wise?" Rosalyn asked solemnly. "We know nothing about this man. How do you know we can trust him?"

"He put himself in harm's way to protect us. I think we can trust him. We have no other choice!"

"But what if something happens to you? I agree with Isaboe that we shouldn't be separated."

"If either of ye can provide me with another way of getting to Euphoria, on the other side of the realm, with no map to go by, using only our own legs to travel, then I'm open to hear it." Connor shot glances at both of them, but neither woman had anything to offer. "Then we're sticking with my plan."

"No!" Isaboe threw her arms around Connor's waist, burying her head in his chest,

Gently pushing her back, he looked into her terrified face. "It'll be alright, *Breagha*. I'll be back before ye know it. Trust me." Kissing her hard and quick, he nodded to Rosalyn and then ran back down to where Klute waited anxiously.

"Alright, so how do I ride that bird?" Though the idea of flying on the back of a giant eagle gave Connor more than a little trepidation, he pushed it aside.

Klute didn't immediately respond. He was looking at the two women that he would now be responsible for. "That small younger one—she's your mate?" he asked with an odd expression.

Looking back up the hill, Isaboe did look small, frightened, and completely out of place. Nodding in response to Klute's question, Connor cursed himself for letting her come, and he hated leaving her now, but he also knew there was no other way. He turned his focus back to riding a bird that was as large as a dragon, looked just as fierce, and could easily kill him in a number of different ways.

"Are you certain about this, mortal?" Klute asked one more time, obviously seeing the hesitation in Connor's face.

"I've got a Jarcadian warrior to rescue. Ye've got my two charges to transport to safety. Let's be about it, aye?"

CHAPTER 3

DEN OF TROLLS

The flight on Loca's back was almost as intimidating as fighting the trolls, but despite the giant bird's initial reluctance, Connor managed to keep himself in the saddle. Under different circumstances, a ride across the sky on the back of a giant eagle could be exhilarating. It wasn't much different from galloping across the plains on the back of a quick steed, with the obvious exception being a long and most likely fatal landing should he fall out of the saddle. But now was not the time for joy rides.

From his vantage above the ground, Connor easily spotted the location where Nyia had been taken as the bird hovered over the bodies of three dead trolls just outside the opening of a cave. Circling in quietly, Loca lowered to the ground for a stealth landing less than fifty yards from the den.

After stumbling awkwardly off the eagle, Connor drew his axe in one hand and a sword in the other. Moving cautiously toward the cave, he examined the bodies of the dead trolls sprawled outside of the entrance. The arrows plunged mercilessly into their now-vacant eyes made it obvious that Nyia was an expert in hitting her mark. A slight grin crossed Connor's lips as he stepped over the corpses, realizing that Nyia hadn't been taken easily. On her own, she had taken down nearly a dozen of the beasts, but was she still alive? Stepping past the carcasses and toward the cavernous opening, he quietly entered into the dark cave, and Connor was instantly assaulted by the rancid odor of rotting flesh. It clung to the walls like invisible curtains, burning his nostrils and making his stomach turn. He'd been held a prisoner of war for two hellish weeks in a British dungeon, and the stench reminded him strongly of that horrific experience. He was all too familiar with the smell of death and decay. Silently, he followed the dimly lit path that led deeper into the heart of the ugly beasts' den. Keeping his senses alert and his footing light, he carefully made his way through the dark recesses of the underground tunnels.

From deeper within the cavern, Connor heard grunts and raspy growls as he crept his way down a stairwell of roughly-carved stones that descended into the earth. Stepping onto a landing at the bottom of the stairs, he froze when he saw light flickering off the rock wall ahead. Realizing that the light wasn't moving, he continued on cautiously. With deliberately placed steps, he made his way toward the sound of the grunting trolls, vocalizing in their guttural language. Holding his breath, Connor slid up against the outside wall. Attempting invisibility, he cautiously peeked around the corner to take a closer look.

Two torches cast flickering light over the six hideous beasts who filled the small cave. Scattered around the floor were piles of animal bones, some covered with rotted, half-eaten flesh. Strange otherworldly beings hovered above the remnants of the troll's previous meal, small scavengers that looked like a cross between a rat and a dragonfly. As the odd creatures fluttered from one decaying mound of leftovers to the next, one of them fluttered too close to a troll, who reached out with a meaty paw and snatched it in mid-air. Stuffing the screaming insect into his morbidly disgusting mouth, he crunched down a few times before spitting the jumbled remains onto the floor. A stream of dark slimy liquid hung off the troll's repugnant mouth until he wiped it away with the back of his hairy arm. Instantly, the once-flying predator was now on the other end of the food chain and was being ripped apart by its former peers.

Tearing his focus from the grisly sight, Connor scanned the rest of the room. With his eyes now accustomed to the dimness, he could make out the dark outline of Nyia in the back corner of the cave. A troll on each side held her arms, and she was dwarfed in comparison to their bulk. In the middle of the cavern, two bull trolls shouted guttural noises at each other, gesticulating wildly at their prisoner. They appeared to be in a heated debate, and the Jarcadian warrior was the subject of their argument. Making a quick move, one of them grabbed Nyia and pulled her into the center of the poorly lit cave. It was then that Connor saw that her hands were bound behind her back. Forcibly bending her forward at the waist, the troll mockingly humped her, setting some of the other beasts into a roar of guttural approval. But not everyone saw humor in his act of domination, and a swift fist from the other troll landed hard and brutal across the defiler's face. As he lost his grip on Nyia, she tumbled to the ground.

When she landed near a pile of broken bones, Connor was amazed to see Nyia's nimble tail reach around until it found the perfect weapon. Yanked to her feet, the unsuspecting troll didn't even see the piece of jagged femur whirling through the air before it plunged ruthlessly into his eye.

Roaring in pain and rage, the creature lost his grip as Nyia quickly dropped and rolled across the room. Jumping up, she slashed at another troll caught off guard by the warrior's swift movements, strength, and incredibly agile tail that served as a third arm and was just as accurate.

Taking the opportunity Nyia had just provided, Connor joined the fight with a slash of his sword and the swish of his axe, then disarmed a club by slicing off the fist that held it. The battle dance took place in a matter of seconds as the lithe Jarcadian warrior and Scottish rebel danced with ease around the larger trolls in the enclosed space. After the last troll dropped, Connor barely had time to catch his breath before Nyia rushed forward and slammed him up against the wet cave wall. During the battle she had cut the binds that bound her hands, and now held the jagged edge of a troll's knife pressed against his jugular.

Buhota aqur Klute?" she shouted her strange and angry words into his face, and Connor could see the puffiness under her right eye and the bruising on her right cheek. "Where is Klute?" she growled again, but this time she used old Scots Gaelic.

Now, using that ancient tongue, Nyia's beautiful, yet threatening face was only inches from his own. Connor also saw that she carried a split and swollen lip, yet her dancing crystal blue eyes were now black menacing slits.

Struggling to push her off, Connor was surprised to discover that the warrior, who was as tall as him, was also as solidly built. She didn't budge. "He's deliverin' the women to Sashtonia," he replied. "I came to rescue ye," he hissed, finding it difficult to speak with the pressure of the knife against his throat.

"I did not need rescuing," she snarled, her warrior's grip on the knife never easing.

"Aye, I see that. But ye can take the blade from my throat now. I'm not the enemy."

"You are a mortal. That makes you my enemy," she growled viciously, and for a moment, Connor seriously wondered if this beautiful warrior would take him down just as easily as she had the trolls. But Nyia finally released her grip and stepped back. "However, it appears that Klute does not see you that way." Though she had relaxed her stance, her demeanor had not changed, and her steely gaze remained deadly. "Why is Klute delivering your females to Sashtonia?"

"Because I asked him to. Now, before I answer any more of yer questions, let's get the hell out o' here. I dinnae ken about you, but I dinnae wanna be around when the rest o' this group shows up." Connor pointed the tip of his blood-stained sword toward the carnage that now lined the small cave floor.

Apparently in agreement, Nyia grabbed her weapon-belt lying on the floor amongst the filth and snapped it around her waist. Sliding the troll's knife into the belt, she grabbed her bow and quiver, which were also lying on the floor. Slinging them over her back, she led the way up and out of the stinking hole and away from the smell of death. Moving quickly, they ran back up the stairs, and Connor did his best to keep up with his companion's longer stride.

"How did you know where to find me?" Nyia asked over her shoulder as she took the steps two at a time. Her tail whipped behind her, and more than once Connor had to dodge to keep the tip from striking him in the face.

"That giant bird of yers brought me here," Connor answered, but jolted to a stop when Nyia came to an abrupt halt and turned to face him.

"Loca? Loca let *you* ride her?" Nyia stared incredulously at Connor. "Since my bonding with her as a Jarcadian warrior, Klute has been the only other one that Loca has allowed on her back. Until now." Nyia cocked her head to the side, as if she suddenly saw him in a different light.

"Well, I dinnae think she was keen to the idea, but Klute did somethin' to her, and, well, here I am," he said with a quirky smile. But before Nyia could respond, a loud angry roar echoed from deep within the dark cavern behind them. "Let's move!" Connor shouted as they sprinted toward the cave entrance. The sound of a stampede could be heard coming up from the depths of the earth. By the vibration he felt rippling through the ground from their stomping hooves, he surmised that there were more than just a few of them.

Daylight up ahead indicated they were close to freedom. Running for the exit and back out into the fresh air, the two warriors found Loca waiting impatiently, shifting her weight from one enormous claw to the other. Her anticipation of being reunited with her rider, and her determination to be up off the ground away from the advancing trolls was palatable. The Jarcadian warrior's battle eagle screeched her warning as she dropped low to the ground. Placing the tips of her wings on the earth, she created a plank that Nyia flew up in three strides of her long legs. Following her closely, Connor ran up the wing, but not quite as quickly or as gracefully. Meeting on the back of the giant bird, he took his place in the saddle behind Nyia.

As she dug into the earth with her incredible talons, Loca flapped her wings and took flight. The two warriors clung to her back as she accelerated upwards at a daunting angle, while below them the angry trolls hurled stones and spears, along with insults and threats. Connor could feel the ripple of the giant bird's enormous muscles as the Shekar climbed high enough to be out of range from the projectiles, and out of the enemies' sight.

Eventually, when the air was cold and the trolls were far beneath them, Loca leveled off and returned to an easy flight above the land. Connor could finally relax, but the exhilaration of being so high above the Earth and the wind whipping across his face kept his pulse rapid. As much as he was thrilled by the experience, he seriously doubted that Isaboe shared this feeling. Thinking of her riding above this strange land on the back of Klute's Shekar suddenly made him start to worry. Seriously questioning why he had given in when she insisted on being part of this desperate mission, he hoped that his wife's focused character would serve her now and push her into doing what was necessary. After all, it was Isaboe's grandson whose life was at stake.

A couple of hours had passed flying high above the land when Loca began a slow descent, matched by the sun sinking into the horizon. Purple hills in the distance, rose-colored clouds and the coolness in the air were all signs of dusk's imminent arrival.

"Is this Sashtonia?" Connor asked over Nyia's shoulder.

"No, but we are landing for the night. With the extra weight Loca is carrying, she needs to rest, and so do we. We'll make camp near the mountains over there," she announced, nodding to a wide plateau cut into a mountain side and surrounded by a few sparse clusters of trees.

"How much farther is it to Sashtonia?"

"If we set off early, we should be there by midday tomorrow, though it might be later. Having you along is slowing us down. Loca cannot fly as far or for as long with two on her back." Nyia's words matched the look she shot Connor over her shoulder, and she made no attempt to hide her annoyance.

"Oh, well, ye're most welcome for comin' to yer rescue," Connor replied using the same tone.

"I already told you, Mortal: I didn't need you to rescue me," Nyia snarled. "Until I am reunited with Klute, I will put up with you, but I do not have to like it."

Their silence continued unabated after they landed, broken only by the discussion necessary to set up camp and gather firewood. Although Connor had put himself in harm's way and given over charge of the woman he loved in order to save her, Nyia showed no appreciation for his efforts. She made it clear, that to her, he was merely an unwelcomed interloper.

From within his jacket, Connor pulled out a small cloth pouch of dried pork strips and stuffed one of them into his mouth. Still chewing, he began to offer a strip to Nyia but found her busy digging through Loca's saddlebags. As soon as the Jarcadian warrior had gathered her supplies, the battle eagle took a few steps away before flapping her wings and returning to the sky. When Nyia finally joined him by the campfire, she was carrying a cask, a pot, and several things he did not recognize. Pouring clean water from the cask into the pot, Nyia placed it over the flames. After the water was warm, she filled a small metal cup and stirred in a yellow powder before handing it to Connor.

"What's this?" he asked.

"Kimorush."

Connor sniffed it cautiously and found a pleasant savory scent that made his mouth water. When he braved the first sip, it curled warmly over his palate, tasting a lot like chicken broth. This brought to mind another fowl creature. "What became of yer giant bird?" he asked between sips in an attempt to break the uncomfortable silence.

"She is out there somewhere in the dark, watching over us," Nyia finally answered.

"Once we reach Sashtonia, how do we locate Klute and the women?"

"He will have taken your females to the castle. They will not be hard to find."

"What land are we in now?"

"This is Silverleaf, home of the Elves." Nyia glowered at Connor. "And they don't like humans. That is why we are up here on this mountain, where our presence is less likely to be noticed."

"Why dinnae the elves like humans?"

"Do you not know the history of your own race?" she snapped. When Connor only shrugged, Nyia snarled at him, shaking her head before she continued. "Thousands of your mortal years ago, humans and elves fought a bloody war for control over the land of Silverleaf. The elves were able to drive the mortals out of their realm and back into your own world, but only at great expense."

"Why did humans want control over Silverleaf?"

"For the silver, of course," she stated, as if it should have been obvious. Connor silently encouraged her to continue, and she obliged him. "Veins of silver run through the land. The trees literally drink it up through their roots, and it turns their leaves silver, hence the name. The humans, in their greed, almost wiped out the elven race trying to acquire it."

"A thousand years is a long time to hold a grudge. They must have forgotten it by now."

"Elves have long memories, and they are not known for forgiveness. If they capture you, they will not be kind."

"They couldna be any worse than the trolls we encountered today."

"That kind of thinking will get you killed. Trolls may be large, but they're dumb beasts with simple minds. Elves, on the other hand, are keen, intelligent, and skilled in the art of war." Nyia took a drink of her kimorush. "But you would probably take out a few in the process before they kill you. For a mortal, you put up a good fight."

"Thanks… I guess," Connor replied suspiciously to her backhanded compliment, but he could not deny that being a mortal in this world was not to his advantage. Downing the last swallow of his kimorush, Connor wiped his mouth on his sleeve. "Why are the trolls attacking at the border of Silverleaf? Do they want the Elves' silver too?"

Nyia shot him a suspicious glare before she finally answered. "No. They are trying to increase their hunting grounds. They have been pushing hard into the three lands that border their own: Silverleaf, Sashtonia, and Teremenia. We, the Jarcadian warriors, have been commissioned to halt their advance, but during these last few months, the trolls' tactics have become more aggressive."

"How so?"

"For centuries the trolls have fought primarily with brute strength, making use of only club and ax. But those flying boulders you experienced today were enchanted to explode upon impact. That kind of warfare is too sophisticated for the likes of a stinking cave troll."

"Maybe they're adapting?" Connor suggested, thinking of his Jacobite brethren back home. They had learned quickly that open warfare against the British was not viable and had turned to guerrilla tactics.

"Trolls are simple-minded, yet their attacks have become more organized and their weapons more advanced. Just before you arrived to *rescue* me, they were arguing." Nyia's sarcasm was biting. "I heard one of them say that a live Jarcadian warrior would make a valuable trade. He wanted to turn me over to Kaegron."

"Who's Kaegron?"

"The leader of the trolls. As stupid as those beasts normally are, Kaegron actually has half-a-brain, and that makes him dangerous."

"Seein' ye as a valuable trade commodity sounds like someone or somethin' is helping 'em. Any idea who that could be?"

When Nyia's expression changed to one of suspicion, Connor wondered if he had gotten too close to the truth. The Jarcadian warrior silently glared at him across the fire before she finally asked her own question. "What are you humans up to? Klute said you want to go to Euphoria. Why?"

"We're here because Lorien snatched a baby boy from our family. We've come to take him back."

"Why would the Queen of Euphoria take a mortal child?"

"She's using him for leverage. Threatenin' to kill him if we dinnae hand over our daughter."

"Why does she want your daughter?"

"Lorien wants her because she's... special." His voice grew quiet. "Different. Like her grandmother." Connor still wasn't sure how he felt about his daughter's unique talents. She was still just a baby, only six months old. Though he knew their lives would be a far cry from normal, he'd hoped they could at least provide her with an ordinary childhood. That dream seemed to be drifting farther and farther away from his grasp, but that was a concern for another day. First, he and Isaboe had to get back to her.

"Special, how?" Nyia asked with renewed interest.

Connor hesitated before responding, but he knew there was no point in not telling her the truth. "Our daughter, Kaitlyn, well, she was conceived in Euphoria."

"Wait," Nyia interrupted. "You and the child's mother have been there before?"

"Aye. Lorien manipulated the conception, so our daughter ain't just mortal. The queen has some twisted plans for her, and has already attempted to take Kaitlyn from us. So far, we've prevailed, but now that fey bitch has taken the game to a whole new level. She kidnapped a boy from our family, Isaboe's grandson, and threatened to kill him if we dinnae hand Kaitlyn over to her. So we're bringing the fight to Lorien and takin' back what's ours."

Nyia had no response. The light from the campfire danced off her dark skin, making her crystal blue eyes look as black as the dark sky surrounding them. But the flexing of her jaw told Connor that there was something else behind that covert silence. Strange noises in the dark temporarily distracted him as Connor threw a bundle of dried sticks into the fire, sending sparks into the night air.

"So, those females you were with, was one of them your mate, the mother of this special child?" Nyia finally asked.

"Aye, and right now I wish I hadn't let her come. I canna protect her or Rosalyn if I'm not with 'em."

"As long as they are with Klute, you need not worry. They will be safe."

Connor only nodded, feeling a little less anxious by Nyia's assurance, but what followed was a long uncomfortable silence.

Nyia stared into the flames of the campfire before she finally looked up at Connor. "So, warrior, I have a question. Why does a soldier with your skills have a mate like that puny female I saw in the tree line?"

Connor scowled at her. "I dinnae understand the question."

"I am a warrior. Klute is a warrior, and he is my mate. He is my equal. Your mate is not your equal. She is small and fragile looking, obviously unable to defend herself. Are there no female warriors where you come from?"

Chuckling to himself, Connor slowly shook his head. "Aye, a few, but none I'd want to mate with."

"Why? Do you not find them appealing?"

"Let's just say that where I come from, female warriors dinnae look like you," he murmured with a cautious smirk. "And dinnae underestimate Isaboe. That's a fiery stubborn lass, that one, and there's nothing puny about her. She's a lot stronger than she looks. She's been to hell and back and lived to tell about it. Ye're right, she's not my equal. She's better than me. She's the opposite of everything I am, and I'm eternally grateful for that, even when she challenges me. I *literally* wouldna be alive today without her. Isaboe is my partner, and she makes me wanna be a better man."

Nyia had no response, but her penetrating stare said plenty, and Connor felt as if she were examining him.

The night sounds were different in the realm of the Underlings. In the distance, squeals and screams like he had never heard before sent a chill of discomfort down Connor's spine. Being high on the mountain top, the full moon looked larger than normal, and its bright light illuminated the land, casting eerie shadows. Even back in his world, scary things came out at night. All of his senses told him to be aware of his surroundings, to be on calm alert, but when the recognizable sound of Loca's screech erupted into the night, it brought both Nyia and Connor immediately to their feet.

Running in the direction of the animal's screams, it sounded like a battle was taking place. The two warriors dropped over the edge of the ridge to find Loca moving in on a trapped animal. Taunting it with her razor-sharp talons, her snapping beak, and lethal flapping wings, Loca was planning to have a late-night snack. The terrified animal appeared to be trapped with its back leg wedged between two large boulders. Though it struggled furiously, the unfortunate creature was unable to free itself. The moonlight offered enough illumination that Connor could make out the creature's form and was shocked at what he saw. As the animal reared up, its hooves sliced the air, missing Loca's beak only by inches, but what Connor found so incredible were the huge wings attached to its back. *"It's a winged horse!"* he exclaimed.

Nyia shot him a curious side-glance before shouting a command at her Shekar. A few loud disgruntled screeches in Nyia's direction made it clear Loca wasn't happy with her rider's demand. As she repeated her command with more authority and aggressive hand gestures, the battle eagle eventually backed down. Taking a few steps backward, Loca dropped her head low between her massive wings. Her large brown-speckled skull swung aggressively from side-to-side, looking just as deadly as she did in battle.

With the imminent threat of being devoured by a giant eagle seemingly at bay, the trapped animal resumed its efforts to free itself, but it was under obvious distress.

"It is called a wallabock; also known as a ghost-runner, but I've never seen a dark one before. I have heard of such, but they are rare. Wallabocks are usually light colored. They live in herds throughout the realm on mountaintops like these. When they take flight, the light ones blend in with the sky, making them hard to see. Hence the name, ghost-runner. They're also a delicacy of the trolls. That's why dark ones are rare. They can't hide as well as their white relatives. See the troll's sling wrapped around its back leg? By all appearances, it was intended to be a troll's meal. But his missed opportunity looks like Loca's good fortune."

"*What?*" Connor reeled around. "Ye canna let Loca eat it!"

"Why not? She needs nourishment too."

"Then let her find it elsewhere!"

"Why do you care if she eats this animal?"

"It's a *bloody* flying horse! A horse, *with wings!*" Connor's over enthusiastic rant had no effect on the Jarcadian warrior.

"And you point out the obvious because…?"

"*Seriously?* My God, I am in a foreign land," he grumbled. "A flying horse is pretty damn amazing! Ye canna let yer giant bird eat it."

Loca was slowly inching her way back towards the trapped beast. It was too easy a meal to let pass by. The wallabock did not miss Loca's intentions either, and it began to screech and whinny again, desperately trying to free itself.

"Nyia, *please!*" Connor shouted urgently.

"Why? What do you want with it?"

"I'll ride it!" he hastily announced. The excitement and the urgency to save the beautiful beast momentarily blocked his rational thinking.

"Ride it? A ghost-runner? What makes you think that animal will let you climb on its back?"

"It's a horse, regardless of what ye call it. If it's a horse, I can ride it," he boasted with over-zealous confidence.

"Even if by some chance you are able to mount that beast, as soon as it takes to the sky, it will dump you at its first opportunity."

"Not if I break it first. If I can ride it, I can fly it." Though Connor's words sounded confident, deep down he knew he had no idea what he was getting into, but he couldn't let the magnificent animal become the eagle's dinner. "Look, Nyia, I ken ye dinnae want me around, much less on the back of yer bird, and my extra weight is slowing us down. If I had my *own* flying horse, I wouldna have to sit behind ye with that wicked tail o' yers slapping me in the face!" Connor knew she had complete control over her incredibly nimble tail, and a slight smirk crossed Nyia's face, confirming his suspicion. Loca was preparing to pounce, and he also knew this was his last chance to convince Nyia. The great eagle was a predator and the prey was ready for the taking. All she needed was a signal from her rider.

"Nyia, call Loca off *now*! *Please!*"

The Jarcadian warrior gave Connor another curious look, staring at him for an uncomfortable moment before she turned toward the battle eagle and barked out a command. The Shekar reared up in defiance, squawking and flapping her armor-covered wings and stirring up the dusty soil. But Nyia repeated the words more aggressively, making her demand clear. Loca finally conceded and shot up into the night sky, shrieking her angry cry.

"There you go mortal. The animal is all yours. Do what you wish with the beast, but I am going back to camp to get some sleep. You are on your own." Nyia turned and walked away, but not before Connor heard her mumble; "Stupid foolish human."

CHAPTER 4

A NEW RIDE

Having had no idea what to expect in the realm of the Underlings, Connor had the foresight to pack some essentials before leaving his world; an extra waterskin, a hammer, a knife, and now most relevant, a length of rope. But it was obvious that only one rope would not be enough to hold a beast with wings.

Though it took a while in the dark, he discovered a thicket of thin wispy trees. Their vine-like branches had twisted around themselves as they grew, creating a strong union as they reached toward the ground like long, slender fingers. Finding the tender ends still pliable, Connor cut multiple bundles and twined them into a crude rope.

Connor took the rope he'd brought from home and swung it overhead so he could lasso the magnificent animal. Even though its leg was lodged between two boulders and anchored by a troll's sling, Connor still missed its thrashing head three times. But on the fourth attempt, he was successful, and the rope finally slid down onto the horse's neck. Pulling the rope firmly, he anchored its head with its snout to the ground, then tied the rope to a nearby tree. Though it kicked and snorted, he had the beautiful animal securely roped and restrained, but now, what to do with those massive wings?

Jerking and stomping its hooves furiously, the flying horse was too restrained to damage itself or Connor as he gingerly climbed onto its back. Ducking under the thrashing wings, he secured himself on the animal's back and began pulling in the first wing—a six-foot span of bone, muscle, and feather. Catching the wing at its base, he worked his hands up the bone and forced it down to the horse's side, holding the wing there with a leg while he did the same on the second. The sheer strength of the wings took Connor by surprise, and by the time both were wrapped with his vine-rope and secured to the animal's sides, he was drenched in sweat.

"There. That oughta' hold ye," Connor muttered before jumping down. With the rope that held the horse's head tethered to the ground still wrapped around the tree, he sliced the strap on the troll's sling that had restrained the animal, then quickly leapt out of the way. Stepping in front of the beast, he loosened the rope, giving it room to move, but kept the rope wrapped around the tree.

Finally released from its restraint, the frantic animal kicked out its front legs and reared up, but Connor yanked the rope hard, quickly bringing it back onto all fours. When it tried to bolt, its newfound freedom was brought to a sudden halt when the rope snapped tight around the tree trunk.

"Whoa, boy! Ye're not goin' anywhere right now, so ye might as well calm down." The creature turned and attempted to run the other direction, only to suffer the same fate. Realizing that it was confined to the length of the rope, it turned toward Connor and reared up, screaming in fury, its mouth foaming and its eyes wild as it kicked out."

As he jumped out of the way of the deadly hooves, Connor quickly reeled in the rope, bringing the animal closer to the tree. He held the rope fast to keep it from rearing up. "I ken ye're angry right now, and maybe a bit scared. But I saved yer life tonight, so I'll thank ye for not tryin to take mine."

The animal stomped and snorted, but Connor seized the rope until it finally became less agitated and ceased its struggles. When he felt he had waited long enough, Connor slowly let out the rope from around the tree, but kept it taut around the animal's neck. At first, it attempted to bolt, but Connor held the rope tight until it calmed down and allowed itself to be led—albeit reluctantly. As the beast continued to stomp and snort in protest, he brought it back near the campfire and again restrained its head to the ground and tethered its front legs

He did it. Connor had captured and contained his prize. Taking a deep breath, he wiped the sweat from his brow and stepped back. "I'll let ye stay like that for a few hours. Later, I'll give ye some food and water, and maybe then ye'll appreciate me a bit more." Connor felt the exhaustion of what he'd just accomplished and knew he was in need of some sleep. Walking over to where he'd left his bag, he pulled out a blanket, and created a make-shift pillow. But as he tried to get comfortable on the ground, Connor could hear the animal only yards away, snorting and clawing at the dirt with an occasionally desperate whinny.

Just before closing his eyes, he glanced across the fire to where Nyia lay on the ground. She was watching him—more like glaring, with narrow slits for eyes that glowed amber in the fire light, but she said nothing. Silently she rolled over, turning her back to him, and Connor watched as her tail snapped in the air a few times before finally coming to a rest.

At the first light of dawn, Connor was up and working with his prize. The rope that had held it restrained throughout the night now worked as a lead. Using a long stick as a prod, he ran the animal in circles, lunging it into submission. He had broken many horses in his time, but that had been back in Scotland, his homeland, where he knew the nature of the beasts and what to expect. But here, in the realm of the Underlings, he'd already encountered creatures the likes of which he had never even imagined. Connor decided to put his skills to the test, hoping that a horse with wings was still just a horse. Guiding the animal in closer, he tied the lead around its snout. The horse stomped and tossed its head, but Connor held firmly and continued his patting until it stopped reacting negatively to his touch.

"Yeah, ye're alright, everything's gonna be just fine," Connor murmured to the creature, letting it sniff him. He continued patting down the length of its back, and each time it reacted to his touch, Connor soothed it with calm chatter. The muscles in the large black wings flexed as they tested the strength of the makeshift rope that held them secure. Keeping firm control until the animal relaxed, Connor stood near its flank and laid his upper body over its back with his feet hovering just above the ground. Protesting from the weight on its back, the powerful creature stomped and tossed its head, but Connor continued tapping on its side, speaking softly until it again relaxed. Sliding off, he gently stroked its coat a few times before jumping back on. He continued repeating the process until the beast no longer reacted to his weight. It was then that he slowly slid one leg over its flank and sat atop his future steed's back.

As Connor had anticipated, it bucked, attempting to throw him off, but when he didn't fall, the animal reared up and kicked furiously at the air with its front legs. Shrieking in protest, it jumped, kicked, and snorted, but Connor wasn't giving up. After a few more useless attempts to toss its new rider, the reluctant beast apparently realized that wasn't going to happen, and its bucking began to transition into a struggling gait. With additional mummers and gentle prodding, Connor finally managed to coax it into taking a few controlled steps. Squeezing his legs around the animal's middle, he pulled on the lead, and with a slight kick of his heels, had it moving as directed. As they trotted along for several minutes, Connor kept his course unpredictable, teaching the animal to comply with his will. After it finally stopped fighting his instructions, he gave it a rest and slid off its back. Slowly, he approached the beast's head and again let it sniff him, allowing it to become more comfortable with his scent.

Nyia, who had been watching from a distance, took a few steps in his direction, shaking her head, but Connor noticed a slight upturn to her lips. "I must admit, you have surprised me, human. I did not think that the beast would let you on its back, much less ride it."

"As I said; if it's a horse, I can ride it."

"But the real question is: can you fly it?"

"That is the goal, aye?"

"What makes you think the moment the restraints on those wings are cut, that animal won't take to the air and dump you to the ground?"

"Well, there's only one way to find out," he replied with a cocky smile. "That's why I'm working him, hoping he'll trust me enough so that won't happen." Connor returned to walking the beast in circles, then stopping and turning it in the other direction, patiently working it into submission.

After a few moments of merely watching, Nyia again broke the silence, "Have you eaten this morning?"

"No, and I'm right starvin'."

"Here." Nyia tossed him something round and yellow, and he grabbed it out of the air.

"What is this?" he asked. His mystery breakfast was fuzzy and round, the size of a small apple.

"It's a bolacot. Use your knife to split it open."

Following her instructions, Connor found that inside the odd vessel was a tasty treat. Small, yellow sections that resembled an orange were pulled out easily, and the juicy fruit was a pleasant surprise. "This is *damn* good! What'd ye call it?" he asked, licking his lips and wiping his mouth with the back of his hand.

"Bolacot. The fruit only grows up here on these mountains where it's closer to the sun. Here, have a couple more." Nyia tossed another two in Connor's direction. "Speaking of the sun, it has been up for a while now. How much longer are you going to mess around with this beast? I would like to be on my way."

"Just a bit longer. I need to see how he'll respond when I push him into a run."

"Well, do not take too much longer. It is still a long way to Sashtonia, and we are wasting daylight."

Nyia had started to turn away when Connor called out to her. "Hey, Nyia. Thanks much for the bolacot, and for waiting. If I didnae ken better, I'd think ye actually care."

Nyia's normally serious expression turned even more intense as she shot Connor a cold steely glare, her eyes narrowing into piercing slits. "*Tondt cho!*" she spat viciously, followed by a presumably rude gesture she made with her forearms. She then turned and stalked away, her tail switching behind her in defiance. Though Connor may not have understood the words, her message was loud and clear.

After a few hard runs across the ridge and back, Connor had the magnificent beast responding to his directions—for the most part. When he pulled back sharply on the reins, his newly-trained steed skidded to a halt, puffing and snorting as it tossed its head wildly in protest, stomping and switching its tail. "Aye, ye're gonna be a fine horse," he reassured the animal, patting and stroking its neck. As he continued speaking softly, the horse seemed to settle, actually soothed by his words, and in that moment, Connor felt rather confident in his skills as a horseman.

But his moment of pride was interrupted by a terrifying scream as a hideous creature with huge jaws full of sharp jagged teeth came charging over the ridge on a direct path to his campsite. Instantly, the horse screamed out before bolting into a dead run, but the snarling beast was already on their heels. Holding tight onto his steed's mane and falling into rhythm with its pumping hooves, Connor felt the strength of its muscles beneath him as it galloped across the open field. But his panic rose as he looked over his shoulder and saw the monster gaining on them. Snarling and snapping its razor-sharp teeth as it tried to chomp onto his ride's unprotected flank, Connor's anxiety spiked to an all-time high. If he could reach his knife and slice the vine rope holding down the horse's wings, they could take flight and escape, but with each pounding stride the deadly creature was gaining on them. Realizing that his only choice was to outrun the hideous beast, Connor had to keep all of his focus on pushing the animal hard and fast.

In the next moment, he heard the sound of arrows sinking into flesh; *thunk, thunk,* followed by another of the monster's unholy screams. He saw Nyia standing in the distance, locked onto her target and reloading her bow.

Looking over his shoulder, he saw that the beast had two arrows protruding from its torso, but the arrows hadn't stopped its progress. Still on its long legs and picking up speed, the terrifying predator would not be swayed from his prey. Two more arrows zipped over Connor's head, and he heard the sound of them hitting the monster. But despite Nyia's successful hits, it barely slowed the creature down. As Connor pushed his ride and tested its strength, it became clear that arrows and speed alone were not enough to protect them.

Suddenly swooping down from above, Loca descended from the sky and sunk her huge talons into the attacker, causing it to scream out in anguish. The Shekar screeched her war cry as she flapped her wings hard enough to drag her mark into the sky. The once-predator had now become the prey, screaming and thrashing in the talons from which it could not escape. They heard an audible crunch, even from across the field, and the monster let out one last keening wail as it died. A moment later everything went quiet as Loca carried away her prize, now hanging limply in her clutches, until Connor lost sight of the incredible battle eagle.

Both horse and rider were steaming with sweat from the exertion of running for their lives as they made it back to camp where Nyia was packing her gear. "What the hell was that thing?!" Connor asked as he brought his steed skidding to a halt. His chest was heaving from the rush, and his mount stomped around nervously, its eyes still full of fright from the panic-induced run.

"That was a velaripper. And if it had caught you, it would have eaten you and your wallabock while you were still alive," she snarled, repacking her bag and dousing the campfire.

"Well, that's not a pretty thought. I owe ye a debt of gratitude for savin' our lives."

"I did not save your lives. Loca did."

"But ye're an expert with that bow, Nyia. It was yer arrows that slowed the creature down," he paused and gave her a cocky grin. "And Loca finally got her meal." But it was clear that Nyia was done waiting. She was breaking camp.

"I am leaving," she said, confirming his thought. "So, unless you plan on riding that beast all the way to Sashtonia, you had better figure out how to get it into the air, and now." She tossed Connor's bag at him.

"What's the hurry?" he asked, catching his bag and placing it in front of him. "Do you expect more of those velarippers to show up?"

"It's not those beasts I'm most concerned about at the moment." Nyia nodded at a distant point on the horizon where a wide, billowing cloud of dust was traveling quickly across the land. From their vantage point atop the mountain, they could see for miles in all directions.

"Aye, looks like a storm is brewing, throwin' debris in the air." It looked to Connor as though several small tornados were heading in their direction.

"You could say that." When Connor turned to look at Nyia, the crystal blue of her eyes danced and swirled with a crisp intensity. "That storm cloud is a group of elves on their way here, and they are not ordinary elves. Those are warriors."

"Why are they coming here?"

"Because of you, human. I told you last night that elves do not like mortals, especially not in their land."

"But, how did they ken I was here?"

Nyia glared at him and shook her head. "You really are a stupid man." Picking up her quiver, she tossed it over her shoulder. "Loca and I are taking to the sky. I do not intend to be on this mountain top when those elves arrive, and I suggest you do the same. If you plan to fly that beast, now is the time to do it," Nyia snapped at Connor before barking a command into the sky. Moments later, Loca swooped down and landed on the ground near to where Nyia stood.

Instantly, Connor's mount reared up at the sight of the giant bird and bolted in the opposite direction. Taking advantage of the animal's fright, Connor tucked his legs under the folded wings and leaned forward over its neck. Wrapping fingers into its mane, their bodies again moved as one. He felt the animal's strength resonate all the way up into his own legs, flexing and extending as it ran faster and faster. When he finally felt ready, Connor slipped the knife from his boot and reached back, sliding the blade under the vine-rope. With two quick slices, the restraints snapped open, and the massive black wings unfolded.

Burying his hands into the horse's mane, Connor clutched on tightly as the wings stretched out to each side of the galloping steed. As the flapping increased, so did the animal's speed as its hooves pounded into the ground. With the wings now fully unfurled, it ran straight for the edge of the cliff.

"*Ohhhh… fuckkk!!*" Questioning his sanity, Connor screamed as he closed his eyes and buried his face into the magnificent animal's neck. But in the next moment, the sound of its hooves pounding into the earth went silent.

When they immediately dropped, the fall took Connor's breath away, but in his next heartbeat, the animal finally adjusted to the additional weight, and its struggling gait transitioned into a fluid rhythm as it gained control. Lifting his head, Connor looked down and saw the land beneath him dropping away. The rush of the run, the heart-stopping take off, and the wind in his hair were exhilarating. A smile of pure joy broke out across his face.

He was riding a flying horse!

Turning to look over his shoulder, Connor saw Nyia and Loca not far behind, but higher in the sky. From his vantage point, he couldn't help but be impressed by the majestic bird, not to mention Nyia's strength and boldness. The two looked like one creature, exotic rider and battle eagle, and it was clear that their bond went deep.

Connor kicked his heels into his mount, and the swooshing sound of wings flapping up and down instantly intensified as the winged horse with its new rider climbed steadily up into the sky.

When Connor met Nyia's eyes across the distance, she gave him a slight nod. If he didn't know better, he might have called it approval. In any event, he was pretty damn proud of himself as he shot her a wide smile. But a gesture from the Jarcadian warrior made it clear that she was still in charge. A quick tug on the reins, a booming command from Nyia, and a shriek from Loca had the two immediately in an upward ascent and taking the lead.

CHAPTER 5

THE PALACE OF SASHTONIA

When she dared to glance over the side of the giant eagle, Isaboe's anxiety spiked and her stomach did summersaults, so she kept her head down and her eyes focused on her lap. But each time the amazing bird dipped, lifted, or banked to one side, Isaboe would gasp and squeeze the Jarcadian warrior who sat in front of her. After the first half-dozen squeals in his ear, Klute shot a scowl over his shoulder, accompanied by a low grumble of disapproval.

She could hardly believe she was riding on the back of an eagle, sitting behind this strange furry man. *People aren't supposed to fly!* But here she was, high above the land, flying through the vast wide sky as her mother sat silently behind her, seeming much calmer than she.

When she wasn't panicking about her situation, Isaboe's thoughts kept drifting to Connor, wondering where he was, how he was, and if she would ever see him again. She still couldn't get over the undeniable fact that he had left her. Yes, she understood that he felt a sense of obligation for the female warrior being captured, but to leave her mother and herself with this barbaric creature in a completely strange land? His heroic sense of duty had once again overridden his common sense.

However, Connor's sense of duty and obligation to commitment was something she was very familiar with. It was the reason that he felt compelled to follow her across Scotland for three long months in the middle of winter and that she was still alive. Plus, she had begged to come with him and Rosalyn on this excursion into the world of the Underlings, unable to bear the thought of being away from him for even a week, let alone forever, should he never return. But leaving her and Rosalyn alone was completely unacceptable. They should be Connor's first priority, and he should be here now, keeping them safe, *damn him!*

Not knowing when or if she would see him again amplified her anxiety, and when the giant bird suddenly banked left, Isaboe couldn't stop the shriek that slipped past her lips.

This time, Klute not only looked over his shoulder with a vicious glare, but also growled menacingly at her. Isaboe wasn't sure if she was more frightened of the warrior who sat in front of her or falling off the giant eagle and plunging to her death.

"You will have to relax, Isaboe," Rosalyn muttered, placing a hand on her daughter's shoulder. "You're making our driver a bit cranky."

Isaboe turned to look at her mother. "I can't help it. This is insane!" she hissed, and the edge of panic was clear in her voice. "How can you be so calm? Aren't you nervous?"

"Well, I'd be lying if I said I was happy about climbing up on the back of this bird, or that I didn't pee myself a little when we took off, but now that we're up here, I find it rather exhilarating," Rosalyn replied with a satisfied grin.

"Yes, both exhilarating and terrifying! And I can't wait until he lands this thing." Isaboe tried not to glance down at the land passing so far beneath them that it made the trees below look like tiny bushes. "Do you think Connor's alright?" she asked, looking back at Rosalyn.

"Connor is one man who can take care of himself. I'm sure he's fine," Rosalyn replied with a comforting smile and a pat on her shoulder, but Isaboe knew that was just to make her feel better. Neither of them had any idea what Connor's current condition was, or if they would ever see him again, and she reluctantly nodded before her eyes went back to her lap.

The sun threw out coral streaks across the few clouds hovering in the sky as it made its descent toward the horizon, and at some point Isaboe noticed that her anxiety had lessened some, but she still couldn't look down, nor could she wait to put her feet on solid ground.

In the distance, she could see the last rays of sunlight glinting off a tall structure that reigned over the land, now covered in dusk's shadow. Though still a long way off, it looked like an etheric structure as the sunlight caught its edges, creating bright iridescent flashes of color. Glancing over her shoulder, she saw that Rosalyn was looking in the same direction. "What do you think it is?"

"I have no idea, but it's certainly very large. The way the sunlight is creating these amazing flashes of color, it could be made of glass."

Just before the last traces of sunlight waned into darkness, the magnificent building came into full view, revealing an enormous castle lit by hundreds of lamps. Brilliantly illuminated from within, spires of glass and metal reached into the sky, and their glow could be seen for miles. Majestic towers stood atop the stone castle, and stretching for miles around its perimeter was a beautifully manicured garden. From her vantage point atop the eagle, the few people Isaboe could see walking the grounds looked as small as ants.

As the great bird slowly passed over the spires and began its descent, Isaboe realized that the castle was their destination. She was nervous all over again, but this time about their reception. Still, she was grateful for the opportunity to finally put her feet on the ground. However, a new realization washed over her when the eagle flew behind the castle and dropped down into a dark, overgrown courtyard. Since Klute wasn't taking them in through the front door, she assumed that he didn't want whoever was in that castle to know they were there.

When the giant bird made a surprisingly soft landing, Isaboe was grateful to be back on land. After Klute gruffly assisted them down, the two women fell in behind him as he made his way toward a back entrance into the building. It was dark, and there was little light to see her footing, but Isaboe managed to keep up with the warrior's longer stride. Soon, they found themselves inside a long hall with oil lamps jutting out of the walls, casting flickering shadows down the hallway.

They continued down the hall until Klute stopped at a door and opened it, motioning for them to step inside. The room was black as pitch before they heard a popping sound, and a light began illuminating the darkness. In his hand, Klute held a round object that glowed like fire. When he placed it on a small table, Isaboe was surprised to see that the fiery object didn't burn the table but lifted slightly and then hovered as it continued to glow.

Klute walked back toward the door and then turned. Making a sharp gesture, he spoke a few words that the ladies couldn't understand, but it was clear that he wanted them to stay in the room. When he walked out and closed the door behind him, Isaboe heard the distinctive click of a lock.

Looking at her mother, Isaboe saw the same look that must have been on her own face. "What do we do now?"

"We wait." Rosalyn announced, glancing curiously around the small room.

Isaboe followed her mother's sweeping gaze of their holding cell. Next to the table, there was a cushion on the floor that looked comfortable enough to sleep on. There was one chair, and she watched as Rosalyn took a seat, folded her hands in her lap, and looked up at her daughter.

"How can you be so calm?" Isaboe almost shouted, unable to control the fear that flooded out with her words. "We have no idea where in the hell we are! We don't know where Connor is, or if he's even still alive! What are we going to do, Rosalyn?"

"Let me remind you, my dear; you insisted on coming along. You knew we had no idea what we would be walking into when we passed over into this realm. So, calm down, get a grip, and have a little faith, in both me and your husband. This hysteria isn't doing us any good. Now please be quiet and let me think."

Isaboe stared at her mother, but the chastisement did nothing to calm her nerves. She soon began pacing the small room, wringing her hands and mumbling under her breath. "I can't believe Connor abandoned us. I'm so *angry* with him right now. Where in the hell is he? God, I hope he's alright."

"That's not helping, Isaboe."

Upon hearing the lock click in the door once again, they both looked up, hoping to see Connor. When Klute abruptly opened the door and reentered the room, he was carrying two leather straps, each with a red stone embedded in the center. After closing the door, he walked up to Isaboe and held out one hand, making a gesture indicating he wanted her to do the same. Tentatively, she raised her arm as he proceeded to buckle one of the leather straps around her wrist.

"*Rasto undondte unjken,*" he spoke in his foreign tongue. "*Ochthack yaket tilvan…*and let me know if this is too tight."

"No, it's fine," she said before the realization shot across her face. "Hey, I understood that!"

"Yes, this is a translation stone. It will allow you to understand me now." Klute then proceeded to attach the other strap onto Roslyn's wrist. "These are usually only given to kings, queens, high elders, and Jarcadian warriors. However, in this case, it would be best if we can communicate. Just make sure not to lose these. They are very rare."

"Thank you," Rosalyn added, now able to join the conversation. "I believe Connor told us your name is Klute. Is that correct?"

"Yes."

"Klute, my name is Rosalyn, and this is my daughter, Isaboe. First, we owe you our deep gratitude for rescuing us from that war zone and delivering us safely here. But, if you please, *where* are we? What is this place?"

"This is the Palace of Sashtonia."

"But since we came in through the back door," Isaboe injected, "I can only assume that you don't want anyone to know we're here. Is that right?"

He met their eyes briefly before answering. "It is best if you stay out of sight. There are those who would not be pleased to know there are mortals in the realm. This is for your own safety."

"Do you know where Connor is?" Isaboe doubted that he knew but had to ask.

"Connor, your male companion, he is your mate?"

"Yes, Connor is my husband."

"He briefly told me why you are here, and that you intend to travel to Euphoria. He said Queen Lorien has taken a mortal child that you have come to retrieve. Do I have this correct?"

"Yes." Isaboe and Rosalyn answered together.

"What is so special about this child? Is it yours?"

"No, but he is family. My granddaughter, Anna, is his mother," Rosalyn answered. "Lorien is using the boy as ransom, threatening to kill him if we don't give her what she wants."

"What does she want?"

"She wants my daughter, Kaitlyn," Isaboe replied.

"Why?"

"Because Kaitlyn is…gifted. The queen is using the baby boy as leverage so we will hand Kaitlyn over to her."

"But if it is your daughter that she ultimately wants, why is the queen playing this game?"

"Lorien can't locate Kaitlyn in the mortal world," Rosalyn answered. "I have her hidden."

The warrior scrutinized Rosalyn for a moment before addressing Isaboe. "I still do not understand. What makes your gifted-daughter so unique that the queen would go to such extremes?"

Isaboe took a step closer to the intimidating warrior, whose armor and weaponry hid his battle-hardened fur-covered body. Beneath his lion's mane, Klute's eyes were dark under a furrowed brow. Though he stood at least two heads taller than her, Isaboe lifted her chin stoically and answered his questions. "This is not the first time I have been in your realm. Many years ago, Lorien abducted me, and while I was here, I conceived my daughter. Kaitlyn is mortal, but she carries fey blood."

"And not just any fey blood," Rosalyn interjected. "We believe Lorien added her own essence to the child's conception, and that's why she wants possession of Kaitlyn. It is her intent to raise my granddaughter as her own, to be used for whatever vile purposes the queen has in mind."

The warrior went silent, as if absorbing what he had just heard. He then took a step closer toward Rosalyn and stared at her. "How did you arrive here? It has been more than a thousand summers since mortals have been able to cross over without our assistance. And how is it that *you* can keep the child hidden from Lorien?"

"Just as Isaboe was taken, many years before, my mother was also abducted and brought to this realm. I, too, have fey blood in my veins, and that has provided me with abilities that other mortals do not possess. We passed through a portal that I created."

The Jarcadian Warrior stepped back and glared at Rosalyn before shooting the same dagger-like gaze in Isaboe's direction. "You must leave here immediately," he growled. "When your male companion finally arrives, you must all return to your own world and forget the mortal boy."

"*What?* No! We can't do that!" Isaboe shrieked. "We can't leave without the child. That is not an option!"

"It is not an option for you to stay!" Klute snapped back at her, his words laced with a growl. "You are not welcome in this realm, and your ridiculous attempt will only get you all killed! Queen Lorien shows no mercy to those who challenge her. You have no idea what you are up against."

"Oh, but I do," Isaboe replied. "I know the Queen very well, and she almost destroyed me once. But she underestimates us, and she's in for a fight."

"Then you are all fools, and you will never succeed!" Klute barked, glaring at the women as an uncomfortable silence fell between them.

"Are you returning for the female warrior, and for Connor?" Isaboe finally asked.

"No, not yet. I was planning to go back this evening, but I do not think it is a good idea to leave the two of you alone tonight. If I do not hear from Nyia by morning, I will go back and look for them."

Though Isaboe had no idea how he would be able to hear from them, she took some comfort in knowing that at least there was some sort of a plan. "So, what shall we do now? Just wait here?"

The man with a lion's mane nodded and turned toward the door.

"Wait," Rosalyn called out. "Before you leave us for the night, may we please have some water, and something to eat? And if it would not be too much to ask; we're both covered in dust, and it's been a long hard day. Is there anywhere we could wash up?"

A look of realization washed over the warrior's face as he nodded. "Yes, of course. You must be famished. I will bring you some food, and then I will take you to a location where you can bathe. You are right—it has been a long day." His lips twitched slightly, and Isaboe thought he may have been attempting a smile, but just as quickly it was gone. Klute turned and swept out of the room, and once again they heard the click of the lock from the other side.

CHAPTER 6

A LUCKY BLACK HORSE

After a restless night, Isaboe felt no better the following morning, and her anxiety lay just under the surface of her false sense of calm. But she kept it to herself as she quietly nibbled off the plate of food Klute had brought them the night before. Some of the fruit she recognized, like apples and pears, but there were fruits whose colors she'd never seen before and tastes she had never experienced. Dried meats and hard bread finished off the plate.

She had prayed that during the night Connor would arrive, and she would wake to find him by her side. But that didn't happen. Nor had they seen Klute yet that morning, and she wasn't sure she wanted to see him. He had made it very clear that they were not welcome in his realm, and Isaboe knew that if the warrior had his way they'd be gone today.

"You've been rather quiet this morning," Rosalyn broke the silence. "I know you must be worried about Connor."

"Yes," Isaboe said with a forced calm, but unable to stop it, her anxiety came spewing out, "What if he doesn't come back, Rosalyn? What if something—*God forbid*—happened to him? Then what would we do?"

Rosalyn studied Isaboe for a long moment, as if choosing her words carefully before answering. "If Connor doesn't show up, then we'd have to make another plan. Fortunately, I do have allies in this realm."

"Can't you locate Connor? You picked up his vibrations and tracked him before."

"Yes, in the mortal world. But here the air is charged with strange energy. It's more complex than I've ever experienced in our world. I can't pick up Connor's vibrations, at least, I haven't been able to yet."

Her mother's statement about the air being charged with energy rang true, as Isaboe had felt it more than once. When they first arrived, the blue stone that lay next to her chest had felt warm and tingling, as if radiating with its own power. A gift from Queen Brighid, the amulet's warmth had given her an unusual sense of comfort that she couldn't quite identify. But now it felt cold and lifeless, and Isaboe felt certain that this shift had something to do with Connor missing from her side.

The Fey Queen had given her the amulet when she had first appeared to Isaboe in the mortal world disguised as an old crone, telling her it could enhance her communication with the Underlings. When they were planning this desperate journey through the portal, she had known it wouldn't be as easy as arriving at the perfect place, walking in to grab the baby, and then walking back out without encountering any resistance. But she hadn't expected to become separated from Connor so quickly or having to face the possibility they could be forced to return empty-handed.

A rap at the door pulled Isaboe from her disquieting thoughts.

"It is Klute," the warrior's voice came from the other side of the door. "May I enter?"

"Yes," Rosalyn replied, just as a distinctive click was heard when the key turned in the lock.

The warrior entered and nodded at them before closing the door. "Good morning. I hope you rested well, though I know these were not the most pleasing of accommodations."

"It was quite fine. Thank you," Rosalyn said.

"Have you heard from Connor?" Isaboe asked anxiously.

"I have just made contact with Nyia. She and your male companion are on their way and should be here shortly."

"Oh, thank God!" Isaboe let out a heavy sigh of relief as she saw a matching sense of ease on Rosalyn's face. "Are they meeting us here?"

"No. I will take you to where they will be landing. It is off the palace grounds, but not far. Leave your belongings and follow me."

"Wait, are we walking to this place of rendezvous, or must we get back on your giant bird?" Isaboe knew she sounded a bit pathetic, but she was sincerely hoping they wouldn't have to fly again.

Klute's lips twisted into something that hinted at mirth, but then it quickly disappeared. "I am afraid we will be flying on Rohan." Isaboe's enthusiasm melted back into anxiety, and it must have shown on her face. "Do not worry. It will be a short trip."

From their vantage point on top of the ridge where they waited, Isaboe could see the land spreading out for miles in all directions. In the valley below, a sparkling lake sprawled wide and lazy under the morning sun, fed by mountain waters. Orange and yellow wildflowers dotted the landscape, and in the distance, craggy purple mountains stood dark and ominous against morning's light blue sky.

When the breeze picked up on top of the ridge, Isaboe pulled her cloak tightly around her neck and let the wind whip her hair wildly as she stared into the distance, trying to locate anything flying their way.

"There," Klute said, squinting as he pointed. "They are coming in from the south. Reaching into a pouch that hung around his waist, he pulled out a wooden cylinder that resembled a telescope and held it to his eye. After staring for a moment, he lowered the looking glass. "Why are there two of them?"

Isaboe shot Klute a curious look. "Aren't you expecting two of them, your female warrior and Connor?"

"No, I mean, there are two flying beasts; one is Loca, and the other is…" Again, Klute held the telescope to his eye.

"The other is what? Do you see Connor?"

"Yes, and he is flying a…a wallabock!" Klute seemed astonished as he dropped the instrument. "Your mate is flying on the back of a ghost-runner!"

"What is a ghost-runner?" Rosalyn queried as she walked over to join Isaboe staring into the horizon alongside the Jarcadian Warrior.

"Here, see for yourself." Klute handed Isaboe the looking glass.

Hesitatingly, Isaboe held it to her eye, and within a few moments, she found her targets. First the female warrior on the giant eagle, and then… "Oh my word!" Isaboe exclaimed when she could finally make out what Connor was riding. "It's a flying horse!"

"A horse with *wings?*" asked Rosalyn.

Isaboe lowered the glass and looked at her mother. "Leave it to Connor to find a horse in this crazy place!" She was equally surprised, and relieved as Rosalyn took the telescope to see for herself.

Within moments, the specks on the horizon came into full view. Connor's light-brown hair and cloak flapped in the wind, and even this far away, Isaboe could see the smile on his face without the help of the looking glass. Nyia and Loca circled overhead twice before making their descent, but Connor appeared to be having difficulty convincing his ride to cooperate as they flew past the landing spot. Making another attempt, Connor worked the horse toward the ground, but away from the giant battle eagles.

After dismounting from her ride not far from where they stood, the female warrior gave Isaboe a disapproving glare. Though she was sure that the scowl on Nyia's face was meant for her, Isaboe didn't care. When Nyia turned to greet Klute, Isaboe returned her attention to the sky and watched as Connor finally brought the winged horse to the ground a good distance from where she stood waiting for him. Picking up the hem of her skirt, she bolted in his direction.

Though initially it didn't look that far, now that Isaboe was running, it was further than she had thought, and she was soon winded. Stopping to catch her breath at the top of the mound, she watched Connor carefully wrapping the horse's lead around a tree, making sure it was well secured. She then began running at full speed toward him as she shouted his name.

When he saw his wife running in his direction, Connor's face split into a huge grin. "Isaboe! Isaboe!"

After sprinting across the grassy terrain, she gave a wild shriek and jumped into his arms. As he spun her around, she held tightly with her face buried into his neck and his arms wrapped around her waist. "Oh, thank God!" she beamed as he gently lowered her back to the ground. "I was so worried about you, you crazy rebel! Are you alright?" Glancing quickly across his body, she saw no sign of injury, but plenty of dried blood on his clothes. "That's not your blood, is it?"

"Nah, I'm fine." Connor held her at arm's length and took a good look at her as well. "Are ye alright?"

"Yes, Rosalyn and I are both fine." She then grabbed onto his shirt, and her earlier look of elation melted into fury as she pulled him closer. "Don't you ever leave me again!" she snarled, "especially not in this place!"

"Did Klute not treat ye well?"

"No, he's been kind to us, but that's not the point." Isaboe released her grip.

"Ye look like ye survived alright."

"I was scared, Connor, and worried that I would never see you again!"

Wrapping his arm around her shoulder, he gave her a kiss on the forehead as they started walking back toward where the others were waiting. "I'm sorry that ye were scared, but I did what I had to do."

"But this will be the last time we're separated, agreed?"

He smiled down at her, and squeezed a little tighter. "Agreed. I missed ye, too." This time he kissed her full on the lips.

"Wait!" She drew away and turned around. "Connor, a *flying horse?*" she asked, pointing at the beautiful black animal, stomping around and tugging at its restraint.

"Isna' he a beauty? I found 'im on a mountain top in Silverleaf, stuck with his back leg lodged between two boulders. I managed to save the amazing animal and break it. Now we have our own ride!"

"You don't expect me to ride on that, do you?"

"If ye survived riding on the back of a giant eagle, ye can ride on a winged horse just as well."

"But I hated every moment of it! People aren't meant to fly, Connor."

"Ye mean to tell me ye dinnae find it just a *wee* bit exhilarating?" he chuckled with a flash of excitement in his eyes. "I admit that at first it was a bit terrifying, but being high up in the sky with the wind in my hair was thrilling. It made me feel alive!"

It was completely obvious to Isaboe that this was a subject they would not agree on, and a sick feeling told her she hadn't taken her last aerial trip.

"Good to see you again, Connor!" Hearing Rosalyn's greeting as she walked toward them, Connor raised his hand in response. "Hey, Rosalyn."

When she finally reached them, Rosalyn gave Connor a quick hug. "You had us a bit concerned," she said, taking a step back. "We're glad to see you again, and in one piece."

"Aye, me too." He nodded as they moved toward the Jarcadian Warriors. "On the way here, we passed over what I assumed was the palace o' Sashtonia. Is that where Klute took ye?"

"Yes, but we stayed in a dingy little room in the back, like a couple of prisoners." Isaboe answered sourly.

"It wasn't that bad," Rosalyn added. "But it is obvious that Klute doesn't want whoever lives in that castle to know we're here."

"He told us that as soon as you arrived, we would have to leave, immediately!" Isaboe felt the panic in her words.

Connor stopped and turned to look at Isaboe, "What'd ye mean, he told ye?"

Pulling back the sleeve of her cloak, Isaboe exposed the red-stoned leather strap on her wrist. "Klute gave us these. They're translation stones that allow us to communicate here." Following suit, Rosalyn showed her wrist as well.

"And ye can talk to him now, and he understands ye as well?"

"Yes. And though he's been a decent host, he did make it very clear he doesn't want us here," said Rosalyn.

"Aye, Nyia's made that quite clear as well."

Isaboe looked up at Connor, hoping he had some ideas. "What are we going to do? How can we continue on to Euphoria without their help? And we certainly can't go back without Gabriel."

Watching Connor clench his jaw, she could see the look of frustration under his furrowed brow. "We'll just have to convince them otherwise," he said, continuing his course as his features finally softened.

"Connor, where did you pick up that flying horse?" Rosalyn asked.

"Pretty amazing, aye?" he said with a flourish. As they all turned back around, Connor's grin was hard to miss. "I saved 'im from being Loca's dinner and then spent most of the morning breakin' 'im. We had to run for our lives from a velaripper, but he has a lot a fight in 'im. He's a real beauty, aint he?"

"Running for your lives?" Isaboe asked, as her concern jumped a whole new level. "What's a velaripper?"

"It's a very nasty looking creature that almost had us both for lunch, but fortunately he's a fast horse, and Nyia's damn good with that bow. She and Loca saved both our lives."

"Have you named him?" Rosalyn asked.

"I've been tossin' some names around, cause, well, I canna just call him horse, aye? Since it was most fortunate that I found him when I did, and we both survived the morning's attack, I think the name *Sonas* fit's him well."

"Sonas. Isn't that the Gaelic word for lucky?"

"Aye. Kind o' fits, dinnae ye think?"

"Well, it may be lucky for the horse," Isaboe added, "but there's no way all three of us will fit on that beast." Whether on a giant eagle, or on the back of a horse with wings, she didn't favor the idea of traveling through the air on a flying animal.

But pointing out the obvious didn't seem to deter Connor's intentions. "No, but there's still Klute and Nyia with their rides."

"Weren't you listening? They want us to leave. They are not going to help us."

"We'll just havta see 'bout that," Connor said with a cocky grin, placing one arm around Isaboe's shoulder and the other around Rosalyn's as they walked back to where the Jarcadian Warriors waited with their eagles.

CHAPTER 7

A WARRIOR'S DUTY

From the ridge they had landed on, the majestic palace was hidden by a dense forest, but the spires of the castle could still be seen above the treetops. As Connor, Isaboe, and Rosalyn crested the rise, they saw Klute and Nyia in a heated discussion. Nyia's gesticulations, facial expressions, and sharp tone made it clear that she was not happy. And, based on how often she had pointed in their direction, Connor had no doubt that the three of them were the cause of the warriors' argument. Slowing their advance, he waited until there was a lull in the squabble and then gingerly approached as Isaboe and Rosalyn trailed behind.

"*Thank ye, friend,*" Connor spoke in Old Scots Gaelic. "*I'm in yer debt for deliverin' the women to safety and keepin' them in yer charge.*"

Nyia's attitude oozed with defiance as she turned her face away, but not before shooting Connor an angry glare. Klute watched this silent exchange for a moment, then reached into a pouch and withdrew a red stone embedded into a strip of leather that matched Rosalyn and Isaboe's, securing it to Connor's wrist.

"Now we can all understand each other," Klute said, nodding to Connor. "I appreciate your bravery, mortal, for going into the dungeon of the trolls to assist Nyia in her escape. She tells me you fought well."

Nyia had no response to Klute's compliments, and her lips were pulled into a thin angry line as she scowled at her partner.

Ignoring her hostility, Connor nodded respectfully at Nyia. "Did she also tell ye that she didnae need me? Nyia's the brave one, and scrappy as hell! I'm glad *I* wasn't fightin' against her, especially with that wicked tail of hers." For a second, he thought Nyia's lips may have twitched into a hint of satisfaction, but it quickly vanished.

"Now that you are here, we must talk." Klute glanced sideways at Isaboe and Rosalyn who had joined Connor. "I understand that your motives are noble, but there is no realistic chance of rescuing the mortal child, and just by trying you would suffer your own demise. Since we cannot be of assistance, you will never make it to Euphoria on your own. Your cause is futile. It is in your best interest—and the best interests of this realm—to leave here now." Klute's words were as firm as his expression.

"It's not in our best interest to leave here empty-handed," Connor hissed, taking a step forward. "We'll gladly leave this realm, but not without the child." He looked into the warrior's eyes, holding his defiant glare. "We'll find our own way if ye're not willing to help. Though we all ken that we'd be out of here a lot sooner if ye did."

When Klute glanced at his mate, she shook her head firmly. "I see no other alternative, Nyia. Having them stand before the Council is the best way."

Hissing at Klute as she stormed away, Nyia's tail whipped behind her like a vexed cat. Klute sighed as he watched his mate retreat to her battle eagle and run up the wing to take her seat. At Nyia's barked command, Loca flapped her wings and rose quickly into the sky.

"I think Nyia's startin' to like me." Connor said, shooting a grin at Klute, but the other warrior didn't respond to the jest.

After Nyia and Loca had disappeared around one of the castle's many towers, Klute readdressed the mortals. "In two days, the Council of Elders will meet here in Sashtonia. It is a gathering of the heads of state from every province, some of whom will arrive tomorrow. This may be why Nyia finds your timing to be so suspicious. I, on the other hand, find it advantageous. This takes the matter of what to do with you out of my hands. The elders will decide."

"The elders will decide what?" asked Isaboe.

"If they agree that you may continue on your mission, then yes, we will help you. But if they do not," Klute turned toward Connor, "you and your women will be subject to whatever the elders decide to do with you."

"Well, just so it's clear," Connor grumbled, taking another step forward. "We're not leaving without the child, regardless of what yer elders decide."

As Connor and Klute glared each other down, the tension between them filled the silence until Rosalyn stepped forward, gently pushing Connor aside. "Klute, until we meet with the Council of Elders, do you have other accommodations for us? The room you provided last night will not be adequate for the three of us."

Tearing his gaze from Connor's, Klute nodded. "I shall see what I can do. But now, you must all accompany me."

"Where are we goin'?" Connor asked.

"To seek an audience with King Enoch. He is the absolute ruler of Sashtonia."

"Why do we need to see him?"

"Because he is already aware of your presence, and the longer I delay in addressing this issue, the greater my retribution will be."

"What do ye mean *yer retribution?*"

Klute glared at Connor for a moment before answering. "As a Jarcadian warrior who has knowledge of intruders in our realm, I am required to take you prisoner and report your presence immediately." When he wavered, Connor saw something pass over the warrior's face that he couldn't identify. "I did not do that."

As a warrior himself, Connor understood the consequences of disobeying orders and was surprised that Klute had broken his own law. At that moment, a newfound respect took hold for this man who resembled a lion. He now also understood Nyia's anger. Klute's decision not to immediately inform the superiors of their presence may have put both him and his mate in a difficult position.

"Well, can we get something to eat before we meet King Enoch?" Connor asked. "I'm right starvin'!"

Klute stood at the entrance to the small room as he waited for the group to accompany him to the king's hall. Leaving their bags at the door, Connor found a plate of food that Rosalyn and Isaboe had left unfinished and quickly began shoving fruit and bread into his mouth. Though the Jarcadian warrior remained silent while he stood guard at the door, Connor could read the anxiety in his face. He knew that Klute was anxious about having this audience with the king, but, as a soldier, duty took precedence.

After Connor had stuffed the last piece of bread into his mouth, he nodded. "Let's get this over with."

As the mortals followed Klute through the dimly lit corridors of the palace, they all walked in silence, though their footsteps echoed loudly off the stone floor. More than once, Connor thought he saw something moving along the walls, but when he looked closer, it appeared to be only a flickering of light. As Isaboe slipped her hand into his, he glanced down and saw fear written across her face. Giving her hand a slight squeeze, he flashed her half a smile when she turned her eyes up. He wished he could assure her that everything was going to turn out fine, but he couldn't lie. He had no control over this situation, nor any idea what the outcome would be.

They turned a corner to face a large, intricately-carved wooden door. Klute gripped a metal ring attached to the door and pulled it slowly open. As light flickered off the carvings, the image of a strange, two-headed beast seemed to slither along the surface of the door, as if alive. Only when the door swung to a stop did the effigy once again blend into the woodwork, as if it had been nothing more than a decorative etching.

The room on the other side of the door was blindingly lit compared to the dark corridor through which they had passed. Sunlight streamed through the high glass ceilings overhead, casting rainbows around the hallway. When they looked up through the panels of cut glass, the sky was broken up by thousands of tiny, illuminating crystals, and sunrays shot across the hall in a brilliant display of color. At the opposite end of the hallway stood another large, ornately-carved door. Composed of white marble, this massive entrance was even more impressive than the first. Dragons in hues of green, orange, and blue flew across the stone slab, belching out red flames and etching their fire into the image.

Two heavily armed guards glared at them from either side of the great door, and Connor quickly took account of their weapons: spears in their hands, swords at their sides, and several daggers tucked into their bandoliers. Upon their heads were bands like the one Klute wore. As Connor observed their pointed ears and fierce-looking features, he surmised that these were warrior elves, like the ones Nyia had warned him about. And their solidly built frames, steely glares, and defiant postures were a far cry from the playful creatures he recalled from his childhood tales. These elves were dangerous, and Connor was sure they could be incredibly challenging foes.

Stepping up to the platform, Klute approached the armed elves with confidence. They exchanged a few muttered words, too quiet for Connor to hear, and after shooting angry glares in the mortals' direction, the guards finally stepped aside. The large door slowly swung open, causing the dragons to once again fly across the surface of the stone, bringing the carved images to life. When Klute gestured for them to follow, the three travelers cautiously stepped over the threshold into the king's throne room.

The first thing Connor noticed were two more armed guards standing at the top of a staircase on the second-floor balcony. Sitting between them was a well-dressed figure who Connor assumed was King Enoch. When he glanced down at his dirty boots and blood-covered clothes, Connor wished he had cleaned up before appearing in the king's hall, but then, he'd never really had a high opinion of royalty. Lifting his head and jutting out his chin, he let his defiance push away any inadequacies he might have been feeling.

As they continued across the polished black-and-white stones, the mortals came to an etched image in the middle of the ebony floor. It was a circle separated into six equal parts by lines of silver, and the image of a unique animal was etched into each section: a deer, a boar, an eagle, a monkey, a snake, and finally, a dragon. Arching down to meet the walls at smooth, rounded corners, the ceilings in the throne room were even higher than those in the hall. Slightly below the ceiling and placed strategically along the walls, a row of rectangular windows shed light into the large open hall, as well as the empty balcony that encircled the throne room.

The room was utterly silent, and only the echo of their footsteps broke the stillness. Connor, Isaboe, and Rosalyn followed the Jarcadian warrior across the large room until he stopped at the base of the king's dais and turned, ordering them softly, "Wait here." After ascending to the dais alone, he addressed the king.

As Connor watched the interaction between the warrior and his monarch, though he couldn't make out the words, he recognized by the tone that Klute was being reprimanded. With the exception of his large pointed ears, His Highness looked like a mortal man. He wore a dark purple robe with an ornate crown upon his head, and by the command in his voice, it was clear King Enoch was not pleased.

"What do you think they're talking about?" Isaboe whispered.

"Well, I'm pretty sure he's not offering us a key to the castle," Rosalyn replied, quietly. "And I'm starting to get the feeling that our venture here may be short-lived."

Connor saw a seriousness in Rosalyn's face that belayed her sarcasm. If she was having doubts about their ability to complete this mission, how could he find the courage to keep going? They had entered this strange land on an incredible rescue attempt only because the sorceress seemed so confident in her ability to pull it off. It was Rosalyn who had created the portal that brought them here, and now it sounded as if she was ready to give up. "Then why did we come at all?" Though he tried to keep his voice down, Connor felt his irritation rising.

"Because we had no other choice," Isaboe whispered. "You know that."

"Then we canna accept defeat and retreat, regardless o' what we may be up against," Connor hissed back, meeting her concern-filled eyes. "We'll get what we came for, and then get the hell out o' here. But not until then!"

A resounding crack on the stone floor caught their attention, and they looked up as one toward the throne. Holding a staff in one hand, King Enoch stood and glared down at the mortals who had dared to appear in his hall, but he said nothing to them. Instead, he barked an order at Klute, who made a gesture of royal respect before retreating back down to join the mortals. As he stomped down off the last step, Klute's expression was rigid and his fierce stare was locked onto Connor. "You do not speak in the king's throne room unless you are spoken to first. Is that clear?"

Returning the warrior's glare, Connor only nodded.

"We are done here now. Follow me," Klute snarled, pushing Connor aside.

Following Klute out of the hall, Connor thought the brevity of their audience with King Enoch a bit odd. The way he glared at them made it hard to believe that he would support their cause. Nyia had mentioned that the elves held a hatred for humans, and he wondered if that was a feeling shared amongst all Underlings. If so, that would make their challenging mission even more difficult.

Stopping first to collect their bags from the small room that Isaboe and Rosalyn had stayed in the night before, the three mortals followed Klute through the dark corridors of the castle. Though he was a man of few words, the warrior was more silent than usual as he guided them to their new accommodations. "You should find these arrangements more suitable," he finally said as he pulled open the door to a large, well-furnished room. "As you have requested, there are two separate rooms with a bed in each. Fresh food and water will be brought to you, so make no attempt to leave."

"What, we're prisoners?" Connor growled, standing outside the open door and refusing to enter.

"These are not accommodations for prisoners," Klute snarled back.

The two men stood glaring at each other in defiance for several seconds before Connor spoke, "I left my horse tied up. I havta go tend to him."

"I don't know why you want to keep the ghost-runner. You will not be here that long."

"Long enough to accomplish what we came here for, and until I ken if ye are gonna help us, he may be our only ride."

Klute glared at Connor for another uncomfortable moment. "Then I will accompany you to a location where you can keep it. But since you will be leaving soon, I do not expect that you will be seeing this wallabock again."

Connor struggled to guide his unruly wallabock through the winding forest path as he tried to keep up with Klute. Not until the trees gave way to a clearing and the Jarcadian warrior slowed down did Connor finally catch up to him. Together, they stepped out into a wildflower-dotted meadow through which a sparkling creek flowed. Klute led the way to the trunk of a very large old tree that sat along the water's bank. The roots of the decaying tree had grown out in long slender fingers that clung to the land as the water slowly washed away the earth it sat upon. A door had been cut into the face of its trunk.

Klute stepped up to the small door and knocked, but after waiting a moment with no response, he walked around to the back of the tree, stopping in front of what appeared to be a ram's horn hanging from a hook that had been embedded into the tree's trunk. After lifting the horn, the Jarcadian warrior put the small tip to his lips and blew. The horn's call was deep and rich, cutting cleanly through the clearing. Klute waited a second, and then blew the horn a second time before replacing it on the hook.

Relaxing his grip, but keeping a secure hold on the wallabock's lead, Connor let the flying horse nibble on the grass as they waited. When a sound caught the horse's attention, its head immediately was up and its ears forward. Connor looked over his shoulder and saw a number of small deer running into the clearing as if fleeing from some danger. Not much bigger than hunting dogs, the animals sprinted on twig-thin legs. Connor watched in shock as a few leapt high into the air and then unfurled delicate wings. Their wings didn't take them far, and, after cresting the treetops, the tiny deer floated back down and rejoined the run. No sooner had the deer vanished into the forest on the far side of the clearing when another sound caught Connor's attention, but this time it was not prey on the run. It was the hunter.

Connor watched as a short squatty man emerged from the trees and waddled in their direction. He couldn't have been more than three-feet tall and was cloaked in expertly woven leaves and twigs. Upon his head sat a green cap also made of the sort of things one might find on the forest floor. The would-be hunter carried a bow and had a quiver of arrows slung across his back. When he came close enough, he raised a hand in welcome.

"Lo, there, JoJo!" the stout little man shouted his greeting as he continued his course. With such short legs, it took a few moments for him to reach his destination.

Klute lifted a hand in response. "Greetings, Titto. It appears we have interrupted your hunting. Sorry about that."

"I be truly craving some fresh meat, but no mind. I'll get one on the next go," Titto said as he joined his guests. "Fish and nuts get to be a bit old, dontcha' know?" Speaking in a voice cracked with age, the little man gave Connor and his wallabock a scrutinizing look as he slipped the quiver off his back and laid it on the ground in front of his door, where it was quickly joined by the bow. "A black ghost-runner? Oh, for sure, that be a rarity!" Curiosity was etched on the man's face, which Connor thought resembled a dried-up apple, all wrinkled and squished together. "How'd ya come by such a prize?"

"That is not important," Klute retorted. "I need you to watch over this ghost-runner for a short while."

"How long be a while?"

"It should not be more than a few days. But if we do not come back," Klute paused and shot Connor a steely glare, "you will not have to hunt for your fresh meat."

Connor had no reply. He just held Klute's cold stare until Titto broke the uncomfortable silence.

"Well, that be no problem, JoJo." Having picked up on the tension between his visitors, Titto offered a guarded nod to the stranger. "And who be you?"

"This is Connor," Klute answered for his companion.

"You be neither fey nor elf," the gnome scowled at Connor.

"No, I'm mortal."

"A mortal?" The gnome's bushy white brows shot up in surprise. "By Gypsum and by Golly! A mortal's not been seen in this realm for longer than I've been alive! What brings ye?" As the gnome paused, a look of recall lit his face. "The Council of Elders be meeting at the castle of Sashtonia in a few days, hey? Is that why the mortal be here? Something big be happening?"

"That's no concern of yours, Titto," Klute answered firmly. "And how is it that you know about the Gathering?"

"Uh—well, just because I live in a tree, JoJo, don't mean I live ignorant. I be keeping an ear to the ground. It's easy enough for us wee folk!" The gnome chuckled outright at his own joke, but the Jarcadian warrior did not seem amused. When the little man realized his guests did not find him humorous, Titto suddenly looked nervous, and his smile was strained when he spoke again. "Would the two of ye be interested in a mug o' brew? I cracked open last year's barrel, and it fermented right nice, if I don't say so meself."

"No. We need to return to the castle," Klute replied firmly. "But I do appreciate the offer." As Connor observed this exchange, he thought the warrior's stiffness seemed to soften.

"Oh, well, since you can't stay, JoJo, I have something for ye," Titto announced before he turned and waddled into his tree-trunk house.

"Why does he call ye JoJo?" Connor asked after Titto had disappeared.

"I am not entirely sure," Klute replied. "But I think it has some meaning of reverence. He has been referring to me as JoJo since I first found him here a few summers back. This is the king's land, and Titto is a squatter paying no tribute. Though I should have thrown him off, I took pity on him. He has come in handy a time or two."

"Here it is." Titto had left his hat and coat inside, though a few remnants of greenery remained stuck in his bristly white hair. Red suspenders held up his dust-covered pants, and the little man looked almost as round as he was tall. A sparkling green stone hung on a chain around his neck, an unexpected luxury that seemed out of place on the squatty little gnome. Titto proudly presented a bundle of what appeared to be chainmail armor to the Jarcadian warrior. "All stitched up; be just like new."

Klute took the garment and turned it over in his hands, examining it closely. "Nicely done, Titto. I cannot even find where the hole was. Even the king's best tailors could not do a finer job. Thank you."

For a second, Connor thought he saw the hint of a smile cross the Jarcadian warrior's lips, and there was sincerity in his eyes as he spoke to the little man. Titto beamed with pride at the warrior's praise, showing a wide smile that was missing a few teeth.

"That is a fine gem you are wearing, Titto," Klute said. "Is it new?"

"Oh, this?" Titto asked, grasping the sparkling green gem. "I just found it," the gnome said before dropping the stone under his shirt.

"You found it?" Klute repeated, and Connor immediately heard the suspicion in the warrior's voice. "Where did you find it, Titto, and why are you hiding it from me?"

"I not be hiding it, JoJo! I found it, just like I said. Lying near the creek it was, as if it had washed ashore, or… or dropped from the sky, just for me to find!"

As Klute paused, some of the skepticism drained from his voice. "That is a very lucky find, Titto. But you do know that this is the king's land, and therefore that gem also belongs to the king."

"Oh, no, please, JoJo! It be just one small stone. King Enoch will never miss what he don't know about." The gnome chuckled nervously. "You know us gnomes. We be rather partial to our pretty stones and sparklin' gems, dontcha' know? No harm, no foul, hey?"

Klute looked hard at the little man before he continued. "Alright, I will let you keep it for now. But do not forget whose land it is you are living on, Titto. Everything here belongs to King Enoch," the warrior said firmly before nodding at Connor. "Secure the wallabock so we can return to the castle."

"Oh, I not be forgetting, JoJo!" The gnome chimed, looking even more at ease. "And your kindness be beyond measure, my friend."

Glancing around the clearing, Connor led the ghost-runner toward one of the slender trees that grew near the water's edge, not far from Titto's tree-trunk home. Wrapping the rope multiple times around its trunk, he did his best to secure his newfound ride. "I'll be back," he promised as he patted the wallabock's flank. "Dinnae go anywhere." By the time he turned around, Connor saw Klute already heading back out of the clearing the way they had entered.

"I'll be back for the horse, so dinnae let it fly away," Connor said as he sprinted past the gnome. "And don't eat it!" he shouted. Though anxious about leaving his new steed, he really hadn't a choice in the matter.

On the quick walk back to the palace, Connor again struggled to keep pace with the Jarcadian warrior's longer stride. He was sure Klute was intentionally keeping the distance between them to limit any conversation and to avoid sharing what King Enoch had told him privately. Not knowing made Connor anxious; in this strange world, he needed to know what he was up against.

"Klute," Connor called out, causing the Jarcadian warrior to look over his shoulder but not to slow his pace. "Wait up, I need to ask ye," he spoke while hurrying his stride to catch up. "Why did ye not report our presence to King Enoch when ye arrived last night with the women?"

When Klute didn't respond for several seconds, Connor wondered if the warrior's lips would be sealed to any question he might have, especially after meeting with the king. "I had my reasons," Klute finally mumbled.

Connor fell into step beside the lion-man, whose eyes were focused on the path before him. "And what are those? That ye ken our cause is just? Is that why ye dinnae tell 'im right away?" But Klute didn't reply, so Connor kept talking. "As a soldier myself, I understand duty and orders, and yet ye made a choice to disobey yer own law, which I can only assume ye did on our behalf. That tells me there's more goin' on here, and I need to know what it is. What are ye not tellin' me, Klute?"

Again, no answer, so Connor kept pushing. "I ken ye have a heart. Ye just showed it with that little man back there squattin' in a tree! And I know that ye're torn about what to do, but I need to ken what we're up against."

The warrior only glowered at Connor.

"Yer silence is killin' me, man! And I have to tell ye, I'd rather face another pack of trolls than the Council of Elders in two days." Seeing that his rant wasn't making a difference, Connor blurted out his next thought. "With ye on yer bird and me on Sonas, we could fly to Euphoria and find the child. Then we could go back to our world, just like ye want us to and we'd never have to face the Council."

"You have no idea of what you speak, mortal, so just shut up," Klute growled without turning or slowing his march. He seemed grimly determined to be rid of Connor as soon as possible.

"Then tell me; why are we so unwanted here? I'm aware of the war with the elves, but that was over a thousand years ago. Yer people can't really still hate us so much that ye're willing to let an innocent child be killed by that fey bitch. Are ye all so afraid of Lorien that none of ye are willing to stand up to her?"

That stopped Klute in his tracks, and he turned around with a murderous look. From beneath his heavy brow, the lion-man's amber eyes looked dangerous as he stepped closer to Connor. "I will not dignify that question with a response. But I will tell you this, mortal: sometimes it's best to sacrifice one for the sake of the many. It would be wisest to let the child die rather than risk the future of both our worlds." Klute's tone softened, and his eyes said more than his words. "Go home, Connor. Take your women and leave this place."

When Klute started to turn, Connor grabbed ahold of his arm, but in the next moment, he had to jump out of the way of the warrior's blade as it sliced through the air, barely missing his fingers.

"I told you once before, mortal; if you want to keep that hand, never ever lay it upon me again!" Klute hissed, still holding his weapon ready to make good on his threat.

Throwing his hands up in surrender, Connor stepped back.

"And no more talk!" the warrior snapped, stomping toward Connor. "You are just a stupid human who has not figured out that you are in over your head. You do not belong here, you cannot survive here. More importantly, I will not be helping you. Are we quite clear on that?" Klute's words escalated with the intensity Connor saw on his face.

"Aye. We're clear," Connor said, keenly aware of the defeat reflected in his own voice.

CHAPTER 8

A NIGHT AT THE POND

By the time Connor and Klute made it back to the castle it was almost dark, and when they entered the room, Isaboe let out a deep sigh of relief. But she couldn't help but notice Connor's foul mood and the rippling tension that had floated in with the two warriors.

"If your attendance is required, I will come for you. Otherwise, you will remain here," Klute said firmly as he turned toward the door.

"Wait," Connor stepped into Klute's path, forcing him to an abrupt stop. Isaboe watched nervously as the two men stared at each other, challenging the other without words before Connor finally spoke. "I'm tired and hungry, and I want answers. But since ye won't answer my questions, and it appears we're being locked up for the night, I'll settle for a hot bath and a decent meal."

"The meal has been provided for you." Klute gestured to the table laden with plates of food. "And, while you are most certainly in dire need of a bath, the wash basin in the other room will have to suffice for now."

"I'm covered in dirt, sweat, and the blood of trolls. I'll not crawl into my woman's bed smellin' like a butcher," Connor snarled.

"Let me take him to the pool," Isaboe offered as she stepped between the two men.

"What pool?" Connor asked suspiciously.

"There's a bathing pool not far from here that Rosalyn and I were able to use last night after we arrived."

Connor shot Klute a suspicious glare.

"They had a female chaperone at all times," Klute answered Connor's silent accusation. "As promised, your companions have been protected, and treated with nothing but respect."

"Klute is right, Connor. He's been very decent and respectful to us," Isaboe said, placing a hand on her husband's arm in an attempt to soften his guard. "And you'll like the pool. It's quite lovely." She turned back to Klute. "Please, may I take him?"

"But no chaperone," Connor growled. As Klute started to protest, Connor silenced him. "I dinnae need a chaperone to take a bath, and besides, where would we go?"

"And don't forget, I'm still here," Rosalyn added from across the room. Munching on a piece of dried fruit, she took a seat on the sofa. "I'm sure they'll not leave me behind. I'm their way home," she chimed with half a smile.

"See, nothing to worry about," Connor jested as he raised his hand to pat Klute on the shoulder, but he quickly pulled back, and once again, Isaboe saw the unspoken exchange between them.

"I will have an attendant wait for you at the entrance to the pool," Klute finally agreed before looking down at Isaboe. "Do you recall how to get there? It winds down through the brush, and night has fallen."

"Yes, I remember."

"Leave your communication stones here so they do not go missing."

Removing the strap from her wrist, Isaboe placed it on the table, then spun back into the room. Opening her bag, she pulled out a change of clothing and a bar of soap. "You'd better fetch some clean clothes," she said, shooting a furrowed glare at Connor's attire. "Klute is right; you smell something awful, and those clothes most likely can never be saved."

Leading Connor by the hand through the trees, Isaboe pushed aside the branches that reached out into the path. "Come along, it's not much further."

"Are ye sure ye ken where ye're goin'?" Connor's uncertainty caused Isaboe a twinge of doubt. But when they passed the twisted oak she recalled from the night before, with roots that bulged up out of the ground and threatened to trip the unwary traveler, she knew she was on the right course.

"Yes, I know where I'm going. And be sure to watch your footing." As they silently followed the path to the pond, odd sounds in the night brought Isaboe's senses on alert, but it wasn't the unknown that was bothering her. "Connor, did something happen between you and Klute? You were both very tense tonight," she muttered over her shoulder.

"Yeah, well, there's something he's not tellin' me, something related to us being here. When I tried to push him for information, he got a bit defensive—pulled a knife on me."

Isaboe spun around. "Pulled a knife on you! Are you alright?"

"Oh, aye. He didna cut me, just gave me a warning to quit asking questions."

"What do you think he's keeping from us?"

"I dinnae ken. But there's more going on here than them finding out that Lorien has taken Gabriel. I think we're only part of a much bigger problem."

Isaboe only nodded and swallowed her anxiety before continuing down the path. Around another bend she ducked under a low-hanging branch, and slowed her progress as the trees thinned. She led Connor down a small slope that opened around what looked like a black hole in the ground, dark and endless. The night sky was full of stars whose light, along with the half-moon, lit up the lazy steam rising from the surface of the pond, giving away its wonderful secret.

"Why is the water steaming?"

"Because it's warm." Isaboe had barely answered Connor's question when splashing sounds drew their attention to the other side of the pond. Even in the dark, Isaboe could make out two figures quickly slipping out of the water and into the underbrush. She could hear strange, chastising words coming from even stranger voices as the figures faded into the trees.

"Sorry," Isaboe called out. "We didn't mean to intrude," she added apologetically. But suddenly feeling a sense of unease, knowing that others were around, she made a quick decision to let Connor bathe alone.

"Apparently we're not the only ones who use this bathin' hole," Connor muttered. Having already removed his boots, socks, and shirt, he was obviously less concerned about a potential audience. "*Ahh*, it feels like bath water," he confirmed, as he stood near the edge and dipped one foot. "What makes it so warm?" he asked, unlacing his blood-covered breeches and dropping them to his feet before kicking them up onto the bank.

"Klute said the water bubbles up from an underground hot spring. Rosalyn and I spent a long time here yesterday evening, and obviously the locals like it."

Tossing his last piece of clothing aside, Connor was down to just his skin. "Are ye joinin' me?"

Isaboe watched him hesitate at the water's edge as he waited for her. "No, go ahead. I'll just keep you company from here."

Facing her, Connor placed his hands on his hips. "Come on, Isaboe. It was yer idea to take a bath."

"No, it was my idea for *you* to take a bath. I had one last night."

Taking the few steps to stand before her, Connor started to unlace her dress. "And ye'd like to take another one tonight, right?" His eyes held a playful smile.

"No." Isaboe pushed his hands away. "I'm not taking another bath."

"But it'd be so nice to feel yer soft skin against mine," Connor whispered before starting to plant little kisses down the side of her neck as he continued unlacing her dress.

Though his kisses were sweet, the stench of dead trolls and the sweat that wafted off of him was nauseating, and she pushed him away. "Connor, I don't mean to be rude, but you smell like the back end of a mule!"

A look of insult crossed his face, but only for a moment. "That's the sweet smell o' victory, *boireannach*, and it dinnae come without a lil' sweat and blood." A cocky smile crossed his face as he leaned in closer. "And now it's time for my reward."

Again, Isaboe blocked his advance. "No. Bath first. Get into the water, *now!*"

Stepping back from the bite in her words, Connor's expression melted into disappointment before he extended his arms and took a stance, giving Isaboe a flirtatious smile. "Are ye sure ye dinnae want some of this?"

Isaboe rolled her eyes at her husband's over confidence. "I'm quite sure I can hold myself back." Bending down, she retrieved the soap and tossed it in his direction. "Here, don't forget to wash off the stink."

"Hey!" Connor snarled, deflecting the soap before it hit him in the face. "Ye really ken how to crush a man's ego, *Breagha!*" Now sullen, he snatched up the soap from the grassy bank and turned into the steaming water. Wading in hip-deep, he proceeded to do as instructed.

As Isaboe watched him wash away the troll's blood, she listened to the chorus of the night, and it felt cold and eerie. When Connor dove into the liquid darkness, she took a seat on the water's edge, wrapped her arms around her knees and waited for him to surface. But a sound coming from the trees drew her attention. Looking over her shoulder, she saw the dark outline of rustling bushes but no sign of what was causing the movement. When the sound came again, she jerked her head in the other direction and this time caught a glimpse of her company.

Staring at Isaboe from only an arm's length away was a small being with starlight twinkling in its enormously wide eyes. The limited light of the night sky cast enough luminance to see that the being had a slender body and matching arms and legs, but a rather round and bulbous head.

Feeling trapped by the large strange eyes staring back at her, Isaboe was startled when the little figure abruptly snarled at her, exposing a set of nasty-looking teeth. She jumped to her feet before the creature darted into the trees as it sang its deadly song.

"If a water faerie comes along, best ye break into a song. If she likes what you give, she might just let you live. But sing the song out of tune, and death shall come on the next full moon!"

As she heard the threatening limerick, Isaboe felt a slither of fear run down her back. Fumbling with the laces of her bodice, she couldn't pull her dress off fast enough. "Connor, where are you?" she muttered nervously. "Why haven't you come back up?" Hearing the anxiety in her voice, Isaboe quickly finished undressing and tossed her bodice and knickers onto the shore. But stepping into the warmth of the water did nothing to ease her shivers. "Connor! Where are you?" she called out again.

Startled when she heard voices on the shoreline, Isaboe saw the silhouettes of lithe figures dashing along the water's edge, but when something touched her back, panic slammed into her stomach and she let out a shriek. Spinning around, Isaboe found Connor leaning away from her swinging arms.

"*Whoa!* It's just me, love," he said calmly before wrapping her into his embrace. "Looks like ye changed yer mind, aye?"

Isaboe threw her arms around his neck. "Uh…yeah, well, you were under the water for so long, I was starting to worry."

"Oh, ye were worried about me, aye? Are ye sure it wasn't that ye were afraid of that wee creature on the bank?"

Isaboe shot a glance over her shoulder before looking back at Connor, her eyes wide. "Did you see it? I heard it say some sort of warning about a water faerie, and it didn't sound very pleasant."

"Dinnae worry, Isaboe. I won't let those bad water faeries get ye."

"It's not funny, Connor. I don't like it here. I just want to get Gabriel and go home. Do you think Klute will help us?"

"I know ye'd love to go home with little Gabriel in your arms, but it's not gonna be that easy, *Breagha*. I think Klute is torn at what to do. He may want to help us, but he's sworn to his duty. And after the meeting with King Enoch, he ain't saying much."

"What about Nyia? You spent some time alone with her. Do you think she would be willing to help us?"

Connor scoffed. "Not likely. Nyia's made it real clear we're not wanted here. She dinnae care much for humans, nor does she give a damn about our problem. No, I still think our best chance is with Klute. He *wants* us to meet with the council. I'm just guessing, but maybe he thinks there's a chance they'll be willin' to help us, and he's waitin' to see how the ruling goes."

"But we've already been here for two days. The council doesn't meet for another two, and we're no closer to finding Gabriel than when we first arrived." Though Isaboe had been attempting to calm her fears, they were starting to get the best of her.

"As long as Rosalyn has the portal locked in that ring, time is standing still, so it dinnae matter how long it takes here. We'll figure it out, somehow. I hate to see ye worry like this. It pains me to see so much angst on yer beautiful face, my love." Connor's soft words were followed by his hands around her waist, bringing her closer. Even in the dark, Isaboe could see the compassion in his eyes, now intimately close and dancing with hers. "Every moment I was away from ye it hurt my heart. All I could think about was getting back to ye, holding ye, and keeping ye safe." His words came barely above a whisper, just before he kissed her. Sinking into his embrace, Isaboe wrapped her arms around his neck and lingered in the kiss—soft, wet, and passionate.

When Isaboe pulled back, she ran a hand across his face and looked closely into his eyes. "I was so afraid the whole time you were gone. You were off somewhere in this strange land fighting trolls!" Isaboe struggled with the concept that the creatures from her childhood stories were real, but they looked much more ominous in real life then in her picture books. "I was so frightened you wouldn't come back, or that you might come back missing pieces!"

He chuckled softly. "Ye shouldn't worry 'bout me so much, *Breagha*. You know I can take care of myself." The mirth left him and was replaced with tenderness. "It's you I'm worried about. I dinnae ken what's in store for us at the Council of Elders, but we need to be prepared for the worst-case scenario; that they send us home empty-handed."

"That's not an option, and I never want to hear those words again!"

"I agree, and we'll do everything we can to make sure that dinnae happen. But in this place, and with these people, we canna predict the outcome."

"And if the ruling doesn't go in our favor, then what?"

"Well, I guess we'll have to convince Klute not to follow the council's orders."

Isaboe felt a lump rise in her throat at the idea of not being able to come home with her daughter's baby boy. She had promised Anna that she would, and this was a promise she was desperate to keep.

"Enough talk for now," Connor whispered as he peppered kisses down the side of her neck. Closing her eyes, Isaboe let her head ease back in the water while Connor continued moving lower with each kiss until she felt his lips on the curve of her breasts. As much as she enjoyed his touch, it wasn't enough to overcome her worries, or the fact that something was out there in the trees, probably watching. When Connor's touching became more intimate, she pushed him away.

"No. Not with an audience."

"Oh, come on, *Breagha*. Maybe we can teach the little critters a thing or two." Connor reached for her with a sly smile, but she continued to hold him at bay.

"I have a question to ask you," Isaboe stated, pushing his hands away. "Connor, I'm serious," she said firmly, trying to redirect his focus, but to no avail.

"So am I," Connor whispered, reaching for Isaboe again and pulling her close into his body.

Though his kisses were tender, this was not the time, and so she pushed him away once more, holding him at arm's length. "No. I need to ask you something."

A look of defeat flashed across Connor's face as he heaved a heavy sigh and let his head drop back into the water. "Fine. Ask yer question," he grumbled.

"Lift your head and look at me, please."

Letting out a sigh, Connor lifted his head, brushed the water from his hair and met her stare. "What?"

Isaboe paused for a moment, seeking the right words. "Do you think I'm…weak? I mean, do you think I'm *too* dependent on you? What I'm trying to ask is if you think I'm…puny?"

She watched her husband's lips curl slightly. "Why do ye ask?" he finally said with a restrained smile.

"It was something Klute said. He asked why a warrior like you would be mated to a puny woman like me. Maybe those weren't his exact words, but that's what he meant. And it got me thinking. Maybe I *am* too dependent on you. I don't even know how to defend myself or how to use a weapon properly. I think you should teach me, so if I ever need to I can defend myself."

"Well, that's wise, and I'll be happy to show ye a few things, but ye're not built for fighting, my love. That's my job."

"But Nyia is Klute's mate, and she's a warrior. She doesn't need Klute to defend her. I feel as if they both look down on me because, well, I'm not your equal."

"These are different people, Isaboe. They have different customs, so dinnae take it personally." Connor stroked the side of her face, letting his fingers linger on her skin. "I dinnae think yer puny. Petite, aye, beautiful and sexy, yes, but yer too damn stubborn and fiery to be considered puny. And I wouldn't want ye to be like Nyia. I like ye just the way ye are, soft and warm," he confirmed with a coy smile, sliding closer and wrapping Isaboe back into his arms.

When his wife slid her arms around his neck and kissed him, Connor again reached for places she didn't want him to go, and she was back to blocking his advances.

"Ye ken, it's not fair that ye come into the water, all naked and beautiful, and expect me to keep my hands to myself."

Pushing out of his embrace and grabbing ahold of his offending hands, Isaboe turned toward the bank. "Well, then we're done here," she said as she dragged him reluctantly from the warm water and into the night air. Back on the bank, Connor retrieved his bag and began pulling out clean clothes. Wet, naked and shivering, Isaboe felt around on the ground for her clothing. A twinge of panic started bubbling in her stomach when only the smock could be found. "Connor, I can't find my dress or my knickers, or any of my underclothes!"

"Are ye sure this is where ye laid 'em?" Connor asked, now standing next to her as he laced up his breeches.

"Yes, I'm sure! I was standing right here when I tossed them and…" but the sound of a devilish chuckle coming from behind the bushes stopped Isaboe in mid-sentence. "That wicked little creature stole my clothes! You bloody bastard!" she shouted toward the bushes. "I can't believe how rude you are, taking someone else's clothes!"

"It's a good thing ye brought a change with ye. Here, put this on." Connor helped Isaboe pull the smock over her head while she continued to complain.

"Well, at least it left yer shoes." When Connor handed Isaboe her slippers, she heard the ring of humor in his words.

"It's not funny, Connor," she snapped, grabbing her shoes from his hands. "That horrible creature not only scared me, it stole my best clothing!"

"I dinnae think it's funny that it scared ye, but it's a wee bit funny that it took yer clothes."

Isaboe could hear the mirth in Connor's voice, but she wasn't finding any of it amusing, and she shot him a look that told him so. "As you most certainly know, I didn't bring many clothes with me. That was one of only two dresses I have to my name in this crazy realm!" Turning toward the bushes, she shouted, "It won't fit you, you filthy little bugger!"

Once again, a mischievous cackle came from the underbrush along the bank and they heard the sound of scattering. The thief was gone.

"Alright, I think ye made yer point, but ye'll never see that dress again. Ye havta let it go."

Trying to calm her rage, Isaboe finished lacing up her smock. "Well, I may have to let it go, but I don't have to be happy about it!"

CHAPTER 9

THE COUNCIL OF ELDERS

When the knock at their door jarred them awake, Isaboe sat up in bed, rubbing the sleep from her eyes. She watched as Connor scrambled to pull on his breeches before opening the door to their room. At the same moment, she heard Rosalyn greeting their guest.

Slipping out of bed and into some proper clothing, Isaboe found Klute awaiting them in the antechamber. Behind the Jarcadian warrior was another bizarre-looking fey creature who was tall and lanky with blue skin under his brown tunic and leggings. Instead of hair, he sported a set of sharp, black pointed horns above the equally pointed ears on his bald head. Holding a tray of food and water, the strange man walked over to the table to replace yesterday's empty tray with refreshed offerings. As the fey was turning to leave, he caught Isaboe's eye with a look of curiosity that matched Isaboe's as she stared back at him.

Klute grumbled something at the boy, who quickly recovered, scurrying from the room and closing the door on his exit. Connor and Rosalyn had already strapped on their communication stones, and Isaboe hurried to do the same. Klute waited until they were all able to understand him. "I apologize for the early morning intrusion, but there has been a change of plans. The Council of Elders is meeting today. You have one hour to prepare."

"What?" Isaboe exclaimed.

"I thought they weren't meetin' til tomorrow," Connor added.

"Most of them have arrived early and do not wish to wait."

"For some reason that doesn't surprise me," Rosalyn said, stepping up to Klute. "Can you please tell us what we are to expect at this meeting?"

"Will we have a chance to present our case?" Connor asked.

Klute's stoic gaze swept over them before he answered. "I do not know what you can expect today, nor do I know if you will have the opportunity to argue your case."

"And what'd ye think the chances are that they'll help us?"

When Klute met Connor's stare, something like regret flashed behind his eyes. "I have enough respect for you, mortal, to speak honestly. The truth is this: I do not believe your chances are good. But I will do what I can to find a few moments for you to have your say." As he paused, Isaboe saw what looked like defeat cross his face before he spoke again. "I will be back to escort you to the king's hall. Be sure to pack your belongings—just in case."

True to his word, Klute returned for them an hour later. As they followed him down the hall, Isaboe held Connor's hand tightly, but it did nothing to ease the anxiety bubbling in her stomach. On his other side, Rosalyn was unreadable, her expression stoic and aloof. But Isaboe knew her mother also had to be feeling anxious, even if she was better at hiding it. Everything hinged on this meeting with the council. She hated how quickly this mission had spun out of their control and had a heavy feeling that they would be leaving today, but not the way they had hoped.

Just as before, the flying dragons embedded in the doors came to life as the travelers were escorted into the king's throne room, but that was where the similarities ended. The last time they were escorted here the room had been empty, save for the king seated high on his throne surrounded by his armed guards. Now, the balconies were filled with the elaborately adorned council members, each more striking and extraordinary than the last. These Fey Kings and Queens looked stranger and more beautiful than anyone Isaboe had ever seen, or even imagined. Her heart thundering in her ears, she clutched Connor's hand a little tighter as they followed Klute into the room. The council's muted conversations faded as the mortals crossed the polished black floor, and Isaboe thought the echo of their footsteps sounded almost intrusive against the heavy silence. As the amazing creatures looked down upon them in judgement, she felt small and plain in their presence, yet she couldn't tear her stare away from them.

The first to catch Isaboe's attention was an aged woman with pale green skin. She wore a dress of shifting rainbow colors, and her silvery hair flowed around her slender form like rippling water. A crown of twisted vines sat proudly on her brow. Next to her sat an ebony-skinned man with hypnotic black eyes and a dark red robe. He was crowned in antlers. At his side stood a tall, slender hairless woman with polished skin the color of Maplewood. Her tight suit appeared to be made of snakeskin, and it outlined every curve of her body. The fey woman's cheeks were hollow, her lips dark red, and her judging eyes challenging. As the woman leaned over the balcony railing to get a better look, Isaboe met her gaze, and it sent a shiver down her spine.

Escaping the strange woman's stare, Isaboe averted her eyes to the other side of the balcony, which was filled with just as many bizarre-looking figures. When a tall rough-skinned man with a long narrow face and willowy arms lumbered up from his seat, Isaboe noticed leaves and twigs sprouting from his body. There was a woman with green skin whose crown of twisted horns grew right out the top of her head. Inside the tangled cage of bone fluttered a twittering songbird.

As they approached King Enoch's throne, Isaboe couldn't look away from the strange group of beings that would decide their fate. Her eyes fell upon an elegant looking woman with fair skin and flaming red hair. When she leaned forward, Isaboe saw that the exotic creature's crown was swirling with dancing lights. Another form suddenly materialized beside her. The woman only took proper form when she stopped at a chair, and then became transparent again before she moved into her seat. Once seated, her solid form reappeared, shimmering like a liquid jewel.

Toward the back of the balcony, separate from those seated, stood a dark figure sheathed in shadow. Though Isaboe couldn't make out his features, she shivered when she felt his eyes on her. Was there no end of dangerous and deadly creatures in this realm? Glancing up at Connor, she found him looking in the same direction, but his expression was unreadable.

They came to a halt in the middle of the throne room, and Klute looked back at the mortals. "Stay here," he commanded, "and be quiet." Klute continued alone until he stood at the foot of the stairs to the balcony. King Enoch glared down at them, even as the warrior made a gesture of respect to the king. Determined to stand strong against the glares of the congregation, the mortals silently huddled together. Set against all this regality, Isaboe felt naked and powerless. She hoped that Connor and Rosalyn were feeling stronger and more confident than she was.

"Your Highness," Klute began, "all good kings, queens, and elders in attendance." His voice carried easily around the throne room, and he spoke with reverence as he turned his face up to address the audience. "I know that in this place, sound decisions and laws are decreed. Wise and sound leaders are gathered here within these walls, and I have the greatest confidence that your decision today regarding the request of these mortals will be fair and just." Introductions complete, Klute made another gesture of respect, and then stepped back, taking his place next to Connor.

King Enoch glared at Klute before tapping his rod, a signal to the robust man at his right to rise. Wearing a bright red jacket over his ornate vest, the man's barrel-chest seemed much too big for the garment, pushing at the fabric and testing its buttons. His skin was tinged an unhealthy green, and his wide mouth and bulbous eyes reminded Isaboe of a toad.

When he cleared his throat, it did nothing to dissuade her of the notion. "This special gathering of the Council of Elders is hereby called to order." The toad-man's bloated jowls jiggled when he spoke, and Isaboe was sure he hopped in lieu of walking. "I, Bolticush, Counselor of Citizens," he continued, "speak for the council. We recognize King Enoch's authority here in the Palace of Sashtonia," he paused and made a gesture of acknowledgment toward the king. "However, this is no ordinary meeting, and all elders in attendance will have an equal opportunity to speak their minds regarding the mortals' request."

With these words, Bolticush took his seat and King Enoch stood. Still holding his staff, the king offered the mortals only a sour glare before turning his attention to those seated in the balcony. "My friends and fellow dignitaries, I thank you for your early arrival to this year's meeting of the Council of Elders. I know we all have important matters from our own lands that must be addressed. However, at this time it seems we must first deal with this pressing matter which requires our attention." When the king glared down at them again, Isaboe could feel the accusation in his eyes before he even said a word. "These mortals," he said, pointing at them with his staff as he continued, "have come into our realm uninvited in order to attempt an impossible mission. They have asked that our Jarcadian warriors assist them."

"What is their mission?" asked a bald man with large eyes, blue skin and wearing a dark green suit. The shiny gold crown that sat upon his head caught the sunlight as he leaned forward.

"More importantly, *how* did these *filthy* mortals even get here? There hasn't been a human in our lands for over a thousand years!" Isaboe didn't see who spoke, but that in no way lessened the sting of the insult.

"You are not seriously considering helping them, are you?" The odd, high-pitched voice came from a little man who needed to stand on a crate to see over the balcony railing. He was only about two feet tall, a bit on the round side, and wearing a tidy little red suit with a large black buckle. Over his wispy white hair a cone-shaped cap was pulled down to his pointed ears. More mumbled questions began spilling out of the gathered council before King Enoch forcefully tapped his staff, causing silence to fall over the large room. "All of your questions will be answered," he spoke with command, "but we will keep this meeting orderly and address one question at a time." He let his gaze wander across those sitting in the balcony before finally looking upon the intruders. "These mortals have all been equipped with communication stones, so they are able to understand everything spoken in this room."

Instantly, all faces in the balcony turned toward the mortals standing alone in the middle of the floor, and once again Isaboe felt the silent judgment in their eyes.

"From what has been shared with me," King Enoch continued, "the mortals are here on a rescue attempt. Queen Lorien of Euphoria has kidnapped one of their own, a human boy-child, and they have come to take him back."

A faint gasp was heard across the balcony, followed by uncomfortable silence. When Isaboe shot a glance to both Connor and Rosalyn, she saw her uncertainty mirrored on their faces.

"They have asked for assistance in this mission," King Enoch continued. "We need to consider the consequences that could arise if we honor their request. We must make the best decision for *all* concerned," the king paused, "even the mortals."

Isaboe could hear the distaste with which he said the words, as if having to deal with them fairly was repugnant.

"May I ask a question?" A thin man whose skin glowed in iridescent hues of green and blue stood up, catching everyone's attention. His nose and ears were long and pointed, and his large slanted eyes were deeply menacing. The lights dancing through his crown were purple and gold, and his gem-embroidered coat glimmered in the sunlight.

"The council recognizes King Bogknocken, Lord of the Pixies," Bolticush announced.

"How did these mortals enter our realm?" asked King Bogknocken. "As Queen O'desha has pointed out, a mortal has not passed into our realm since before the existence of Luminara. It was my understanding that mortals no longer possessed the ability to cross between realms. How did they arrive here?"

"Yes, how is it that they are here?" a disconnected voice asked. "What other powers do they have?" said another. "What's so special about the boy child?" These questions caused a flood of muttering from the balcony, and the audience turned toward King Enoch, awaiting the answers.

Pointing his staff at Rosalyn, the king commanded, "You! Step forward." Enoch paused while the sorceress did as instructed. "From what I have been told, this one created a portal that they all passed through."

"Where is the portal now?" a voice shouted, but there was no reply. Apparently, this was something King Enoch didn't know, and he turned his attention down to the group of mortals.

"It is kept in a ring I wear on my hand," Rosalyn replied quickly.

"Then use it now and go back!" demanded the slender woman in the snake-skin suit who was standing at the railing and glaring down at them. "You are not welcome here and your mission is a death sentence!"

"Thank you, Lady Jobetha, for your impassioned statement," replied a man whose head resembled a goat, complete with curled horns, floppy ears, and a beard. But when he stood upright, he was dressed in the clothing of a scholar.

"The council recognizes Lord Pagganot: High Elder from Teremenia," the frog-man announced.

Lord Pagganot nodded before continuing. His oration was measured and thoughtful. "Before we dismiss the mortals and their mission, I would like a bit more information. Why did Queen Lorien take this mortal child? He must be of great value for her to do so, and for the humans to risk such a dangerous rescue mission. I should certainly like to know the answer before I pass judgement."

"Nothing good has ever come from having mortals in our realm," Lady Jobetha snarled at Lord Pagganot before turning to address the congregation. "And there is certainly no reason why we should put *our* warriors at risk for these mortals!"

"Lady Jobetha, please take your seat," King Enoch demanded. The woman shot him a cold glare before sulking into her chair. "It is my understanding," the king continued, "that Lorien is only using the child as leverage. She has threatened to take his life if these mortals do not give her what she really wants."

"What does Lorien really want?" another voice in the crowd demanded. King Enoch once again pointed his staff, but this time at Isaboe. "You, step forward."

Still holding Connor's hand, she looked up at him nervously before releasing her grip, then stepped forward to stand next to her mother.

"These two women are mother and daughter. I have been told the younger one was recently abducted by Lorien and brought here to Euphoria for the purpose of conceiving and birthing a female child. It is this girl child that Lorien wants, and the boy's life is being held in exchange."

There was an audible silence in the large room, and the air felt cold and heavy as Isaboe instinctively slipped her hand into her mother's. It was the first time she had ever done so, but in that moment Isaboe needed her mother's strength, and just holding Rosalyn's hand gave her a small bit of courage.

"Don't these people have names?" asked the woman who sparkled like water when she moved. "Can they not speak on their own behalf?"

"The council recognizes Idora, Lady of the Lake," Bolticush announced.

"Lady Idora, the mortals will not be speaking further in this Gathering of Elders," King Enoch answered with reproach.

"I thought we would have a chance to speak." When Isaboe heard Connor grumble behind her, she glanced over her shoulder to see Klute snarl at her husband, obviously encouraging his silence. Though Connor said no more, his scowl said plenty.

"But are we seriously prepared to cast them out," the Lady of the Lake continued, "without completely understanding why they have risked so much to come here?

"We all know why they are here, Idora," snarled Lady Jobetha. "Put aside your *pious* attitude. The only decision this council can make must be for the good of the realm, and that is to *send them back*! Now!"

"Let us not be so hasty," said the tall, willowy-looking fellow. His words came almost as slowly as his movements, so lethargically that it was almost agonizing.

"The council recognizes Lord Mordackian, representative of the Tree Spirits from the land of Sashtonia," Bolticush announced.

"So that we may have a more complete understanding and make an informed decision," continued Mordackian, "I would like to know what the mortals' plan was upon arriving here. As you say, mortals have not been in our realm for over a thousand years, yet here they are. Somehow these three were able to cross over into our realm intending to rescue their human child, and then slip back into their own world. But without an army of soldiers to assist them, they have discovered that their mission is in jeopardy before it could even begin." The tree-man paused and looked around, holding the gaze of his peers. "But I present this question to the council: If these three mortals can find the courage to stand up against Lorien, with no idea how to accomplish that task, then why can't this great gathering of minds find even a small bit of bravery to consider their request? Speaking for myself and my people, isn't now the time to take action and make an effort to stop Lorien's reign of terror, once and for all?"

The silence that fell over the hall was heavy as Lord Mordackian took his seat. Isaboe glanced at her mother, then back over her shoulder at Connor, but she couldn't read the blank expressions on either of their faces.

King Enoch had been seated while the tree-man made his speech, but he now rose up from his throne to address the congregation. "I think we have heard enough. The council will adjourn for the mid-day meal and meet back here later this afternoon to make our decision."

"*This is bullshit!*" Connor shouted. "We're being ram-rodded out of town without having a chance to say a goddamn word?"

Klute slapped a meaty hand against Connor's chest and shot him a cold hard stare before he turned toward the king. "Your Highness, I would like to speak on the mortal's behalf."

"You are out of line, warrior," growled a large intimidating-looking man as he stepped out of the shadows from under the balcony. He wore a decorated metal chest plate and spoke with authority.

Klute turned toward the commander. "I mean no disrespect, General Renwolf, but I have spent a good deal of time with the mortals, and since the council will not allow them to speak, I beseech all of you: give me a moment to speak on their behalf."

King Enoch glared down at Klute and held his stare for several long heart-pounding moments before finally nodding at the general. The decorated man stepped back, once again disappearing into the shadows.

Klute shot a glance at Connor before taking a step forward. "First, I cannot agree more that the mortals' mission here is foolish and most likely futile. But we cannot ignore that even without a plan and having no idea of what they would encounter when they crossed over, they came anyway, because of their courage. They may be foolish, but these three brave mortals have risked everything to save the life of one boy and to keep Lorien from achieving her goal." Klute paused and let his gaze drift across the balcony. "Maybe now is the time to join these mortals and put an end to Lorien's reign. I have seen the disgraceful way she treats her own people and her ruthlessness in dealing with those who are unfortunate enough to cross over into her land uninvited. How long will this council continue to ignore the atrocities she commits?"

"That will be enough, warrior," King Enoch snapped. "The council has heard all it needs to hear. We will adjourn for now and give our decision after ..."

"*Move out of my way!*" A woman's voice echoed through the hall, interrupting the king's decree as an impressive looking fey-woman wearing a sparkling crown and a long blue and white robe pushed aside the guards standing at the throne room doors. The woman's face was full of anger, and she was closely followed by a well-armored Jarcadian warrior who matched her quick steps before joining the other soldiers standing in guard around the room.

Though the royal woman strode past the mortals without a glance, Isaboe recognized her immediately. The heated fey stomped over to the stairs that led up to King Enoch's throne and stared up with a reprimanding glare. "Why was I not informed that the gathering had been moved a day early?"

"The council recognizes Queen Brighid from—"

"*Oh shut up, Bolticush!* Everyone knows who I am!" Queen Brighid snapped at the frog-man who, appearing intimidated and flustered, immediately took his seat.

"Welcome, Brighid," King Enoch finally replied. "I apologize that you did not receive your message in a timely manner, but a messenger was sent out to all the lands."

"Really? Mine seems to have gone astray, and I nearly missed the entire gathering. Or perhaps that was the council's intention all along." Queen Brighid's voice was filled with accusation, as were her eyes as she scanned the balcony.

"I assure you it was not," confirmed the king. "But we have already heard enough here today to make a decision, so unless you have something to add..."

"Oh, you know I do, Enoch!" Queen Brighid barked. "But before I have my say, I will speak first to the mortals."

Isaboe stepped back as she watched the queen spin on her heels and then march toward Rosalyn while shooting quick glances to Connor and herself. "When I learned that mortals were in the realm," the queen said quietly, "I knew it had to be you. Though I wish you hadn't come, it is very good to see you, Rosalyn."

"And you also, Your Highness. Though it seems we have found ourselves in quite a bad situation."

"Let us see what I can do about that." Queen Brighid smiled quickly before her gaze jumped to Connor. "I see you have brought your strongarm with you. That was wise." She then turned her eyes to Isaboe, and the judgment in them was not missed. "But you? I do not understand why you are here. *You* are the mother of the child. *Your* place should be back in your own world where you can protect her." Queen Brighid's tone was chastising, and the accusation in her eyes sent a shiver down Isaboe's spine.

"She is protected," Isaboe said, attempting some defense. "She's with family."

"And I've placed a cloaking-spell over her location," Rosalyn added. "Lorien can't find her."

"Then you underestimate Lorien!" Brighid turned a heated glare on Rosalyn before looking back at Isaboe. "What happened to your pious motherly-love that drove you to the ends of your world, looking for your *mortal* children? Why would you now leave this child, a very special child, without the support of her mother?"

Slipping her hand into Connor's for support, Isaboe cringed from Brighid's accusations, but she could think of nothing to say in her defense.

"*Ohhh,*" Brighid said smugly, glancing down at their clasped hands. "Now I understand. You made a choice."

"It wasn't an easy choice to make, believe me." Isaboe's words sounded weak and defensive, even to her.

"But you did choose, and once again, you thought only of yourself," Queen Brighid murmured as she leaned in, and Isaboe dropped her gaze to the floor, unable to meet her reprimanding glare. "You forget, little human, that I spent two seasons following you around in your world watching you make choices that almost cost you and your unborn child your lives. I just hope this poor decision hasn't cost more than I can fix," Brighid snapped before spinning away and moving toward the center of the throne room as her gown swirled behind her in a brilliant pool of blue.

Isaboe's body began to shake as she fought a wave of renewed anxiety. When Connor squeezed her hand, she looked up at him. "It's gonna be alright, and dinnae worry about Kaitlyn. She's fine," Connor mumbled, as Queen Brighid continued her reprimands, but this time they were directed at the congregation of elders.

"I heard this warrior's words from the foyer," she said, gesturing toward Klute, "and he speaks the truth." Queen Brighid stepped into the center of the throne room and stared challengingly up into the council's balcony. "I too would like to know how long you will turn a blind eye to Lorien's reign of darkness." Receiving no reply, she continued. "We all know her intentions, and this council has been silent about her abuses for too long. We must now take a stand. If these three mortals have the courage to face her, then what excuse can we possibly have? Now is the time to take action! If we come together, we have the power to end Lorien's reign. But to do so, we must put our differences aside." Brighid turned her attention toward the throne. "We cannot ignore this opportunity, Lord Enoch. Like it or not, the pendulum of war is in motion. The mortals have already done their part. I beseech you all; let us join these tenacious humans and finally take Lorien down!"

The silence that followed Queen Brighid's speech was heavy. She stood ridged and resolute as she waited for a response, but none came. Finally, King Enoch cleared his throat. "Thank you, Queen Brighid, for your impassioned lecture. As I already mentioned, we are now breaking for the mid-day meal. Before the sun begins its descent, we will return here to make our decision." When Enoch stepped away from the balcony and disappeared into the shadows, the rest of the council followed suit, leaving the mortals in doubt about the fate of their mission.

CHAPTER 10

STRATEGIES
AND STRANGERS

Rosalyn gave Queen Brighid a gracious nod as she stepped up next to her. "Thank you for speaking up on our behalf, Your Highness, though I doubt it will make any difference. It appears as if the esteemed council has already decided to send us back. But why take this break and delay the inevitable?"

Queen Brighid's expression was opaque, and she hesitated before answering. "The day is still young, and this fight is not over yet." She glanced around at the fey funneling out of the hall. "I have a few friends among the Elders who may yet be swayed. But your sudden appearance in the realm has made many of the council members uncomfortable."

"Yeah, that was obvious," Connor grumbled.

"Well, you have accused Lorien of high crimes; kidnapping a mortal child and threatening murder. Now they must address this malignancy to which they have turned a blind-eye for far too long. You are forcing them to act, and they're not happy about it."

"And how many of the members might actually vote in our favor?" Rosalyn asked. "The overall consensus in this room was to send us home. What chance do we really have?"

Isaboe heard the concern in her mother's voice, and the silence that followed only compounded her fearful uncertainty. Observing Queen Brighid's stoic gaze, Isaboe too panned the room, watching the remaining council members take their leave. As they paraded out of the king's throne room, she noticed their judging glances as they muttered to one another.

"Don't lose hope," Brighid said at last. "The fact that you are here has created a ripple, and that weighs in our favor. Let me take care of the politics. Keep your heads down and I'll find you later." Giving them a quick nod, the queen then spun away with her warrior shadowing her and fell in with the crowd exiting for lunch. Having apparently spotted her first target, Brighid intercepted two of the council members coming down the stairs, holding them in brief conversation. A moment later, they followed Brighid in the opposite direction of the dining hall, leaving the small group of humans standing forlorn on the throne room floor.

"Now what?" Connor asked.

"You heard King Enoch," Klute replied, "we eat." The warrior took a few steps before he stopped to look back and urged them forward with a gesture. "That means you as well."

Following Klute from the throne room, the three mortals fell in beside a group of fey who had suddenly appeared from beneath the balcony, all headed toward the foyer. As Isaboe saw them emerge, she realized that they must have been there all along, watching from the shadows. Once again, the eyes of these strange and beautiful creatures followed them as if they were just as fascinating. Holding Connor's hand, she dropped her gaze to avoid meeting any of their condemning looks, just as Brighid had suggested.

"Wonder what's for lunch 'round here," Connor mumbled.

"Whatever it is, I won't be able to eat," Isaboe replied. "I'm too nervous to keep anything down."

Rosalyn scoffed, "I just hope it's edible. This might be our last meal."

"What do you mean by that?" Isaboe gasped as she felt her remaining courage slipping away like water between her fingers.

"Ye make it sound like we're headed for the gallows," Connor said. "Is there something yer not telling us, Rosalyn?"

Rosalyn shrugged. "No, I just think the council has already decided. This break is just to make us sweat it out."

Listening to her mother's words, Isaboe tried to keep her anxiety in check, but so far everything about this rescue mission had gone horribly wrong. Even though they'd had no idea what they would encounter when they crossed over into this strange world, she had never expected that so many forces would be aligned to prevent them from reaching their goal.

"Maybe we should bust out on our own and not wait for their decision," Connor whispered, leaning in toward Rosalyn. "I think Klute might decide to help us."

Rosalyn glanced at the stoic Jarcadian warrior who was only a few steps in front of them as they promenaded toward the dining hall. "I'm not so sure," she murmured, keeping her voice low. "Though he may want to, his hands are tied. He'd have to break his own laws and I don't see that happening."

Trying to avoid the judging glares from the others in the foyer, Isaboe felt the lump of doubt in her gut growing. She was struggling to hold onto the hope that she would be able to keep her promise to Anna and actually bring Gabriel home, but her hopes were quickly slipping away.

"Well, there are *some* intelligent minds here," said a breathless Brighid, suddenly appearing at Rosalyn's side. "But unfortunately, not enough of them." As the queen's voice dipped, she shot both Rosalyn and Connor a quick covert glance. "If the council doesn't rule in our favor, I have a backup plan," she whispered.

"Let's hear it," Connor muttered, keeping his steps short as he focused on the queen. "I think it's highly unlikely that enough of this council can be swayed. Not from what we heard today. So what's yer backup plan?"

Brighid didn't answer. She was scanning the faces in the crowd. As the queen made eye contact with another member of the council, she ignored Connor's question in favor of her next target. "Go grab a bite to eat and I'll meet up with you soon, hopefully with better news." With those departing words, the queen sprinted away to mingle with other royals and high elders.

The crowds converging on the dining hall had bottlenecked at the entrance, making their progression come to a slow crawl. Dropping Connor's hand, Isaboe slipped behind him to protect herself from the strangers swarming around them. The smell of food drifted out and teased Isaboe's nose only moments before someone bumped into her, forcing her to step back or be run over.

"I wonder what her backup plan could be?" Connor whispered, "and if it will come down to a fight."

Rosalyn's jaw tightened. "As divided as this council appears, I just hope that our mission to rescue Gabriel doesn't start a civil war in this world." Isaboe strained to hear her mother's hushed voice over the low murmur of the crowd and the sound of clattering dishes drifting out from the dining hall.

"It won't be our fault if this council refuses to act." Connor's words and expression were firm, but his voice was hushed. "I've dealt with the likes of this group before. They're just like those arrogant British assholes back home. If it comes down to a battle, I'm ready."

"If you haven't noticed, Connor, you're just one soldier against a whole troop of Jarcadian warriors. What we need now are cool heads and persuasive words. Try to remember that."

"I dinnae start this fight, but I intend to be part o' finishing it," Connor argued defensively, but Isaboe was distracted from Rosalyn's response by a quick jerk on her arm that had her stumbling back several paces before she finally found her balance. She was now in a covered alcove, only steps from the foyer but hidden from sight. And she was not alone. Turning to face the instigator, she found herself looking into a pair of wide, shining black eyes. The woman was a petite thing whose eyes seemed much too large for her face; an effect that was only exaggerated by her dark-red cloak. Before Isaboe could demand an explanation, the stranger threw her arms around her in a fierce bear-hug.

"Alaina! I can hardly believe you are really here!" the stranger gasped before drawing back to look closely at Isaboe, as if she was seeing an old friend. "We thought you were dead!"

Confused and unsettled by the fey woman's bold embrace, Isaboe stared into her unusual eyes. They resembled a deer's eyes, almost black and wide with fright. "W-who are you?"

"Alaina, it's me; Petrina," the young fey insisted.

"I am not Alaina. My name is Isaboe," she said firmly, "and I don't know you." She was already beginning to back away toward the foyer when Petrina reached out, stopping her escape.

"Wait, Alaina! You don't remember me?" The fey woman seemed almost insulted.

"I told you: I'm not who you think I...," but before she could finish,

Petrina grabbed Isaboe's right arm and pushed up her sleeve. "Hey! What are you doing?"

Exposing the starburst mark in the crook of Isaboe's right elbow, the fey smiled in confirmation before releasing her. "I knew it was you. Whatever name you go by now—Alaina or Isaboe—I'm just happy you came back."

"Why? What do you want with me?" Isaboe asked nervously, pushing down the sleeve of her dress. She glanced over her shoulder at the crowd, now thinning as they funneled into the dining hall, but saw no sign of Connor or Rosalyn.

Petrina's darting gaze also scanned the foyer before she clasped onto Isaboe, holding her from escape. "Ever since you left Euphoria, we have all suffered under Lorien's rule, just as the warrior said." Her voice dipped and her face grew solemn before she released her grip. "The council won't help us, and they most likely won't help you either."

"How do you know that?" Isaboe asked, although she was suspecting the same.

"It doesn't matter. Even if they were willing, they cannot help us. Only you can. Now that you have returned, *you* can help us bring Lorien down." Though the fey kept her voice low, her words were intense, matched by the fright Isaboe saw in her dark eyes as she once again grabbed Isaboe's arm. "You must come back to Euphoria with me!"

"What are you talking about?" Isaboe's anxiety spiked as she jerked her arm out of the fey's grip. "Leave me alone!"

"What are ye doing in there?"

At the sudden sound of Connor's voice, Isaboe spun around. "There's a woman in here, and she's telling me…" Isaboe turned back around, but the alcove was empty. There was no sign of Petrina.

Connor glanced into the alcove. "What woman?"

"There was a strange woman just here. She said her name was Petrina. She said she knew me as someone named Alaina."

"Who's Alaina?"

"I don't know," Isaboe muttered, confused and unsettled. But that was not the whole truth. The name Alaina did mean something to her, although Isaboe didn't know why. "She said she was from Euphoria, and that she wanted me to go back there with her. She said that only *I* could bring Lorien down."

"What does that mean?"

"I have no idea. I just hope I don't ever see her again. I didn't care for the way she looked at me."

"Well, she's gone now. Come along, love, and try not to fall behind again," Connor said, taking her hand and leading the way.

The encounter with the strange fey only added to Isaboe's heavy feeling of foreboding as she walked beside Connor with a new sense of dread chewing away at her heart.

CHAPTER 11

A ROYAL REBEL

When Isaboe crossed over the threshold of the dining room, the smell of food filled the large open area, but it didn't settle well in her nose. The encounter with the woman in the alcove only added to her roiling stomach, and she was sure she wouldn't be able to keep anything down.

Isaboe's gaze was drawn to the front of the large dining room where the council members were being seated. The nobles were dining at tidy round tables that were noticeably separated from the commoners. An elaborate banquet had been spread out before them on polished silver plates.

The remainder of the congregation took their place at long dining tables that filled the rest of the hall. Isaboe noticed that the eating utensils provided for those of lesser status consisted mostly of wood and bone, as did the bowls, plates, and mugs. Apparently, silver was reserved for the heads of state. The class divisions were clearly defined, not only by the dishes they ate from, but by their position in the front of the hall, closer to King Enoch.

Taking a seat at the end of one of the long tables, Isaboe settled between Connor and Rosalyn. On the back of her neck, she could feel the curious looks and silent accusations from the other diners. Trying not to stare, Isaboe let her gaze continually skim the room. Most of the beings were oddities, unique from any creature she'd ever seen before. One group had horns growing out the sides of their heads, and though they had upright human-like bodies, they strolled on muscular fur-covered legs with hooves that clicked on the stone floor with each step. Others fluttered into the room on the power of their own wings. Isaboe was startled to see a small man roll across the floor like a boulder before he came to a stop at his seat and jumped up onto the bench using his powerful little legs.

A willowy well-dressed fellow with blue skin paraded into the dining hall wearing a jaunty leather cap that sported an enormous peacock feather. As he sauntered across the floor, his large dark eyes exchanged Isaboe's curious look, until he became distracted when another man in court attire slid up beside him, linking arms with a warm smile. At once, the blue-skinned man's attention was focused entirely on his partner; a shorter fey with snow-white hair and skin, and whose large translucent wings draped to the floor. After exchanging an affectionate kiss, the newcomer took his partner's arm and escorted him to one of the smaller tables. Isaboe watched curiously as they took their seats, whispering intimately together. Floating a glance to Connor, she could see that he too was shocked by the men's unconcealed affection, as such things were heavily frowned upon back home. Both of his eyebrows were raised in surprise. Yet, when Isaboe glanced around at the other diners, she found herself alone in her bewilderment.

Rosalyn laughed quietly at them both. "There is a woman made entirely of water over there, a man who looks like a tree, and a goat who speaks like a scholar, yet you two act as if those gentlemen are the strangest things here."

Isaboe blushed shamefully and was happy to be distracted by the entrance of the kitchen staff; a mix of elves and fey. She watched them scurry from one table to the next, delivering steaming bowls of soup, along with serving platters overflowing with meats, cheeses, fruits, and breads. When a whizzing noise overhead caught her attention, Isaboe was surprised to see a number of small fey flying over the tables with pitchers used to pour a golden liquid into the diners' tankards. The fey servers were tiny and childlike as they fluttered all over the room, stopping only long enough to refill their pitchers. But from Isaboe's experience, age was something hard to determine in this world of the Underlings. Since time didn't move the same here, these young-looking fey could very well be older than herself.

Klute took the empty spot on the bench next to Connor but said nothing as he dug into his meal. Connor studied the lion-man for a long moment before he finally spoke. "How's this goin' down today, Klute? Will the council help us or not?"

Still chewing, the warrior shot Connor a glare and swallowed his bite before answering. "I doubt that it will be today. I can tell you that," Klute said before stuffing another hunk of meat into his mouth.

"What'd ye mean it won't be today? The king himself said they would all meet back before sunset to make their decision."

Klute scoffed. "That is what he said, but it is not likely that will happen. This council is not known for making quick decisions, and you may not have an answer for days, if at all. If you had not noticed, achieving an agreement of minds within the Council of Elders can be," he paused, choosing his words carefully, "challenging at best. Even now, those who oppose your cause are moving to sway those who are unsure. They will stall, hold closed-door meetings, and wrangle favors. Until then, nothing changes. This is the council's way."

"Then where does that leave us?" Isaboe asked.

"Stuck in the middle o' a pile of political bullshit," Connor grumbled.

"Unfortunately, that seems to be the case," Klute mumbled around another mouthful.

"Please answer the question. What is to become of us?" Rosalyn demanded.

"Does that mean they'll send us home empty-handed?" Isaboe couldn't even imagine returning home without Gabriel. How could she face Anna and Jared?

"No. Since they know you have the ability to cross back over whenever you wish, they most likely will not let you leave until the decision is final."

"*What?* We're prisoners now?" Connor growled as renewed fear bubbled up in Isaboe's stomach.

For a long moment, Klute only glared at Connor before he spoke, "I told you to take your women and go home. You should have listened to me while you had the chance."

From seemingly nowhere, Queen Brighid leaned over Rosalyn's shoulder, her guard hovering half-a-step behind. "Come with me," Brighid said, gesturing for the group of mortals to follow. "All of you, gather your plates and come with me." Isaboe, Connor and Rosalyn quickly stood and picked up their plates, but no one moved as the queen stared down at Klute, who still sat stiffly in his place. "That means you too, warrior."

Klute swallowed hard on a mouthful as he met the queen's stare, but he didn't rise. "That was not a request," Queen Brighid added sternly. Immediately, Klute gathered his meal and fell into step behind the queen as she led her strange band toward the front of the hall.

As Queen Brighid led them across the room, Isaboe couldn't help but notice the looks they were drawing. Conversation ceased, and all eyes watched as the mortals and two Jarcadian warriors silently followed Queen Brighid toward the front of the dining hall. Stopping at a small vacant table, uncomfortably close to the nobility, the queen motioned for them to take a seat. Doing as she was told, Isaboe watched Brighid return the challenging glares and shocked proclamations of the elders with haughty defiance, snubbing her nose at them and their protocol.

Once they were seated, everyone's focus returned to their meals, and the low murmur of voices resumed, though Isaboe kept her eyes on her plate to avoid the condemning glares.

"Not everyone who has power in this realm attends these gatherings," Brighid said, breaking the uncomfortable silence. "Many of them feel it is a waste of their time, and I'm sure you can see why. However, I do have allies who are willing to help stir things up," Brighid whispered with a mischievous grin. "What is your name, warrior?"

Clearing his throat, Klute met the queen's stare before giving a quick glance to the other warrior at the table. He then mumbled, "Klute, Your Highness."

"So, Klute, I would like your opinion on General Renwolf. Amaroth has given me her take," the queen said, floating a glance to the warrior sitting at her side. "I would like to know where you think his loyalties lay."

It was only then that Isaboe realized the other warrior was female. Beneath her armor and musculature, Isaboe wouldn't have guessed. Only upon second inspection did she notice the fuller curve of Amaroth's lips and the roundness of her face. It was time, Isaboe was quickly realizing, to recalibrate her expectations for the people of Euphoria; they did not follow the same norms that she was used to back home.

"He rules by the law," Klute answered firmly. "No exceptions. If you go looking for help in that direction, you are asking for trouble."

"Hmm, that's what I thought," Queen Brighid said. Picking up a piece of soft cheese, she tore off a tiny bite and chewed on it thoughtfully for a moment before speaking again. "So, if an order came down from the highest authority in the realm, even if it was contradictory to what the Council of Elders had decided, then General Renwolf would have to obey, yes?"

"Are you referring to The Cloud People?" Klute questioned, surprise clearly written on his stoic face.

"Who are The Cloud People?" Rosalyn asked.

But before Brighid could answer, they were jarred from their conversation by a piercing whistle that filled the hall. Even the Underlings seemed surprised, and Isaboe detected a hint of fear in them as well. As one, all the Jarcadian Warriors jumped to attention, a fighting force ready to protect those in their care at a moment's notice.

"What's goin' on?" Connor asked as he also leapt to attention.

Amaroth and Klute were preparing to join their fellow warriors, but Klute paused long enough to say, "That alarm means something dangerous is happening near the palace grounds, and it is not good. You and your women need to go back to your room and stay there."

Just then, a young blue-skinned server ran into the hall with wide eyes and panic written across his face. "The trolls are attacking from the south! They've already crossed the river!" he shouted.

An audible gasp filled the dining hall. "Everyone who is not a warrior, to your rooms!" a disconnected voice shouted. "Lock yourselves in!"

Chaos exploded through the dining hall as elders and heads of state, who had earlier looked so regal, now ran like scared jackrabbits.

Klute caught Connor's attention. "Go now!" he shouted, but Connor grabbed his arm, ignoring the fury in his feline face.

"Let me help."

"No! Take your women and go back to your room. This is not your fight!"

"Ye've seen me stand up against em'. Let me help!"

Klute's glare turned steely cold. "I do not have time for this," he growled.

"If the council sees that I'm willing to jump into the fight to defend the castle, it might make 'em more willing to help us." As Connor held Klute's furrowed glare, Isaboe could see conflict in the lion-man's eyes.

"He may have a valid point," Brighid said. "Go with them. You might be right, and this could be just what the council needs to see."

Klute hesitated, looking to Amaroth for support, but he only met her steely stare. "You heard the queen," she said. "The mortal goes with us." Isaboe watched closely as Klute silently challenged his fellow warrior, but when he saw the queen's determined glare, he accepted defeat.

Turning toward Isaboe, Connor spoke hurriedly, "Go back to your room, my love, and lock the door!"

"No!" Isaboe shouted, grabbing Connor by his jacket. "You promised you wouldn't leave me again!"

"This is something I havta do, Isaboe. It could make all the difference on whether the council will help us get Gabriel back." He placed his hands on her shoulders, and his voice softened. "I'll be alright. Ye know I can take care of myself," he declared, looking into her frightened eyes, "as long as I'm not worried about you." He released her and looked at Rosalyn. "Take her back to the room and lock the door, then wait for me to return."

"No," Isaboe repeated, feeling the anguish in knowing there was nothing she could do to stop him.

Beside them, Brighid and her warrior were also having a quick, quiet conversation. "Amaroth, please be careful and watch over him," she said, placing a hand on the warrior's powerful arm.

"You can count on me, Your Highness," Amaroth said as she took the queen's hand in her own, bowing gracefully and dropping a lingering kiss on her knuckles. "I'll return as soon as possible, my queen. Until then, stay safe." Just before Amaroth turned away and bolted toward the exit, Isaboe thought she saw something that resembled fondness pass between them.

As she watched Connor, Amaroth, and Klute running from the dining hall to join the other Jarcadian warriors who were heading to the southern border of Sashtonia, Isaboe felt her anxiety spike as her husband and protector disappeared into the crowd. She shot a desperate look at her mother, who offered nothing but an order.

"You heard him," Rosalyn said firmly. "Let's return to our room."

Grasping Isaboe's hand, the sorceress started to turn when Queen Brighid caught their attention. "Wait, Rosalyn!" the queen said, her mischievous eyes alive with schemes and plans. "Actually, we must take advantage of this opportunity."

"What do you mean?" Rosalyn asked.

"My allies are far from here, but they are powerful and capable of pushing the council into action. We must use this distraction. It's time to go," the Fey Queen said excitedly as she ushered Rosalyn and Isaboe toward the exit.

CHAPTER 12

DESTINY AND PURPOSE

Holding tightly to her mother's hand, Isaboe struggled to keep up as they pushed and bumped their way through the foyer. She could hear disconnected voices shouting over the throngs of people but couldn't make out the words. They only blended into the clamoring cacophony of people running for safety.

I can't believe Connor left me again! Isaboe's frantic thoughts only fed the panic building in her chest. *He promised he wouldn't do that. Damn him!* She knew she was being selfish, but they were under attack and Connor was her protector. Now he was gone, again!

"Rosalyn, wait!" Brighid shouted as she stepped in front of her companions and gestured toward a figure in the crowd. Lord Mordackian, the fey who resembled a tree, emerged laboriously from the crowd and joined the queen. His height was so impressive that Isaboe's head had to drop back as she gazed up into his wood-grained face.

"Is the carriage ready?" Brighid asked.

"Yes, ready and waiting for you," Lord Mordackian answered in his calm baritone voice.

"I can't believe the castle is under attack!" Rosalyn exclaimed. "Does this happen often?"

"The last time it happened," Lord Mordackian replied, his voice deep and commanding, "I was just a sapling. And that was a very long time ago."

"Does this have anything to do with us being here?" Rosalyn asked.

"I don't know," Brighid answered. "But most of the council members are scurrying back to their own lands."

"But they can't leave," Isaboe interjected. "They haven't given us their decision yet!"

Brighid shot a glare at Isaboe but didn't offer a response. Instead, she stepped closer to Rosalyn and her voice dipped, her bright eyes darting around suspiciously. "We are going to the Floating Island of Luminara where the Cloud People live." Her words were just above a whisper. "There are people there you need to meet, allies who may be able to help you."

"A floating island?" Isaboe asked, not sure she'd heard the queen correctly. But once again, Brighid ignored her.

"Who is it you want me to meet?" Rosalyn asked.

Isaboe heard the apprehension in her mother's voice as the queen paused, choosing her words carefully. "The time for change is long overdue. Your presence here has pushed the first stone over the edge. It's just a matter of time before the whole rocky hillside comes crashing down." Placing a hand on Rosalyn's shoulder, Brighid stepped even closer, her face softening but still holding a speck of mischief. "I think now is the time to give it a little nudge."

Finally turning toward Isaboe, Brighid's expression melted into a stern glare. "You, however, are not needed at this time. The best place for you is back in your room where you can stay out of trouble. Do you think you can do that?"

Isaboe began to protest, only for Rosalyn to stop her. "Isaboe, please just go back to our room and wait for Connor. Lock yourself in until he returns."

"*What!?* You're leaving me *too?*" Isaboe's anxiety jumped to a whole new level.

"You'll be fine, just as long as you stay put."

"But—"

"There is no time to waste," Brighid interrupted. "We must go now. The castle will soon be in lockdown, and we have only a short window of time before we won't be able to leave at all. Please, Rosalyn. Come with me, now!"

When Rosalyn turned toward her daughter, Isaboe saw conflict written on her mother's face. The sorceress's gaze dropped briefly to her hand before she met Isaboe's eyes again, then she pulled the Ring of Odin off her finger, the ring holding the portal that would allow their return to the mortal world. Placing it firmly in Isaboe's palm, she wrapped her daughter's fingers around it. "In case I don't make it back."

"*What? NO!* Don't leave me, Mother, please! I…I have no idea how to make the portal open!"

"If it comes to that, I'm sure you will have no problem finding someone who can help you." Rosalyn softened, taking a step closer and placing a hand on Isaboe's shoulder. "I'm confident I will be back, but if not, just go home. Go back to Kaitlyn." Forcing a smile, she quickly hugged her daughter. When Rosalyn stepped back, her face and tone were firm. "Now, go to your room and lock the door!"

Then Brighid and Rosalyn turned and disappeared into the throngs of people madly rushing through the foyer, just as Connor had done only moments earlier. Isaboe was suddenly, and horribly, alone.

"Would you like me to accompany you to your room?" Lord Mordackian's words startled Isaboe, and she glanced up at the giant tree-man hovering above her.

"No. I can find it myself," Isaboe muttered, feeling the tears welling. She did not want him to see her cry. Turning away from the lumbering Lord, she made haste down the hallway that led to her room before the first tears could spill down her cheeks. She was terribly frightened. So much was happening all at once, and both Connor and Rosalyn had abandoned her in this strange land! The agony of when—*or if*—she would see them again was almost more than she could bear. It was all too familiar. She couldn't face that nightmare of separation again, the horrible anguish of losing her loved ones. Not all over again. *Please, God, no!* She cried her silent prayer.

Her vision blurred by tears, Isaboe bumped and pushed her way through the crowded hallway. When she finally reached her room, before she could open the door, a hand fell on her shoulder.

Spinning around, Isaboe found herself face-to-face with Petrina. The young fey she had encountered earlier in the covered alcove now stood only inches away, and Isaboe could see fear in her wide eyes. Startled, Isaboe took a step back as she wiped the tears from her cheeks.

"Alaina, my escort is waiting, so I must go now. The castle is going into lockdown, and we're all being told to leave. Please, come to Euphoria with me! Only you can stop Lorien," the fey pleaded.

"I told you: I am not Alaina. I'm Isaboe. Now leave me alone!"

"Wait! Regardless of what name you call yourself, you are the only one who can open the vault."

"What vault?"

"Lorien has something hidden in a vault that she doesn't want the council to know about, and it is sealed by blood. Only the same blood can open it—your blood."

"What? No. I…I can't go to Euphoria with you. Not without Connor." Isaboe turned away from the fey's pleading expression and again reached for the door handle, but Petrina's long pale fingers darted out and wrapped around Isaboe's wrist.

"Please, wait. I know where the boy is. I can help you get him back."

"Gabriel?" Isaboe exclaimed, spinning around. "You know where he is?" A flash of hope rushed through her chest.

"Yes. I can take you to him if you agree to help us. Only you can open the vault and expose Lorien's secret." Dropping Isaboe's hand, Petrina's voice softened. "You may not remember, but Euphoria is your home too. We are your people as well, and there is more that the council doesn't know." Pausing, the fey's expression grew hard. *"Damn* the council and damn the prophecy!"

"What prophecy?"

"I don't have time to explain!" Petrina glanced around nervously, then again lowered her voice. "There is a reason you've come back, Alaina…I mean, Isaboe, and it's not just to rescue the mortal child."

Hope lit a spark in Isaboe's chest, momentarily overshadowing her fears, until another dark thought took seed. "But she will know I'm in Euphoria. The queen always knew how to find me back in my own world. Lorien will certainly know the moment I step into her domain."

A disconnected voice filled the foyer and echoed down the hallway, announcing that the castle was going into lockdown. Everyone who wanted to leave must do so immediately.

"You do have some fey in you. Draw on that, and we'll figure out a way to hide your presence. But we must go, now!" Petrina pleaded.

"But how can I get in and out of Euphoria without her…" Isaboe stopped in mid-sentence and opened her hand. The answer was lying on her palm.

The first time she had seen the Ring of Odin was when Connor had shown it to her as they sat around the campfire on their journey to Kirkwall, shortly after Kaitlyn had been born. The wizard Demetrick had given it to him, and the magic it contained kept the fey from knowing he was in their realm. That memory was immediately followed by another; when Lorien's accomplice, the dark muse Lilabeth, had arrived in Gabriel's nursery and stolen him to use as ransom. Lilabeth had transformed from a black cat into a slick lethal woman to deliver the Fey Queen's demand that they hand over Kaitlyn or the boy child will die. The kidnapper had grumbled that Lorien still didn't know how Connor had slipped in and out of Euphoria without her knowing.

It was the ring! It had blocked Connor's mortal vibrations, his presence. If it had worked for Connor, it had to work for her, too. Was this the reason Isaboe had come on this mission? Maybe it was more than just to save Gabriel. Maybe it was even bigger than that.

When Isaboe thought about Queen Brighid's demeaning words, and how Nyia and Klute had made her feel small and insignificant next to Connor the warrior and Rosalyn the sorceress, she knew what she had to do. She would prove to all of them that they were wrong. She did have a purpose, and this was it. She would go with Petrina into Euphoria and rescue Gabriel herself. That would show them all. "Wait here," she breathed, throwing open the door to her room. She grabbed her cloak and slipped it on, then stopped for a second to question her actions. Connor's instruction to lock herself in her room flooded her memory. When he returned to find her gone, he would be both livid and worried sick.

"Sorry, Connor," she muttered to herself. "This is something *I* have to do." Slipping the ring into her cloak pocket, she found a morsel of courage and stood taller. Walking out of the room and closing the door, she faced the young fey. "Alright, Petrina, take me to Euphoria."

CHAPTER 13

PETRINA

Outside the castle walls, the air was filled with a cacophony of whoops, whistles, and whinnies as the fleeing feys' coaches took to the sky. Isaboe found herself staring at chariots that varied from wobbly wooden structures covered with vines to giant polished shells adorned with gold and sparkling jewels. As much a part of the aesthetic as they were practical, the creatures pulling each vehicle took flight as soon as their passengers rushed into the safety of the cabs. The sound of flapping wings and shrieking animals was all-encompassing, and Isaboe wondered if Petrina would also be flying in one of them to Euphoria.

Skirting the main crowd, Petrina led Isaboe into a protected courtyard behind the castle which was surrounded by flowering hedges. When they emerged into the clearing, Isaboe stumbled to a halt at what she saw.

It was a carriage made of some sort of metal and upholstered in dark red leather. Gothic lanterns hung from twisted and pointed spears that were anchored at the front corners of the coach. Seated between the lanterns was a thin, hunched-over and hairless man with ashy skin and large bulbous eyes. He peered out from beneath a dirty leather cloak, and the hand that Isaboe saw grasping the reigns was long-fingered and boney. Attached to the far end of the reigns was a creature that could have been spewed from her worst nightmares.

The dark furry creature stood on four stocky legs and had a large body similar to an ox, but its wide head seemed almost lupine. With its lower jaw hung slack, the creature exposed rows of sharp jagged teeth, and a long black tongue dripping saliva that hung out the side of its mouth. As she had feared, whatever the creature was, it also had huge muscular wings and emitted a low rumble as it shifted its weight, swinging its enormous head from side-to-side as it pulled taunt on the bridle buckled around its impressive chest.

Realizing that her guest wasn't at her side, Petrina stopped and turned back. "Isaboe, come along!"

But Isaboe didn't move. "Oh, my God," she gasped, staring at the beast and wondering if she was making the correct decision.

Petrina glanced back at the carriage. "Isaboe, if it's Toblet and his grockmusk that you're afraid of, you needn't be. They won't harm you, I promise." Petrina grabbed Isaboe's hand and pulled her toward the carriage. At the same time, the driver—who was closely watching the two women moving toward him—pulled back his gray lips. Isaboe wasn't sure if it was meant to be a smile, but the driver's jagged grin did nothing to ease her anxiety.

Reaching for the handle, Petrina opened the coach door and ushered Isaboe inside. As soon as she cleared the threshold, the young fey slammed the door shut, enclosing them in cool darkness. Before Isaboe's eyes could adjust to the low light inside the coach, she felt it rock into motion. The sound of a snapping whip was followed by a low guttural screech, then a loud roaring howl that Isaboe felt all the way to her bones. With a sudden lunge forward and the sound of hooves digging into the gravel, they lifted from the ground in jerky motions that nearly made her lose her stomach. Still trembling, Isaboe dug her nails into the leather of the seat, feeling her entire body tense up. As much as she tried, she couldn't slow her heartbeat or calm her frantic breaths. When she licked her dry lips, she tasted the salty tears that had slipped down her cheeks during takeoff. At the same moment Connor's face flashed through her mind. Torturing herself, she already regretted her decision, but it was too late now. *My God, what am I doing? I should have stayed at the castle in my room as Connor told me! He'll be so angry I wouldn't blame him if he killed me—unless I die first!* After a few jarring lifts and drops, the carriage eventually leveled out, and Isaboe slowly grew less intimidated, although she hadn't released her nails from the leather.

Abruptly breaking the silence, Petrina asked, "Why don't you remember me?"

Staring hard at the fey, Isaboe attempted to calm her racing pulse before she finally answered. "Rosalyn told me it has something to do with the Veil of Forgetfulness. It prevents mortals from remembering what took place in your world when we pass back over into our own."

Petrina only nodded, as if it now made sense, and then gestured toward Isaboe's white-knuckled grip. "Please try to relax," she said with a compassionate smile.

Looking into the fey's large eyes, Isaboe knew that with so many unanswered questions, it wasn't possible for her to feel at ease, and it was the most prominent question that gave her the most anxiety. "Petrina, what is your connection to Lorien?"

"I am Lorien's emissary. Since Lorien is no longer allowed to attend the Council of Elders, I represent Euphoria."

"If you're Lorien's emissary, then why should I trust you?"

"I only report to Lorien, but I have no loyalty to her, though she believes otherwise. She demands allegiance from all of Euphoria. Since we live in fear of her, most of us pretend to give it. Any who oppose her are killed without mercy." Her words were laced with hatred and sorrow, and Petrina's bright eyes were dimmed with remembered horrors. "Shortly after you left, she went mad with power. When people fled to the skies, she had our wings cut off." Seeing the pain reflected in the fey's eyes, Isaboe knew that she too must have been a victim of Lorien's madness. "When they tried to escape by land, they discovered the deadly spell that Lorien had placed on our borders. Most died before they could cross out of Euphoria."

Having been deceived for months in her own mortal world by the Fey Queen's bewitching spells, Isaboe knew firsthand how heartless Lorien could be. Suddenly the idea of her own bloodletting twisted Isaboe's insides. "And this vault you mentioned: just how much of my blood will you need to open it?"

The fey chuckled lightly, and her eyes softened as a smile graced her face. "Don't worry, it's not much. Just a prick of your finger will do. From what I know of blood-locks, all that is required is to let a few drops fall upon the latch, and it springs open."

"But why my blood?"

"Because Lorien used your blood to seal something in the vault that she doesn't want the Council of Elders to know about. With you gone, there was no way the vault could ever be opened." As Petrina went silent, Isaboe saw a slew of emotions cross her face. "Lorien never expected you to return."

Isaboe pondered the fey's words as she recalled all those months when she had traveled alone with Lorien back in the mortal world while her unborn daughter grew in her belly. The Fey Queen had said that Isaboe's destiny was to live in the land of Euphoria as the beloved mother of the gifted child. But she had known even then that Lorien had no intention of letting her be revered as the mother to Kaitlyn. She wanted Isaboe out of her daughter's life. Lorien wanted Isaboe dead.

The sound of the beast's large wings swooping through the air distracted Isaboe's uneasy thoughts in another uncomfortable direction, and she tried not to focus on how high they were flying. She turned in her seat to face Petrina. "You claim that you hold no loyalty to the queen, but you seem to know a lot about Lorien's secret, one that even the council does not know about and is somehow locked in a vault." Isaboe paused and examined the fey with intensity. "Why should I believe you?"

"I'm taking a huge risk by bringing you back to Euphoria, but I believe you have returned for a reason. Seeing you has renewed my hope for the first time in so long."

"But you report to Lorien, and she apparently trusts you. If she's so horrible, why have you stayed so close to her?"

"Do you think I actually have a choice?" Petrina's voice turned angry and hard. "She cut off my wings!" Releasing the clasp on her cloak, she let the red fabric slip down to the bench. After fumbling with the laces and loosening her dress, she turned in her seat, exposing her skin. Two ragged scars ran down her back, just below her shoulders. "That is where my wings used to be," Petrina snarled as she pulled her clothes back into place. Her large eyes were angry slits as she hissed, "Lorien did this to me."

Remorse flooded Isaboe, but even this confession didn't completely eliminate her fears about her companion's loyalty. "When you were here last time," Petrina said, softening her posture, "Lorien put this whole façade into play, and we all thought that she had changed, really changed. She even resumed the gathering of the Maidens of the Oracle, something that hadn't been done in centuries. When she called upon all the young fey to bring back the old ways, of course, we were all clamoring to get in line. Everyone wanted to be chosen for the queen's court and be trained in the old magic. We even allowed ourselves a glimmer of hope that one of us could possibly be the next High Priestess." Petrina's voice dipped, and Isaboe could hear the innocent desire of a young girl's dreams.

"While you were still here it was wonderful," the fey continued. "But then you left, and it all fell apart. When Lorien turned against us, most of us tried to escape, but we didn't get far. She killed enough of us to make an example to the rest. Those who kept our mouths shut and did what we were told were allowed to live, but we were never allowed to leave the castle and return to our homes. My family believes that I chose to stay. They do not know that we were lied to, that Lorien lured us to the castle with false promises of learning the old magic, but we never did. We became her…entertainment."

When their eyes met, a flicker of shame appeared beneath the fey's carefully constructed mask. As Petrina's face shifted, hardened by old wrongs, Isaboe felt a stab of sympathy for what her new acquaintance had experienced at Lorien's hands. "If you want my help with this plan, I need to know what's in this vault. What is Lorien hiding?"

Petrina shook her head. "I don't know. But whatever it is, Lorien doesn't want the council to know about it for fear of being dethroned."

"How do you know this?"

The fey was silent for several heartbeats, then she let out a long sigh. "One night, when I was chosen to be her source of entertainment, I was summoned to her chambers. By the time I arrived, Lorien was already heavily under the effects of Malie juice, and she was ranting about how the people didn't love her and how sad it made her feel. And, of course, Lorien doesn't like to feel sad. It makes her angry. It was my job to make her feel better, but I wasn't pleasing her properly, so Lorien threw me off her bed. I hit my head on a stone table and blacked out. When I came to, I was lying on the bed while she blubbered over the top of me. My head hurt something terrible, and blood was running into my eyes from a gash on my forehead, but Lorien didn't seem to care. As soon as she saw that I could sit up, she went back to her whining. She even put her head in my lap!

"I still remember how stunned I was, sitting on her bed, half-naked and bleeding while she whined about how no one loved her. She actually said that if the people would just worship her as she deserved, she wouldn't need to hurt us. Can you imagine?" As Petrina went quiet, Isaboe watched the anger wash across her face. "If I had had a weapon that night, I would have killed her," she hissed. Both her words and the look in her eyes were lethal. "So instead, I just kept listening. She was so drunk on Malie juice that she was stumbling over her own tongue, and that's when she said it."

"Said what?"

"She was complaining that the council didn't support her rule, and then she said something I will never forget. 'If the council knew what is in that vault, I'd be deposed immediately! But that bitch Alaina is dead, so they'll never get past the blood-lock.' Then she laughed and turned her anger onto me. But she was more crazed than usual and slapped me around for what seemed like an eternity. Sometimes she would cry and apologize, but she never stopped. Sadness makes her angry, and anger arouses her carnal instincts. She savagely abused my body throughout the night. By the time I returned to my room, I was covered in blood and bruises and drained of my spirit, but I've never forgotten what she said." When Petrina went silent, Isaboe saw more hurt and shame slip through her mask, but only for an instant. "Shortly after that, for some unknown reason, Lorien made me her emissary. But she never acknowledged that night, nor has she ever called me back to her chambers. I'm not sure if she remembers, but I think she wants to keep me close, just in case."

"Back at the castle you mentioned a prophecy? What does this prophecy have to do with me?"

"My mother told me that many winters ago, Euphoria was a beautiful land. We were peaceful and prosperous when we were ruled by King Nicholi and Queen Alaina."

"*Queen* Alaina?" Isaboe exclaimed.

"Yes, and she was a good queen. The people loved her. After she and Nicholi left, darkness fell over Euphoria."

"Why did Alaina and Nicholi leave Euphoria?"

"Lorien is Nicholi's sister, and she hated Alaina. Lorien always believed that she should be queen, but when Nicholi took Alaina as his bride, his sister was forced to take her place as a princess, never to be queen. But it wasn't just Nicholi's marriage that pushed Lorien into madness; it was that he took a mortal woman as his bride. Lorien vowed revenge."

"Alaina was a mortal woman?" Isaboe asked, although for some reason she wasn't surprised.

"Yes. And when Lorien discovered Alaina was with child, she dug up an ancient prophecy that had long been buried and presented it to the council, forcing them to take action."

"Take what action? What was in the prophecy?"

Petrina studied Isaboe's face for a long moment before she finally spoke. "The prophecy states that a female child born into royalty, with both fey and mortal blood, will rise up in the realm to become a powerful leader, but her heart will be black. Great famine, disease, and darkness will cover the world while she is in power, and there will be no force strong enough to bring her down."

As she listened to Petrina's explanation, Kaitlyn's innocent face flashed across Isaboe's mind. Could Kaitlyn be the child of the prophecy? Was that why Lorien wanted to raise her as her own, to be molded into the black-hearted ruler the council feared? "So, when it was discovered that Alaina was with child, what action did the council take?"

"Lorien had The Mundahli—The Keeper of the Knowledge—deliver the prophecy to the council, so of course they had no choice but to accept Lorien's conclusion. They forced Nicholi to send Alaina back to her own world before the child was born."

All at once it fell into place. It was as if the missing piece of the puzzle that Isaboe had been unconsciously trying to solve had suddenly manifested. It had been there all along and she just hadn't seen it before. "Oh my God! It is Rosalyn. My mother is the child of Nicholi and Alaina. Alaina was my grandmother!"

Rosalyn had been born with special gifts, which she had assumed were fey in nature, but even she didn't know her parentage. She had shared with Isaboe that the fey had tried to take her on the night she was born, but the nuns at the convent had kept the demons away. Since Lorien had failed to recover Nicholi's child, she had tried again with Isaboe, and manipulated Kaitlyn's conception to create the circumstances she needed. Isaboe's next realization had her shrieking. "I am related to Lorien!"

"It appears so," Petrina confirmed. "When you were here last, Lorien told us all that you were Alaina. Since she and Nicholi ruled long before my time, we believed Lorien. She told us that you had returned to bring life back to our lands. She told us that Euphoria would once again be glorious, now that you had come home."

"But it was all a lie," Isaboe murmured.

"Yes, it was. And shortly after you went away, Lorien went completely mad. She created an army of monsters to do her bidding, and if anyone was fool enough to ask what happened to Alaina, the poor soul was immediately beheaded. That's when she had everyone's wings removed to stop us from fleeing. No one was allowed to even utter the name Alaina without fear of death. Lorien accused Alaina of having done horrible things, but of course no one believed her. She demanded that the people acknowledge her as the true and only Queen of Euphoria. She announced that Alaina was dead, never to return, and those who did not bow down and kiss her feet were killed—or worse."

"Didn't the council try to stop her?"

"Yes. They sent representatives to reason with her, but they never made it back out alive. So the council placed a spell around the boundaries of Euphoria, and Lorien can never leave. It has become her prison. In turn, she cast her own nasty spell, and anyone who tries to enter or leave Euphoria without permission suffers a horrible death."

"What about the people of Euphoria? Did the council just turn their backs to what Lorien is doing to them?"

Petrina slowly nodded. "Yes, they have. Lorien must have some leverage against them, because they refuse to take action against her. You heard them in the king's hall. They are terribly divided, and most refuse to deal with her at all." Petrina's eyes grew wide with fear. "But we can't escape her! Our only hope is to reveal to the council whatever is in that vault, and you're the only one who can open it." As Isaboe searched Petrina's pretty face, she saw a slim thread of hope dance in her eyes. The fey was counting on her, certain that Isaboe could defeat Lorien and save her homeland. But this was a frightening task. Isaboe's actions would not only affect her life and the lives of her family; this could change the lives of people in both worlds. Although for better or worse, she did not yet know.

As anxiety flooded over her like a rogue wave, Isaboe dropped her head into her hands, fighting back more nausea. After a few moments, she sat up and looked into the anxious eyes of the fey. "Petrina, I—I don't think I can do this. It's way too much to ask of me." Isaboe could hear the fear in her voice, and it matched the panic brewing in her chest. "What if something goes wrong? What if Lorien finds me? What if…?"

"You can do this!" Petrina grabbed Isaboe by her shoulders, forcing her to focus. "It is why you are here. *This* is your mission, your purpose. When I saw you in the king's hall today, I knew it was the sign I've been waiting for. What we've all been waiting for." Petrina dropped her hands, placing them in her lap and softened her voice. "Everything happens for a reason, Isaboe, even if we don't always understand why."

Staring back into the determined eyes of the fey, Isaboe felt her pulse beating rapidly in her temples. But in the next moment, the blue amulet lying against her chest began to feel warm, and for some reason it gave her comfort. From somewhere deep within, a small but flickering spark of strength washed through Isaboe, calming her just enough to keep her grounded, and possibly even prepared for what she was about to do.

CHAPTER 14

A TORTURED SOUL

Meanwhile, back in the mortal world, the moon was nearly full as Anna looked out into the night sky. A gust of wind swept up from the canyon floor as she sat quietly on a chair. With her feet on the seat and her knees pulled up to her chest, her arms were wrapped around her legs. Though the wind cooled the air in the cave, the fragrant evening breeze left her chilly and shivering with anxiety.

Three nights prior, Isaboe, Connor, and Rosalyn had disappeared into a vortex of magical energy that was said to be a portal into another world. They had crossed over to retrieve her son, Gabriel, but had not yet returned.

The dark muse who had stolen her baby almost two weeks earlier had made it clear: give Kaitlyn, Anna's baby sister, to the Fey Queen of Euphoria, or she would kill Gabriel. They had until the mid-summer full moon to make the exchange—tomorrow night.

Anna's eyes ached from crying, and her insides were tied in knots. She knew she should eat, but she hadn't been able to keep anything down except a few crackers and some dried meat. When she had managed to sleep, it was restless, and her dreams were dark. Each time she awoke, Anna rediscovered that her worst nightmare was her reality. Gabriel was still gone.

Startled when a hand landed on her shoulder, Anna jolted in her chair before looking up into the sleepy eyes of her husband. "Anna, you should come to bed." Jared sounded weary. "It's late."

"I can't sleep."

"You must at least try."

Anna didn't move. She knew this had been hard on Jared too, but if he was devastated about losing his son, he hid it well. She turned to look back at the dark sky. "You know what tomorrow night is."

She heard him take a deep breath and let it out slowly. "Yes. I know."

The silence hung around them like a heavy blanket until Anna spoke again. "What do you think we should do?" she whispered as she stared out into the night.

Jared pulled up a chair and took a seat beside his wife. "What do you mean?" he asked, leaning in toward her.

Feeling the intensity of his eyes on her, Anna turned to look at him. "You know what I mean."

"What? Take Kaitlyn to the standing stones and trade her for Gabriel?"

"You're thinking it too," Anna said, more as confirmation than a question. She searched her husband's eyes for approval, for understanding.

"No, Anna. Though I'd be lying if I said the thought hadn't crossed my mind, you know we can't do that. We have to trust that Connor, Isaboe and Rosalyn will bring him back."

"Why? Why do we have to trust them?" Anna dropped her feet to the ground and swiveled in her seat to face her husband.

Jared appeared taken aback by her question. "Anna, I didn't see the cat-woman in the nursery, but you did. Do you believe what you saw? Do you believe, that by some sort of faerie magic, Gabriel has been taken to another world?"

Again, Anna searched his face, trying to figure out what he was looking for. "My son is missing, and, yes, I saw and heard that cat-woman in his nursery. From what Rosalyn has told us, I suppose the only answer is, yes—I do believe that Gabriel is in the world of the fey."

"And we both saw them walk into that whirling spiral they called a portal and disappear, even though they have no idea what's on the other side. They did that to save our son, Anna. Why can't you believe that they'll bring him back?"

"They haven't returned yet, so what makes you believe they can?"

"You're not giving them a chance. They need time."

"We don't have the luxury of time, Jared," she snapped. "The full moon is tomorrow."

"Anna, think about what you're saying. You're talking about handing your sister over to a monster."

"Two weeks ago, I didn't even know I *had* a sister!" she spat sourly. "I also thought my mother was long dead and my son was still here. I didn't ask for any of this!"

"Keep your voice down. The others are sleeping."

"How lovely for them," she sneered.

"Anna, just come to bed," he sighed. "This line of thinking must stop."

"Jared, listen to me," Anna pleaded, grabbing his arm to keep him from walking away. "If we leave before dawn, we can be at the standing stones by nightfall." Jared shook his head and started to pull away, but Anna held tight. "Jared, wait! That fey, the cat-woman, she said Kaitlyn would be next in line to be queen. Even in another world, that can't be a bad life. At least she would be alive. But if we don't give the Fey Queen what she wants, Gabriel dies. How is that fair?"

Jared sat back down and grasped his wife's hands as he looked into her face. "Nothing about this is fair to any of us, but you can't hand Kaitlyn over to the creatures who kidnapped our son! You're not thinking straight, Anna."

"And you're not thinking like a man, much less a father!" Anna spat as she stood. "If you really cared about our son, you'd be willing to do whatever it takes," she snarled, then turned toward the cave. But she came to a sudden halt before stumbling a step back.

"Margaret. I—I didn't see you in the dark," she stuttered. "How long have you been standing there?"

"Long enough," Margaret's words held an icy edge, but her posture softened after a few heartbeats. "Anna, I know you're frightened, and you're scared you won't see Gabriel again, but we can't give in to the queen's threats. We have to trust that they'll bring him home."

"But how do you know they can pull it off, Margaret? It all seems too impossible to comprehend." This friend of Isaboe's was kind, but in Anna's mind, she was wrong. Deadly wrong.

Jared came over to stand behind his wife as Margaret replied. "I've already seen the impossible happen right before my eyes," she confirmed, taking a step closer. "The things I've seen and experienced since your mother has come back into my life have not always been comprehensible, but I can't deny that they've happened. The fact that Isaboe is alive today is a bloody miracle! She should have been dead three times over, yet, even in the face of what seemed improbable *and* impossible, she still lives."

Margaret regarded both Anna and Jared carefully before continuing. "Isaboe has gone through hell at the hands of that Fey Queen, and she would *never* give Kaitlyn up without a fight, just like she wouldn't give up searching for you, Anna, all those long dark months." Margaret let out a deep sigh before grasping Anna's hand. "We must wait, dear one, and have faith that they will bring your son home. As hard as that is for you to hear, we don't have another choice."

As Anna looked into Margaret's eyes, for a moment she felt a small thread of hope. Jared's hands softly found her shoulders again, and she turned her gaze up to her husband.

"Let's go to bed, Anna," he said. Lowering her face, she allowed him to escort her back into the cave. Just before they reached the hallway leading to the sleeping coves, he stopped. "You go ahead, my love," he muttered. "I'm going to get a drink of water first."

Anna glanced back at Jared and then at Margaret, who was still lingering at the opening to the cave door, hugging herself against the night air. The moonlight silhouetted Margaret's body against the cool silver backdrop of twilight.

"Go ahead," Jared repeated. "I'll be right there." Placing his hand at the small of his wife's back, he gently encouraged her down the dark hallway.

Anna reluctantly shuffled toward their sleeping cove until the light from the main cave could no longer reach down the hall. She then pressed her back up against the stone wall and listened. At first, she heard nothing but her heart beating, but just as she had suspected, Jared wasn't just getting a drink of water.

"Margaret, I'm so sorry," she heard her husband mumble. "I really thought she had given up on the idea. She told me she had. I...I," he stuttered for something to say.

"You needn't apologize, Jared," she heard Margaret reply. "I know Anna is torn about what to do. Actually, what I overheard doesn't really surprise me."

Margaret doesn't know me well enough to make an assumption like that, Anna thought coldly. They were quiet for a moment before Jared spoke again. "Please, don't judge her, Margaret. Ever since Gabriel disappeared, she's not been herself."

"I understand, and I don't blame her for how she feels. I love her like family, and my heart breaks for her suffering. I can't imagine the agony she must be going through."

For a moment, Anna felt a tinge of guilt at Margaret's honest concern for her. The woman didn't know her that well, yet she had embraced Anna like a long-lost family member.

"I'm not sure what I believe anymore," Jared confessed, "but I know that what Anna is contemplating would destroy us for the rest of our lives, regardless of the outcome." Jared lowered his voice, and Anna had to strain to hear his words. "I know there's a good chance I may not get my son back, but I can't lose my wife too."

Hearing the pain in her husband's voice made Anna wonder if all this craziness that had been forced upon her, all the agony she felt about her missing son, was making her lose her mind. *Was she going mad?*

"This fight isn't over yet, and you won't lose either of them," Margaret stated firmly. "Let's turn in now and make sure Anna gets a good night's sleep, aye? Lord knows, we all could use one."

Hearing their footsteps, Anna hurried from her eavesdropping spot and ducked quickly into the sleeping cove she shared with Jared.

After lying awake for what seemed like hours, Anna finally heard Jared's rattled snoring, knowing that he was now deep in sleep. Slipping quietly out of bed, she found her smock and silently pulled it over her head. Walking out of the sleeping room, she picked up her cloak and her bag before grabbing her shoes. Finding a hard roll and a piece of dried meat, she stuffed them into her bag, along with a full waterskin.

Tiptoeing back into her room, Anna went to the bassinette where Kaitlyn was sleeping soundly next to the bed and scooped up her little sister. Wrapping a blanket around the baby and holding her close to her chest, Anna looked back at her husband, knowing how upset he would be when he discovered what she was doing. But she had to do everything she could to save Gabriel's life. As much as Anna wanted to have the same faith Margaret did, she was convinced that if her son was to be saved, it would have to be by her hand. Pushing away the last traces of doubt, she snuck out of the room, fighting back tears.

Dawn was brushing the horizon in a rose-gold tint, lightening the sky just enough for Anna to see her footing as she made her way to the outbuildings, her breath ghosting before her in the chilly morning air. After hooking William's buggy up to one of the horses, she tugged at the reluctant animal's lead, slowly pulling it from the shed where the other horses were stabled. Having laid the still-sleeping Kaitlyn in a basket on the seat, Anna took her place on the bench and looked down at her sister. The child looked like a sleeping angel, and for a moment Anna wondered if she could go through with this. She would be handing over this innocent child to be raised by the vicious Fey Queen, but she would be getting her son back.

Anna knew she would have to push the horse hard in the first few hours to make it to Glochmoor before sunset. She also knew that Jared, Margaret, and Will would be on her trail as soon as they discovered she was gone, but she had already made her decision, right or wrong. The thought of having to face them and justify her actions was frightening, but she truly felt she had no other choice. She had to do this.

Fighting back another wave of tears, Anna slapped the reins. Begrudgingly, the horse moved into step, pulling the buggy out of the shed before the first rays of sunlight broke over the horizon.

CHAPTER 15

THE FLOATING ISLAND OF LUMINARA

Staring down through the transparent floor of the Fey Queen's sturdy glass and metal carriage, Rosalyn felt her anxiety levels rise as the ground below her fell further and further away. Logic told her she was completely safe as she sat across from Brighid on the bench, made plush by the soft pelt of an animal. But looking down and seeing only empty air and passing clouds between her and the ground kept Rosalyn from relaxing, and she kept her feet firmly on the footrest, away from the nothingness that comprised the floor. From this perspective, the land looked like a giant patchwork quilt, now at least a mile below. She suddenly felt a little sympathy for Isaboe's fear of flying.

"Are you alright?" Brighid asked.

"Other than some discomfort in my ears," Rosalyn replied rubbing her ear and giving a forced smile, "I'm fine," she lied.

"Oh, that's right. You're not adapted to these heights." The queen made the statement as if it was a shortcoming Rosalyn was cursed with. "Not to worry. It will pass, and you'll adjust to the altitude, eventually."

The popping in her head actually made her ears hurt, but Rosalyn wasn't about to admit it. "What type of creature is pulling this coach?" she asked to distract herself. "It looks a bit like those giant eagles of the Jarcadian warriors, but it isn't an eagle, is it?"

"No. It's a griffin. And I know this mode of transportation must be a bit unnerving for you."

"Well, to be completely honest, yes, it is. Flying is not something I normally do. Up until we arrived here, the idea was a foreign concept." Rosalyn glanced back down again, and her vision tunneled as she sat back up, trying not to let her fear show. "Doesn't it bother you, just a bit, to be this high off the ground?"

Brighid tossed her elegant blue cloak from her shoulders, letting it fall to the bench as her blue wings unfurled, filling the carriage. The soft tips were bent over where they met the ceiling, and at the clear floor below. Rosalyn was amazed at the size of the queen's wings, despite the coach's restrictions. Startled and awed, she closed her mouth before meeting Brighid's smiling eyes.

"I was born to fly," the queen replied with an air of haughtiness in her voice.

"Of course you were." Rosalyn suddenly felt silly for asking. With an uneasy grin she watched the queen fold her wings back into place. "Flying must be second nature for you, and for most everyone here. If I had to, I'm sure I'd get used to it, eventually," Rosalyn added as the queen offered an agreeable nod. Feeling the need for a distraction, she switched topics. "Your warrior, Amaroth, you seem quite fond of her, as I can tell she is of you. She's more than just your bodyguard, isn't she?" At first Brighid only stared at her, and Rosalyn wondered if she was being too bold in asking such a question. "Please, forgive me, Your Highness. I am out of line."

Brighid looked slightly taken aback, and then she laughed. "No, no, not at all. I was merely surprised by the question. You humans are always so prudish," the queen berated, but then softened with an understanding smile. "I have needs like everyone else, Rosalyn, and trust is a big issue for someone of my status. I trust Amaroth, and she takes care of *all* my needs. We take care of each other." A confident smile grew across Brighid's face before she continued. "Amaroth has been my personal guard and lover for many years now. You needn't worry about your son-by-law; she will protect him."

As Brighid's smile grew more confident, Rosalyn chuckled, certain Connor would loath being spoken of thusly. She glanced around the coach, seeking another topic. "This is a beautiful carriage, but this glass floor, well, it is a little unsettling. It is glass, right?" She wasn't sure she could take anything at face value in this world.

"It started as crystal," Brighid replied. "The Dwarfs of Edelstock, a small village in Teremenia, mine the crystal and melt it down into sheets. I commissioned the Elves of Silverleaf to create the frame, and then the dwarfs cut and fit the sheets of crystal to create this beautiful coach." Brighid pulled back the cream-colored curtain to expose the side construction of intricate scrolled silverwork, married perfectly with the sheets of crystal to create the queen's sparkling vessel. "I don't like to feel closed in when I travel. I want to be able to look out at where I am and where I'm going."

Rosalyn nodded as she glanced around the vehicle. It was a thing of beauty, a true work of art. Both sides, along with the top and bottom, were made of crystal sheets, walls she could see through. At the edges of the panels were delicately scrolled etchings, and the crystal sheets were held together by intricately twisted silver rods. Elegant blue fabric sashes accented the entire inside of the carriage, softening the corners and adding a sense of comfort between the silver and crystal layers. When she looked up through the clear ceiling, Rosalyn saw a flock of birds pass only a few feet above before glancing back down at the ground, now even further away. "Just where is this floating island?"

"If you look up, you'll see it."

"So, it's really up here, in the sky?"

Brighid only nodded.

When Rosalyn looked up once again through the ceiling, she strained to see anything but the wide-open sky. "I only see clouds."

"That's why those who live in Luminara are called the Cloud People. From this side, that's all anyone can see. But it's there. Trust me."

Rosalyn swiveled back to face the Fey Queen. "Who is it you want me to meet?"

"There are people in Luminara who want Lorien brought to justice for her crimes. It was almost expected that the council would fail to act, and they knew that eventually they would need to involve themselves. It's not their preferred choice, as most of them are above being involved in the daily on-goings of what happens down below. Some land-walkers think the Cloud People are Gods. Who Knows? Some of them just may be. They spend most of their time in meditation, making connections with other enlightened beings, or trying to unlock the mysteries of the stars. But they've been waiting for a sign, for the right time to make a move against Lorien. Your presence, and your mission, cannot be ignored. I believe that now is the time."

Rosalyn nodded, but she felt an uneasiness bubbling in her stomach as she and the queen fell into silence and the coach continued to rise. But when she noticed that the daylight was quickly dimming, Rosalyn again looked through the coach's crystal walls and saw only whiteness. Glancing below, she could no longer see the ground. They were surrounded by a misty white nothingness, and Rosalyn noticed water droplets forming on the outside of the crystal panes.

"We're inside a cloud," Brighid answered Rosalyn's unasked question. "And those are rain drops."

Rosalyn only nodded as she felt the cool dampness penetrating its way through the coach walls, causing a shiver to crawl up her spine. But she wasn't sure if it was from the cold, or from trying to wrap her brain around the idea that they were miles above Earth and passing through a cloud. She crossed her arms in a vain attempt to ward off the chill, but when the whiteness suddenly fell away as fast as it had appeared, the sun's warm light again filled the carriage.

As Rosalyn pulled back the curtain from the side window, she was awestruck by what she saw. In the distance, a magnificent palace stood like a golden beacon against the whiteness. The sun glinted off the structure's gold-and-glass spires as it reached toward the heavens from atop a high craggy pillar of rock. Lifting straight up out of the cloud, the incredible acropolis was blended into the natural rugged landscape with such remarkable elegance, it could have sprung up organically. Across the white swirling mist, the sun gleamed off the palace's intricate architecture in rainbow spears of light. Rosalyn wondered at the magic it must have taken for this impossible beauty to exist here floating among the clouds.

As the coach flew closer, Rosalyn had difficulty absorbing the grandeur of Luminara's size and beauty. She'd found the Palace of Sashtonia to be impressive, but this spectacular breath-taking sight made it look like a child's doll house by comparison.

The golden towers were encircled by rounded rooftops, wide and smooth, perfect landing sites for carriages and winged creatures. Covered bridges and walkways connected the floating castle to other smaller floating islands, many of which also supported buildings, although of a less dramatic stature. But what Rosalyn found even more amazing were the cascading waterfalls spilling off the sides of each floating island and down through the air into the swirling white clouds at the base of the fortress.

"This is completely amazing," she gasped softly, but Rosalyn realized she was alone in her astonishment when Queen Brighid offered no response.

In the distance, coming from the opposite direction, Rosalyn watched two very large birds, or at least that's what they appeared to be, soaring above the structures, gliding on the air currents that formed around the massive palace compound. But as they grew closer, Rosalyn saw that the length of their whipping tails was equal to their massive wingspans, and their heads appeared to have pointed snouts. When she realized that their large bodies and long necks were graced with colored scales, Rosalyn finally knew what they really were. "Are those...*dragons?*" she gasped, amazement coating her words.

Brighid nodded with a slight smile. "Yes, the Sordorian Dragons belong to Lord Ruz-Zambia, a highly respected and enlightened fey who resides here, though he claims he does not own them and that they are their own free spirits, able to come and go as they please. But everyone in Luminara knows that the dragons wouldn't be here if it weren't for Lord Ruz-Zambia."

"Why? Who is Lord Ruz-Zambia?"

"At one time he too was a dragon. Those are his brothers."

"A dragon? Seriously?

"Yes. However, no one knows if the dragons are planning to join their brother and shed their scales and fangs for the life of a fey, or if they're just checking in on him, making sure he is well and happy in his choice. Ruz-Zambia engages very little with others and keeps mostly to himself, high in the mountain tops."

"How does a dragon turn into a fey?"

"You'll have to ask the dragon," Brighid answered, and Rosalyn heard the hint of mirth in her voice.

Rosalyn understood only some of the mystery and magic of the fey, and since arriving in this world of the Underlings, she realized just how little she really knew. The ability to completely change into another species was so beyond her scope of understanding that it made her head spin. She watched the two dragons soaring over the castle's spires and then out across the cloud-covered terrain until they flew between two mountain peaks and disappeared. *Searching for their rebellious brother, no doubt*, she thought.

After a noticeable drop, Rosalyn saw that they were headed toward a wide landing platform on the main palace rooftop. Awestruck by its enormity, she watched the glimmering gold surface come ever closer, and she unconsciously lifted her feet just before the carriage touched down with a slight jolt.

As she stepped out of the coach, Rosalyn was no less awed when she saw the palace up close. Peering up at the spires atop the palace, she could barely make out the tips. Tall, golden statues that looked like giant chess pawns stood as silent sentinels around the perimeter of the landing area, and two elaborately decorated doors had been pulled open to permit their entrance into the building.

Rosalyn followed Brighid's lead as the two women made their way across the landing area toward the large doors that led to the inside. Sunlight filtered through the glass ceilings, filling the foyer with a luminance so bright that it was difficult to see beyond the opening. A small amount of uneasiness began to flicker in Rosalyn's chest at what might be waiting for them on the inside.

Rather than entering the palace, Brighid walked toward the edge of the platform and stood at the railing before glancing down. "Come." She gestured for Rosalyn to join her.

Stepping up next to the Fey Queen, Rosalyn glanced over the side but had to grab onto the railing. The sheer distance to the lower floating island made her dizzy, and she felt light-headed looking down at it.

After stabilizing, Rosalyn was able to look again and noticed a pond on the island far below them. What appeared to be a beautiful white swan was swimming on the surface of the water, and two young women sat at the bank watching the graceful bird swim.

"Greta!" Brighid shouted as she waved her arm. "How fares the water?"

The two girls looked up, and one of them twisted her torso to reveal not legs, but a large tail spread out behind her. In the next moment, she dove into the water.

"A mermaid?" Rosalyn exclaimed, and when the other young girl placed her hands to her mouth and shrieked loudly, what appeared to be a large fish instantly rose to the surface. After the girl climbed onto the water-creature's back, it dove down, causing them both to disappear. Then the swan began creating ripples by flapping its long white wings, the tips barely brushing the water, until it lifted and took flight. Up soared the elegant bird, circling once overhead before landing on the platform only yards from where Rosalyn and Brighid stood.

When it touched down, the swan transformed, and Rosalyn now saw a beautiful woman striding toward them. Her flowing white hair framed her torso as she walked on long willowy legs. Her white dress clung to her every curve, and the woman's alabaster skin was radiant in the sunlight.

"Welcome, my good friend," the swan-woman called out.

"Hello, Greta!" Brighid returned the greeting. "I hope we didn't interrupt anything. Were those your lovely daughters we saw on the rock?"

"Yes," the swan-woman replied as she sauntered over to embrace the Fey Queen before stepping back. The elegant woman acknowledged Rosalyn with a slight head nod. "We were doing some training, but I fear the girls are not as interested as I wish them to be. Transformation is not a simple task. It takes discipline and consistent training to control the magic that's required."

"I can only imagine," Rosalyn said incredulously, but then wondered if she spoke too soon.

"Greta, this is Rosalyn. She's a mortal."

"A mortal?" Greta's eyes widened. "There hasn't been a mortal in this realm for ages. What brings you here?"

"It's rather a long story, but in short, I'm here to rescue my grandson."

The curious expression on Greta's face prompted Brighid to elaborate. "The child has been taken by the Queen of Euphoria. Lorien is using the boy's life as ransom to get something she desperately wants."

"And what is it that she wants?" asked the swan-woman.

When Queen Brighid glanced at Rosalyn, she took that as a sign that it was up to her if she chose to share. "About a year ago Lorien abducted my daughter, Isaboe, in order to impregnate her with a child of both mortal and fey blood—specifically *Lorien's* blood. It is Kaitlyn, my granddaughter, who she ultimately wants to possess. She is using the boy's life as ransom."

Greta only stared at Rosalyn as she absorbed the weight of their quest, and it showed on the graceful woman's face before she finally spoke. "A half-fey-half-mortal female child," Greta said, more as confirmation than question, and she glanced at Brighid before readdressing Rosalyn again. "Then may the Goddess Mirarish see favor on your mission."

"Thank you." Though Rosalyn had no idea who Mirarish was, if the Goddess could offer help, Rosalyn would be happy to accept any divine intervention.

"We're on our way to the atrium," Brighid added. "Will you join us?"

"No, but perhaps I'll see you again before you leave," the swan-woman said before she turned and stepped up to the railing. "It's hard enough to keep my daughters focused these days. I had best get back to see if they are still practicing, or if they've found something less challenging to waste their talents on."

Standing tall and balanced, as steady as the sentinels beside her, Greta stood on the railing and blew them a kiss. "Take care, my friends, and I wish you well in your endeavor." She smiled over her shoulder and then leaned forward to leap over the edge. Astonished, Rosalyn ran to the railing and watched Greta freefall for several heart-pounding seconds before she transformed back into a white swan in mid-drop. With her long wings unfurled and catching the air currents, she circled a few times before landing back on the surface of the water.

"That was amazing!" Rosalyn announced as she turned to Brighid, but when the queen looked almost impatient, she realized that, once again, she was alone in her astonishment.

"We should go," the Fey Queen gestured toward the palace doors. "There are other people you need to meet."

CHAPTER 16

AN OLD FRIEND

When Rosalyn followed Brighid through the palace doors, she was surprised to see that the space inside was grand, but simplistically so. The wide-open area was bathed in sunlight, which flooded in through high stained-glass windows. There were no dividing walls inside the palace, only stone archways and glass panels that opened into other areas of the enormous structure, creating an airy, celestial feeling inside the sweeping architecture.

On her left, Rosalyn saw a magnificent garden with foliage so large and abundant that the plants filled the space, the tips of their fronds swaying as they brushed against the glass ceiling. She could see people tending the garden, almost hidden by the giant leaves. A gentle breeze rustled through the swaying branches and teased the colorful oversized flowers as birds fluttered around them, filling the air with their song. A small river gurgled between the plants, weaving intricately through the tangle of roots. Upon further inspection, Rosalyn realized that the water was flowing through some sort of transparent pipe. She stopped to get a closer look, and was even more surprised to see small creatures inside the water tunnel. At first, she wasn't sure what she was seeing, but after a moment of focused concentration she watched what looked like hundreds of tiny fish-fey darting around the root system. Busy as honeybees, they appeared to be simultaneously inspecting the underwater entanglements and feeding the plants.

Stepping away from the massive garden, Rosalyn hurried to catch up with Brighid's brisk steps. Glancing down at the plain and unpolished stone floor, Rosalyn thought it seemed out of place against the brilliance that it supported. But when she glanced up, the library came into view, and the floor was suddenly unimportant.

Shelves filled with books lined the walls from floor to ceiling, and they covered not just the walls, but flew through the air itself. Rosalyn's jaw went slack, and her eyes widened as tomes and tablets zipped overhead, magically transported to their destination. On a ladder leaning against one of the book-filled walls stood a little man who appeared to be organizing the shelves. Rosalyn watched the bearded fellow pull a book from the shelf, shake his head in disapproval, and toss it carelessly over his shoulder. The moment the book left his hand, a number of minute winged figures swooped in and plucked it from their air just as it was about to hit the floor. When the little man barked out an order, the dainty beings fluttered their wings furiously as they reshelved the book on the other side of the room. Rosalyn remembered Isaboe talking of pixies, the tiny folk who had followed her in her misadventures across Scotland. Could these miniature librarians be pixies as well? Rosalyn wondered as they set the book on the shelf and gave it a push, cheering proudly as the book wiggled itself into place.

Astonished, Rosalyn turned toward Brighid, whose destination was apparently not this miraculous place, but elsewhere. The Fey Queen was already disappearing into a far passageway, and Rosalyn had to jog to catch up. Brighid led the way through another arched passage, this one lined with a mosaic of clear green stones that invited them to gaze into the next chamber. The intricate pattern continued toward the center of a garden, where an elegant fountain of white marble bubbled. More large-leafed foliage, like what she had just seen in the garden, shaded the space, hiding the fountain's source.

Standing in various states of repose around the water feature, several people were holding a hushed conversation. As Rosalyn and Brighid approached the fountain, they noticed that one figure seemed to hold the reverent attention of his peers. Blue-skinned, hairless and delicately featured, this one sat alone with crossed legs and closed eyes. Even as Rosalyn watched, the being began to rise. Slowly the space between him and his marble seat grew as he lifted into the air. Still maintaining perfect posture, the blue-skinned fellow stopped at his audience's eye-level. It was clear, even from several paces away, how seriously the fey was concentrating in order to manage the feat.

"Practicing the art of levitation," Brighid whispered, finally coming to a stop. "This is where the most brilliant minds come to teach the old magic."

Rosalyn only nodded. She couldn't tear her eyes away from the person still floating on air. Then, one of the men sitting on the bench at the fountain's edge turned to look over his shoulder. As the elderly man stood, letting his blue robes fall around his figure, Rosalyn found herself studying his somehow familiar countenance. His white sash and gait also reminded her of someone…of an old friend. When he was close enough to make out his features, Rosalyn blinked at what her eyes were trying to tell her, because logic said it couldn't be possible.

Coming to a stop in front of her, the elderly gentleman's face broke into a bright smile as he took her hand. "Rosalyn, it's wonderful to see you again, my dear! I'm happy to see that you were able to decipher my manuals. I was hoping you wouldn't find the formulas too challenging, but I see now that I needn't have doubted you."

"Demetrick?" Rosalyn exclaimed. "I…I thought you were dead!" Rosalyn threw her arms around the man, who at one time had been as close to a father-figure as she had ever known, as well as the most brilliant wizard to ever walk the Earth.

Demetrick squeezed her tightly for a moment and then drew back. "If I had stayed in the mortal world, I most likely would have died by now. But here, I have been able to keep my disease at bay. I've managed to cheat death, for a time at least." The wizard turned back toward the fountain and placed his hand against Rosalyn's back, gently escorting her. "I have decided that as long as I have the breath and the mind to do so, I will spend my last days here, sharing my knowledge. I hope to leave this world a better place than I found it," he finished with a soft smile on his aged lips.

"So, you've been here all this time?" Rosalyn still couldn't believe that Demetrick walked beside her. As a young woman, it had been Demetrick who had opened up the world of magic and of the fey to her. His teachings had certainly saved her life many times over.

"Yes. I am a High Elder, a teacher here. I was invited into Luminara, and it is a great honor to use this opportunity to teach these students. I can but hope to do some good with my borrowed time."

"If the people can learn from a master such as you, then there is no doubt of the good you'll do, my lord." Rosalyn smiled widely and then gave Demetrick another hug.

Drawing back, the old wizard slowly began to lead the way back to the fountain. Sitting on the edge around the water feature, he gestured for Rosalyn and Brighid to join him.

"I am curious though," Demetrick continued, "how you were able to decipher those formulas and build the portal. Most of them were written in Latin."

"Oh, yes, and thank you for that," Rosalyn said sarcastically. "Fortunately, we recruited a brilliant young man from the university who was able to read your Latin scribble, and between the two of us, we pulled it off."

Chuckling, Demetrick nodded. "I really didn't believe you would ever make the attempt," he paused and looked directly at Rosalyn, "but if you needed me, I knew you would find a way."

"I couldn't have done it without Hamish," Rosalyn admitted. The young physicist was quite cunning, and together, with her magic, they had accomplished something truly remarkable when they had opened the otherworldly portal. "The thing that baffles me is how time can stand still within the portal. I understand that it's magic, but..."

"What do you mean, time can stand still?" Demetrick asked, interrupting her.

Rosalyn shot him a curious look. "Your manual said that as long as the portal remains housed within the Ring of Odin, the same ring you gave to Connor, that time will hold still for us. So, regardless of how much time passes here, we will return at the exact time we left. Isn't that how the spell works?" Feeling a quick stab of doubt, Rosalyn stared at the wizard, waiting for him to confirm what she hoped was correct.

"Rosalyn, you can't hold time still. Time is always moving. It might twist and turn back on itself, but it can't be stopped. Trying to stop time is like trying to stop the movement of the oceans or the turning of the seasons. It simply can't be done."

Jolting to her feet, a sense of horror rushed through the sorceress. "No! I thought we read in your manual that time would remain the same within the portal."

With a deep sigh, Demetrick pushed himself to his feet. "Rosalyn, you and your brilliant student misunderstood. As you know, time in the mortal world moves at a different pace than time in this world. When I wrote that time would remain the same within the portal, I meant that time would remain in tandem between both worlds for those who pass through. Therefore, if you stay here a year, when you return, a year will also have passed in the mortal world. What that portal does is hold time between the two worlds at the same pace for the voyagers. Nothing can keep time still." Accurately reading the distress written across Rosalyn's face, he added, "I can see that causes a problem for you."

"By the time we were able to cross, we had only three days to make the trade—Gabriel for Kaitlyn—before Lorien makes good on her threat to take my grandson's life. Today is the third day; mid-summer's eve is tonight. Since we haven't returned yet with Gabriel, we might already be too late."

"I don't think so," interjected a new voice. The stranger who joined them was slightly shorter than Demetrick and clean-shaven; his dark hair was greying at the temples, but other than the lines around his mouth and eyes, he didn't look much older than she was. Made of a fine cloth that looked like spun ivory, his tunic was simple but elegant.

"Rosalyn, this is Nicholi the Wanderer. He is a trusted advisor here in Luminara." As Demetrick made the introduction, Nicholi held out his hand, and she instinctively took it. Holding her hand for a long, uncomfortable moment, the man called the Wanderer stared into her face, and Rosalyn began to feel awkward under his scrutiny.

"Why do you think it's not too late?" she asked, finally drawing her hand free.

"Because right now Lorien thinks she has the upper hand. As long as she underestimates us, this will play in our favor."

"How do you know this?" Rosalyn asked, scrutinizing the man. "How do you know what Lorien thinks?"

"Lorien is my sister." Nicholi smiled self-depreciatingly. "At one time we ruled together."

Rosalyn stepped back. "You are Lorien's brother?"

"Do not worry. I hold no loyalty to her, nor she to me." His odd smile twisted sadly. "My sister actually wishes me dead."

"Why?" Rosalyn asked as Nicholi and Demetrick shared a quick glance. When something inscrutable passed between them, she wondered if she really wanted to know the answer.

Nicholi was the first to look away, and after taking a deep breath he finally addressed Rosalyn. "Hundreds of your mortal years ago, our parents were both killed in a troll attack at the Gathering of the Elders, thrusting Lorien and I into leadership of Euphoria. Young and foolish as we were, we vowed to never marry and that we would rule together forever as Prince and Princess of Euphoria. But as I grew out of my childhood, I began to desire the company of beautiful women, both fey and mortal. Being in my position, my guests were never questioned, and I enjoyed their companionship for as long as I wished. But I never intended…" He hesitated, gathering himself before continuing. "As much as this heart is capable, I fell in love with one of my companions, a mortal woman named Alaina. Against everything I had promised my sister, I took this woman as my wife. In doing so, Alaina became the Queen of Euphoria, stripping Lorien of her ruling powers and turning her against us." Drawing another deep breath, he wavered. "It is against the law for mortals to remain in the realm, much less to become head of state. But I was able to convince the council that this kind, mortal woman could cause no harm, and they dismissed Lorien's demands that Alaina be deposed. That was until Lorien discovered that Alaina was with child, and she finally acted, revealing how black her heart had become." Nicholi had begun to pace, and while his back was turned, Rosalyn shot Demetrick a questioning glance, but his face gave nothing away.

"Lorien again went before the council," Nicholi continued, "and brought forth a long-forgotten prophecy of a half-mortal female child born of royal blood who would rise up to become a great leader. However, this child of mixed blood would also start both our worlds down a path of decay and destruction. Should this prophecy come to pass, war, famine, and death would become commonplace for both Underlings and mortals. By this time, my sister had learned how to manipulate the council, and they were driven to take action."

Stepping forward to stand in front of her, Nicholi hesitated before looking into Rosalyn's face. "When I was presented with the horrible choice of either taking your life upon your birth, or sending your mother away before you were born, I did what I thought was best for both of you. At least back in the mortal world, I had hoped that you and your mother would have a chance for a new life."

The shocking reality of Nicholi's identity crashed over an unprepared Rosalyn, leaving her breathless. "You—you're my *father?*"

"Yes. Though not a very good one, it seems."

"That's certainly an understatement," Rosalyn blurted.

"My child, you must understand that I had no choice but to send your mother back. It was the only way I could hope to give you a life together."

"But I didn't *have* a life with my mother. She died shortly after I was born, and I never knew her." Rosalyn didn't try to stop the angry hurt from infecting her words.

"Yes, Demetrick informed me. My dear, I cannot begin to tell you how sorry I am."

"Sorry? You're *sorry?* I'm having a hard time believing that. You seem to have found yourself a very comfortable life after casting your wife out, along with your unborn child! Why should you give a damn now?" The words came out full of vile, a wound built up from a lifetime of unanswered questions.

"Rosalyn, please, let me explain…"

"Did you have any idea what it would be like for her when she returned to the mortal world? After ripping her from her previous life, did you even wonder how she would survive when you sent her back with no memory, no family, and pregnant?"

Rosalyn glanced at Demetrick, then caught a glimpse of Brighid standing quietly behind him. The Fey Queen had mentioned there were people in Luminara who Rosalyn needed to meet. Brighid had to know this confrontation would take place, but both she and the wizard remained silent, content to let father and daughter settle their differences uninterrupted, so Rosalyn continued. "I was raised to believe that my mother had been raped by a demon, and I was treated like a thing created by evil." She took a step closer to Nicholi. "For some reason, you fey seem to believe you have the right to play with the lives of mortals for your own selfish entertainment. My childhood was a nightmare because of what you did. Then, my daughter's life was almost destroyed thanks to your sister. All of this because of your lust for a pretty face! No, *Father*, I don't accept your explanation, or your apology," Rosalyn spat.

"Rosalyn," Demetrick finally interjected, his voice placating.

"It's alright," Nicholi interjected. "Anything she has to say, I deserve to hear." Meeting Rosalyn's eye, he continued. "I never thought the day would come when you would be standing before me. But now that it has, you have made it clear just how selfish I have been." He drew a deep breath before speaking again. "Lorien also demanded my death for breaking the law, but the council would not grant her that wish. They did, however, remove me from my throne, which without Alaina by my side, I gave up freely. I have been here licking my wounds ever since. I turned my back on not just my family, but my own people. It gives me great sorrow to know the pain I have caused. I don't expect you to forgive me, but please, give me the opportunity to offer you aid, and in the process, help my people as well."

"And what do you have to offer?" Rosalyn asked sharply. She didn't know how to feel about this fey, even if he was offering his assistance.

"I know every inch of Euphoria," Nicholi replied. "Though Lorien has cast a nasty spell around the perimeter to keep out the uninvited, there is a tunnel that runs beneath the border of Euphoria. For years it has been sealed by magic, but I can open it and allow you to pass through. If we can draw the attention of Lorien's guards away from the tunnel, we could sneak in, as long as Lorien hasn't sealed it from the other side."

"But," Demetrick added, "the tunnel is quite small, and we couldn't easily move a large group of people through it."

"And what could we use for a distraction?" Brighid asked. "How do we distract her patrols when we can't cross through her spell to draw their attention?"

"And what if the tunnel opening is sealed on the inside?" Rosalyn said. "Do you have an alternative plan?"

No one replied.

"Then explain to me how any of you are helping us," Rosalyn almost shouted. "How is it that the greatest minds in the realm can't seem to break through Lorien's magic? I've considered you to be a great wizard, Demetrick. Are you telling me that even you can't get through?"

"The spell Lorien has placed on the borders of Euphoria is so potent that no one has yet been able to counter it," the wizard answered humbly. "Anyone who has attempted to cross into Euphoria uninvited has died a horrible death."

"Well, this is just great! I come all the way up here to find out that time in the portal hasn't stood still as I thought it would, and today is mid-summer's eve, meaning we are out of time. I also meet my father, who, I discover, threw me and my mother away because we were *inconvenient*," she snarled, glaring at Nicholi. "And now we have no plan to save my grandson." Rosalyn felt the heat rising on her face as she glared angrily between the wizard and her father. "I'm no better off than when we first arrived in this crazy land. I don't know why I even tried!" Fighting furious tears, Rosalyn turned and walked away.

"Rosalyn," Demetrick called out, but she didn't stop. After running from the room, she passed the library and the garden before reaching the doors to the landing platform. When she stepped out into the air, Rosalyn hurried to the railing and grabbed on. Drawing long deep breaths, she willed her tears from falling as she struggled with her feelings of failure.

CHAPTER 17

LORD RUZ-ZAMBIA

Rosalyn was allowed only moments to herself before she heard footsteps following her to the railing. Though she didn't turn to face him, Rosalyn acknowledged Demetrick as he stepped up beside her, with Brighid and Nicholi quietly standing a few paces behind him.

"Rosalyn, I understand your distress, but we will find a way in. There are many brilliant minds here, and they will lend us their aid. If you will just join us in the atrium, I am certain that we can find a solution."

Demetrick's face was open and optimistic, but Rosalyn knew that he was only telling her what she wanted to hear. It was becoming painfully obvious that this rescue mission was a disaster, and they would not be bringing her grandson home as she had promised. How would she ever be able to face Anna and her husband?

"Look who's decided to grace us with his presence," Brighid said, distracting Rosalyn from her spiraling thoughts.

Following the Fey Queen's gaze, Rosalyn saw a cloaked figure crossing one of the many suspended bridges that linked their island to the next. He entered from the opposite side of the landing platform and was on a direct path toward their party.

"Who is that?" Rosalyn asked.

"That is Lord Ruz-Zambia," Brighid whispered. "I told you about him in the carriage."

"The fey who was once a dragon?"

As Lord Ruz-Zambia approached, Brighid's only reply was a mischievous smile. The impressive fey drew everyone's attention like moths to a flame, and even the air felt charged with his presence. A long charcoal-colored cloak, appropriately decorated for someone who carried the title of Lord, swept behind him in an impressive wave of fine cloth, and Rosalyn thought the magnificence of his elegantly embroidered garment matched the imposing figure of the fey himself.

With a tiny shiver, Rosalyn realized the lord's eyes were fixed only on her as he strode across the vast platform. He carried a golden staff that clicked on the tiles with every other step. Even from a distance, she was struck by his dark countenance, by the dusky color of his skin and the sharp points of his ears. His brow and jaw were both sharply defined, giving him a regal and mysterious air. Beneath his elaborate cloak he wore only trousers and boots, which left his bare chest exposed.

Rosalyn felt a slight rush as she let her eyes wander over his nakedness, admiring the flex and pull of his muscles beneath his warm amber skin. She wondered if this unusual creature always drew so much attention when he made an appearance, or if she were alone in her amazement.

"He's quite impressive, isn't he? You might want to pick your jaw up off the floor," Brighid whispered in Rosalyn's ear. "His Lordship very seldom makes an appearance, but when he does grace us with his presence, he usually has something profound to say. If he chooses to, I'm sure Ruz-Zambia could really *fire* things up."

Ignoring Brighid's pun, Rosalyn only nodded. As the dragon-lord came to stand next to them, Rosalyn's gaze was once again drawn to his face. She could now see his eyes properly, and they were as captivating as the rest of him. Each eye sported two irises, one inside the other. Swirling in opposing directions, they were the color of mountain streams, green circling blue in a hypnotic dance. As he looked at Rosalyn with curiosity, it was clear that he was intrigued. Bringing his handsome chiseled face close to hers, he studied her as intently as she was studying him. But he seemed to have no sense of personal space, and Rosalyn took a step back.

"I feel a vibration in the air, something I've never noticed before." The dark fey's voice was deep and smooth, and Rosalyn thought its rich tone sounded like a finely-tuned instrument. "You are different. Why is that?"

"Lord Ruz-Zambia," Demetrick stepped forward, "I would like to introduce you to Rosalyn. She is half-mortal."

"Explain mortal."

"I'm from another world, Your Lordship," Rosalyn answered, "the world of mortals, or humans, as we are also called."

"How are you different from a fey?" Ruz-Zambia leaned forward and sniffed Rosalyn's hair, causing her to take another step back. The dragon-lord's presence was intimidating enough without him sniffing her. "Why is your vibration so much stronger than every other being here?"

To this, Rosalyn had no answer, so Demetrick interjected. "Forgive me, Lord Ruz-Zambia, but our guest is not familiar with your direct approach." He then turned to Rosalyn. "As you can see, Lord Ruz-Zambia speaks rather frankly, but he means no disrespect, I assure you."

"None taken." When Rosalyn met Ruz-Zambia's penetrating stare again, it seemed as if he were trying to read her very soul.

"Welcome, Lord Ruz-Zambia," Nicholi stepped forward to address the recent arrival. "It is a pleasure to have your company on this beautiful day. I wish I could say that all is as pleasant in the lands below. Sadly, there is a malignant growth that has gone unchecked for far too long. We were just discussing what actions we should take, and I believe I speak for all of us when I say that your opinion on this matter would be greatly appreciated. Would you care to join us in the atrium? The others are gathered there, and we were just on our—"

"Not yet," Ruz-Zambia cut Nicholi off, his eyes never leaving Rosalyn's face. "I would like to have a moment alone. That is, if you would grant me the honor of your time, Rosalyn of the mortal world."

"Uh, well, I suppose."

"Excuse me, Lord Ruz-Zambia," Brighid interrupted. "But I need to speak with her first." The queen offered a forced smile and left no room for argument before clasping onto Rosalyn's arm and pulling her aside.

When they were just out of hearing range, Brighid whispered, "For some reason, Ruz-Zambia seems to have taken an interest in you. This could play in our favor. To have the dragons on our side would be a huge advantage, but until now, no one has been close enough to him to make such a request. Maybe you're the one to do the asking."

Rosalyn looked back at the three men and saw that Demetrick was bending Ruz-Zambia's ear, but she noticed that his hypnotic eyes frequently strayed in her direction. "I just met the man," she whispered. "I can't ask him to have his dragon-brothers go into battle for us. Besides, if he has taken an interest in me, it's only because he's never met a human before. I'm just a novelty," she said defensively.

"If you want to stand on protocol and take your time getting to know him, that is up to you. But let me remind you, my dear, it's your grandson's life at stake, and we don't have the luxury of time." Spinning around, the queen strolled toward the door that led to the foyer, her blue cloak sweeping behind her as she disappeared through the doors. A moment later, Nicholi and Demetrick followed her into the brilliantly-lit hall, but the wizard floated Rosalyn an encouraging grin before he disappeared.

Suddenly, Rosalyn felt nerves fluttering in her belly as the dragon-lord approached. Dropping her gaze, she had an abrupt, yet almost humorous feeling, of what a shy school-girl at her first dance might feel like, had she ever been one.

"Nicholi tells me that the evening meal will soon be served in the dining hall. Would you like to eat?" Ruz-Zambia asked.

"No. I'm not hungry." Rosalyn doubted she would be able to get food down, not after everything she had learned this day. And now, an incredibly handsome fey—who was also a *dragon*—had taken a special interest in her. She wasn't sure how she felt about any of it. "But if you would like to eat, please, don't let me stop you, Your Lordship."

"No, I'm good for now, and please, call me Norvik. Though, I do admit that this body requires frequent nourishment, which can be quite inconvenient. When I was a dragon, I could eat once and be sustained for a month. This form is much less efficient."

Rosalyn felt a genuine smile pull up the corners of her mouth. "In comparison, I suppose not." She gave him a curious look. "But what did you eat that would hold you over for a whole month, an entire cow?"

"Explain cow."

"It's an animal, it's a…oh, never mind." Rosalyn felt her anxious frustration growing as she turned away from the mysterious Ruz-Zambia. When she walked over to the railing and glanced over the side, the sheer drop made her feel a bit light-headed, and she held onto the bar to stabilize herself. She felt the dragon-fey's eyes on her as he came to stand next to her, but she didn't want to meet his penetrating gaze. Something about his scrutiny made her feel uncomfortable, as if she were under close examination.

"Where is the world of the mortals?" he asked.

Finally turning to look directly at him, she searched for an answer. "It's in another realm, in a place you can't easily reach from here."

"How did you arrive? Did you fly?" He leaned around her to take a quick glance at her back. "Do you have wings?"

Rosalyn chuckled. "No, I don't have wings. Before he left our world, Demetrick left me the instructions for building a portal that allowed us to cross over."

Ruz-Zambia gave Rosalyn a look as if he were trying to visualize a doorway into another world. "What is the mortal world like?"

"It's a lot like this one. Well, not really like this." Rosalyn gestured to the towers around them. The spires of silver reaching for the heavens atop the palace and the ring of golden sentries that guarded the landing platform were a far cry from anything she had ever seen in Scotland. "There's no place in my world that looks like this, at least not that I know of. Up here, everything seems so peaceful, so calm and serene. It's nothing like where I come from. My world is complex and full of people, both good and bad. Most of us have to make difficult choices just to survive, and sometimes it's hard to know who to trust."

"What threatens your world? What is the cause of this strife?"

"We are driven by the same things that drive the fey, Your Lordship. Just like the fey, we often have to fight for our rights to live freely, and sometimes we are forced to make the only decision that is available to us, even if it isn't a good one." She felt a pang at those words, recalling the choice that Nicholi had been presented with all those years ago, and for a brief instant, her loathing of her father melted into something that felt like empathy, but she quickly shrugged it off. "What we want are the same things all beings want: the opportunity to have quality of life, to raise our families peacefully, and to not live in fear of one another."

"I don't understand. What causes your species to turn on its own?"

Giving him a confused look, Rosalyn spun away. She was done with his questions that she didn't know how to answer. After taking a few steps, she turned and looked back at him. It was time to turn the tables. "If it is not too bold, my Lord, may I ask how a dragon becomes a fey?"

He seemed a bit surprised at her question, but then took a step forward. "My grandfather provided the magic for me to make the transformation."

"Is your grandfather a dragon?"

"Of course. What else would he be?"

"I—" she paused, feeling rather silly. "What kind of magic turns a dragon into a fey?"

"A very old and guarded magic. Grandfather is the keeper of the old ways, of the dragons' secrets. He lives high up in the mountains. I had to travel a great distance to find him, and then I had to prove myself worthy of taking on such a task."

"But why did you want to become a fey?"

"Dragons live a very long life, and I had learned everything there is about being a dragon. But I knew nothing of what it felt to live as a land-walker, to experience the world in another form and see life through another's eyes."

"And have you done that? Have you actually experienced life through another's eyes?"

"Yes. In this fey body I am beginning to understand what is important to their way of life, and what brings them enlightenment."

"And you're discovering that by what means? Living away from others like a hermit? Connecting only with other highly intelligent beings? Do you really expect to find what you're looking for by hanging out in this paradise and having your ideas repeated back to you in an echo chamber?"

"You seem annoyed."

"If you haven't been off this floating island, how can you experience what real life is like unless you interact with real people? If you came down from the mountaintops to be a land-walker, don't you need to get down on the land, my Lord?"

Ruz-Zambia stared silently at her, his face giving nothing away, and Rosalyn wondered if she had been too brash. But the dragon-lord once again seemed more curious than affronted, and he finally broke the silence. "Nicholi and Demetrick told me of your mission to rescue the mortal child. But since you are here requesting assistance, you obviously have been unable to accomplish this task on your own. Why would you take on such a risky endeavor unprepared?"

"Are you always so blunt?" Rosalyn heard the sharpness in her words, but at the moment, she didn't care.

"Have I said something offensive?"

Turning away, Rosalyn decided that this conversation was going nowhere. His words had struck a nerve. When she, Connor, and Isaboe had made the choice to cross over and rescue Gabriel, they did so blindly. She had hoped that her powers, which she now realized were insignificant in this realm, would allow her to lead this rescue mission and escape victorious. But she now knew how arrogant that had been. They were in completely over their heads, and only now when it was already too late did she realize how ill prepared she really was. There had been no plan. They had just jumped. Lord Ruz-Zambia had simply pointed out the flaws in their thinking, feeding the self-doubt that was rapidly filling her mind.

Lifting her chin and swallowing her pride, Rosalyn turned to face him. "Your Lordship, thank you for pointing out my short-comings. Unfortunately, you are correct. We arrived with no plan of attack. But we are here, and I have no intention of leaving without my grandson. So unless you have something beneficial to add, I believe I'll take my leave and join the others in the atrium."

Spinning away, she had gone only a few steps before he called out, "Are you always this passionate?"

"*What?*" Rosalyn spun back around with a steely glare. Ruz-Zambia didn't appear intimidated, but once again he stepped too close, peering down into her eyes.

"Are all mortals as passionate as you are?"

"I don't know. Are all dragons as annoying as you are?" she snapped.

"It is not my intention to be annoying. I only wish to know you, to understand more about mortals. I apologize if I have offended you in any way."

"Why do you wish to understand me?"

"You intrigue me. The people I've met here in Luminara take their roles very seriously, and their decisions and conclusions often take a great deal of contemplation before any action is taken or a judgment made. As you confessed, you and your team of would-be rescuers came into this foreign realm with no plan. But you came anyway, because you felt you had no other choice. I find spontaneous behavior interesting. I desire to know more about you, to understand what makes your kind so impulsive. What is it that gives mortals purpose?"

Empowered by her anger, Rosalyn stood up straighter and thrust her face close to his. "You became a fey so you could understand them, and yet, you still don't," she challenged. "How can you possibly expect to know what gives me or any mortal purpose when you can't even walk in the shoes of the being you have chosen to become? Have you done anything but hide up here in this oasis meditating on the mysteries of the universe? Meanwhile, just a few miles beneath us, there are important matters happening *right now* that could use your attention! If you weren't hiding up here in the clouds, you would know that!" Rosalyn spat, fully energized. But as quickly as her rush of fury had come, it left her. Realizing who it was she was yelling at, she awkwardly adjusted her posture. "Forgive me, Your Lordship. I've spoken out of line."

"No, you did not. You simply spoke your truth. And please, call me Norvik." His swirling blue-green eyes danced with hers before he spoke again. "Dragons have very large hearts, and with a large heart comes a great deal of passion. The heart of the fey is not the same. I do not refer to their size so much as their limited ability for compassion."

"Oh, I am very familiar with their lack of compassion," Rosalyn said dryly. "I have first-hand experience with their egotism." She heard the spite in her own words, but Ruz-Zambia only nodded.

"But I do feel your passion. It is something I have not experienced here before. You are correct that I haven't really walked the land of the fey. Perhaps there is more to experiencing the life of a land-walker than just taking on his form." Ruz-Zambia did not bother to put more space between them, even as the heat of their conversation cooled. Instead, he continued meeting her eyes directly as he spoke, while Rosalyn stood her ground. "The reason I chose to transform is so that I could think like a fey. I wanted to experience the feelings and emotions of a land-walker, but I've always felt that something was missing." He leaned back, but created only enough space to brandish his staff between them, holding it up so that the large red stone at the top was at eye level as he looked at it with reverence. "A dragon's heart is so big that it cannot be contained in this body. My grandfather had to store my heart in this gem. Occasionally, I still feel it beating."

Drawing his other hand to his chest, he continued, "But for the first time, I feel the beating of this heart." The dragon-lord stepped nearer again, so close Rosalyn could feel the heat radiating off his body. "It feels something like fondness, and this feeling is being directed toward you."

"What?" she exclaimed, taking a step back. "I just insulted you, and you tell me you feel fondness toward me? Are you insane?"

"Explain insane."

"It's what I am right now for having this conversation with you!" Rosalyn spat before she spun around. Stomping toward the foyer doors, she met Demetrick and Nicholi who were walking out. The pointed intent on both their faces brought her to a stop. "What's wrong?" she asked.

"You need to come with us." Demetrick gestured for her to follow, and the look on his face did not put Rosalyn's mind at ease.

CHAPTER 18

BATTLE OF THE TROLLS

"This way!" Klute shouted to Connor. "We will get there faster on Rohan!"

Following Klute's lead, Connor had no time to think as he sprinted to catch up with the lion-man's quick pace. The other Jarcadian warriors were either in a heated run toward the conflict or scrambling to mount their battle eagles.

As he scurried up the Shekar's wing, Connor literally fell into his seat behind Klute at the exact moment Rohan began flapping his wings. Lurching into a run, the battle eagle was off the ground in seconds, and Connor had to hang onto Klute's middle when Rohan banked hard to the left heading toward the southeast border of Sashtonia.

From their height, it didn't take long for Connor to spot the battle unfolding beneath them as dust rose up in a foreboding cloud around the combat. The trolls had come through the southern mountains, detected by the watch only as their force was descending into the forest. General Renwolf had launched his defense from the southern watchtower, the warriors' primary guard post in the southern reaches. Standing on the bank of the Talverde River, it towered proudly over even the massive trees of the king's forest, providing sweeping views of the mountains to the south and the river which bisected Sashtonia to the west. A dark scar had already been ripped into the pristine forest as the earliest skirmishes were fought.

Leaning low over the neck of his battle eagle, Klute pulled hard on the bird's lead, and they plunged toward the ground. As Connor felt the rush of battle ignite in his veins, his heartbeat quickened, and the fear that had been plaguing his mind turned to thrill. From above, he could see the chaos surging on the ground below, ground that was rapidly growing closer. "Klute, what's our plan?" Connor called over the roaring wind.

"Behind the saddle!" the warrior shouted over his shoulder. "Grab your weapons!"

With only seconds to react, Connor turned in his seat and found a woven basket strapped to the saddle. When he flipped open the lid, he saw an array of war tools, some of which he'd never seen before. Connor grabbed a long-jagged knife, which he shoved under his belt. He then clutched onto a weapon that resembled an ax, heavy and deadly.

As soon as Rohan began to level off, the Jarcadian warrior retrieved a spear, two long daggers, and a shield that had been strapped to the side of the saddle. With a terrifying war cry, he leapt out of the saddle and onto an unsuspecting troll. Klute's charge into combat inspired Connor to do the same, and he jumped into action the moment Rohan hit the ground. Once off the Shekar's wing, he had only a second to prepare before the first troll came charging through the dust with a battle cry of his own. As Connor raised up his axe to challenge his foe, Rohan beat him to it. The angry Shekar reached out with its lethal beak and snatched the troll off its feet. Though the troll screamed and pounded its club against the giant eagle, Rohan had only to snap his beak to slice the beast in half.

Having faced trolls twice before, Connor was beginning to learn the lumbering beasts' limited tactics. The trolls charged erratically, seemingly bent on destroying whatever was in their path. He watched one do just that, roaring through the dust toward the back of a Jarcadian warrior who was entirely caught up with the troll he was currently battling. Connor intervened, his ax meeting the troll's shoulder with a meaty thud, forcing the beast to drop its club and bellow in pain. The Jarcadian warrior, whose life Connor had most likely just saved, threw off his own attacker and spun around, plunging his spear into the wounded troll. After kicking the troll over and ripping his spear from the beast's corpse, he and Connor had only a moment to acknowledge one another before they saw an enormous hairy troll barreling toward them with its club held high. But as Connor drew up his ax to catch the beast's attack, it never came. Instead, the troll changed course, avoiding Connor and targeting another victim.

Something about this seemed incongruous, but Connor did not have time to dwell on it, as the dust parted just enough for another skirmish across the battlefield to catch his attention. Amaroth stood alone against two massive club-swinging trolls, her sword flying as she battled them both. Running in her direction, Connor could only watch helplessly as one of the beast's weapons found its mark, striking Amaroth from behind and sending her tumbling.

Though he struggled to reach Amaroth, Connor's path was interrupted by another troll, who took a swing at him with the blunt end of its ax. Connor dodged to avoid taking a direct hit, but his feet became tangled beneath him, and he tumbled face-first into the dust. After quickly recovering his balance, Connor saw the troll looming toward him with its hairy fist balled up and cocked for a brutal punch, aimed directly at Connor's face. But he rolled out of the beast's way and kicked at its ankles, bringing it down to join him in the dust. Unlike his opponent, Connor did not hesitate to put it out of its misery, and sliding the knife from his belt, he plunged it into the troll's throat to end the struggle. But the fight left Connor disquieted. Why would the troll hesitate to kill him? He was confused by the oddities of these trolls who seemed reluctant to face the lone mortal on the field of battle. The beasts tried to avoid him, and those few who did face him used only non-lethal methods of attack, to their detriment. If they could bring down as powerful a warrior as Amaroth, why did they change tactics against him?

Connor was pulled from his thoughts when a silver flash zipped past his head, and he barely had time to dodge the second flash. Tumbling to the ground, he looked back over his shoulder in time to watch the flash of silver slice through the pauldron of a Jarcadian warrior who screamed and flinched, dropping his weapon. As the warrior's opponent took advantage of his distraction to pound him into the dust, Connor saw three more silver lights shoot up toward an unsuspecting battle eagle. She and her rider had been circling the conflict overhead, but when the weapon clipped the eagle's wing, both bird and rider were sent in a screeching dive toward the ground.

As he scanned the dusty landscape behind the fallen battle eagle, Connor could see additional Shekar swooping down to join the skirmish.

Their numbers were growing, and it was clear that the Jarcadian warriors were mounting a successful defense.

Spinning to find his next target, Connor spotted the largest troll he had ever seen. Covered in fur and supporting a massive set of horns, he wore a crown of antlers upon his giant head signifying his place as leader; this must surely be Kaegron. The intimidating beast was also scanning the battlefield, and when their gaze's met, Connor felt the weight of Kaegron's stare settle over him. The troll hefted his ax and began to march purposefully in Connor's direction. As he scrambled to put space between himself and the oncoming troll, the waves of battle worked in Connor's favor, and Kaegron was soon swallowed up by the chaos. When the dust settled, the troll leader was gone.

Scanning the skirmish to find wherever he could make himself most useful, Connor spied Nyia taking on two trolls at once and leapt to assist her. Swinging his ax high, he charged toward one of the beasts and brought the blade down hard across its neck, severing its head from its body. No longer outnumbered, Nyia easily took out the other troll, her swords and tail slicing through the beast's entrails. Nyia and Connor had only a moment to acknowledge each other before two more trolls rushed up behind them. Lunging at the mortal, one of them grabbed onto Connor's upper arm with a bruising grip and twisted, forcing Connor to drop his ax and bringing him to his knees. He struggled in vain for several seconds until Nyia's tail whipped across the hand holding Connor down, instantly drawing blood and making the troll howl in pain as it stumbled backward. This gave Connor the opportunity to wield his knife, and he slashed out wildly, feeling the blade meet flesh as it sliced across the troll's throat. As black fluid spurted out of the open wound, the beast gurgled in its own blood and dropped into the dirt.

Without a flinch, Nyia slid her sword through the middle of the second troll. Although the battle had clearly taken its toll on her, as evidenced by her bruised face, she gave Connor a confident nod. There was still a lot of fight left in her.

"Is it my imagination, or was that troll trying to capture you?" Nyia asked, catching her breath as she continued scanning the battle unfolding around them.

"Aye, and that's not the first time. Something fuckin' weird is goin' on."

Nyia nodded, but her attention was suddenly fixed on a distant skirmish. Following her gaze, Connor spotted Kaegron's crown of antlers towering above the battle. They were not the only ones who had seen the troll, and as they watched, General Renwolf himself moved to confront the enemy's leader. When Connor looked back at Nyia, it was as if she were reading his mind. "Let's end this," she growled.

Grinning viciously, Connor followed the Jarcadian warrior as she descended back into the chaos. They stayed low to the ground, slipping through the mayhem and taking advantage of their stealth to hamstring a few trolls as they went. After finding a safe position, they waited for the opportune moment to strike.

As Kaegron and General Renwolf charged one another, the clashing of sword and club was lost to the cacophony of the battle. Although Renwolf was an experienced combatant, Kaegron was a giant among his peers. Bringing his club down upon the general's shield, the force of his blow split the bronze sheet in twain. Renwolf tossed his now worthless shield to the side and faced the troll with his spear alone. They bobbed and wove for a few heart-pounding seconds until the troll leader seemed to grow bored. Connor saw a flash of sliver as Kaegron tossed something down between them, and a dozen sharp streaks zipped toward Renwolf's face, slicing through his helmet and into his flesh. When the general clutched his face and fell backward, Kaegron loomed over him sensing victory and raised his club to finish the job.

"Get him from behind!" Nyia shouted as she charged to intercept the troll's attack. Placing herself between Renwolf and Kaegron, the Jarcadian warrior shoved aside his club with a well-placed swing of her own sword. When he stumbled backward, she pressed her advantage, slicing her sword at the troll's gut. But Kaegron soon found his feet again and retaliated with a swing of his mighty club, knocking Nyia off her feet.

Realizing that this was his moment, Connor charged Kaegron from behind, dropping his axe low and aiming for the back of the troll's knees. As his blade sliced through bulging tendons in Kaegron's right thigh, the troll leader's legs gave out from under him. With a furious roar, he crumbled, and his crown of antlers went flying.

Immediately, Renwolf was up and taking advantage of the opening Connor had provided. With blood streaming down his face, the general dug the tip of his spear into Kaegron's throat. Within seconds, the general was surrounded by other warriors, their spears directed toward the stunned troll. "Surrender now or die!" the general commanded, as he placed a blood-soaked boot on his opponent's chest. "Call off your warriors! NOW!"

Though the giant troll clearly did not want to admit defeat, Connor and Nyia, and all the other warriors who now surrounded him, proved that they were more than willing to follow through with Renwolf's threat. At long last, the beast finally stopped thrashing and threw back his head. Opening his grotesque mouth, he bellowed out a roar that made Connor's ears ring.

Instantly, the battles around them ceased as all the trolls stopped their attack and began fleeing back the way they had come. Leaving behind a battlefield scattered with dead or wounded trolls and warriors, they abandoned their captured leader.

The Jarcadian warriors were eerily silent as they marched their limping prisoner through the halls of Castle Sashtonia. The only sound was their heavy footfalls echoing off the walls of the nearly empty fortress, and the few people they did encounter scattered like frightened mice. Connor was intimately familiar with the bitter taste of victory. Rather than celebrating their victory over the trolls, the warriors were grim and solemn. Still covered with the blood-and-dust of the battlefield, they led their badly wounded prisoner directly to the king's throne room.

Although the battle had been short-lived, the carnage was significant. Fortunately, the trolls' mad rampage onto enemy territory had resulted in them taking the majority of the casualties. Their attack had been ambitious and aggressive, yet the larger beasts could not compete with the quick-footedness and skill of the Jarcadian warriors, nor the bone-crushing beaks and ripping talons of their Shekars. However, the defenders had also suffered heavy losses.

Connor took account of the injured warriors, seeing blood seeping from nasty gashes, soldiers limping on wounded legs, and more than one warrior being carried by their comrades. Klute, who had found Connor and Nyia soon after the battle's conclusion, had also taken his fair share of blows, sporting a bloody, swollen cut on his face. As they walked together, Connor could see the concern Klute had for his partner. Assisting Nyia through the hall, she leaned heavily against him, limping. For the proud warrior, this was admission enough of the pain she must be suffering. Recalling the force of the hit he had seen her take from Kaegron's club, Connor privately thought that Nyia was lucky to have escaped with only bruises and broken bones. Glancing to his left, he caught a glimpse of Amaroth, who also wore the bloody signs of battle. But she, too, had survived.

Though he wasn't sure if anyone besides he and Nyia had noticed the trolls' attempts to capture the lone mortal in combat, Klute's silence was filled with suspicion. Even the man he had helped to save, General Renwolf, seemed to look at Connor with skepticism. Approaching the throne room at last, Connor felt less prepared for this battle than he had fighting the trolls.

The doors to the throne room were thrown open, and the dirty blood-covered soldiers funneled in, stomping across the polished floor and coming to a stop in the center of the room. Renwolf grabbed a fistful of fur on the back of Kaegron's neck, and with his warriors' spears keeping the growling prisoner in line, forced him to his knees. King Enoch had risen upon their entrance, and he, along with those few elders who had not fled the castle, gawked down at the scene from their balcony. Connor, Klute and Nyia stood toward the back, watching.

"So, this must be Kaegron," King Enoch finally said, breaking the tense silence, "the mighty leader of the trolls." The king descended the stairs to stand before his prisoner, but Connor noticed that Enoch wisely kept his distance. "Has he told you what provoked such a bold attack on the palace grounds?" the king demanded of Renwolf.

"No. He said he'd only speak to you, Sire," the general replied.

"Then speak!" Enoch demanded. "Why have you attacked my castle? Why do you push at your borders?" When the troll only glowered at

Enoch, the king began to shout. "You will answer my questions, or my warriors will end your worthless life and mount your head on a stake before sunset!"

"Your Lordship," General Renwolf began. "The trolls were using these—star-discs." Producing the weapon from inside his armor, Renwolf presented it to the king. "We took these off of him and found more on the dead. This is a perfect example of these trolls using weapons and tactics of which they should not be capable!"

"Where did you get these? Who is helping you?" King Enoch demanded. But when Kaegron remained silent, at Renwolf's signal, two of his warriors stabbed their spears into the prisoner's back. Roaring from the torture, Kaegron finally found his voice. Although Connor was still wearing his translation stone, the troll's deep guttural words were challenging to understand.

"I earned 'em!" was Kaegron's gruff reply.

"From whom? Who's helping you?" the king demanded again.

"Kaegron need no help," the troll hissed. "Trolls need no one."

"Yet, somehow, you have acquired these weapons," said one of the elders from the balcony. Connor looked up to see King Bogknocken, the Lord of the Pixies, glaring furiously down at the troll. His pointed ears and long pointed nose might have looked comical, but the deadly seriousness in his large eyes was anything but humorous. "As General Renwolf has already pointed out, your kind do not have the capacity to create such weapons. How do you explain this?"

"If I may, Your Highness," said Idora, the Lady of the Lake, as she moved toward the railing, shimmering like a liquid jewel. "Though we've always believed they do not have the intellect to create such weapons, this evidence would prove otherwise. This then raises an important question; are they being assisted, or are the trolls evolving in their knowledge?"

"And if there is someone behind the trolls' advancements," added Reania, the red-haired elf princess from Silverleaf, "we all know who has the motivation."

"We must also take note of how timely the troll's attack was; they took these drastic steps right after the arrival of the mortals," spat Lady Jobetha, the Prime Minister of Nacmorid. Connor did not miss the vile tone that coated her words. "And by their own admission, the mortals are here to stir up trouble with Lorien. Now our warriors are bloodied and battered in the name of their agenda!"

Connor felt the fey woman's glare like venom in his veins, and suddenly her snakeskin suit seemed appropriate. He felt his hackles rise at Lady Jobetha's accusation. They would have never been in this realm in the first place if Lorien hadn't forced their hand.

"I believe you are correct, Lady Jobetha," said Lord Pagganot, the High Elder from Teremenia. "The timing of the trolls' attack most likely does correspond with the mortals' arrival. But you cannot deny that the trolls have been growing in strength and numbers for years, pushing their borders long before the humans' appearance. Can you not see that both of these things have been brought upon us by Lorien's machinations? I suggest we follow their lead and take this opportunity to launch a campaign against the Queen of Euphoria."

"And put us all at risk of war?" cried Bogknocken. "Lorien has had years to create her army and fortress, to say nothing of the spells she has placed on her borders. We would do better to keep the peace. Send the mortals back from where they came. Do not instigate trouble with the Queen of Euphoria."

"Sending the mortals away will solve nothing," argued Lord Pagganot, his goatlike ears flopping about in his passion. "We must address the malignancy that exists in Euphoria! If we deal with Lorien, the mortals will have what they came for, and then they will leave."

"We've had this discussion before, Pagganot, and it always ends the same."

"Well, maybe now is the time to change that," interjected Princess Reania. "With help from Luminara, we could finally bring Lorien down!"

"The Cloud People have no place in this council, Reania!" shouted Lady Jobetha. "You know that!"

"Yes, I've heard that over and over again from this council, yet no one will explain why. Why do we not allow the greatest of all the minds in all the realm to offer us their advice and assistance, especially now? *Wake up people!* We already are at war! Now is the time to unite!"

"That is enough!" King Enoch roared. "We will continue this

discussion later, in a more appropriate setting and in a more organized manner." The king let his disapproving gaze float over his fellow leaders.

After an uncomfortable silence, General Renwolf spoke again. "We also took this from him, Sire." He produced a leather pouch on a long rough-looking belt and offered it up to the king. "It held star-discs, and something unusual for a troll to possess."

Connor watched as the king opened the leather bag and lifted out a chain. Dangling at the end was a familiar green gem. When Kaegron saw it, he struggled and roared, "That's *mine!*"

A sudden recall forced Connor to turn toward Klute and whisper, "Isn't that the same green gem we saw on …?" A swift glare and a threatening hiss from the lion-man instantly shut Connor's mouth.

When King Enoch reached out to touch the stone, one of his royal ministers rushed forward and slapped the gem from the king's hand, leaving Enoch staring and aghast.

"Forgive me, My Lord," the minister said quickly, offering a nervous bow. "But that charm is enchanted! I can feel its dark energy." As fear crossed his face, the man paused. "It is a foul and malignant magic!" The minister backed away in revulsion as he stared at the charm, now laying innocently on the floor.

"Who is helping you?" King Enoch again demanded, but Kaegron refused to answer. "Take him to the dungeons and torture him until he talks. I want answers!" King Enoch shouted. "And summon my personal wizard! I want this vile enchantment removed from my castle *immediately!*"

As the king's ministers scrambled to do his bidding. General Renwolf nodded and drew his fist across his chest in a gesture of respect before leading his warriors back out of the throne room.

Once out in the hallway, Connor stood alongside Klute and Nyia as Renwolf directed the wounded to the infirmary and sent others to escort Kaegron to the dungeon. Then the general's glare found Connor, and he felt a lump grow in his throat as the general began to march directly toward him.

When the battle-scarred and blood-covered warrior finally stood before him, the general held Connor's anxious gaze for several long seconds before he finally spoke. "You fought well today. You helped to save my life and the lives of my warriors. You have earned my trust."

"Thank you," Connor bowed his head respectfully, and felt relief wash over him knowing they now had the general's support. That was until Renwolf spoke again.

"Unfortunately, that does little to help your cause until I have proof." Renwolf glanced at Nyia, who straightened beneath her general's scrutiny. "It has been brought to my attention that the trolls attempted to take you captive."

"Aye. If what I think is true, the trolls are bein' helped by Lorien, and my guess is that she wanted me and my women to be taken alive."

"I agree. But I can't prove Lorien's involvement unless we can make Kaegron confess. So, for now, rest and recover. I have a troll to torture." The general turned toward Klute. "This mortal is your responsibility, warrior. Do not let him out of your sight."

With those parting words, Renwolf turned and followed his warriors to the dungeons. The general, Connor thought with quiet reverence, was now a valuable ally to their cause. He only hoped that they could indeed force the truth out of Kaegron. From the discord he had just heard among the council members, Connor doubted that even Renwolf's support would be enough to sway the council into action without a confession.

With a respectful nod, Nyia joined the injured limping off to seek medical attention.

"I'm gonna check on Isaboe and Rosalyn," Connor said, but the li-on-man reached out to stop him.

"Not now. We have a gnome to see, and you heard the general. I am not to let you out of my sight. You are coming with me."

"But, Isaboe—"

"Your women are not my concern right now," Klute growled. "They are perfectly fine. Now, come along!"

CHAPTER 19

A GNOME'S CONFESSION

On the back of Rohan, it took only a few minutes for Klute and Connor to arrive at Titto's meadow. Jumping off the battle eagle the moment he touched down, Klute stomped toward the door nestled at the base of the tree's trunk and threw it open. Connor fell in behind him as Klute ducked down to look inside but found it empty. As he quickly scanned the meadow, the Jarcadian warrior shouted, "Titto, you traitorous bastard, show yourself!"

Stepping around the old tree trunk that was Titto's home, Connor expected to see the wallabock where he had left it tied to a sapling by the water's edge the day before. But it too was gone. Crouching down to examine the ground, Connor found a trampled path leading through the grass and into the forest. "Hey, Klute!" he shouted, drawing the Jarcadian warrior's attention. When Klute saw what Connor had found, they followed the trodden path, and it didn't take long to find what they were looking for. As soon as they entered the tree line, the gnome gave his presence away.

"Hold still, ya damn beast!" Connor heard Titto's grumbling voice, followed by a horse's snort. In the next step, Klute and Connor saw the gnome with a stuffed bag slung across his back making a pathetic attempt to climb a tree. The wallabock tugged angrily at its lead, which Titto had tied to the tree's trunk. The little man had already reached the lowest branch and was now trying to inch his way to the next one higher, bringing him up closer to the saddle. But the would-be horse thief was too short, and Titto was so focused on his task that he didn't realize he was being watched. That was until Klute made his presence known. "Hey Titto. Where do you think you are going?"

The startled gnome lost his grip and dropped to the ground with a thud. Fortunately, he hadn't gotten very high, and the drop was short. Scampering up, he stared with wide frightened eyes at his two tall visitors. "Oh—JoJo, I—I didn't expect…" the gnome stuttered nervously.

"Yes, you did not expect me to find out that you are a lying little traitor!" growled the furious lion-man as he stomped forward and jerked the gnome off his feet with one hand.

Titto's little feet kicked uselessly as he tried to defend himself. "I—I'm not a traitor, JoJo! I swear!"

"Where's the gem, Titto?" Klute pulled at the gnome's shirt, searching for the green stone.

"I—I don't have it anymore! I lost it!"

With both hands, Klute grabbed the cuffs of the gnome's jacket and shook him violently. "You're a liar and a traitor! I should break you in half right now!" he spat in the gnome's terrified face.

"No, wait! It be that wicked fey—she made me do it!"

"What wicked fey?" Klute snarled as he put the gnome down and held him in place by glare alone. "Start talking. And you had better give me a damn good reason why I shouldn't stomp you into the ground."

"She—she just showed up one day, right after you left," Titto started his tale. "You remember, JoJo? It be the same day you brought me the battle shirt to repair."

"Who was she?"

"Well, she came first as a black bird soaring overhead, but when it landed, it changed. It changed into a woman!"

"A woman? What woman?"

"Oh, she be a striking beauty, for sure, but with a heart full of blackness. She must have seen you leave here that day, JoJo, and she said that if I didn't do exactly as instructed, she'd be turning me into stone!"

"But instead of telling me about this, I find you trying to sneak off. I am not buying your story, Titto. Trolls attacked the castle today, and many good warriors were seriously injured, or killed! And that same gem, the one I saw on you just yesterday, was discovered in Kaegron's possession. So, start talking, Titto! What are you not telling me?" Klute roared as he reached out again to grab the gnome, but Connor spoke up.

"Wait, Klute." Turning his gaze on the frightened gnome, Connor said, "Tell us more about this fey woman. Did she give you a name?"

"She said her name be *Lilabeth,*" Titto uttered the vile name cautiously, as if he feared to say it aloud.

Connor knew that same fear intimately. Letting out an exhausted breath, he turned toward Klute. "He's tellin' the truth; Lilabeth is a shape-shifter, a dark muse, and she can make a good man do bad things. Take my word on it, and show him some mercy, man."

Klute shot a questioning glare at Connor. "You know this Lilabeth of whom he speaks?"

"Unfortunately, I am familiar with her. Lilabeth is Lorien's hench-woman, the bitch who came into the mortal world and stole the baby." Connor paused, then looked down at the gnome. "Alright, Titto. Tell us everything. Lilabeth gave ye that green gem, aye? What did she want?"

"Well, like I said," Titto started again, his terror easing some with Klute's temper temporarily allayed. "I had found the gem on the creek bank, and right after I put it around my neck, she came flying in as a bird. It be her who informed me of the upcoming Council of Elders, and… and she wanted me to be her spy! Said that if I didn't do what she be asking," the gnome paused, and the fear that crossed his face was certainly honest, "that she be going to the king. She said she'd blame you, JoJo, and tell him that you be providing the council's private information to Queen Lorien… through me."

"That's a lie!" Klute bellowed.

"I know! I know, JoJo. But then that horrible creature changed into another form! Right before my eyes I watched her change into General Renwolf! Then she said, in his own voice, 'And the king won't question an accusation made by his commanding officer.' That's when I felt the power of the green stone, as if it be alive! The moment I felt its magic, something changed, and… and I wanted to do as she asked, but at the same time, I—I knew it be wrong! I didn't want to be bringing you any trouble, JoJo!"

Connor watched the realization wash over Klute's face that his kind-hearted gestures toward the gnome had made them both pawns to the deceptive black-hearted muse.

"How did Kaegron end up with the gem?"

"Uh, well, I—I wasn't sure what to do, but thought if I be telling the shapeshifter about the mortal, well, then maybe that would satisfy her, and—and then she'd leave me be. So, I did. Holding the gem in my hand, I called out her name, and in only a few moments, there she be. Oh, and, JoJo, the moment she heard the mortal's name, her face twisted up into an evil grin, impure and wicked like, it was! She said, in a very nasty sort of way, 'So, Connor has come to rescue the boy. Marvelous! I can't wait until Lorien hears this.' And that's when she took the gem from me!"

Klute turned a confused look to his companion, but Connor brushed off the unasked question and instead suggested, "Well, General Renwolf said he needs proof that Lorien is behind the troll attack. I think we got it."

Looking back at the gnome, Klute snarled, "So, instead of telling me about this, you decide to take the coward's way out and run."

"I be too frightened to tell you, JoJo!" Shame coated the gnome's face before he continued. "When she took the gem, that be when I realized what I had done." Looking horribly apologetic, the gnome muttered, "I couldn't face you, JoJo. I be really sorry."

After a moment, Klute turned toward Connor, a new resolve on his stern lion-man's face. "Grab the wallabock and head back to the castle." In one fell-swoop, Klute reached down and grabbed the startled gnome, pulling him off his feet and then tucking him under his arm.

"Hey, what are you doing?" Titto protested.

"You're going to tell King Enoch what you just told us."

"And I need to check on Isaboe," Connor said, finally sensing a moment of opportunity. Taking the strap from the tree that held Sonas, Connor led him out of the tree line before mounting up. He watched as Klute plopped the gnome on top of Rohan' saddle and then took a seat behind his new passenger.

Kicking his horse into a quick run, Sonas had his wings out and flapping hard in seconds. With a rush of wind across his face, Connor soon had the wallabock in the air, eager to return to Isaboe.

The sun was on its descent toward the western horizon as Connor swooped toward the castle, realizing with some chagrin that he had left Isaboe and Rosalyn alone and afraid for too long. Though the rush of the battle and the encounter with the gnome had held Connor's undivided attention, it had also been more than a few hours since his interrupted lunch, and he was beginning to feel the effects of the long day on his body. He hoped Isaboe had something edible in their room.

After bringing his wallabock down on the palace's manicured grounds, he secured it well away from where the battle eagles were held and joined Klute, who was rapidly ascending the castle steps with Titto tucked under his arm, looking small and frightened. The palace halls were still nearly empty as they stormed toward the throne room, seeing only harried-looking servants racing to-and-fro. Suddenly, they heard the rhythmic clattering of armor and marching boots that preluded the appearance of a squad of Jarcadian warriors, also marching toward the throne room. In the lead was General Renwolf, whose canny gaze immediately found the gnome tucked under Klute's arm. He drew his troop to a halt before them. It was then that Connor saw Nyia and Amaroth among the warriors following Renwolf, and he felt a strong sense of relief to see them both walking on their own.

"Care to explain yourself, soldier?" the general asked Klute.

"The king needs proof that Queen Lorien is behind the attack. This is it."

For a moment, Connor was afraid that the general would begin asking uncomfortable questions, but the questions never came. Instead, he only added, "With the confession I've managed to force out of Kaegron, and whatever this gnome has to say, we may have a chance at convincing the council to take action. I would need a royal proclamation to lead this campaign, and that requires a majority agreement among the council members." Renwolf turned his glare on Connor, surveying him with a stern expression. "And that will not come swiftly or easily."

"I understand, sir," Connor replied politely. "I gotta go check on my women, but we'll join ye shortly. They'll want to hear what the council has to say."

Renwolf nodded, and Klute fell in with the other warriors as they continued their march toward the throne room.

The light in the corridor that contained their rooms was low as Connor hurried to be at Isaboe's side, certain that the women would be thrilled when they learned of the conspiracy he had uncovered. Surely, with so many important voices speaking up and so much evidence placed before them, the council would be forced into action. He threw open the door to their assigned living area. "Isaboe! I have information about...," but Connor went silent when he saw the room was empty.

"Isaboe, are ye here?" he called as he peered into their private bedroom. It too was empty, the bed made and their bags exactly where they'd left them that morning. Connor's heart began to pound, and he struggled to swallow his instinctual panic. Clinging to his last shred of hope, Connor knocked on and then opened the final door, which led to Rosalyn's room. The empty darkness inside scared him more than any troll could have.

Dashing back out of their room, Connor glanced down the hall in both directions but didn't see what he was looking for. Where could they have gone? He had no idea where to begin his search. Running blind, he could feel the thread of fear growing in his gut. Lorien and Lilabeth knew that Connor, at least, was in the realm. Instigated by the murderous Fey Queen, the troll attack had drawn all the Jarcadian warriors away from the castle. What if it had all been a ruse so that Isaboe and Rosalyn would be left alone and vulnerable to the wicked queen? The thought that he had fallen for her tricks one more time, and had again left Isaboe utterly unprotected ate at Connor's gut. But whatever had happened, someone in the castle must have seen them. Stopping to ask the few people he encountered if they had seen the women, Connor received only negative responses, and his anxiety grew with each step.

Running toward the dining hall, he glanced in but saw only a few workers cleaning tables and mopping floors. Turning back the way he came, Connor thought to look outside in the courtyard before retracing his steps toward the front entrance of the castle. Rounding a corner, he found the castle doors wide open and then began jogging toward the spacious foyer. But after catching a glimpse of Lord Mordackian strolling down a breezeway toward the west wing of the castle, he changed his course and sprinted to catch up with the giant tree-man, who came to halt and turned to address him.

"Oh, good! You've returned!" Lord Mordackian greeted him pleasantly. "I hear the Jarcadian warriors were successful in their… "

"Yeah, yeah," Connor interrupted, "It was a victory for the good guys," He knew he sounded rude, but he had a more pressing issue. "Have ye seen Rosalyn or Isaboe? I cannae find 'em anywhere!"

"Oh, Rosalyn and Queen Brighid went to Luminara. I believe they seek to recruit the Cloud People for your cause."

"Luminara?" Connor felt a bit of hope, but it warred with his concern over Isaboe. "Who are these Cloud People anyway?"

"Well," Lord Mordackian began slowly, "Luminara is a floating Island where the most enlightened and magical beings in all the realm reside."

"And where is this floating Island?"

The tree-man pointed his long and willowy finger upward. "Their island drifts above the land on a group of clouds, hence the name, Cloud-People."

Glancing up, Connor was truly confused, but Lord Mordackian still hadn't answered the question that concerned him the most. "Did Isaboe go with them?"

"No, she did not. And she was quite upset when Rosalyn left with Queen Brighid. I was concerned for her and offered to escort her to her room, but she refused, quite rudely, I must say."

"But she's not in our room! I canna find her anywhere!" Connor cried as panic slammed into his gut. "I dinna even ken where to start lookin'!"

"Oh, dear," muttered the tree-man. "Would it help to speak with Rosalyn?"

"Aye, it would, if she were here!" Connor snapped. "Did she say when she'd be back?"

When Lord Mordackian chuckled, Connor was even more confused. "She need not be here physically for you to communicate with her."

"What?"

"Come along, mortal," the tree-man turned and gestured for Connor to follow. "Let us go see someone who can help."

Befuddled, but otherwise without a lead, Connor fell in behind the tree-man. Fortunately, they didn't have to go far before they found Mordackian's someone.

CHAPTER 20

A NEW COMPLICATION

"Have you discovered a way into Euphoria?" Rosalyn asked as she followed Demetrick back into the golden foyer.

"Not yet. But there's a message for you. Please, follow me," Demetrick gestured, but Rosalyn didn't move.

"A message? From who?"

"That's what we're about to find out. Please." Once again, Demetrick gestured for Rosalyn to follow, and this time she conceded.

Glancing over her shoulder, she saw Ruz-Zambia and Nicholi trailing behind them.

After passing both the indoor botanical paradise and the library, the wizard opted instead to turn down a dark hallway. He directed Rosalyn into a more private room where two figures stood in the dimness, their faces obscured. Entering the dark alcove, it took another minute for her eyes to adjust, but when they did, Rosalyn recognized the taller one as Queen Brighid. The petite figure next to her was wrapped in white linen like a monk with the hood pulled up and covering her face.

Demetrick introduced the stranger. "This is Nrog. She is an Octipuru."

"What exactly is an Octipuru?" Rosalyn asked directly, feeling weary now of introductions and niceties.

"Nrog can relay messages across great distances with her twin, Kaya, another Octipuru. Through Nrog, we will see and hear as Kaya does. Kaya is currently in Sashtonia, and she has a message for you."

Rosalyn only nodded, feeling a bit overwhelmed by all this new magic.

"Now, let us hear her message," Demetrick concluded as he turned toward the robed figure and invited her to proceed. Nicholi, Brighid, and

Ruz-Zambia also gave the Octipuru their undivided attention before she tossed back the hood, exposing a completely bald head.

Her skin was the color of chalk, as if she had never seen the sun, and her eyes were void of color except for a small dark pupil in their center. Without uttering a word, the Octipuru closed her strange eyes, and for the first few seconds nothing happened. Then, the frail woman began to twitch, at first slowly and then with greater intensity. Soon, the twitching became full convulsions, though somehow she remained upright, as if her feet were anchored to the floor. Then the Octipuru's body began thrashing around so rapidly that it started to lose clarity. Stepping back, Rosalyn watched intently as the image of Nrog swirled, blurred, and distorted until it became completely unrecognizable. It was a subtle shift, but undeniable. After a few more convulsing movements, Rosalyn blinked in disbelief at the new figure that stood where only moments before Nrog had been.

"Connor?" she asked incredulously. "Is that you?"

"Rosalyn?" She heard the same surprise in his voice as Connor's image fully came into view. "The tree-man says ye're in a place called Luminara, to recruit some Cloud People?"

"Yes, I'm here with Queen Brighid. Were you able to protect the castle?"

"Aye, and we captured the leader of the trolls. But Isaboe is missing!"

"What? Are you certain? Before leaving, I gave her firm instructions to return to our room and stay there."

"Well, she's not there, and our bags are still sittin' in the same spot, as if no one's been there all day. And her cloak is missing."

"Where could she be?"

"Well, I canna confirm it, but I'm pretty sure I ken where she's gone." Connor paused to gather himself, and Rosalyn didn't miss the fear hiding under his angry scowl. "I think she's gone to Euphoria."

Rosalyn let a small gasp slip past her lips. "What makes you think that?"

"Before the troll attack, when we were on our way to the dinin' hall, Isaboe fell behind. When I found her, she told me about a strange encounter she'd had with a fey woman. She said that this fey wanted Isaboe to go to Euphoria with her. She'd told Isaboe that…" Trailing off, Connor was lost for a moment in his anxiety.

"She told Isaboe what?" Rosalyn prompted.

"The fey told her that only she could bring Lorien down!"

Rosalyn gasped. "Oh, my Lord! Did you see this woman?"

"No. But either Isaboe left with that fey of her own free will," Connor swallowed hard, "or she's been abducted by Lorien. Either way, I am more worried than I've ever been in my life, and this has just become a more fucked-up mess!"

Rosalyn watched the image of Connor's face twisting with frustration as his hands balled into fists. *"Damn it, boireannach!"* he spat. When he looked back at Rosalyn, his fear was now hidden behind a mask of rage. "How soon can ye get back here?"

"We can be back in Sashtonia within the hour, before sunset." As Brighid spoke, Rosalyn turned to look at the group that stood behind her.

"And we'll bring reinforcements with us," Demetrick added.

"Who said that?" Connor asked.

"You'll have to see for yourself," Rosalyn said, somehow finding some bitter humor in the moment. She stepped aside, bringing Demetrick forward to occupy Connor's view.

"Hello, Braden. Rosalyn tells me you've taken well to the task that I'd assigned you, just as I'd had hoped you would. I'm pleased to hear that I chose wisely."

Connor blinked a few times before his eyes shot open wide and his jaw went slack. *"Demetrick?"*

"I understand that you now go by the name Connor. Did I provide you with that name, or did you come up with it on your own?'

"I thought ye were dead, ol' man! How—how is this possible?"

"We'll explain later," Rosalyn interrupted, stepping back in front of Demetrick and into Connor's line of vision. "Right now, we must return to Sashtonia and put together a plan of attack. Obviously, this news about Isaboe has just made this rescue mission much more complicated."

"The reinforcements Demetrick mentioned, what do they consist of?" Connor asked. "Cause we're gonna need all the help we can get."

"Don't worry," Demetrick soothed. "We'll come prepared. This is a battle we have been anticipating for some time now." He turned and looked at Rosalyn, placing a hand on her shoulder, and in that moment, she saw pride in the wizard's eyes. "We just needed a commander to lead us."

Shaking her head, Rosalyn scoffed. "I'm no commander. I'm just trying to save my family." Glancing back at the image of Connor, she saw that it was starting to waver as the connection slipped. "Connor, do you think you can convince the Jarcadian warriors to join us? I don't know what to expect, but I'd rather be over-prepared."

"I'm on my way to the throne room now to find out. Just get back here as soon as ye can. Regardless of what the council decides, I'm gonna find my way into Euphoria, even if I have to do it alone."

Rosalyn had no doubt that Connor would make good on his promise. "You won't have to go alone. We're on our way," she promised. Connor said something more, but it was lost as his image rippled and twisted, disappearing in a swirling effigy. Once again, Nrog the Octipuru stood where Connor had been only seconds before. After taking a long cleansing breath, she opened her eyes and pulled her hood up over her head. Clasping her hands in front of her robe, she turned and silently took her leave.

Spinning around, Rosalyn looked into the faces of her allies. "What now? Do you really have reinforcements, Demetrick? Have you figured out how to get past the spells Lorien has placed on her borders?"

Brighid glanced at Demetrick and Nicholi, but they all offered nothing but apprehensive silence.

Rosalyn threw a frustrated glare at the group. "It doesn't matter how heavily we are backed if we can't get through!"

"We haven't been able to find a way in as of yet," the queen eventually responded. "So far, every emissary, every troop of warriors we've sent in has not returned. Whatever spell she has cast, it is deadly to everyone who tries to enter her land uninvited."

Rosalyn couldn't believe that they had come this far, only to run into yet another dead end. And it wasn't just about Gabriel anymore; now Isaboe's life was also in danger. "Since no one knows how to counter the spell, it sounds like our only option is to hope we won't be noticed when we pop up through the tunnel on the inside. Do I have that right? Demetrick, you're a great wizard. Are you sure you don't have some magic that can get us through?"

Demetrick started to reply but Nicholi interjected. "To keep up a spell this strong, one that surrounds her entire lands, Lorien must be exhausting her magic. I'm sure that if we could draw her attention in another direction, it might weaken the spell enough that we could break through."

"Then the distraction better be a big one, and you'd better have the best minds at the ready in order to break through that spell," Rosalyn demanded.

"We could use the Jarcadian warriors to distract attention from the tunnel," Demetrick suggested. "If we can locate a weak spot in her spell and have a large enough coalition to attack Euphoria while they are distracting the queen, that might give us the opportunity to slip through undetected while her forces are focused on defending her borders."

"Connor is determined to enter Euphoria, with or without us," Rosalyn spat. "And I'm still hearing a lot of ifs. This is not a solid plan!"

Again, all Rosalyn received was silence and disconcerting glances, until Lord Ruz-Zambia stepped forward. "You could let me help."

When she gave the dragon-lord her attention, Rosalyn found herself momentarily lost in the deep swirling colors of his eyes. His words from earlier, his professed fondness, had baffled her. He now wore the same expression he'd had when saying those words. Rosalyn didn't know how to feel about any of it, and she quickly brushed the distraction aside. "And what do you suggest, my Lord?"

Ruz-Zambia held her gaze. "I will lead the coalition into Euphoria."

Feeling her heart begin to quicken, Rosalyn didn't know how to respond, so the Fey Queen did it for her. "And how do you propose to do that, my Lord? We certainly appreciate your offer, but Lorien will know an army is coming long before we reach her borders. No one is getting in through the front door."

"I am not suggesting we go through the front door," he replied. "I am suggesting we burn the door down. One simply must utilize the correct forces."

"The correct forces?" Rosalyn repeated, although she was confident she already knew what he was implying.

Turning away from their watching faces, Ruz-Zambia stepped toward Rosalyn and took her hand. Though she felt a slight shock at his touch, she pointedly ignored the feeling. "Meet me back here before the sun dips beneath the treetops. We will make our way to Euphoria to rescue your family, and hopefully change history in the process." He turned to the others. "I will return shortly. Prepare yourselves for battle."

Forty minutes later, Rosalyn found herself standing once again on the landing platform. As promised, Lord Ruz-Zambia was not gone for long, but in that time his countenance had changed drastically. As he strode toward her now, he seemed much more intense, much more focused than during their initial meeting. When sudden movements in the sky drew her attention, she saw two small objects on the horizon, sparkling like colored jewels as they caught the sun's setting rays. With Ruz-Zambia standing directly before her, Rosalyn didn't know what to say, but knew that her opportunity to address him was quickly slipping away. "So, Norvik, what is your plan?"

Rosalyn saw an unreadable expression cross his face when she used his name for the first time, rather than his title. "As I said," he continued, "I will be leading the direct assault on Euphoria's gate." As Rosalyn watched him focus his magnificent eyes on the horizon, she followed his lead and found that the glittering objects were close enough to make out wide wings and long necks.

"With your dragon-brothers?" she guessed.

"Yes." Easily marshalling behind their appointed leader, the others came to stand behind Rosalyn, listening to Ruz-Zambia's instructions. "We will set the whole west side ablaze. That will not only burn down Lorien's spell, it should also keep her beasts occupied so your rescue team can get in and back out of the castle during the chaos."

"You will be taking back your dragon form?" Something in Rosalyn twisted unhappily at this reality.

"Yes. That is the only way," he confirmed before addressing the others. "There is no spell that can hold up to the fire of a Sordorian Dragon. With the three of us destroying her borders and attacking her beasts, your odds of success should be quite high."

Rosalyn knew that it was a good plan, but at what cost? If Norvik would be giving up his life as a fey to return to the sky, to his true form, would she never again see him as Lord Ruz-Zambia? Though her first and most important obligation was to Isaboe and Gabriel, she felt torn about her feelings. If this incredible fey could help them, why should she care that he would become a great lizard once more? Rosalyn didn't know what this revelation meant, but the truth was she did care.

"Before we take our leave," Lord Ruz-Zambia's voice softened. "Once your daughter and the child have been rescued, will you return to your own world?" he asked, and Rosalyn could see that her answer meant a great deal to him.

"I suppose so. I mean, you will be a dragon again, and we will have what we came for. So, yes, I intend to return home." Rosalyn saw something that looked like disappointment flash across his face. "Why do you ask?"

Raising his staff, he placed the end on the floor so that the red jewel was at eye level. Rosalyn thought he stared at the sparkling stone almost longingly before he finally looked back at her. "When I take my dragon form, I'll be taking my dragon heart from this vessel," he paused and placed a hand on his chest, over his fey heart, "and I'll be replacing it with this one. I am hoping that you would…hold it for me."

Feeling a slight flutter in her chest, Rosalyn suspected that the implication of his request was great. He was asking something very intimate of her. "Will you be coming back for it?"

One corner of his mouth pulled up and his eyes softened. "Yes."

"You can do that?" she asked incredulously.

"Yes," he repeated as a slight smile spread to both corners of his mouth.

Though his smile was subtle, Rosalyn found it beautiful, and she felt a tingle all the way to her toes. "Then I would be honored to hold your heart for you, Norvik."

He nodded wordlessly, but the fondness in his amazing eyes spoke volumes. Rosalyn watched as he slipped his cloak from his naked shoulders, and she felt another rush at the sight of Norvik's beautiful musculature. "I won't be needing this." He held out his cloak. "Would you mind?"

Taking the cloak, she felt a subtle magical energy shoot through her fingertips and up her arm. She wondered if the fabric was enchanted or if it was the dragon-lord himself that sent shivers along her skin. "Of course. And Norvik," she placed her free hand in his, "thank you for doing this. Please, be careful."

He held her gaze for a long moment, but now they could hear the wingbeats of his brothers, and their moment together was cut short by necessity. With one last enchanting smile, he gently squeezed her hand. "Take care of my heart."

After releasing his grip, Lord Ruz-Zambia walked toward the center of the landing platform. Turning to face the war party, he brandished his staff overhead and waived it in a circular motion toward the dragons before leaning it against the railing. Rosalyn then watched transfixed as Norvik removed his boots, then his pants. Though he seemed to have no reservations about standing on the platform completely bare, Rosalyn felt a flush rise to her cheeks before she finally managed to avert her gaze.

But when he brought the butt end of his staff down hard, startling them all with an intense impact, Rosalyn could see that the red jewel on top of Norvik's staff was now glowing, and a small cloud of dust had begun to lift around him. Again, he slammed his staff on the ground, and this time Rosalyn felt the vibration of its impact spread through the entire platform. As the dust cloud rose and thickened, the light from the red jewel began to shimmer, and sparks of energy could be seen in the billowing fog of magic that now engulfed him up to his shoulders. Small bolts of lightning emitting from the red jewel shot out into the mist that was growing around Lord Ruz-Zambia.

After raising his staff for a third time, the dragon-lord slammed the butt-end down onto the platform, creating a sudden explosion of sound and a blinding burst of light, accompanied by a shock wave that rippled through the stone beneath their feet. As Rosalyn felt its intense power rushing through her body, Ruz-Zambia became completely engulfed in the magical cloud of smoke and heat that swirled out from where he had been standing.

Startled by the blast and having lost sight of Norvik in the smoke, Rosalyn soon saw a majestic brown head rising above the fog. As the cloud began to dissipate, the rest of the dragon's incredible body came into full view, and he was breathtaking.

Stretching his huge wings to their full expanse, their tips touched the golden sentries on either side of the platform. The dragon-lord's equally massive reptilian body was covered in blue-green scales all the way to the tip of his tail. His legs were as thick as tree trunks and were the same rich iridescent brown color as his head. From the back of each of his eyes to the tips of his short-pointed ears ran a line of glistening turquoise scales. His long snout was full of deadly-looking teeth that flashed in the sunlight. When he threw back his head and roared, the sound shook the platform, and Rosalyn felt its vibration all the way up her spine.

Crouching down, Lord Ruz-Zambia beat his enormous wings and launched into the sky, sending a dusty swirl of hot air blasting across the onlookers. Rosalyn was forced to squint from the flying dust as she watched him lift off the ground and soar up to join his brothers.

When the three dragons met in the sky, they seemed to almost dance with joy. Soaring about gracefully, they flew in a circle so close that their wings touched. Rosalyn wondered if this was their language or merely the way Lord Ruz-Zambia chose to greet his kind. But whatever it was, it was an obvious moment of bonding between brothers.

After separating from his siblings, Norvik continued to circle above the war party, and Rosalyn could sense that he was looking down at her. Dropping her gaze to where he had been standing before his transformation, she saw his staff lying on the ground. When she picked it up, she noticed that the red jewel on top was now smaller, though it still sparkled in the sunlight. Glancing back up, she saw the dragon soaring overhead, watching her. Apparently satisfied, Norvik then circled one more time before rejoining his brothers.

Standing on the platform, Rosalyn watched the three dragons soar across the sky until she could no longer see the blue-green sparkles gleaming off Norvik's scales. She then turned and joined the others, ready to fly back to Sashtonia and prepare for a surprise attack on Euphoria.

CHAPTER 21

A SCOTSMAN'S FURY

Fueled by rage and panic, Connor rushed through the castle corridors on his way back to the throne room. The large doors to the king's room were open, but upon entering, he stepped into the middle of a heated argument.

"This is still not enough to justify risking our warriors' lives to rescue one insignificant mortal boy!" argued King Bogknocken from the balcony. Surrounded by the few other council members who hadn't fled the castle when the trolls attacked, the pixie drew himself up to his full height. "I admit that Lorien aligning with the trolls is alarming, but she has been creating havoc like this for centuries. It's no reason to go to war!"

"Her ongoing crimes are undeniable!" bleated Pagganot. "Do we not have the courage to hold Lorien accountable?"

"I must agree with King Bogknocken," said King Enoch. "A border dispute with the trolls is no reason to start a war with Lorien."

"We'd be as stupid as the trolls to openly attack her lands!" cried Lady Jobetha. "Has this council forgotten that her borders are cursed? No, I will not agree to this campaign, regardless of what General Renwolf and this stupid gnome have said. The sacrifice of our warriors is not worth the life of one mortal child!"

"Lady Jobetha," Princess Reina argued, "For just a moment, let us disregard the mortals' role in this. What I hear you really saying is that it doesn't matter to you that Lorien has been mutilating and killing her own people for centuries. You do not care that she has been using the trolls as puppets to create chaos in our realm and to expand her reach into lands that are not her own. Is that correct? What is this power,

Lady Jobetha, that Lorien has over you? Why do you refuse to stand up against her?"

Connor watched as Lady Jobetha coiled back, offended and ready to strike out at the princess, but Lady Idora drew everyone's attention, shimmering as she moved toward the railing. "From what I have observed," the Lady of the Lake spoke softly but with conviction, "all this council ever does is clean up after Lorien's messes. It is time to be proactive and bring the fight to her."

"If we had the capability to do so, dear ladies," King Enoch interjected, glaring at both Lady Idora and Princess Reina, "we would have already done so."

"But if we could accept help from the Cloud People, maybe we could work together and find a way!"

"Oh please, Reina! Give it a rest! The Cloud People are not coming to assist the mortals!" Lady Jobetha hissed.

A pause in the debate gave Connor the courage and the opportunity to move forward. He pushed his way through the crowd of Jarcadian warriors to stand before the king and the council members seated in the balcony. "What the hell is wrong with you people?" he shouted. Movement out of the corner of his eye revealed Klute stepping up beside him. Though Connor expected a reprimand for his outburst, it never came.

Empowered by Klute's silent support, Connor continued his tirade. "This council ain't no different than the goddamn arrogant British assholes I havta put up with back in my own world! While ye've been standing 'round flappin' yer geggies and arguing with one another, my wife has gone to Euphoria to save the boy!"

"What?" Klute asked, aghast. "Your mate went to Euphoria?"

"Aye, she did!" Connor turned his anger on King Enoch. "Because this goddamn council cannae agree to do what's right and she ken there'd be no help comin' from ye cowards, Isaboe must've decided she had to do it herself! And though she'll probably die in the attempt," Connor paused as he glowered at the council members, "my wife has more bloody courage than all o' ye bastards put together!"

"Mind your tongue, mortal," snarled King Enoch. "It would behoove you to remember in whose castle you stand!"

Connor had to regather himself before he could continue but refused to be cowed. Puffing out his chest, he glared back at the king.

The tense moment was broken by Klute's deep voice as it echoed around the chamber. "You speak of wanting to protect the lives of your warriors and yet you continue to let us die in the trolls' attacks." Klute paused and turned toward Renwolf. "I say we follow the brave mortal woman's lead and take the battle to Lorien so we can end this altogether!"

Before General Renwolf could speak, the king asked. "How do you know that your wife has gone to Euphoria on her own? Did she tell you this directly?"

"No, but she's not here, so either she got sick o' waiting for ye, or she dinnae go o' her own free will. While we were out fighting trolls to save *yer castle*, Isaboe was unprotected, and there's only one place she could be." When Connor glanced at the stoic warrior standing at his side, Klute silently encouraged him to continue. "If the council is waiting on help from Luminara," he addressed the elders in the balcony, "ye won't have to wait long. Rosalyn is on her way back here now with reinforcements from the Cloud People."

"What?" Lady Jobetha exclaimed. "How is it that a mortal woman was able to recruit assistance from Luminara?"

"And what sort of assistance do they offer?" asked Lord Pagganot.

"I dinnae ken! All I ken is that they're willing to act even if this council won't." Connor glanced around at the battle-hardened warriors who stood not far behind him and saw that many were nodding along with his words. Emboldened, he again addressed the elders. "With the help of these Cloud People, I'm gonna rescue my wife and the boy, with or without yer approval!"

"You will not go alone," Klute promised. Connor was surprised by Klute's offer of support, but he doubted that just one Jarcadian warrior's opinion could sway the council.

"No," agreed Nyia, limping forward to stand beside her partner, "you won't."

And Nyia wasn't alone. Soon Amaroth came to stand by their side, and then another soldier, and another. One-by-one, a handful of other warriors, many of whom Connor had assisted on the battlefield, also stepped forward to join his quest. Connor suddenly felt a small seed of hope take hold.

But when General Renwolf joined the volunteers, Connor felt that seed of hope germinate as the leader of the Jarcadian warriors addressed the king. "All we need is a royal proclamation, Sire. With help from Luminara, a single well-placed strike could bring Lorien down once and for all."

After a tense moment of silence, King Enoch sighed in defeat. "Such proceedings require a majority vote." Turning toward his fellow politicians in the balcony, he met each of their gazes before he spoke again. "What say you, King Bogknocken?"

"Nay."

"Lady Jobetha?"

"Nay."

Connor cursed under his breath. Couldn't these fools do the right thing for once in their lives? It was no wonder Lorien and Lilabeth had played them all for fools; they made themselves easy targets.

"Lord Pagganot?" Enoch prompted.

"Aye."

"Lady Idora?"

"Aye."

"Princess Reina?"

"Aye."

All at once, the tide of the tally had turned. Would this be it? Connor waited anxiously for Enoch himself to cast the final vote.

"I am afraid that there is not enough justification to make such a sacrifice, even with help from Luminara. My vote is nay."

"Well, that leaves us at a tie," Lord Pagganot announced the obvious. "And nowhere closer to resolving this matter!"

"Not entirely," boomed a voice from behind. Connor spun to find Lord Mordackian lumbering into the throne room. "I have not yet cast my vote." The silence was deafening as everyone stared at the towering tree-man. "And since the Cloud People are on their way here to lead this campaign, I vote in favor."

With the final vote cast, all eyes turned back to Enoch, who jutted out his chin and cleared his throat before he was finally forced to make the vote official. "Very well. This *one time* we agree to accept assistance from Luminara." He glared down at Connor and General Renwolf. "You have your royal proclamation, General. Be swift, be accurate, and bring back as many warriors as you can. But know that the loss of any warriors, saving these witless mortals, is on you!"

CHAPTER 22

BABA DENOVA

It was dark by the time they reached the border of Euphoria, and Isaboe had insisted that Petrina take her to see Gabriel first. Before sneaking into the Fey Queen's castle and offering up her own blood, she had to see with her own eyes that the child was still alive and well.

"I told Toblet to take us in through a different entrance," Petrina explained as she closed the slider between the coach and the driver. "It will be closer to where the child is being held, and you will see for yourself that he is well." When Petrina sat back down on the bench, Isaboe only nodded, not knowing what else she could do. "Normally, I check in with Lorien as soon as I return from the gathering of the Council of Elders," the fey continued. "I give her a summary of events and issues addressed at the gathering, that sort of thing."

"Are you going to do that?"

Petrina hesitated a moment before speaking. "I've been trying to decide the best way to do this. I never want to face Lorien again, but she has spies everywhere. She probably already knows that you and the other mortals were presented to the council today, and she'll be expecting me to relay that news. If I don't appear before her, Lorien will know that something is amiss."

"What are you going to tell her?'

"Well, I am certainly not going to tell her that I brought you back with me, if that is what you are worried about."

"How do I know I can trust you?" The doubt that Isaboe had been quietly nurturing sprang forth. What if Petrina's story of being a victim was all a sham, and she was actually loyal to Lorien? This fey might be leading her right into a trap. "What would happen if you didn't check in with her? Would she come looking for you?"

"She might, especially if she suspects that you are in the realm. If I don't show up, she may conclude that the two of us are together."

"Petrina, I can't take the chance of having a random encounter with the queen."

"I will check in with her, but I'll only tell her what I want her to know. Don't worry. I know how to deal with Lorien. I promise I won't give us away."

Isaboe shuddered when she felt the carriage making its descent, and a few moments later, she jolted in her seat when it touched down. The sounds of the grockmusk's hooves and the carriage wheels on the rough roadway were jarring after the silence of traveling through air.

"I can leave you with Baba Denova when- ,"

"Baba who?"

"Baba Denova is the old elf who's been caring for the child. I'll leave you with her while I report to Lorien. When I come back, we'll sneak into the castle and wind our way down to the lowest level of the main tower so we can open the vault."

"You make that sound so easy, but where will Lorien be while we are sneaking into her castle and opening her vault?" Isaboe raked her hands through her hair and felt her anxiety bubbling. "How do you know she won't be aware of us? I'm still not sure about this, Petrina. I don't know if I can do it."

"You told me that the ring you have will block your vibrations. Do you doubt that it works?"

"I don't know." Isaboe reached into her dress pocket and slipped the ring onto her index finger. "You're a fey. Do you sense my vibrations?"

When Petrina didn't immediately reply, Isaboe watched sadness melt across her face before she finally spoke. "Since Lorien took our wings, most of us have lost the abilities we once had. Our wings not only gave us flight; they were the very source of our magic. I haven't been able to sense your vibrations, Isaboe, so I can't tell you if the ring is working." Reaching into a pouch at her waist, she pulled out a small glass vial. "But I still have this," Petrina said with a mischievous grin. Inside the vial, Isaboe could see what looked like swirling blue sand.

"And what is that?"

"It's the last of the pixie dust I possess. Lorien doesn't know I have it."

"What can you do with that?"

"Whatever I want," Petrina boasted, and Isaboe didn't miss the mischievous spark in the fey's eyes.

But before Isaboe could ask any more about pixie dust, the carriage rolled to a stop. She heard the driver shout something, and then the carriage rocked as he climbed down from the bench. After following Petrina out of the coach, Isaboe stepped out into a night sky full of stars. The air was cool compared to the stuffy coach, and she pulled her cloak a little tighter about her shoulders as she waited for Petrina to finish her muttered conversation with the driver.

"Follow me," Petrina murmured before leading the way off into the darkness. "And keep quiet," the fey hissed over her shoulder as Isaboe scampered to keep up. .

Staying close to Petrina, Isaboe silently followed her into an overgrown, wooded area. More than once she felt the slap of a branch across her neck and arms as they pushed their way through the trees. Strange sounds in the night kept her on alert, and more than once Isaboe questioned her sanity. She would be much less anxious if Connor were leading the way and holding her hand as they traversed the dark forest. But she was on her own. Thinking of Connor made her realize how angry he would be when he discovered that she was gone, but it was too late now. Her only option was to be brave and finish what she had started.

Eventually the trees thinned, revealing a path that led them to a small cottage deep in the forest. There were lanterns hanging in the windows, and a thin trail of smoke rose from the stone chimney. It was a simple, deteriorating little cabin, but it spoke of home. Isaboe was careful to watch her footing as she followed Petrina up the rickety steps and onto the porch. When the fey rapped on the moss-covered door, it slowly creaked open, and Isaboe found herself looking down at the startled face of an old woman peering out of the door frame. "What do you what?"

she asked as she looked up at the strangers on her doorstep, her voice guarded with suspicion.

"Baba Denova, my name is Petrina." The fey then gestured toward her companion. "And this is Isaboe, a mortal. The child Lorien gave you to look after belongs to her."

There was no reply, only large eyes staring at them through a small gap in the doorway.

"May I see him, please?" Isaboe asked, stepping forward. "I've traveled a long way to find him. Please, may we come in?"

It was another moment before the door pulled open and the old woman stepped back, eyeing them both warily. "Come in," she muttered.

Stepping into the small home, Isaboe had to stoop to avoid knocking her head against the low ceiling. When she saw the host standing next to the fireplace, the size of the dwelling instantly made sense.

Baba Denova stood no more than three feet tall and was a little on the plump side. Her wavy gray hair was pulled back and partially covered with a red scarf. Wide dark eyes stood out in contrast to her pale skin, and on each side of her head were large pointed ears, the tale-tell sign, Isaboe had learned, of an elf. Covering her plain brown smock was a shawl of muted colors that was pulled snugly around her shoulders as she glanced at the two strangers now standing in her home.

Quickly scanning the cottage, Isaboe could see a wood stove with a cooktop, a bed, a rocking chair, and a wardrobe, as well as a few blankets and baskets tucked into the corners.

"What are you going to do with him?" Baba Denova asked, scrutinizing Isaboe.

"I'm here to take him home."

There was a beat of silence before Baba Denova spoke again. "Why didn't Queen Lorien come for him?"

"Because she doesn't know we're here," Petrina answered. "And we need to keep it that way."

The old elf regarded them with perplexity, taking her time to puzzle them out.

"Is Gabriel here?" Isaboe asked. "May I see him, please?"

After another moment of staring, the elf finally turned and shuffled to the back corner of her small home. She reached down into a basket and lifted out a bundle, cradling the child in her arms. However, rather than offering the boy over, she stood her ground and closely studied Isaboe's face. "Is this your boy?" Feeling as if her character was somehow being measured, Isaboe found some comfort in the idea that Gabriel had been in the custody of such a protective soul.

Hoping that the elf would sense her honesty, Isaboe stepped forward, her hands outstretched. "No. He is my daughter's son. I'm his… his grandmother."

Apparently, something in her countenance must have convinced the old woman, for Baba Denova gently placed the blanketed baby into Isaboe's arms. Gabriel was awake, and his brown eyes looked up at Isaboe with silent wonder, his chubby little face full and pink. Even though he had been away from his mother for weeks, it was obvious that her grandson had been well cared for.

A smile spread across her face as Isaboe touched the child's hand, and he immediately clutched her little finger in his tiny fist. "Hello, Gabriel," she cooed, smiling down at the baby in her arms as the joy of holding him fortified her spirit. For all her doubts—about coming to the realm of the fey, about leaving the castle, and trusting Petrina—Isaboe was at least certain that this little boy was worth the fight. "I'm your grandmother, beautiful boy, and I've come to take you home," she murmured.

"He's a good boy, he is." Baba Denova crossed her arms and slowly rocked from side to side, as if she were holding the child herself. "Doesn't fuss much."

"I'm going to leave Isaboe here while I go to check in with Lorien," Petrina announced.

"But you said you didn't want Lorien to know you were here," the old elf said.

"I don't want her to know Isaboe is here." Turning toward Isaboe, she continued, "After I make my report, I'll come back for you." Glancing down at Gabriel, a slight smile brushed the fey's face. "So, you're the little fellow who has caused all the fuss. You are rather cute." Petrina grinned at the child before lifting her eyes to meet Isaboe's. "I'll be back as soon as I can."

Isaboe watched Petrina disappear through the door before looking back at the old elf, who seemed just as uncomfortable as she herself felt. Glancing around, Isaboe noticed a rocking chair. "May I sit?" Baba Denova only nodded.

Taking the seat, Isaboe glanced around the small space and tried not to make eye contact with the elf, who looked as if she felt invaded upon in her own home. If she had become attached to Gabriel in the weeks he had been here, Isaboe knew that letting him go would be difficult. "Have you been in charge of his care this whole time?" she finally asked.

"Yes."

"He looks very healthy and well cared for. Thank you. What have you been feeding him?"

"Vervaina's milk. She has just given birth herself and has plenty."

"Who's Vervaina?"

"She's the faun faerie who lives in these woods. Whenever there is an extra young mouth to feed, a faun faerie will gladly share." Seeming to relax a bit, Baba Denova sat on her bed before continuing. "I'm sure it doesn't taste like his momma's milk, so it did take a few days for him to adjust. But he eventually got hungry enough, and now I think he rather likes it."

Again, an uncomfortable silence filled the small cottage, and Isaboe sensed the elf's uneasiness. She hoped Petrina wouldn't be gone long.

"Did you say his name is Gabriel?" the old elf asked.

"Yes."

"Oh. Well, since I didn't know his name, I've been calling him Finbar."

"Finbar. That's a nice name." Isaboe said politely, but then turned serious. "Did Queen Lorien tell you what she was going to do with him? Did she tell you why she took him from his mother?" Isaboe asked, wondering how much the old elf really knew.

"I haven't spoken with Queen Lorien, so I don't know. It wasn't she who brought the child. It was that wicked dark muse, the strumpet who does Lorien's bidding," Baba Denova spat, as if she had just bitten into something rotten.

"Do you mean *Lilabeth?*" Isaboe asked, venom lacing the name.

"You know her?"

"Tragically, yes. She almost killed me when she tried to pull me through a portal so she could take my unborn child." Isaboe shuddered as she recalled that horrible night. "That wicked muse tried to seduce my husband, attacked my best friend, and murdered my sister. All this in an attempt to take my daughter!" Anger and remorse gripped Isaboe's stomach as she recalled her sister's tragic end. Her friend Margaret had barely survived the wolf attack, and fortunately Connor had snapped out of his trance before coupling with the dark muse and losing his mind to faerie seduction. "Yes, I know her. Unfortunately."

Baba Denova's jaw worked for several long moments before she finally asked, "Why did she take this child?"

Isaboe looked up from her grandson and met the elf's questioning eyes. "Are you familiar with the prophecy that Lorien presented to the Council of Elders? The one that caused King Nicholi and Queen Alaina to be removed from the throne?"

The elf only nodded, silently encouraging Isaboe to continue.

"My mother is Rosalyn, the daughter of Nicholi and Alaina. Lorien abducted me over twenty years ago and brought me here for the sole purpose of creating a half-fey child, one who she intended to raise herself and therefore fulfil the prophecy. But I was able to return to my own world while she waited for my daughter to be born. My friends protected me from Lorien's scheme, but she has been pursuing us ever since." Isaboe softened as she looked down at her grandson. "That's why she took this sweet little boy. She's threatening to take his life if I don't give her my daughter, Kaitlyn."

Isaboe watched the old elf's shoulders slump as she cast her eyes to the floor. "I did fear Lorien's scheming," she said, heaving a heavy sigh as she slowly shook her head. When Baba Denova looked back up, there was a new unidentifiable emotion in her dark eyes. "So, Lorien is trying to fulfill the prophecy with your daughter."

"Apparently. Though I knew nothing about this prophecy until we arrived here and Petrina shared it with me. I only knew that Lorien wanted me out of my daughter's life so she could raise Kaitlyn as her own, in whatever horrible way she chooses. The more I learn, the more her evil plans become apparent."

Silently staring at Isaboe, the old elf finally stood. "Can I offer you a bit of hot broth?" Baba Denova asked as she shuffled over to the fireplace. "It'll warm you up on a cold night like this."

"No, thank you," Isaboe replied. "Why did Lorien put Gabriel into your care, here out in the woods? How do you know the queen?"

Filling her cup with steaming brown liquid, Baba Denova placed the ladle on the hearth before returning to her seat. "I've known Lorien and her brother Nicholi their whole lives. I was their nanny when they were children."

Feeling her heart racing, Isaboe cursed herself for letting her guard down. Did the old woman still hold any loyalty to the queen? Could she be trusted?

"Their parents died when they were both young," Baba Denova continued, "and they took the throne at an immature age. I could tell early on that Lorien had a taste for power, and it always bothered her that she was born second. Her brother would have first position in line to the throne, but only if he married. Somehow, Lorien managed to persuade Nicholi to join her in a childhood vow to never marry, so neither of them would ever take the title of king or queen. They vowed to reign together as Prince and Princess of Euphoria."

"But Nicholi broke that vow when he took my grandmother as his queen," Isaboe interrupted.

"Yes, and Lorien never forgave her brother and vowed revenge against him. Enraged that a mortal woman would take her place as queen, she sought counsel from me, and I tried to calm her, but she would have nothing of it. I watched the bitterness in her heart grow like a wicked weed out of control. When it became known that Alaina was carrying the heir to the throne, something in Lorien snapped, and I saw the darkness in her soul exploding. Hoping she could find purpose in her life, rather than trying to destroy Nicholi and Alaina's lives, I suggested that she seek guidance from The Mundahli."

"The Keeper of the Knowledge?"

"I see you've heard of her as well."

"Petrina told me that The Mundahli had told Lorien about the prophecy which resulted in Nicholi and Alaina being cast out." Isaboe's stomach twisted as she made the connection.

"When I sent Lorien to see The Mundahli," Baba Denova's expression grew stern as she continued, "I did not know of the prophecy, or just how black her heart had become. Lorien immediately shamed Nicholi for breaking the law of the realm and demanded that the council not only remove him and his mortal bride from power, but have them executed, along with their unborn child. Of course, the council would not take Nicholi's life, but as you know, they did force him to send Alaina back to the mortal world before the child was born. It was either that or take the child's life at birth. Nicholi was a broken fey, and he did what he thought would spare Alaina and his child."

"But neither of them were spared," Isaboe declared. "Alaina died shortly after my mother was born, and Rosalyn had a really horrible life. Nicholi might have thought he was doing the right thing by turning his back on his wife and his child, but he sounds as bad as his sister." Isaboe could hear the bitterness in her own words.

Silently sipping her cup, the old elf didn't respond, just stared at Isaboe with sad, weary eyes. "Shortly after Nicholi and Alaina were exiled, Lorien cast me out of the castle as well, and I've been living in this cottage ever since. Though I knew of her madness, I had no idea that she was capable of doing such things as reaching into the mortal world to destroy your lives as well."

Isaboe silently absorbed what the elf had just shared before she spoke again. "I spent a lot of time alone with Lorien back in my own world before Kaitlyn was born. She kept telling me that I should feel privileged to be carrying such a special child. At the time, I didn't completely understand what she meant, but now I shudder at knowing what her true intent really is. When I consider the idea of my daughter being raised by such a monster, a cold shiver runs down my spine."

"Well, I don't know how I might be able to stop it, but I can't stand the thought that this little one could end up with Queen Lorien." Baba

Denova gestured to the baby in Isaboe's arms. "Taking the life of this innocent child would be an unforgivable sin, and it's high time that Lorien account for what she's done."

As Isaboe heard the commitment in Baba Denova's words and saw it in her expression, the earlier fear about the old elf's loyalty to Lorien melted away. Offering a soft smile, Isaboe glanced down at Gabriel, who had fallen asleep in her arms. "Well, regardless of all the horrible things the queen has done, at least she did one thing right. She placed this precious bundle in your care. For that, I am grateful."

Baba Denova had no response, but Isaboe could see the remorse in her eyes. Feeling a deep sense of empathy for the old elf, she could see that no one had been spared from Lorien's demented thirst for power.

CHAPTER 23

BLOOD LOCK

When Isaboe finally heard a quick rap on the door, she rushed over to meet Petrina, who entered the cottage looking flushed. "How'd it go?" Isaboe asked, still holding tightly to Gabriel.

"I think it went well," the fey said breathlessly. "But I was right. She knew you and the others were at the Council of Elders today."

"What did you tell her?"

"After I told her what I saw and heard, she asked what had become of the mortals. I told her that when the trolls attacked, we were all told to evacuate, or we'd be locked in the castle. I said that I had no idea of what happened afterward."

"Do you think she believed you?"

The fey heaved a heavy sigh. "I hope so." Petrina's gaze fell to the bundle in Isaboe's arms. "Give the baby back to Baba Denova. It is time to finish this."

As the old nanny accepted Gabriel from Isaboe, her wide eyes flicked back-and-forth between the younger women suspiciously. "What are you two going to do?"

"It's best you don't know," Petrina answered furtively. "Pack only what you cannot live without, and then take the child to the pond behind the castle. A carriage will be waiting there for you. When we arrive, the four of us will flee. You won't be coming back here, Baba Denova."

Isaboe watched the shocked expression on the old elf's face as she absorbed Petrina's plans and understood her anxiety. Yet, the elf nodded, and when she looked up at them, concern was written in her wrinkled face.

"You two be careful. Lorien shows no mercy to those who betray her."

Those words sent a shiver of uncertainty down Isaboe's spine as she cast a nervous glance at Petrina. Having now found Gabriel, she wanted nothing so much as to leave Euphoria immediately and return home. But Petrina was counting on her and had brought Isaboe to see the baby first, just as she had promised.

"Are you ready?" Petrina asked Isaboe as she turned toward the door.

"No, but I guess I don't have a choice, do I?" The edge of panic in her voice caused Petrina to stop and turn as Isaboe struggled to hold herself together.

"Isaboe, the only one who can end this—who can free us all from Lorien—is you." Stepping closer, Petrina put a hand on Isaboe's arm and offered a strained but supportive smile. "You can do this. I know you can. Do it for your grandmother. Do it for Alaina."

Something about Petrina's words resonated within Isaboe, giving her the smallest bit of courage. Knowing she could not escape Euphoria without Petrina and her carriage, she found her resolve and swallowed her fear. She also knew she had something to prove, not only to herself, but to all of those who doubted her, especially Queen Brighid. If Isaboe needed justification for being on this mission, this was it. She just wished her rapidly beating heart shared the same conviction. Right now, along with her nagging self-doubt, it was screaming *danger*. Was she really capable of such daring?

Isaboe said a quick silent prayer and then took one last look back at Baba Denova and the baby she had come so far to save. Reluctantly turning away from them both, she followed Petrina into the night.

Once outside and on the move, the evening air felt cool against Isaboe's heated face, but the darkness that enveloped them unnerved her, as did the same strange animal sounds that had frightened her earlier. Staying on Petrina's heels, she followed the young fey back through the trees. Isaboe's head was down as she pushed the branches aside and focused on her footing, when Petrina came to a sudden stop. "Don't move," the fey whispered. "Don't make a sound."

Standing silent and frozen, Isaboe felt her heart hammering in her chest. Desperately wanting to run, but warned not to move, she held her breath and peered between the branches. As a distinctive low growl echoed through the trees, she saw a large shadow lumbering into the tree line. A loud snort and a grunt told her that something quite large was pushing through the brush, but then it stopped abruptly, and the forest fell deadly silent all around them.

There was very little light, but Isaboe was sure that the shadow, now so close she could see its hairy shoulders, was watching her. Feeling that she would explode any moment from pure terror, Isaboe silently clutched Petrina's hand, and the fey squeezed back in response. As the distinctive odor of rotten meat wafted past Isaboe's nose, she resisted the urge to throw up and didn't move a muscle.

When a disconnected shout suddenly echoed in the distance, the beast grunted. Again, the frightened women heard the rustle in the trees and the breaking of branches, but this time the heavy footsteps led off toward a clearing and then away, fading into the darkness. Whatever the creature was, it was now gone. Feeling Petrina release her grip, Isaboe finally took a breath. "What was that?" she whispered.

"One of Lorien's wicked beasts. There's more of their kind here in the forest, so stay close and keep quiet."

Back on the move, Isaboe struggled to follow Petrina along the edge of the tree line, and in the dark, it was a challenge to keep up with the light-footed fey who, more than once, had to stop and wait for Isaboe to catch up. When they finally reached a stone wall overgrown with vines, the fey stopped and began pacing back-and-forth in front of the wall, occasionally prodding at the stones as if she were looking for something.

"What are you doing?" Isaboe whispered.

"I'm looking for the way in." Petrina's hushed reply had just faded away when Isaboe heard a distinctive click, and then the scraping of rock. When an opening in the stone wall appeared, it revealed a narrow passageway. "If we follow this, it will take us into the caverns beneath the palace where the vault is. Come on, follow me."

Swallowing hard, Isaboe ducked down through the low opening. She had thought it couldn't get any darker, but she was wrong. Placing her hand against the stone wall, she cringed away from its spongy dampness, but then realized that she needed a guide in the dark and gingerly rested her fingertips back against the lichen-covered wall. Beneath the low ceiling of the tunnel, it was pitch-black, and Isaboe could sense their descent with each cautious step.

Holding her hand, the fey led Isaboe blindly in the dark until the ground leveled off and a small flicker of light appeared out of the inky blackness. As they came closer, Isaboe saw a lantern hanging from the wall that illuminated the first step down a narrow stairwell. Beyond the stairway, the cavern branched into many indistinguishable passages, each lit with evenly spaced lanterns. The corridors seemed to go on forever.

"Where do they all lead?" Isaboe asked.

"All over. Some lead up into the castle. The vault is down here," Petrina said, taking a lantern from the wall and turning toward the stairs. Isaboe followed her down the steps as the light threw their misshapen shadows against the cavernous wall.

When they reached the bottom step, Petrina held the lantern aloft, illuminating a number of moldering alcoves. The light revealed more dark openings leading out from the main room, and Isaboe, wishing she could be anywhere but here, wondered if her next torture would be having to crawl through one of them.

"This way," Petrina muttered, turning away from the small openings in the cave wall. Quickly catching up, Isaboe followed Petrina around a corner, where they found a solid wooden door. Petrina pressed down on the handle, but the door was locked. "The vault is in here." Retrieving her small vial of pixie dust, Petrina pulled the cork and sprinkled a tiny amount of the sparkling blue powder onto the handle. Isaboe watched in awe as the magical dust danced around the metal before working its way into the locking mechanism. Just when the magic seemed to have sizzled away, there was a satisfying *click*. Petrina again pressed down on the handle, and this time the latch released. With Isaboe on her heels, the fey pushed the door fully open and walked into the room holding the lantern overhead.

A stone vault was the centerpiece of an otherwise empty room, and the fey grabbed Isaboe's hand, leading her toward it. The lantern illuminated the large lock that sealed the vault door, and Petrina gave it a tug, but as expected, it didn't release. "This is the blood lock," she said, holding it in her hand so that the keyhole faced upward. "Your blood goes in here. We need only a drop. Do you have something you can pierce your skin with?"

The urge to flee washed over Isaboe as she stared at the lock, but she knew she had come too far to back out now. Frantically checking her pockets for something sharp, Isaboe was only able to come up with a hairpin. "I have this," she said, hearing her voice tremble slightly, along with her hand that held the pin.

"That'll do. Go on then," Petrina urged, holding the lantern higher and angling the lock toward Isaboe.

Isaboe's hands were shaking as she positioned the pin over the soft pad of her middle finger, and she had to take a few breaths in order to steady them. Emptying her mind and closing her eyes, she brought the pin down hard, and jolted at the impact. Quickly turning her hand over so she didn't have to look at her bloody finger, she squeezed a few drops into the keyhole. As soon as it was done, Isaboe wrapped her finger in her skirt, eyes never leaving the unchanging lock. "Was it enough?"

Petrina tugged on the lock again, and this time it snapped open. Shooting Isaboe a grin over her shoulder, she said, "It was enough." After slipping the lock off the latch, she slowly pushed the stone door open.

As she followed Petrina into the cold dark vault, Isaboe heard the sound of something scurrying. With the lantern held aloft, she could see that the space was much smaller than she had expected. When a whimper reached her ears, she followed the sound to a huddled figure in the corner attempting to cover itself with a tattered cloth.

"Turn out the light!" Isaboe heard the crackled voice of an old woman. "Please, turn it out. It is hurting my eyes!"

Lowering the flame on the lantern, Petrina placed it on the floor and exchanged a wide-eyed look with Isaboe before they both turned their focus to the heap huddled in the corner. "Who are you?" the fey finally asked. "How long have you been in here?"

Isaboe noticed that Petrina seemed as truly confused as she was to find an old woman locked in the vault.

When the woman stood, still blocking the dim light of the lantern with her thin, boney hand, she finally answered. "A better question is;

what took you so long?" the old crone asked in a raspy voice that sounded as if it hadn't been used in years. Her eyes still blinking furiously in the dim light, the woman slowly lowered her hand. Her hair, or what was left of it, lay in filthy clumps over her skull. Her skin was paper-thin and translucent. Straightening the tattered remnants of what must have once been her clothing, the creature shuffled to stand before them. "Queen Lorien didn't send you, did she?"

"She doesn't know we're here," Isaboe confessed, and then repeated Petrina's questions. "Who are you? How long have you been in here?"

Startling Isaboe, the old crone reached out and grasped her hands. As feeble as she appeared, the hag had a surprisingly strong grip. "It is you, isn't it? How many years? How many winters have I been waiting for you to return?"

"I—I guess the answer you're looking for is; twenty?" It took Isaboe a moment for her own words to sink in. "Are you telling me that you've been in this vault all this time?" she asked incredulously. "For twenty years?"

"What's your name, old woman?" Petrina asked.

Releasing her grip on Isaboe, the crone turned her focus on the young fey. "I've been known by many names," she said with a toothless smile. "Which one do you prefer?" As she shuffled behind the two women, they swiveled in unison to keep her in their sights. "Some call me the Wise Owl, while others call me the Speaker of the Stars," the hag cackled. "But I've also been called the Seer of Time, the Bender of Destiny, and Keeper of the Fates. Some call me their worst nightmare!" she laughed again.

"But how could you have survived all this time?" Isaboe asked, startled and confused.

"And why would Lorien lock you in here twenty years ago?" Petrina asked. "What is it you know that the queen wants to be kept secret?" Then a sudden realization flashed across the fey's face. "You're the... the Mundahli, aren't you?" Petrina had finally asked the right question.

"The Keeper of the Knowledge?" Isaboe exclaimed.

The old woman only smiled.

"Lorien told us that you died," said Petrina.

"Not surprising," replied the old hag. "That one is a bad seed. She used the knowledge I gave her for her own malicious purposes."

"Do you speak of the prophecy?" Isaboe asked.

"Lorien used that knowledge to destroy her brother, but it's what they don't know that keeps her in power."

"What do you mean? Who is they and what don't they know?" asked Petrina.

But the hag suddenly spun around. "Yes! Yes, I'll tell them!" the old woman shouted over her shoulder, her eyes fixed on an empty corner of the vault. "Stop pushing me! I know you want out, but all in good time. Now, hush, and leave me be!"

Isaboe and Petrina exchanged another baffled glance.

"The council, that's who they be," the Mundahli continued, "and the alternative outcome to the prophecy. That's what they don't know."

"Alternative outcome?" Isaboe asked, as the pieces slowly began to slip into place. "What does that mean?"

Shuffling to another corner of the vault, the Mundahli scooped up a small object and held it to her sunken chest. With a boney hand, she began to wipe away years of dust and grime to expose a crystal the size and shape of a goose's egg. "This is what you've come for. This is the piece of knowledge Lorien couldn't destroy."

"What is that?" Isaboe asked.

"The alternate prophecy; the one she tried to annihilate."

"What is the alternate prophecy?"

"It doesn't matter. It's what will bring Lorien down," Petrina began to grow with excitement. "That's why she locked it in here with you."

"Yes," the crone confirmed. "She locked me in here when this one came to Euphoria." She pointed menacingly at Isaboe with a wrinkled old hand, still clutching the crystal with the other. "Lorien had everyone believing you were Alaina, but I knew better. That's when the prophecy changed to reveal another outcome. But it slithered alongside the original, morphing from one to the other. Up until then, I thought I understood how prophecies worked, but this challenged everything I believed about the course of destiny. *It can be changed!* Knowing that Lorien wouldn't want this knowledge to be discovered, I sought out the grandfather of dragons and asked him for the Eye of Emarus."

"What is the Eye of Emarus?" Petrina asked.

The hag then turned her focus to the crystal and circled her boney hand above it, muttering a few incoherent words. Slowly, a muted light began to emit from the center of the crystal. As she wrapped it reverently in both hands, her half-blind eyes were lit with worship. "This is the Eye of Emarus, the ancient leader of dragons. Within it lies the alternative prophecy."

Picking up the lantern to get a better look, Isaboe was startled to see a reptilian eye staring unseeingly out of the crystal. A penetrating dark pupil floated in a glistening pool of amber. Half-lidded by dark leathery skin, the eye was as big as the Muldahli's fist. *This is the eye of a dragon!* The very thought of it sent a shiver down Isaboe's back.

"After the prophecy was safely protected, and I had hidden the dragon's eye," the Mundahli continued, "I went to the queen and told her we must inform the council. This was too big, too important, for them not to know. They had sent Alaina out of the realm, had removed Nicholi from power and throne, and acknowledged Lorien as Queen of Euphoria, all based upon their fear that the original prophecy would come to pass. But Lorien couldn't take the chance that the Council of Elders might depose her." She paused, glancing back and forth between the two women standing before her, hanging on her every word. "And as I suspected, the queen didn't see it my way. She demanded that I give her the prophecy, but I refused, and she didn't know about the Eye of Emarus! When I threatened to go to the council alone, Lorien tried to silence me," the old hag scoffed. "But those stupid beasts of hers wouldn't attack. They knew better. So she tried to snuff me out by fire; set my whole body ablaze, but my magic kept me from harm. When Lorien realized she could not destroy me, she had me thrown in here without ever knowing where the prophecy was hidden." The Mundahli paused, and a heaviness crossed her aged face. "I've been waiting for you to come back and set me free ever since."

"But…how are you still alive? How did you survive all of her attempts to kill you?" Isaboe asked in amazement.

"Knowledge cannot be destroyed, child, only forgotten." Again, the toothless hag smiled as she leaned in toward Isaboe. "But once known, it can be remembered," she almost whispered. Then, without segue, the old woman demanded, "Did you bring the vessel?" Her wild gaze jumped back-and-forth between Petrina and Isaboe.

Seeing her own confusion reflected in Petrina's eyes, Isaboe could only ask, "What vessel?"

"You do not possess magic strong enough to swallow the eye, child. You need a vessel."

"What? I don't understand what you mean."

"You can't take the prophecy without a vessel!" the Mundahli shrieked.

Isaboe looked at the dragon's eye. "Why do I have to take it?"

"Because you are the one who must reveal Lorien's lie." As the old hag stared long and hard, Isaboe felt as if the Mundahli was looking right into her soul. "You are the chosen one, and I knew you would return. So, where is the vessel?" she asked again.

Uncertain and confused, Isaboe wondered what the vessel could possibly be. What was it that she was supposed to have brought? But then a sudden thought had her putting the lantern down and pulling the ring off of her finger before presenting it to the seer. "Is this the vessel?"

"The Ring of King Odin." The Mundahli's words were spoken with reverence as she took the ring from Isaboe's fingers, examining it in the dim light of the lantern. "The great king commissioned eight of these bands, each laden with powerful magic." Spinning around, she swung her bony fists at the air. "No, you can't touch it!" she shouted and then swung again. "This is a *magic ring!* Now, stay back, or I'll leave you here!"

Once again, the old woman's vitriol was directed at an empty corner of the vault. Isaboe was genuinely unsure if there was really something—or someone—that she couldn't see. Or had the old woman gone completely bat-shit insane being locked up for so long?

"But this isn't the vessel," the old woman said placing the ring back into Isaboe's hand. "It's too crowded. There's too much magic in this ring. No room for the prophecy."

"Then I don't know what it could be." Isaboe confessed, slipping the ring back onto her finger. But in the next moment she suddenly felt a warm tingling against her chest. With each passing second it grew hotter, as if it was burning her skin, and Isaboe couldn't lift the blue amulet up and out of her dress fast enough. Slipping it from around her head, she held it out. "It's this, isn't it?"

Still holding the crystal-encased dragon's eye in one hand, the hag took the green cord from Isaboe with the other, and held the blue stone at eye level, watching it catch the light as it twisted back-and-forth. "Oh, yes, this will do. This will do just fine!" she mused. The Keeper of the Knowledge then dangled the amulet above the Eye of Emarus held in her boney hand and began shuffling in circles, muttering incoherent words. Isaboe and Petrina stood rock still as they watched the cool blue stone begin to spin, slowly at first, but then it picked up speed, fueled by the hag's mantra. Within seconds, the blue stone was spinning so fast that it was a blur above the dragon's eye.

"Cover your eyes," the crone cackled, glancing up from the magic happening in her hands. "Cover your eyes!" she repeated, this time urgently.

Watching Petrina shield her face with her hands, Isaboe followed her lead. In the next second, she heard the crystal shatter and saw an explosive flash, even though her eyes were clenched tight.

When the light finally dimmed, Isaboe dropped her hands. The old woman now held only the blue amulet, which hung innocently from its green cord. Looking around, Isaboe expected to see shards of broken crystal, but she saw nothing. There were no remnants of the crystal that the Mundahli had been holding, or any sign of the dragon's eye that had been inside of it.

When the old woman placed the amulet back over Isaboe's head, and the blue stone dropped against her chest, it felt heavier than it had before, as if the magic it contained actually held weight. As the warmth of the stone penetrated through the fabric of Isaboe's dress, it seemed to emanate heat where it lay against her breast, and when she attempted to lift it, she found that the stone had passed through her dress and was now laying against her skin! She grabbed at it but found that it seemed to have bound itself to her. The more she scratched at the green cord, the more she tried to clutch the stone and rip it away from her chest, the more the amulet embedded itself into her. It felt alive, like the body of a large insect that had sprouted legs and was now digging its way into her flesh. *"What's happening?"* she screamed. Feeling the magic around the stone as it buried itself under her skin, Isaboe scratched wildly at her breastbone, but the amulet had melded into her chest, feeling hot and cold at the same time. *"What have you done?"*

"Now, you are the vessel," the old crone sang with a toothless smile. But the Mundahli's smile quickly melted as she grabbed Isaboe's thrashing hands and pulled her close, so close that Isaboe could only look into the hag's face. "Heed my words, child. Make haste and seek the wisdom of the old ones. Only at the Grove of Raghii can the prophecy be brought forth and revealed. And only you can deliver it. Until the truth is known, Lorien's reign will never end." The old hag stared hard into Isaboe's eyes. "And know this: if you die, the prophecy dies with you."

'Now you are the vessel.' Isaboe had heard those words before, and they triggered the memory of a vision she'd had just before leaving their world. At the time, she hadn't known what the words meant. Now Isaboe had the horrid realization that it had been a premonition of this very moment.

But this was too big, too important to be her destiny. Isaboe was only one mortal woman. How could she possibly see this through? As she began to comprehend the weight of the Mundahli's task, Isaboe felt her heart beat quicken. She couldn't bear the thought of being the chosen one—not again. She jerked her hands from the old hag's grasp. "No! I can't do this!" In desperation, Isaboe turned toward Petrina. "I came here to take Gabriel home. That's it! I didn't ask to be part of your rebellion to bring Lorien down!" She was shouting now, as if she could somehow shout away her own destiny.

"Then go. Go now!" the Mundahli cried, shuffling forward and giving Isaboe a little shove toward the vault door. "Retrieve what you came for and take your leave of this place—the sooner the better. And whatever you do, avoid Queen Lorien." The crone hunched down and looked up at her with wide searching eyes. Isaboe thought the strange old woman suddenly appeared smaller, her face more sunken, as if such a thing were possible. "You have what Lorien wants," the hag continued, "You are in her way, and she wants you dead. It would be best for all if she does not find you here."

a heavy task

The fact that Lorien wanted her dead wasn't news to Isaboe. The Fey Queen had attempted to take her life more than once already. But hearing those words from the Mundahli, the Keeper of the Knowledge, only renewed her sense of dread. She swallowed hard and glanced at Petrina, who offered a grave nod and then turned toward the vault door. But both of them stopped when they heard the strange cackle behind them.

"Okay, little one, it's time," the crone outstretched her hand toward an empty corner of the vault. "I know, I know, but it'll be alright, you'll see. You don't want to stay here all alone, do you?"

Shooting Petrina a questioning glance, Isaboe saw the same confused look on the young fey's face as the crone carried on her one-sided conversation. But then a thin transparent image began to take shape as it crawled out from the corner. "That's it, come along now. We've been sprung, my friend. It's time to take our leave."

In the dim light of the lone lantern, Isaboe watched warily as the faint image of a small willowy figure with a large, round head and bulbous eyes, climbed onto the old woman's shoulders. The creature was transparent, and Isaboe could only see its outline, like a crude sketch without details or color. But the large eyes that darted back and forth at the two intruders were so clear that they stood out like floating black orbs.

"Time is not on your side, child," the Mundahli told Isaboe with a new authority, suddenly seeming taller and less frail. "The window of opportunity is closing. The longer you linger here—the longer Lorien remains in power—the more death and destruction she will bring down upon this land. The council wrongfully believes that when Lorien is isolated and contained within her borders she can be controlled. Their ignorance may destroy the very realm they are trying to protect," the hag spat. Yet in the next moment, she softened, and for the first time since meeting this strange old woman, Isaboe saw what appeared to be genuine concern cross her wrinkled face. "I know you did not choose this fate, my child," the hag murmured, placing a boney hand on Isaboe's. "But you are a strong mortal, stronger than you think you are. And there be faerie blood in your veins too. Have faith in both of those attributes when the road ahead gets bumpy. Fate has chosen you for a reason."

As the Mundahli stepped further into the light, the figure on her back clutched more tightly, like a frightened child afraid to be left behind. "Make haste. Go now. Our time here is done!" With a full-faced toothless smile, the old crone spun around, the tatters of her clothes twirling out around her, but by the time she had completed the circle, she was gone. Free of the fragile body that they had once covered, her rags dropped to the floor. In the next second, Isaboe felt a rush of warm air slither by her as the Mundahli's spirit escaped the vault. There was no fanfare, no bright lights or explosion of sound. The Keeper of the Knowledge had just vanished.

Turning toward her companion, Isaboe saw her own wide-eyed look of shock reflected in Petrina's face. But as abruptly as the Mundahli had left, the young fey clutched onto Isaboe's hand and dashed out through the vault door, leaving the lantern on the floor. After exiting the small room, they quickly found the stairs and began to run back up the stairwell. Petrina took the steps two at a time, leaving Isaboe struggling to catch up. *Were there really this many steps on the way down?* Isaboe wondered as she kept the hem of her dress lifted to avoid tripping.

"Come on, Isaboe, keep up!"

"I'm trying!" Isaboe gasped, sucking air like an old woman, but her mind held the fear of a young girl. She had not sought the responsibility of delivering a prophecy that would affect every life in Euphoria. In the face of it all, her head was spinning, her lungs and legs ached from running up the stairs, and her chest still throbbed where the Blue Amulet had burned its way into her flesh. All she wanted to do was get back to that cottage, scoop up Gabriel from the arms of the old elf, Baba Denova, and fly out of Euphoria as quickly as possible. The fact that her escape would have to involve flying seemed suddenly unimportant. Escaping the Fey Queen's land without being discovered was the only thing Isaboe could focus on at the moment.

Finally reaching the landing where Petrina waited, Isaboe took a moment to catch her breath, but almost at once the young fey was running again, so she reluctantly picked up her own pace until a recognizable voice called from behind them, bringing both women to an abrupt halt.

"Is that you, Petrina?" Isaboe was very familiar with that voice, and it created a burst of panic in her chest. Petrina turned very slowly. The lanterns hanging along the length of the corridor shed enough light that even in the dark hallway, Isaboe could see the fear in Petrina's eyes.

"Queen Lorien, why are you down here?" she asked, exchanging a terrified look with Isaboe.

"I should be the one asking that question," Lorien stated, taking a few steps in their direction. "I thought you said you needed to rest from your travels. What brings you down here? And who is this with you?"

Isaboe could hear the queen's footsteps coming closer, but there were also other heavier footfalls accompanying hers. It took every bit of control for Isaboe not to bolt, but she was shaking so hard she was sure her legs would fail her. And really, just how far could she get? This was Lorien's castle, and they were surrounded by Lorien's guards! Struggling to calm her racing mind and think of a way to get out of this alive, Isaboe remembered the ring. The Ring of Odin had cloaking powers that could mask a mortal's vibrations, and there was a chance that Lorien had not yet realized her presence.

"The cook sent us for some dried herbs," Petrina offered up a lie and a smile, then took a couple of steps toward Isaboe. *"Think fey,"* she muttered just above a whisper, then inconspicuously tossed a bit of blue pixie dust at Isaboe before walking past her to address the queen. "We were looking for the root cellar, but I think we took the wrong passage." Petrina chuckled nervously.

"Why would the cook send you?" Lorien asked.

"Well, I was hungry after traveling all day, so I stopped in the kitchen for a bite to eat. That's when she sent me on this errand."

"Who is with you?"

Feeling the tingle of pixie dust, Isaboe sensed the magic dancing across her skin as its energy sparked throughout her entire body. But would it be enough for Lorien not to recognize her?

"Meredith, you're being disrespectful," Petrina said over her shoulder. "Turn around and address our queen."

Taking a deep breath, Isaboe let it out slowly before turning. *Please let me look like anyone else but myself,* she silently prayed, but the moment her eyes landed on Lorien, she was sure that her trembling would give her away.

There she was—in all of her black-hearted glory. Even in the dim light of the basement lanterns, Isaboe could see Lorien's long blond hair spilling over the shoulders of her elegant dark-purple robe. Two thugs towered behind her, holding spears and small swords. A startling difference from Isaboe's encounter with Lorien in the mortal world was that now the queen sported beautiful lacy wings. Painted in earthy hues of green and brown and accented in white, she looked almost angelic as her wings fanned out behind her. But it was her piercing stare that caused every nerve in Isaboe's body to scream *danger!* Experience had taught her that Lorien was anything but angelic. Though her instincts screamed for her to run, Isaboe did her best to mask the fear and offered up a forced smile, and a somewhat clumsy curtsy. Lowering her head to stare at the floor, she hoped that her actions would appear as a reverential gesture and not be seen as an attempt to cover her obvious terror.

For a moment there was only silence as she held her breath. Then, hearing the sound of Lorien's footsteps pacing forward, Isaboe glanced up and saw the queen peering down the dark stairwell that she and Petrina had just come up. When Lorien nodded over her shoulder, one of the guards stepped out from behind her and headed down the stairs.

Oh, God, no! Don't go down there! Isaboe thought frantically as Lorien turned back toward her and Petrina. After dropping her gaze back to the floor, she saw the tips of the queen's slippers come into view.

"Look at me," Lorien ordered.

Swallowing hard, Isaboe slowly raised her face and immediately felt a rush of anger and fear. She was certain that the queen had to see through her façade.

"Meredith? Why don't I recognize you?" Lorien stared hard at Isaboe. "I know the faces of all my subjects who reside in the castle."

"She's been working in the gardens until recently, Your Highness," Petrina offered. "Now Meredith works in the kitchen."

"I did not ask you, Petrina," Lorien spat, still staring at Isaboe. "Can you not speak for yourself?"

"Yes, Your Highness, I can speak," Isaboe mumbled, trying to make her voice sound different, hoping that the disguise provided by the pixie dust would extend to her words as well. But Lorien continued to stare intently at Isaboe, as if trying to see something that wasn't completely clear.

Two more armed guards joined Lorien's entourage and stopped just behind Isaboe and Petrina, waiting for directions. Lorien had come prepared.

Paralyzed by the sheer weight of the Fey Queen's gaze, Isaboe waited for the guillotine to fall. When heavy footsteps signaled the return of the guard who had gone to investigate, he reappeared from the stairwell, carrying a lantern.

"Well?" Lorien demanded.

"This lantern was all there was in the vault, Your Highness," he reported.

"The vault was open…and *empty?* Are you sure there was no one— nothing else in that vault?"

"Yes, Your Highness, I'm sure. The vault is empty."

Turning her attention back to Isaboe, Lorien's eyes turned black, and her mouth pulled into a thin tight line. "Enough of this game!" the Fey Queen snapped, shooting a burst of energy that hit Isaboe in the stomach, tossing her backward.

After landing hard on her back, Isaboe's head bounced off the stone, and her vision danced on the edge of darkness, speckled with stars. The magic Lorien had used was much stronger than Petrina's pixie dust, and Isaboe felt it crawling over her skin like insects. Her head throbbed as she managed to push herself to her feet. In the next second, Lorien latched onto Isaboe's arm with a vice-like grip as the other guards took Petrina captive.

"*Isaboe!*" Lorien snarled, painfully squeezing her grip. "Where is the Mundahli?" the queen demanded.

"I don't know!" Isaboe shouted back, twisting and struggling to free herself from Lorien's grasp. "She just vanished!"

"You let her out," Lorien shouted, dragging Isaboe closer as she thrashed uselessly. "You have no idea what you've done." The Fey Queen was so close that Isaboe could see the manic gleam in her eyes.

"Leave her alone." Petrina's command quickly drew Lorien's attention, and she turned on the younger fey.

"You do not tell me what to do!" Lorien snarled as she grabbed Petrina's face in a bruising pinch and dragged her in close. Isaboe watched the vile hatred twisting Lorien's face as she spat, "You betrayed me, Petrina. I offered you leniency and made you my emissary. In return, you used that freedom against me. I should have known that you'd betray me after my moment of weakness. After everything I had done for you, I had hoped I could trust you. Obviously, I was wrong."

Petrina was able to shake free of Lorien's grip on her face, but she wasn't strong enough to break the guard's hold. And yet, even restrained, Petrina shouted at the queen. "You have never given me anything but pain! You lured all of us away from our homes with your false promises. We're nothing more than entertainment for your sick pleasure! *You cut off my wings!*"

Lorien slapped Petrina hard across the face. "Of all people, you should know I have no mercy for those who betray me." She returned her withering glare to Isaboe. "I don't know what magic you used to prevent me from detecting your presence, but I intend to find out." As Lorien's dark eyes flashed, Isaboe trembled even more. "Take them to my chambers," she ordered.

After a guard roughly grabbed her arm, Isaboe whimpered as she and Petrina were dragged down the dimly lit hallway before ascending one stairwell, then another. Both women struggled but were no match for the guards' strength. Isaboe was barely able to keep her feet under her as the guard drug her up the steps, but it was the sheer panic exploding in her gut that made her feel truly helpless. Facing Lorien was the last thing she had wanted, yet here she was—Lorien's prisoner. And this time there would be no rescue. No one knew where she was.

In her attempt to prove that she was worthy of her place on this quest, Isaboe had made herself a casualty. She hadn't even left a message, nor did she have any way to contact Connor or Rosalyn. Her foolish plan to save Gabriel would see both her and her grandson dead by Lorien's hand. Isaboe's tortured thoughts only added to her terror at what she would be facing.

The chambers they were escorted into were luxurious and exquisite in a way that could only make them Lorien's. Elaborate fabrics in reds, browns, and dark greens had been artfully hung on the walls and windows, accenting the intricate woodwork. The thick overhead planks were scrolled with etchings into the dark wood, and from the center beam hung an elaborate chandelier of twisted metal. The stately four-poster bed was draped in heavy red velvet, and the pillows and blankets looked to be made of white silk. The rest of the room was just as imposing: a massive worktable which held unrecognizable objects of metal and glass, a richly decorated sofa, an exquisitely framed dressing mirror, and a hulking wardrobe that was filled with opulent gowns.

Movement drew Isaboe's eye to a serving woman tidying up the room. By contrast, she was dressed in a simple brown smock and looked completely out of place in the midst of the opulence that was Lorien's chambers. "Get out," The Fey Queen snapped. Stopping only to curtsy to her queen, the woman scurried out the door.

"Search her," Lorien commanded, and the guard who had been holding Isaboe began to pat her down. She felt completely violated by the gruff groping hands that roamed over her body. Despite her struggles, he wrestled the strap off her wrist, but when he pulled the ring off her finger, the anxiety in her chest exploded.

The instant the ring was removed, a wicked smile drew up the corners of Lorien's dark lips. "Ahh, there she is." The queen's face took on a look of depraved satisfaction as she stepped forward to examine Isaboe, now revealed once the curtain of magic had lifted away. The guard presented his queen with the artifacts he had taken from Isaboe, and Lorien carefully examined the items in his large hand. "A communication stone? Who gave you this? It had to be someone from the council."

But Isaboe only glared at Lorien, refusing to offer any information. Taking the ring from the guard, the Fey Queen examined the silver band. "So, this is what was blocking your vibrations." Turning it over in her fingers, Lorien seemed to be trying to pick up something from the ring that would help her learn its powers. "Where did you get this? Who is helping you?"

Isaboe stared at the Fey Queen with frightened eyes, certain that if she spoke, her words would betray her. *Lorien had the ring!* The magic ring that Demetrick had given to Connor. The magic ring not only blocked her vibrations, but also contained the portal back to the mortal world, to the very thing that Lorien wanted—Kaitlyn. If the Fey Queen were to open the portal, Isaboe knew there would be no way to prevent her daughter from falling into the hands of this deranged fey. No, the queen would get nothing from her but hatred, of which Isaboe had plenty.

"Unwilling to speak, are we? Or perhaps I'm not asking the right questions." Lorien rolled the ring between her fingers as she sauntered over to a decorated wooden cart which held goblets and a carafe of red liquid, along with a plate of crackers and dried meats. "Leave us," she barked at her guards who still held Isaboe and Petrina.

Finally free, Isaboe rubbed the tender spot on her arm where the meaty paw of the guard had squeezed so hard. She watched as the large man placed her wrist strap on a table by the door before he left. Glancing back at Lorien, Isaboe saw the queen drop the ring into the pocket of her robe before pouring herself a drink of wine. Her dark eyes burning into Isaboe, she seemed to be savoring the wine before placing the goblet down and turning around. "Where is Kaitlyn?" she demanded. "What did the Mundahli tell you? What became of the prophecy?" With each question, Lorien stepped closer, the intensity of her glare growing.

Finally finding her voice, Isaboe shouted at Lorien, "I denounced you! I vanquished you from my life!" These words had once freed her from Lorien's grasp back in the mortal world, and Isaboe hoped, in a vain attempt, that her banishment might still hold some power. Instead, a delighted smile twisted Lorien's lips, and she broke out into titters of false laughter.

"Isaboe, you stupid little fool," she snickered. "You are in *my* land; you are in my home now, and your words mean nothing here." Then, all at once she was too close, their faces only inches apart, and the humor was gone from the queen's face, replaced with fury. "I will ask again. Where is Kaitlyn?"

"I'll never tell you!"

"Then you'll watch the boy child die as I cut off one pudgy little digit at a time."

The queen's sneer was as sickening as her words, and for a moment all coherent thought was driven from Isaboe's mind. "How could you be so cruel to your own family? If it is your brother you want revenge against so badly, go take it out on him and *leave us alone!*"

Surprise crossed Lorien's face. "So, I see you've been educated on your family lineage." When the queen waved her hand in front of Isaboe, she felt Lorien's magic rise up around her feet, anchoring her to the ground. Its constricting grip worked its way up her body like a slithering snake, and Isaboe struggled against the invisible force holding her trapped as Lorien turned her full attention on Petrina.

"Tell me what the Mundahli said before you two let her escape," Lorien demanded.

"You know what she told us," Petrina spat. "And I hope you rot in Fetarus for it!"

Lorien grabbed the young fey by the throat, and with remarkable strength lifted her off her feet. Isaboe could only watch in horror as she fought against the invisible bonds holding her paralyzed.

Frantically clawing at the queen's hand, Petrina's feet kicked uselessly in the air as she struggled to free herself from the constrictive grip crushing her neck. "Yes, I may go to Fetarus for my crimes, but you lied to me, Petrina. You betrayed me. So you can go first, and I'll look forward to seeing you there," Lorien sneered as a ball of light formed in her free hand. It lengthened into a long slender rod that sparked with energy, and then Lorien thrust it into her captive's abdomen before dropping her to the floor. As Petrina doubled over, the rod of energy vanished, but the damage it had done was fatal. When Petrina lunged at Lorien, she only succeeded in clawing at the queen's robe. Kicking out violently, the toe of Lorien's slipper slammed into Petrina's chest, tossing her across the room where she crashed into a rock wall.

Petrina slid down the wall and collapsed into a heap on the floor, and Isaboe watched in horror as a trickle of greenish blood leaked out between her lips. But Isaboe had only seconds to fear for her companion before the Fey Queen was screaming in her face.

"Let's be clear on one thing; you mortals are not my family!"

"Your brother is my grandfather!"

"My brother is dead to me," the queen hissed. "He died when he put a mortal woman on *my* throne!"

"You got what you wanted. You're the queen and Alaina is dead. What more could you want?"

"What I don't yet have, and what I deeply deserve—the council's respect and subservience," she spat, and in that moment, Isaboe saw the queen's raw unhealed anger, something that had scarred her long ago. It rose to the surface of her memory, contorting her features. "Nicholi broke the law by bringing a mortal into the realm. He went even further and made Alaina his queen, handing her *my* title, but the council did nothing. They dismissed my demands for action and enforcement of their own laws. They brushed me aside and told me that such things were family matters, to be handled in private. Nicholi was King of Euphoria, and I was only his sister, forever a princess in my own land!" Lorien screamed. Howling her tantrum, she began to pace back-and-forth before Isaboe's frozen form.

"It wasn't until I brought forth the prophecy of the mortal-born child that they finally listened to me. But even then, they favored Nicholi. The council forced Alaina out, but your cursed grandfather kept the throne. Him! I was the one who revealed his treachery, and I got nothing! However, without his precious bride, my weak brother walked away and handed control of Euphoria over to me. And yet the council would only acknowledge my reign with restrictions. They think that by keeping me contained within my lands they can control me, but they are wrong!" Lorien's voice lowered as another lethal look crossed her face, and she walked over to stand in front of Isaboe. "After I teach Kaitlyn everything

I know, she will reach her full potential, and they will all realize how much they've underestimated me. With her power, I'll make them all pay for their disrespect," Lorien snarled and spun away. Opening the door they had come through, she issued her order. "Go to the cottage of Baba Denova and bring me the mortal child."

"NO!" Isaboe cried as Lorien shut the door and sauntered over to stand in front of her again.

"I'll ask you one more time before you watch the boy die a slow and painful death. Where is Kaitlyn?"

"You'll never get my daughter!" Isaboe shouted.

Lorien slapped her so hard that the pain was dizzying, but it paled compared to the agony of the queen's long fingernails digging into her jaw as she pulled Isaboe close. "You still don't understand, do you?" Lorien hissed into her ear. "You and Connor may have created Kaitlyn, but she carries my blood-line. There is more of me in Kaitlyn than you realize. Allowing her talents to waste away in the mortal world would be a horrible shame. She is destined to rule by my side."

As much as she wanted not to cry, Isaboe could feel the threat of tears, and when she closed her eyes, she pushed them out, letting them flow down her cheeks as despair threatened to engulf her. Would witnessing the death of her own grandson really be her last horrible experience before she died?

The door opened and brought with it a new wave of anguish, but when Isaboe opened her eyes, she didn't see what she had expected. Instead of the guard returning with Gabriel, a familiar slender woman entered the queen's chambers, and a rush of recognition brought on a new wave of horror.

Strolling across the room with arrogant confidence, Lilabeth was dressed in her signature black attire, which served to highlight the perfect curves of her body. Her creamy-white skin stood out in stark contrast to her black clothing, as well as her cunning dark eyes.

Though Isaboe had encountered the dark muse and shapeshifter before, here she looked different. Lilabeth's hair was not slicked down and oiled as it had been when she had morphed into a cat. Nor was it twisted into a long braid as it had been on the night she'd appeared in the form of Isaboe's sister, attempting to drag her into the ring of standing stones. Now Lilabeth's ink-black hair hung down, loosely tumbling over her white shoulders.

The dark muse's eyes were first drawn to where Petrina lay sprawled on the floor, her unimpressed gaze lingering for several seconds on the bleeding body before she shot a curious look in Isaboe's direction. Continuing across the room, she stopped next to Lorien. "Looks like you've been enjoying yourself," she said with a sickening smile, still focusing on Isaboe. "I hadn't realized you'd come along on this failed rescue attempt as well." Lilabeth stepped over to stand directly in front of Isaboe, who couldn't look away from the shapeshifter's dark penetrating stare. "It doesn't look as if this visit is going well for you, does it?" she snickered.

"Why are you here, Lilabeth?" Lorien asked, sounding almost annoyed at being disturbed. "Do you need something?"

Turning from Isaboe, the dark muse strolled over to stand at Lorien's side. "No, I just thought I'd drop by to give you an update on the troll attack you ordered on the Castle of Sashtonia. Those filthy beasts never made it. They got stopped near the river by Jarcadian warriors. But, by the looks of things, I'm going to assume that doesn't matter to you."

"The trolls made it to the river? Impressive. I didn't think they'd get that far, even with the weapons I provided them. And Kaegron? What became of him?"

Turning away, Lilabeth strolled over to the serving table and nibbled on a cracker before answering. "That stupid beast got himself captured. As we expected, Connor was on the battlefield fighting alongside the Jarcadians. I think it's possible that the council may agree to help the mortals."

Lorien scoffed at Lilabeth's comment. "Well, even if they do, it's too late. And Kaegron at least accomplished what I intended: chaos."

"But I instructed Kaegron to capture the mortal, not get himself captured," Lilabeth spat.

"Well, that's too bad. I was hoping that we would both get a chance to torture the bothersome mortal. Though his failed attempt may have robbed you of your prize, Lilabeth, the trolls at least flushed out this little dove, right into my hands."

When the shapeshifter focused a dark stare in her direction, Isaboe felt a shiver shoot down her spine. "Looks like your attempt to rescue the boy has failed. Poor planning on your part it would seem." Lilabeth then sauntered over to stand in front of Isaboe, giving the captive her full attention. When the muse shot her a smug grin, Isaboe could feel the intensity of both her fear and hatred as a wicked smile curled up one corner of Lilabeth's full lips. "Connor slipped out of my hands once before. I'll not let that happen twice."

Isaboe wanted to slap the smug smile off the dark muse's face, but she was in no position to do anything but feel angry and afraid. "Stay away from him!" she shouted in vain.

But the shapeshifter only laughed before she flopped down onto the sofa, making herself comfortable as she leaned her head to the side for a better view of Petrina, who appeared unconscious while her green blood pooled on the floor in front of her body. "I take it this ungrateful fey had something to do with the fact that this one is here," the dark muse guessed, while casually admiring her pointed fingernails.

"Yes, and Petrina has paid the ultimate price for her treason," Lorien scoffed with a vile chuckle. "For some foolish reason, these two sneaked in here alone. Unfortunately, I wasn't quick enough to prevent them from releasing the Mundahli from the vault."

"The Keeper of the Knowledge is out?" Lilabeth asked, shocked. "What about the prophecy?"

"She took it with her." The queen took another step toward Isaboe, and her face was only inches away when a wicked smile drew up the corners of her mouth. "Now Isaboe will watch me slice and dice that little boy until she gives me what I want," Lorien hissed.

Despite the invisible bonds that held her captive, Isaboe could feel her legs quivering.

"Well, I do know how much you enjoy torture, Lorien, but all of this is quite unnecessary, and really rather messy," the dark muse quipped, swinging her long legs casually over the arm of the lounge.

Lorien let out a deep sigh before turning to face the shapeshifter. "Lilabeth, you've given me the report on the trolls, so unless you have some other useful information, why are you still here? I assigned you a mission which you have yet to accomplish. You should be back in the mortal world looking for Kaitlyn," the queen spat.

"Oh, that. Well, I found her," Lilabeth replied casually.

"NO! That's not possible!" Isaboe shouted as panic slammed into her gut.

Lilabeth stood and sauntered back over to Isaboe with a vile satisfied grin on her face. "Oh, but it is. You see, it appears that Anna has more sense than you do. She's on her way to the standing stones with Kaitlyn as we speak."

"No! Anna wouldn't do that!" Isaboe cried, but the words rang false. She didn't really know Anna well, and her daughter was desperate to save Gabriel. Anna's mental state had been questionable when Isaboe last saw her older daughter, and she knew firsthand what horrible choices a person was willing to make when the agony of loss was all consuming.

"Then why are you still here? Go retrieve my heir!" Lorien demanded.

"I will, but now that I know this one is here, I have an idea." Lilabeth stared at Isaboe with a smug sneer on her lips. "I believe that when I meet up with Anna, she'll be more willing to hand Kaitlyn over to her mother, don't you think?"

The moment Lilabeth uttered those words, her image became obscured, indistinct and broken. Through her fear, Isaboe knew what was happening. When Lilabeth's form cleared, it wasn't the dark muse who stood before her, but instead herself, as if Isaboe were looking into a mirror.

"Keep this one alive until I return," the shapeshifter taunted. "Since Connor is in the realm, we know he'll come after you." A slow, wicked smile pulled up the muse's dark lips. "And I'm in need of a new toy."

"You leave my family alone!" Isaboe screamed futilely.

"You're not in a position to demand anything, but don't worry. I'll take good care of him," she snickered. Tossing her hair, Lilabeth blew Isaboe a kiss and disappeared.

CHAPTER 25

DEATH, FIRE, AND MAGIC

"You should be grateful to Lilabeth," Lorien scoffed after Isaboe's doppelganger had disappeared. "She has just spared your grandson's life… for the moment."

It was all unraveling. The mission to save Gabriel would be a one-way trip, and no one would escape unscathed. With the acknowledgement of her failure came the weight of guilt. But at the same time, as odd as it seemed, a wave of warmth pulsed through her, leaving serenity in its wake. It was as if admitting defeat—even only to herself—had freed her from the fear and panic that had taken up residence in her chest. *Maybe this is the calm that precedes death,* she thought. Soon it would all be over.

"Now, I'll finally have revenge against Nicholi and the council." Lorien took a celebratory drink as she watched her plans coming to fulfillment. "They'll beg for my mercy," the queen hissed. She then began to pace the room, moving in-and-out of Isaboe's frozen sightline. "I'll make my brother pay for putting *Alaina,*" she spat the name as if it left a bad taste in her mouth, "a mortal woman on *my* throne." When Lorien turned to face her captive, her beautiful face twisted hideously with each threat. "I'll make all of them pay for their disrespect," she snarled.

As another ripple of warmth passed through her, Isaboe wondered at her own ability to be so at-ease with her captive state. With the next wave of heat, Isaboe began to realize what was happening. The blue amulet was sending out its own magic! It pulsed through her body, tingling just beneath the surface of her skin. As the feeling intensified, she became keenly aware of something more. She felt the invisible bindings that Lorien had used to anchor her to the floor beginning to loosen.

"Everyone loved her," Lorien whined as she paced and her gait had become more relaxed, hinting at just how assured of victory she had become. "'Alaina is so beautiful and kind,' they said, all the while, turning their backs on me—their true queen!"

As Lorien continued her spiteful tirade, Isaboe's focus turned inward to the amulet's growing power. Magic radiated out of it and danced across her skin. But then a slight movement out of the corner of her eye caught Isaboe's attention, and she followed it to where Petrina lay bleeding against the wall. Their eyes met, although Petrina's were distant and glassy. As if she had been waiting for this moment, the fey slowly opened her fist.

The Ring of Odin was in Petrina's hand!

Isaboe's gaze flashed back to where Lorien was still pacing the room, ranting about disrespect and her unchallenged power. She could see that the pocket of Lorien's gown was torn, but the queen had not noticed it. This new revelation gave Isaboe hope, and she could feel it mingling with and strengthening the power of the amulet, dissolving the last binds of Lorien's spell and freeing her completely. Being careful to hold the same trapped pose, Isaboe took the first opportunity to inconspicuously lift her foot, and found that her feet were no longer anchored to the floor as they had been. With this awareness, a renewed wave of strength and fortitude replaced her fear. The words of the Mundahli replayed in her head; *"You are a strong mortal woman, stronger than you think you are. You also carry faerie blood in your veins. Have faith in both of those attributes when the road ahead gets bumpy."*

Suddenly, the door to Lorien's chambers flew open and a guard rushed in.

"How dare you barge into my—!"

"The borders are burning, Your Highness!" the guard interrupted. "Look out your window!"

Isaboe watched disbelief flash across Lorien's face as she rushed toward the windows of her chamber and ripped aside the heavy dark curtains. Instantly, an eerie orange glow filled the room. When she saw smoke and fire blanketing the horizon, Lorien shielded the light with her hand and took a step back.

"What? How is this possible? Who is responsible for this?" The queen shouted hysterically as she stared out the window in horror.

Now was her moment and Isaboe took it. Free of the invisible ties, she scampered to Petrina's side. Up close, she could hear how weak the young fey's breathing had become. They made momentary eye-contact, just long enough for Isaboe to accept the ring from Petrina's weak fingers. With the Ring of Odin now safely on her own finger, Isaboe watched Petrina let the last breath slip past her lips as life left her body.

Though it tugged at her heart, Isaboe knew she had no time to grieve. Scrambling toward the door, she grabbed the wrist strap holding her communication stone off the table before slipping out of Lorien's chambers. As Isaboe sprinted at full force down the hallway, she could hear the chaotic echo of the servants' panic, and it reminded her of the frightening confusion during the trolls' attack in Sashtonia.

She didn't know where she was, but Isaboe recalled that the guards had dragged her up many stairs before they reached Lorien's chambers. She knew that she had to go down, but had no idea which direction would take her to a stairwell. Darting through the hallway, she slowed when she saw the heated glow of firelight piercing the dark through an opening in the wall ahead, and she stopped to take a look.

Red and yellow fingers of fire surrounded the castle, devouring everything in its path. The trees were all ablaze, crackling and snapping beneath the ferocious flames that engulfed the green timbers in a blazing furor. With a roar, the flames raced across the courtyard of Lorien's stronghold as if pushed by a mighty wind. The heat was so intense that Isaboe held up her hand, squinting between her fingers to watch the destruction. Through the fire and smoke, a figure began to take shape. Massive, as large as the very towers themselves, the figure let loose another roar, and the flames parted to reveal a magnificent dragon. As she stared in amazement, the dragon sent another searing stream of fire out of its enormous mouth, torching the ground beneath it. Swooping across the sky, two more dragons came into view, sending down their own streams of fire in spears of red, yellow, and purple, engulfing everything in their inferno.

As boiling smoke erupted in the center of the flames, Isaboe stared incredulously when she saw another figure flapping its way through the smoky haze. But this was a more familiar beast, and Isaboe recognized the battle eagle and the Jarcadian warrior upon its back, their armor gleaming in the firelight. Through the smoke came another, two, three, four eagles, until Isaboe lost count as the air around the castle filled with the screams of eagles and the roar of dragons. Within seconds, a battle had unfolded before her as the beasts darted and dodged the arrows slung at them by Lorien's guards below.

The Jarcadian warriors had come to rescue her, despite what the council might have decided. *But wait… where is he?* Isaboe anxiously searched the chaos, but her darting glances couldn't find what she was looking for. "Where is he?" she verbalized her fearful thought aloud. But she didn't have to worry for long, for coming through the rolling smoke, another form took shape. Though smaller and darker than a Shekar, it was a flying horse dodging the projectiles being hurled from below with ease. Even from a distance, Isaboe could see the cocky confidence with which its rider managed his steed, and Connor appeared as a beacon of hope in the middle of hopelessness and terror. Once again, he'd come for her.

"Connor!" Isaboe screamed out the window, but he was too far away to hear as the roar of the flames and the battle drowned out her cries.

"Isaboe!" bellowed Lorien from far too close, her voice echoing down the dark hallway, bringing with it a new rush of panic. Knowing she had to get out of the castle, and preferably somewhere high and visible, she ran until she found an open breezeway which connected two high towers. After rushing out into the open night air, she slowed to look for a black flying horse. Isaboe's efforts were thwarted when she had to quickly jump out of the way of a burning tree which crashed down onto the breezeway, sending out sparks and burning embers. The fire was so intense that she had to shield her face from the heat with her dress as she inched her way out, trying to see anything through the smoke and burning debris.

"Connor!" she screamed out again but knew her cries would never reach his ears in all this chaos. *How could he be so close and yet so far away?* Even in the midst of the battle, Isaboe had to acknowledge the irony of that thought. How many times had she and Connor almost lost each other? Would this be the one time they wouldn't make that crucial connection? Lorien was right behind her, and there wasn't much time left. He had to come now before it was too late.

"This isn't over." When Lorien's voice came from behind, Isaboe spun around to face the queen. She looked enraged by the light of the fire, the flames dancing in her manic-stricken eyes. "When I have possession of Kaitlyn, I'll rebuild Euphoria, and it will be much grander than ever before."   .

"You will never have Kaitlyn!" Isaboe shouted, feeling a strange sense of confidence and courage as she faced the queen. "I'll never let you get your murdering hands on my daughter!" She felt more hatred for Lorien than she'd ever felt before, and the amulet inside her fueled and amplified this emotion. The warmth pulsing through her this time gave Isaboe a new surge of strength to face the queen. The amulet, she thought with a sort of distant amazement, was much more powerful than she had ever realized.

"Oh, but it's as if I already do, so I don't need you anymore!" the queen sneered as she thrust her hand toward Isaboe, sending a bolt of energy that knocked her over uncomfortably close to the burning branches of the fallen tree. Scrambling to her feet, Isaboe ran toward the railing as she frantically searched the sky. *Now would be a good time, Connor!*

"I should have killed you long ago," Lorien sneered, stalking in her direction. "But I didn't expect you to be so resilient."

Turning to face the Fey Queen, Isaboe shouted, "That is one thing you are right about, Lorien! I am resilient, and I don't give in easily, especially when it's my family you are threatening!"

The Fey Queen poised her hand to toss another spell, but Isaboe had had enough. Feeling another surge of warmth emanate from the amulet in her chest, she was keenly aware of the magic growing inside of her. Extending her arm toward the queen, she shouted, *"No more!"* As the words left her mouth, Isaboe watched a blue bolt arch out from the amulet in her chest and connect to the Ring of Odin on her finger, just before the magic exploded out of her hand toward Lorien.

Hit by Isaboe's unexpected bolt of magic, the Fey Queen was ripped from her feet and flung backward. The impact knocked Lorien halfway back into the castle as she slammed into the wall behind her with a hard crash.

Stunned by her own power and not entirely certain how she had accomplished it, Isaboe almost didn't hear a voice calling out to her over the ringing in her ears.

"Isaboe!" Connor shouted as he flew by on the back of the sleek black wallabock before he banked to make another pass. "Jump out and I'll catch ye!" he shouted.

Isaboe saw the light of the fire reflected in the steed's fear-filled eyes as its rider struggled to keep the animal under control. When she made the mistake of looking down at the blazing ground far beneath her, she knew that if Connor missed her, the fall would kill her before she was consumed by the flames. "I can't jump! You'll have to land!" she shouted. Glancing over her shoulder, she saw Lorien soaring toward her with elegant wings spread wide, and the queen wore a look that promised vengeance. A bolt of panic shot through Isaboe, jolting her into action, and she stepped up onto the railing.

"Jump now!" Connor shouted again as soon as she was in position, and this time Isaboe didn't hesitate. Leaping off the railing, she threw herself into the night sky, hoping this dangerous choice wouldn't be her last.

"*Oomph!*" The air was thrust out of her lungs as she made abrupt contact with the horse's back, landing directly in front of Connor.

"I've got ye!" he said as Isaboe grabbed onto the wallabock's mane. She let out a small scream when the animal dropped with the sudden additional weight, but it quickly adjusted. After Connor pulled Isaboe tightly against his chest, she swung her legs over the animal's back.

"Watch out!" she screamed again when Lorien thrust a ball of glowing energy at them. Jerking on Sonas's reins, Connor banked hard to the right, and Isaboe felt the sizzle of magic on her skin as Lorien's spell brushed by, barely missing them.

Her wings spread wide, the queen dove through the fire-riddled night sky, her blonde hair and dark robe blowing behind her as she continued her attack. But the agile wallabock maneuvered easily through the burning debris and Lorien's flaming balls of magic. Isaboe anxiously watched as her enemy grew closer, until the limb of a burning tree dropped down in front of the queen, forcing her to quickly bank to the right or be struck by the flaming branch. She screamed once more, wordless and threatening, but when Isaboe could next see Lorien, her wings were carrying her away from them; away from the castle and the blazing inferno.

"Hold on!" Connor shouted. "We've got to get out of this hellfire!"

"Not without Gabriel!" Isaboe shouted, clinging to Connor as the horse dipped and dodged the burning debris.

"Where is he?"

But when Isaboe tried to determine which way led to Baba Denova's cottage, all she could see was fire and devastation. "I...I don't know. There's too much fire and smoke everywhere!"

"Then we're outta here!" Connor shouted. "Hold on!"

When Sonas banked hard to the right, Isaboe squeezed her eyes shut. She didn't want to see how far above the land she was, or the flames and destruction on the ground below her. Leaning back against Connor's chest, she struggled with a mixture of feelings warring for dominance. Once again, she had been lucky enough to survive an encounter with the queen and was feeling safe in the protection of Connor's arms, but Gabriel had not been rescued and Petrina was dead. To make matters worse, back in the mortal world Anna was on her way to meet Lilabeth to turn over Kaitlyn. Yes, Isaboe may have thwarted death at Lorien's hand one more time, but at what cost? Feeling the tears of failure burning down her cheeks, she dreaded having to face Connor with this new information when his flying horse finally landed.

CHAPTER 26

RESCUED

Though she was safely nestled against Connor's chest as he held the wallabock's reins, Isaboe's thoughts were clouded with grief by the fact that she hadn't been able to save Gabriel from the fire, and the fear she might lose Kaitlyn too. Keeping her head down, she quietly brushed away the tears that would not stop. Somewhere between Euphoria and Sashtonia, the rhythmic roll of Sonas's muscles finally eased her into a restless tear-filled sleep. As the flying horse began its descent and Connor's weight shifted, Isaboe awoke from her midnight ride. "Are we there?"

"Yeah, hold on," Connor said as he banked Sonas to the left, swooping down toward one of the many glittering rooftops of the Sashtonia castle.

Glancing around, Isaboe could see a thin pink line on the horizon; the sun was rising. The battle and their escape had lasted long into the night, but the dawning of a new day did not lighten her guilt. Her heart was aching, and the agony of her failure and regret hit Isaboe like a punch to the gut.

When the wallabock touched down, Connor slipped off and then reached up for Isaboe, but she could read the disappointment on his face. Quickly averting her gaze, she kept her eyes on the ground and didn't immediately see the people running in her direction.

"Isaboe!" Rosalyn shouted, and a moment later, Isaboe was pulled into her mother's embrace. "Oh, thank God you're alright!" Drawing back, Rosalyn took a quick look at her daughter. "Are you alright?"

Isaboe only nodded, but she couldn't maintain eye contact and dropped her head in shame. "I couldn't save him, Rosalyn," she finally said as her confession unleashed another torrent of tears. Lifting her head, she looked at her mother through blurred vision, letting the pain in her heart flood out. "I had him in my arms! I held him, but I couldn't save him!"

"What are you talking about?" Rosalyn asked.

"Gabriel! He died in the fire! I couldn't save him!" The grief tearing at Isaboe's heart almost brought her to her knees. Her agonized cries stirred those around Rosalyn to action, and the small figure of a woman was shuffled forward. Through her teary vision, Isaboe could see a little bundle in the short woman's arms.

"Miss Isaboe! Oh, thank the Goddess; it is good to see you!"

"Baba Denova?" Isaboe gasped incredulously as she stared at the short round elf in disbelief.

"I went to the carriage like Miss Petrina told me to, and we waited for a long while, but when the fire broke out, the driver took to the air before everything burned up." An apologetic look crossed the old elf's face. "I'm sorry we didn't wait. I was afraid we had left you to die in the fire."

"Oh, no, I'm so glad you didn't wait!" Startling the wrinkled-faced nanny, Isaboe planted a big kiss onto her forehead. "You did well, Baba Denova. Very, very well!"

"You see, Isaboe," Rosalyn whispered, wrapping her arm over her daughter's shoulders, "you didn't fail. You succeeded. You saved Gabriel!" Isaboe looked up at her mother and saw that she was beaming at her. *"You* did very, very well, my dear."

"Aye," Connor added, a hint of pride showing in his eyes as he took his place next to his wife and slipped his hand onto the small of her back. "And though we're still gonna have a little chat about yer decision to disappear without tellin' me," he muttered, unable to manage a disapproving scowl, "ye did succeed, my love, and for that, I am very proud of ye."

Through her tear-blurred vision, Isaboe saw the same approval reflected on the unfamiliar faces of the congregation that had formed around them, quietly observing their reunion. For one blissful moment, Isaboe allowed herself to bask in the praise, until the old elf asked, "But where is Miss Petrina?"

Isaboe was wracked with a wave of guilt as she thought about Petrina's brutal end. "Lorien killed her," she finally muttered, a mix of anguish and hatred lacing her words.

"And the Queen? Do you know what became of Lorien?" Brighid asked.

"No, she flew off during the fire." Turning her attention to the sleeping baby in Baba Denova's arms, she was relieved to see that at least Gabriel appeared healthy and completely unaware how close his little life had come to ending. Still lost in the whiplash between defeat and success, Isaboe released a whimpered giggle that seemed to intensify her tears. Going beyond what she thought herself capable of, she had succeeded, and that victory gave her a new sense of accomplishment.

But the moment was shattered when Rosalyn spoke again. "Let's take this little guy home," she said, taking the sleeping baby from Baba Denova, "and deliver him back to Anna."

"ANNA!" Isaboe was instantly pulled from her temporary illusion of success. "Anna is on her way with Kaitlyn to the standing stones!" she blurted. "She is going to make the trade for her son!"

"How do you know that?" Rosalyn asked as both she and Connor immediately followed Isaboe's mood swing.

"Just before the fire broke out, Lilabeth told Lorien that she had located Kaitlyn and Anna on the road to Glochmoor. Lilabeth will arrive at the ring of stones disguised as me so that Anna will give Kaitlyn to her! We have to stop her!"

"Well, then, what are we waitin' for?" Connor said. "Open that portal, Rosalyn, and let's go home!"

"It isn't that simple," Isaboe muttered, grabbing Connor's cloak. "I can't go back. Not yet."

"Why?" Connor and Rosalyn both asked.

"Because I have been entrusted with a prophecy!" Isaboe announced, almost hysterically, before pouring out the story to her mother. "There is a prophecy about a queen of mixed blood, of fey and mortal, who will rise up in the realm of the Underlings and become extremely powerful. It was first foretold that this leader would wreak havoc over all the world, and that she would bring about years of death and destruction. It was that prophecy that was used to cast Alaina—*your mother*—back into the mortal world before you were born. Alaina had been the Queen of Euphoria, Rosalyn! She was married to King Nicholi, Lorien's brother!"

"Yes, I know," Rosalyn confirmed. "When Lorien went to the council and told them of the prophecy, Nicholi was faced with either taking my life upon my birth or sending my mother out of this realm before I was born."

"You know?"

"Yes. I met Nicholi yesterday and he told me everything."

"Your father is alive?" Isaboe exclaimed.

Rosalyn nodded. "But what does the prophecy have to do with you not going back home?"

Casting her wide-eyed gaze from Rosalyn to Connor, Isaboe gathered her energy before answering. "Petrina begged me to go to Euphoria to help her unlock a vault deep beneath Lorien's castle. She said that the vault held a secret Lorien doesn't want the council to know. Petrina knew where Gabriel was, so she took me there first, and that is how I met this lovely elf," Isaboe cast a soft smile in Baba Denova's direction, "and I was able to hold Gabriel for the first time. As I had promised, I followed Petrina into the depths of Lorien's castle, and we found the vault that had been sealed by a blood lock—my blood. Lorien had taken it when I was first in Euphoria more than twenty years ago, and only my blood could unlock the vault."

"What was in the vault?" Connor asked.

"When Lorien brought me here twenty years ago, all the people of Euphoria thought I was Alaina. It was then that the prophecy changed."

"The prophecy changed?" asked a stranger standing among the assembled, who were all listening intently to her story.

"Yes," Isaboe continued. "The Mundahli told me..."

"The Keeper of the Knowledge?" Brighid interrupted. "She's still alive? You spoke with her?" The Fey Queen sounded shocked. "Where? When?"

"She was being held in the vault. The Mundahli told me that when she originally approached Lorien about the change in the prophecy, she insisted they inform the council, so Lorien tried to silence her. When she couldn't kill the Mundahli, the queen had her locked in the vault with the prophecy. She had been there all this time!"

"She was still alive?" Rosalyn asked, incredulously. "Even after being locked in a vault for twenty years?"

"Yes."

"Did she still have the prophecy?"

"She did, but she doesn't have it anymore."

This brought about a round of panicked muttering from the crowd. "Do you know what became of it?" she heard someone ask.

"And what does any of this have to do with you not coming back home right now?" Rosalyn pushed for an answer.

"This prophecy has the power to end Lorien's reign. The Mundahli told me that only I can deliver the prophecy. She placed it in the amulet and then made me the vessel."

"What do ye mean, she made ye the vessel?" Connor asked.

Grasping Rosalyn's hand, she placed it against her own chest. Locking stares with her mother, Isaboe could see the realization grow in Rosalyn's widening eyes. *"The amulet is inside of you!?"* she exclaimed.

"And to get it out, I have to go to someplace called the Grove of… of…" Isaboe closed her eyes, exhaustion driving the memory out of her grasp. "of Ragnee, or Ragnar, or something like that."

"Do you mean the Grove of Raghii?" asked an onlooker.

"Yes! The Mundahli said that only there can the amulet be removed and the prophecy be revealed." An audible hush fell over the crowd, and Isaboe noticed the suspicious looks they shot each other. "Does anybody know where this grove is?"

"From what I've heard, the Grove of Raghii lies in the center of the Harrow mountain range, on a peak called the Mountain of Ancestors." A tall, white-haired man with a matching beard spoke up as he stepped forward. "The grove is nestled inside this Mountain of Ancestors, but it's nearly impossible to reach."

Shooting a curious and somewhat annoyed look at the elderly man wearing a long dark robe and a scholarly presence, Isaboe wanted to shout at him; *What do you mean it's near impossible to reach? How is that supposed to help?* However, she swallowed her questions and her disrespect.

Fortunately, Rosalyn sensed her frustration. "Isaboe, I would like to introduce you to someone very important to all of us." Placing her hand on the crook of the older man's elbow, Rosalyn first offered him an appreciative smile before looking back at her daughter. "Isaboe, this is Demetrick."

It took a moment for Isaboe to place the name, but then it hit her like a bolt of lightning. "Demetrick, *the wizard?*" she asked, astonished. "I thought you were dead!"

"Aye, so did I," Connor agreed, placing a hand on the wizard's shoulder and giving him a crooked smile. "Apparently he's been hangin' out here all this time, just waitin' for us to show up."

"Since you've heard of it," Rosalyn interjected, turning toward the wizard, "do you know how to reach the Mountain of Ancestors?"

"It is considered inaccessible by man and fey alike. From what I know, the Mountain of Ancestors is surrounded by a wasteland that is rugged and unforgiving. And the air at the peak is so hot and tainted that it's unbreathable. It's near impossible to make it all the way to the Grove of Raghii alive."

"Then how do ye ken it even exists?" Connor asked.

"Because the Mundahli told me to go there!" Isaboe almost shouted. "She said it's the only place I can have the amulet removed from my body!" Feeling her anxiety threatening to choke off her breath, she placed a hand on her chest. "It has to exist."

"What is the Grove of Raghii?" Rosalyn asked.

Before answering, Demetrick held all three of their anxious stares. "The story is that centuries ago there lived a very enlightened fey named Boggle Raghii who traveled both our worlds, questioning everything in his attempt to understand all things. One night he had a dream that a very important message waited for him at the top of the Mountain of Ancestors, and though no one had ever been able to survive the journey, he was determined to discover what the message was. He set out on his own toward the great mountain, but once he was halfway there—cut, bleeding, and barely able to breathe due to the foul air—he began to doubt he would ever make it to the top. So, he shouted his frustration to the universe, and the gods answered. According to the legend, a great firebird came down from the heavens and flew Boggle Raghii to the peak, taking him through a ring of fire. When he arrived on the other side, Raghii found a grove of trees where none should be able to grow, and the trees spoke to him."

"The trees spoke?" Connor questioned. "What was the message?"

"No one knows. When Boggle Raghii returned, his once brown hair had turned completely white, and he said that the message was meant only for him. But whatever message he had received from the trees, it apparently had answered all of his questions. He never traveled again. It seemed that at long last, Boggle Raghii had finally found peace in his search for knowledge and enlightenment. For many years he shared his wisdom with others, until one day he rose for his morning walk and never came back. It was assumed that he had died."

"Well, unless ye have a firebird, how do we get Isaboe to the top of that mountain?" Connor asked. "Could Sonas or a battle eagle manage it?"

Demetrick only shook his head. "No. The tainted air brings them down; it has been tried before."

"Well, maybe a battle eagle can't make it, but I'm sure a dragon could," Rosalyn said with a confident smile. "You can't get much closer to a firebird than a dragon."

"Hmm," Demetrick replied. "You might be on to something." He paused and gave Rosalyn a knowing smile. "And I think you're just the person to ask for that help."

As Rosalyn looked up at the sky, the early morning sun glittering gold, Isaboe followed her mother's gaze. Soaring high above in a graceful dance were three dragons. They must, Isaboe realized, be the same dragons that had besieged Lorien's kingdom.

"Yes, I'm sure Norvik will be willing to help us again," Rosalyn said casually.

Looking back down, Isaboe stared at Rosalyn in disbelief. "You're on a first name basis with a—*a dragon?*" she asked, astonished. "This just keeps getting more and more bizarre!"

"I'll make arrangements with Norvik to take Isaboe and Connor to the Grove of Raghii, and then I'll go to intercept Lilabeth," Rosalyn said, blithely ignoring her daughter's shock. Still cradling Gabriel with one hand, she extended her other. "Let me have the ring of Odin so that I can reopen the portal to the mortal world."

"Wait," Connor interjected as Isaboe handed the ring to her mother. "From what ye told us, that portal will only open from where we left—at yer home. If Lilabeth wasn't lying, and Anna has already left with Kaitlyn on her way to Glochmoor, then ye'll be hard pressed to catch her. It's almost a full day's ride from your home to the standing stones."

"I hadn't thought about that," Rosalyn confessed.

"Maybe I can help," Demetrick added. "May I see the ring?"

Rosalyn placed the ring in the wizard's palm, and he looked upon it with reverence. "It's been a while since I've held this. I'm sure King Odin had no idea when he commissioned these rings that at some point in the future one of them would play such a large part in protecting the prosperity of our worlds." Looking into the faces watching him, Demetrick met them all with a confident smile. "Let see if I can change these coordinates."

Demetrick casually tossed the ring into the air, but instead of falling to the ground, it stayed suspended, hovering in front of him. Gesturing with his hands and mumbling unfamiliar words, the wizard began to weave his magic. In seconds, where there had once been only a ring, now hovered the portal, the same one Isaboe, Connor, and Rosalyn had passed through only days before.

As they peered through the portal and into the human realm on the other side, a familiar landscape took shape. "Isn't that a view of the canyon? And there's my garden!" cried Rosalyn as Demetrick manipulated the position of the portal, and therefore, the view surrounding it.

"Very pretty place, Rosalyn," praised the wizard.

Staring in awe, Isaboe saw what looked like a small circular view around the portal, as if she were looking through a round window on a frosty day, and she couldn't deny the view of Rosalyn's home on the perimeter. Part of her wanted to jump through the portal right now, back to the mortal world and go after her daughters, but she had another important duty and would have to let Rosalyn handle Lilabeth.

"Now, where did you say the meeting place was?" Demetrick asked.

"The Standing Stones of Glochmoor."

"South of Edinburgh?"

"Yes."

The wizard glanced skyward in deep thought and scrunched his brow in concentration before he began to mutter once again. As Demetrick swept his hands to the right, the view beyond the portal began to move.

Slowly at first, and then faster, the landscape sped past their portal, seemingly flying them across the Scottish countryside.

Their strange journey lasted for nearly a minute, and then the velocity began to slow before coming to a complete stop. "There," Demetrick announced, "that will put you in a better position."

With her mouth slightly agape, Rosalyn stared at the wizard, and he smiled at her shocked expression. "I've learned a few things since we were last together."

"I see that!" Rosalyn exclaimed. Then, she turned her attention to Queen Brighid. "Would you be interested in joining me? I wouldn't mind the back-up."

A satisfied grin crossed the queen's face. "I've lost two good commanding officers to that black-hearted muse." She took a step closer. "Nothing would please me more."

"Thank you, my queen," Rosalyn said before addressing Isaboe. "Why don't you two get something to eat while I arrange for your ride to the Mountain of Ancestors. And please, don't worry about Kaitlyn." Rosalyn grasped Isaboe's hand and squeezed it reassuringly. "We'll make sure that Lilabeth and Lorien do not get their hands on her. They will be no match for two pissed-off royal fey," Rosalyn jested, but Isaboe knew the whimsy she heard in her mother's voice was only to cover her own anxiety.

"I'm not worried," Isaboe replied, and somehow saying the words aloud made them feel true. Noticing that the amulet was radiating a warm feeling from her center, it seemed to be confirming their success. Considering what she had been through in the last few hours—feeling certain that her and Gabriel's deaths were at hand—Isaboe found the contrast almost humorous. "No, I'm not worried, Mother. I know you two can handle this," she said assuredly.

CHAPTER 27

A MOMENT OF HONESTY

"I must speak with Norvik," Rosalyn said as she glanced to the sky before dropping her gaze back to Isaboe. "Brighid and I will return after Kaitlyn and Gabriel are both safe. Be careful, and good luck." With her departing words, Rosalyn placed the baby into Brighid's arms and then walked toward the railing. Waving her hands in the air, Rosalyn drew the dragon's attention. Looking slightly uncomfortable while cradling the mortal child in her arms, Queen Brighid followed Rosalyn to the railing.

"Come on," Connor coaxed gently. "When was the last time ye ate, love?" After leading Isaboe through the open palace doors, they walked at a sedated pace toward the dining hall. As their footsteps echoed off the stone floor in the deserted foyer, now void of the citizens who had filled it the day before, she thought about how everything had changed in such a short amount of time. Yesterday, Queen Brighid had criticized her in front of the entire congregation for leaving her child back in the mortal world, unprotected. Now, Isaboe had a distinct purpose for being in the realm of the Underlings, and that validation was both grounding and intimidating.

"Alright, I'm not mad," Connor uttered, calmly breaking the silence, but by the tone of his voice, Isaboe knew a lecture was coming. "Still, I can't help but wonder just what the hell ye were thinkin' when ye wandered off by yerself." With his hands on his hips and a stern pull to his lips, he stopped to face her.

"I thought you said you weren't mad."

"Well, maybe I am, just a wee bit. Do ye have any idea of how close ye came to dying?"

"Of *course* I do! I experienced it!" Isaboe snapped back, distantly aware how their voices echoed loudly in the empty corridor.

"Ye put yer life at risk, Isaboe! And Gabriel's! Ye didn't tell anyone where ye were goin'. That was reckless and foolish."

"A moment ago, you were proud of me. Now you're chastising me?"

"I *am* proud o' ye! But that don't mean yer decision to leave without me wasn't stupid!"

"*Stupid?*" Stunned and insulted, Isaboe shouted back, "Just moments after we arrived in this strange land, you left me to go rescue Nyia! And then you left me again when you went off to fight the trolls!"

"*But I knew where ye were!* We talked about it before I left ye with Klute!"

"No, we didn't! You *told* me what we were going to do. You didn't give me a choice. You left us in a foreign land with a strange man whose language we couldn't speak!"

"That was different. We'd talked about where we would meet up."

"I didn't have time to wait for you to return so we could talk about it!" she shouted. "Petrina was leaving, and the castle was going into lockdown. I had to make an instant decision!"

"But, Isaboe, I dinnae have any idea where ye were!" Connor shouted back. "When I returned and ye were nowhere to be found, I was sure this would be the time I couldna save ye. I had to prepare for the worst. After all the times I saved yer life back in the mortal world, I was sure I had finally lost ye in this crazy place!" Connor ran his hands through his hair and closed his eyes, then took a long cleansing breath. When he finally looked at her and took a step forward, softening the scowl on his face, Isaboe could see that his blue eyes were rimmed with emotion. "There's only a few times I've truly been afraid, and I honestly thought I'd lost ye this time." As he placed his hands on the sides of her face, Isaboe saw that Connor's eyes were glistening with moisture, and it softened her anger. "*Breagha*, you are my reason for livin'. If I lose ye, I got nothin."

Hearing the panic in his voice, Isaboe gently took her husband's hands, holding them in front of her, and she could feel that they were trembling. "Connor, I'm sorry that I frightened you, but I had no choice. When the Mundahli placed this amulet inside of me, I knew then that I was meant to come on this mission." The amulet pulsed warmly, reassuringly in her chest. "I originally thought I was coming along because I couldn't risk losing you to this place, but now I know it was more than that. I was meant to be here."

The image of Petrina's crumpled body bleeding out on Lorien's fine carpets flashed before her eyes, overlaying the amulet's warmth with a new, very personal sense of determination. "Petrina died trying to help me. She died to save her people. I really *am* the Chosen One, and I owe it to Petrina to see that her sacrifice means something. I have to deliver the prophecy that will bring Lorien down, and you've been chosen to protect me." Tilting her head to the side, Isaboe gave Connor a soft grin. "So, soldier boy, are you up for the job? Are you ready to finish this with me?"

Connor seemed more than a little surprised by her confidence, but his crooked smile suggested he rather liked it. "Aye, Ma'am, and I'm ready." Pausing, he studied her face before continuing, "Ye seem different, *Breagha*. Do ye feel alright?" he asked as he gently touched the cut on her swollen lip.

But Isaboe didn't flinch. She'd all but forgotten about the slap and bruised lip Lorien had given her. The truth was, she did feel stronger and more confident as another wave of warm conviction washed through her, confirming the theory. "I do feel different, and I'm sure it has something to do with this," she said, placing her hand on her chest. "The amulet is lending me its strength. But once this is over and I've completed my task, it has to go. No matter how much strength and courage I'm currently experiencing, it's a foreign fey object, and it doesn't belong inside of me."

After having dined, they met Demetrick back on the castle roof-top, along with the most magnificent creature Isaboe had ever laid eyes upon.

The massive dragon took up more than half of the landing platform. Running the length of the creature's back, from the top of its huge head to its pointed tail, were thick blue and green scales as big as a warrior's shield. The rising sun reflected off of them in pools of green-blue light, casting thousands of tiny dancing rainbows all around them. The dragon's dark heavy-lidded eyes made its piercing gaze appear lethal. Out of its flaring nostrils, small puffs of smoke appeared intermittently, but it was the row of razor-sharp teeth in the creature's mouth that sent a shiver down Isaboe's spine. She was quickly distracted by a foreign object which marred the dragon's beauty. Anchored to the dragon's back just in front of his wing-joints, a carriage had been stripped of its wheels and hastily fitted for the journey.

"He's rather spectacular, isn't he?" Demetrick asked mildly, stepping up beside the couple. "Connor, Isaboe, this is Lord Ruz-Zambia. He has graciously agreed to take you to the Mountain of Ancestors." At Demetrick's introduction, the dragon turned its giant head toward them and nodded before grunting his greeting.

The wizard chuckled at the mortals' reaction and then spoke again. "I hope you found something to eat. Was the cook still in the kitchen?"

Awestruck, Isaboe only nodded. "Yeah, we grabbed a bite," Connor muttered, still staring at the dragon. "So, we're gonna ride that thing?"

"Yes," the wizard replied. "But just because the dragon can make the flight without passing out from the heat and fumes doesn't mean the two of you can."

"Well, we certainly can't arrive at the Mountain of Ancestors unconscious," Isaboe said, pointing out the obvious. "How do we prevent that?"

"Come along and I'll show you." Demetrick gestured as he began to stroll toward the railing. It was then that Isaboe noticed two dragon scales leaning up against the handrail, casting their blue-green rainbows in the sunlight. When the wizard picked one up, Isaboe saw that the slightly irregular round-shaped scale was almost as tall as he was. But when he handed it to her, she was surprised at how light it was, considering its size. Mounted on the inside of the scale was a makeshift handle. "When you arrive at the ring of fire, cover yourselves with these scales and you should be able to pass through the flames unscathed."

"Did these scales come off this dragon?" Connor asked, but then quickly corrected. "Uh, I mean, Lord Ruz…uh…?"

"It's Lord Ruz-Zambia, and yes, he willingly offered these scales to protect you from the heat. But they will do nothing to protect you from the tainted air. Apparently, he has made the journey to the Grove of Raghii before, which is fortunate."

Demetrick then reached into his pocket and pulled out a small bottle. Holding it up, Isaboe could see that it held a number of transparent miniature balls, shimmering and dancing inside the clear jar.

"What are these?" she asked.

"When the air starts to become unbreathable, just pop one of these balls into your mouth, and when you bite down, you'll receive a burst of fresh air. But they don't last long, and I don't know how long your flight will be, so use them sparingly," Demetrick said, handing the bottle to Connor.

"When do we leave?" Connor asked, stashing the bottle into the inside pocket of his jacket.

"Immediately," The wizard gestured toward the dragon. "After you, my lady."

Isaboe stared hard at the dragon before glancing at Connor and Demetrick, who both gestured that she should make the first move. "Well then, let's do this," she announced, with more confidence than she felt.

More than anything, Isaboe wanted this whole experience to be over. She wanted desperately to return to her own world, to hold and protect her child while living a simple mortal life. However, something inside told her that even when this task was completed, and she and Connor were finally back where they belonged, life would never be simple and normal again. Being The Chosen One was not a passing event, nor was motherhood, especially for the mother of a gifted child.

Chapter 28

The Grove of Raghii

Although the carriage was comfortable, the air was warm, and she was safely snuggled up against Connor, Isaboe still felt her fear fighting for dominance. She did not like flying, whether it be on the back of a battle eagle, a winged-horse, or a dragon.

She avoided looking down at the scenery passing far below them and instead let her head rest on Connor's shoulder. She fixed her gaze on the pointed tips of the dragon's ears and the way they bobbed up-and-down with each flex of the beast's great wings.

For the most part, she and Connor had both been silent, each lost in their own thoughts. But it wasn't just the act of flying that caused Isaboe's stomach to bubble with nervous fear; she could feel the amulet hot and weighty in her chest. It had to be removed so the prophecy could be revealed, but the manner by which this would be accomplished had been left undefined. What would happen when she entered the Grove of Raghii? Would it be painful to have the fey object removed? The Mundahli's magic had sent out hot tingling waves of energy when the amulet was embedded in her chest. As odd and uncomfortable as it had been, Isaboe couldn't say that it had been extremely painful. Perhaps, she thought with forced optimism, removal would be the same.

With her head still resting on his shoulder, Isaboe slipped her hand into Connor's and tried to focus on the rhythmic beat of the dragon's wings, rather than replaying her fears over and over in her head. The flapping of the creature's great wings sounded different from those of the battle eagle with more gliding between each mighty flap. Gradually she found the gliding through the air to be somewhat soothing and let her eyes slide shut against the bright white of the clouds.

As soon as her eyes were closed, Isaboe's mind conjured Petrina's lifeless body lying on the floor of Lorien's chambers. She shuddered as she tried to push the image away by refocusing on the sound of Norvik's wings. The sound reminded her of the wind caught up in a ship's sails as it blew the canvas taut and thrust the vessel forward. She was intimately familiar with that sound, as she and her friends had often gone to the Port of Glasgow to watch the ships coming and going. A bustling port city, Glasgow had been her home at one time. It was a city full of flavor and culture where ships came and went at all times of the year, bringing fascinating people, exotic spices, and fine fabrics.

Though it seemed only a few short years ago that she had lived there with her previous family—a now-deceased husband and two young children—in reality, it was a lifetime ago. Then, her life had been simple, consisting of tea socials, gossiping about recent events with her equally affluent friends, and concerning herself only with her family and worldly comforts. Although Isaboe no longer saw herself the same and knew she would never go back to that lifestyle, part of her longed for the simplicity she had known then. "Connor," she said, lifting her head to meet his eyes. "Do you think we'll ever have a normal life again?"

When he turned to look at her, the compassion Isaboe saw on his face was sincere and full of affection. He brushed her hair away from her eyes before he answered. "Of course, we will, my love. After this is all over, and we're back home with our daughter, this crazy adventure will be just a memory, and we'll have that simple normal life. I promise."

Isaboe could have gotten lost in the reassuring crinkle of his eyes, and she gave him half a smile for his optimistic words, but she knew this was a promise he couldn't keep. Neither of them really believed that life would ever be simple or normal again. And what new challenges would they have to face as their daughter grew and her magical abilities continue to surface? But that was all secondary. Terrified as she may be, they first had to survive this mission. Even with Connor at her side, Isaboe felt her heartbeat quicken at the unknown that lay ahead. "What if I can't do this?" she asked at last, shame coloring her words. She wished for another wave of her earlier confidence, but none came. "Connor, I'm frightened."

As difficult as it was for her to admit this, it was refreshing to express the fear aloud.

Taking both of Isaboe's hands in his, Connor turned on the bench. When he again met her eyes, his compassion had hardened into intensity. "Ye can do this, Isaboe. And I'm gonna be right there beside ye, all the way."

"But—"

"No buts," he cut her off. "Ye're stronger than ye give yerself credit for, my love. My God, woman, ye just escaped the queen herself! And ye're not alone. I promise ye, *Breagha,* as long as I have breath to give or blood to spill, I'll die before I let anything or anyone ever hurt ye again. I will always and forever have yer back." His eyes silently searched hers. "Do ye trust me?"

"Of course, I trust you,' she confirmed, the words flowing out of her mouth without thinking. But they were true: Connor always had her back. He believed in her, and she would not let him down. His confidence ignited something in her, pushing her fear from the forefront of her mind. "I trust you with my life, my heart, and my soul."

"And that's a gift I promise never to take for granted," he whispered, just before he kissed her.

But their tender moment was short-lived when Norvik banked hard to the right and they were both thrown against the carriage wall with a gasp and a curse. Isaboe made the mistake of looking down and saw the ground rushing toward them, only a few hundred feet below. With a panicked shriek, she threw her arms around Connor's neck in a stranglehold as the unforgiving landscape came into view. The ground was covered with sharp spires of jagged black stone. Turning away, she buried her face in the collar of Connor's shirt, and he hugged her a little tighter.

When the dragon leveled off, flying low over the craggy rocks, Isaboe finally lifted her head to glance around, and that's when it hit her. Throwing a hand over her mouth and nose, she gasped, "Oh no, that smells awful!" Reeking of rot and defecation, the smell burned like acid in her nose, and tears welled up in her eyes.

Also grimacing from the smell, Connor reached into his jacket pocket and pulled out the small vile that Demetrick had given him. "Here." He shook one of the little crystalline pellets out into his hand and offered it to her.

The moment Isaboe bit into the pellet, she felt a burst of fresh air rush into her lungs, replacing the putrid smell. Connor did the same and then quickly put the vial back in his pocket to protect their meager stash. When Isaboe's attention was pulled toward a flicker of light ahead, she focused on a glowing red ring embedded into the side of a lone mountain rising up out of the rocky landscape. She noticed that the dragon was flying directly toward it, and she whispered with wonderment in her voice, "The Mountain of Ancestors."

"And the ring of fire," Connor confirmed her suspicion. Now that she knew what she was looking at, a new fear took hold when she realized that the dragon was on a direct course toward the tunnel of flames.

"*Oh my God!* Are we flying into *that?*" Isaboe stared as if hypnotized toward the circle of fire as it loomed ever closer like an angry red eye.

"That's what these are for." Connor reached behind the carriage where the two dragon scales were secured, but when Isaboe reached out to take her own, he quickly vetoed her action. "No. I want ye to squat down as low as ye can so I can cover us both."

When Isaboe opened her mouth to protest, a rush of hot putrid air hit the back of her throat, interrupting her complaint and causing her to double-over in a coughing fit.

"Here, take another." Connor said, pressing a second crystal into her mouth. The rush of fresh air left Isaboe gasping, and when she glanced up, she watched Connor taking his own clean breath before he turned to face the red ring of flames. It felt as if the mountain's glaring red eye was daring them to come closer. As its searing heat became more intense, Isaboe finally slipped down onto the carriage floor. Moving swiftly into position, Connor embraced Isaboe between his drawn-up knees and safely tucked her against his chest. He then held the two scales directly above them, boxing them into a confined, and hopefully, fireproof compartment.

Looking over her shoulder, Isaboe met Connor's wide blue eyes in the half-light of their compact little cave. His eyes glittered with the same anxious curiosity that Isaboe imagined must be in her eyes as well. But when the first flicker of flames became visible through their makeshift box and the temperature started to rise, the reality of their situation came crashing back down. "Do you think this carriage is fireproof?" she asked, hearing the edge of panic in her voice.

"Aye, I'm sure Demetrick thought o' that," he answered. But Isaboe had her doubts as the heat in the small box continued to increase, and beads of sweat broke out across Connor's forehead and upper lip as he focused on holding the dragon's scales over their heads. Taking a deep breath, Isaboe felt silently thankful that the beads of air were holding up through this trial. Determined to ride out the flames, she buried her nose against her collar, but after a few more uncomfortable minutes, the light from the flames shining through the cracks between the dragon scales began to dissipate, as did the scorching temperature. Connor lifted the scales just enough to peek out and then pushed up off the floor. Placing the scales back behind the bench, he reached out to help Isaboe to her feet.

When she rose and retook her seat next to Connor, what she saw was unlike anything she could have imagined, and the sight took her breath away.

Moments before, they had been flying through vile putrid air over the roughest terrain Isaboe had ever seen. But now she looked upon a paradise—truly a Garden of Eden—and the air smelled so sweet, as if it had just been washed in a crystalline-fresh mountain stream. "What a beautiful place!" she exclaimed. As if in agreement, Norvik began his descent toward the ground. After a gentle landing, the dragon took a few running steps before his forward momentum slowed enough to come to a stop. When Isaboe turned back toward the tunnel they had just flown through, it did look less menacing from this side, but she shivered to see the flames that continued to dance in the terrifying ring of fire.

Their dragon had brought them down in the center of a massive garden filled with a rainbow of flora, the likes of which Isaboe had never seen before. The sky above them was blue and open, but the view was limited by high mountain walls, a fortress formed by nature. Twisting and flowering vines hugged the walls as if reaching for the sun. When Isaboe looked closely to follow their trail, she noticed an abundance of dark round holes that dotted the walls inside of the mountain. Some were small, but others were larger; collectively they implied a rather impressive system of caves.

The sound of trickling water drew her attention to multiple ribbons of the crystal-clear liquid weeping through cracks in the craggy stone walls that encircled the utopia. Green moss grew along the moist edges of the rock wall where the water had formed small ponds, then continued down rocky waterfalls and into a lake that sparkled like a liquid emerald.

Beyond the lake, the land rolled out into a lush meadow that was encircled by a grove of small bushes and willowy vines. Towering over the fern-laden undergrowth and flowering foliage stood the three largest trees Isaboe had ever seen. Nearly as high as the mountain's jagged walls, their branches formed a dappled canopy over a hidden garden.

After hunching lower to the ground, the dragon turned his enormous spiked head to look closely at his passengers. Issuing a strange noise that sounded somewhere between a growl and a bark, the creature gestured with his giant head as one of his wings lengthened out to the side of his large body until the tip touched the ground, turning his webbed append-age into a ramp.

"I take it this is where we get off," Connor muttered as he assisted Isaboe from the carriage.

Upon boarding that morning, they had walked cautiously up the ramp to take their place on the makeshift saddle strapped to the giant beast's back, but it had been a truly awkward walk. Now, looking at her only way down to the ground, Isaboe was even less certain about dis-embarking. As she stared timidly at the loose webbing of the dragon's wing, she felt her anxiety spike. Even though the bony structure inside the wing's flesh made for a sturdy frame, she dreaded the steep descent to the ground.

Cautiously stepping out of the carriage, Isaboe forced herself to stand on the dragon's massive shoulder. Connor quickly stepped behind her, wrapping his arms around her waist before pulling her down to sit on his lap atop the spine of the wing. "I think there's only one good way to get down from here."

"*What!?* Oh my God! We're *sliding* down?" Realizing Connor's in-tention, Isaboe fought to escape his grip even as her husband scooted forward and pushed off.

With his arms holding her tightly against his chest, they slid and bobbed down the rubbery webbing of Norvik's wing, and though it wasn't as bad as she had feared, Isaboe still heard an occasional whimper pass her lips. But it was the whooping in her ear, *all the way down*, that made her realize that, to Connor, this was pure joy.

"Woo-hoo!" he shouted when they reached the bottom, ending their descent with a thump. Throwing his hands in the air, Connor shouted, "I'd like to do that again!"

Isaboe could see the wheels churning in his mind behind those wide excited eyes, but she assumed he was teasing and shook her head before pushing up off his lap. "Once was enough for me," she stated firmly, straightening her tossed skirts. Turning toward the magnificent creature, Isaboe gave Norvik a polite bow. "Thank you, Lord Ruz-Zambia, for delivering us safely."

"Yeah, thanks, old boy! That was exhilarating!" Connor exclaimed, and in Isaboe's opinion, with too much enthusiasm.

Norvik then folded his wing back against his body and began making giant strides toward the lake. Stepping into the water, he leaned his massive head forward to take a long drink. After apparently quenching his thirst, the colorful dragon hovered above the surface, staring intently at his own reflection. He turned his head one way, then the other, examining his image in the water.

But then Norvik suddenly drew his head up and opened his massive mouth, bellowing out a roar that vibrated through the air. Isaboe felt the quiver of the sound all the way to her bones. Yet it was what happened next—after the dragon's roar had echoed throughout the cavern walls— that had her clinging to Connor's arm.

Out of the multitude of holes covering the face of the rock wall, sets of amber eyes began to open one by one. Their escort's call had awoken more of his kind, and they streamed from the caves, filling the air with the awesome sound of their wingbeats and roars.

"It's a dragons' lair!" Connor exclaimed as they watched the sky fill with more and more of the beasts. The brilliant colors of their scales reflected in the broad swatch of sunlight they flew through, making the air sparkle with flashing rainbows. Isaboe stood mesmerized by the beauty of the sight when, over the cacophony, another roar filled the air, so loud that the ground shook and loosened stones at the top of the cavern to tumble down the face of the cliff. This appeared to be some kind of signal, as all the dragons immediately flew back into their caves and a silence fell over the garden paradise. The only sound Isaboe could hear was the bubbling water flowing into the ponds and the intensity of her own heartbeat. She shivered closer to Connor as he slid an arm around her shoulder.

But in the next second they heard heavy footfalls coming from some-where up above. "Look there." Connor pointed toward a particularly large cave at the top of the tower. From the darkness, a dragon began to emerge, and even in shadow, Isaboe could see how much larger it was than its peers. When the creature spread its wings and pushed off, it blocked the sun as it swooped low over the ground. Landing on the grassy meadow with a thud that shook the land, the dark-gray beast lifted its massive head and made eye contact with Norvik, who was standing on the opposite side of the lake. At first, the two gigantic dragons seemed to be taking measure of each other, and Isaboe wondered if Norvik could take the larger more muscular dragon, if it should come to a battle. But when he reached his long neck across the water and dropped his head in respect, the other dragon followed suit, touching its snout to the head of the newcomer. Rather than a confrontation, it appeared to be a greeting with a ritual consisting of bobbing heads, snorts, and grunts being exchanged between the two splendid creatures.

When both beasts simultaneously turned their fearsome gazes upon the two mortals, a shiver ran down Isaboe's spine, but then the larger dragon pushed up off the ground and flew back up to its cave. Landing on the platform, it then took a seat on the ledge, as if preparing to watch a show.

Turning his scaly head to the mortals, Norvik gestured for Connor and Isaboe to follow as he led the way around the lake toward the grassy meadow.

Grasping his wife's hand, Connor took the lead as they followed the dragon. When Isaboe glanced up at the towering black walls, she could see sets of amber eyes looking out of each one of the caves, all watching closely as the humans made their way through their garden below.

Finally coming to the center of the meadow, Norvik stopped and grunted, then made an intricate gesture before turning and walking back toward the lake. Lowering himself to the ground, he began to relax on the grassy bank, crossing his front legs and puffing out a small cloud of smoke from his large nostrils. He too seemed to be waiting for the show to begin.

CHAPTER 29

THE TREES OF KNOWLEDGE

"So, what do we do now?" Isaboe asked, almost in a whisper. But when she met Connor's wondering blue eyes, he could offer nothing but a shrug.

"Why don't you start with why you are here?" a deep voice suggested from somewhere high above.

Isaboe's head jerked about, looking for the speaker, but the limbs of the giant trees appeared empty. "Who said that?"

"Uh…Isaboe," Connor murmured in quiet awe. "Look up."

As she followed Connor's gaze up the trunk of the tree, what Isaboe saw made her gasp.

"Or you could start by introducing yourselves." This time, the voice was a woman's. Isaboe was looking up into an almost-human face formed of bark and knots, which sat about three-quarters of the way up the trunk, just below the canopy. As she watched flabbergasted, the tree's lips twisted into a smile.

"These trees really *do* talk!" Connor exclaimed with an astonishment that matched her own.

"Are you fey?" asked yet another voice, causing Isaboe's gaze to jump to an older man's face embedded into the wrinkled bark of a third giant tree.

Isaboe glanced between the three faces looking down at them before finally finding her voice, "No, we are not fey. We are mortal. My name is Isaboe, and this is Connor."

"Mortals?" asked the tree with the woman's face. "I don't believe a mortal has ever visited our garden before. What about you, Elm? Have you ever seen a mortal here before?"

"No, my dear Ash, I have not. There have been a few fey in my lifetime, but I have no memory of a mortal. Oak? You've been here the longest. Has a mortal ever visited our garden?"

The elderly face of the oak tree had heavily-lidded eyes, and his weighty gaze seemed to fix Connor and Isaboe where they stood, frozen in amazement. "No. But these mortals have quested far and overcome many obstacles to reach us, so their purpose here must be one of great importance." The oak tree's voice was deep and rich with age.

"You speak truly," the ash tree agreed. "Please tell us, Isaboe. What is your purpose here?"

Connor caught Isaboe's hand and squeezed it reassuringly. When she glanced at him, he offered an encouraging, if nervous, smile.

Isaboe swallowed hard before tearing her wide-eyed stare away from Connor. Dropping his hand, she took a few steps forward and lifted her eyes to meet the other-worldly faces above her. "I…I…" she paused to collect herself. "I mean, *we* are honored to be the first mortals to have the privilege of standing before you in your beautiful garden." Isaboe's voice was quivering with nerves, so instead of continuing to speak she offered a respectful curtsy.

Ash chuckled. "This one has manners. I like her," she teased warmly. Ash was smiling again, and Isaboe felt emboldened. "Please continue, my dear."

"Well, uh… as I've already mentioned, my name is Isaboe, and I am the Chosen One." The confidence with which she said those words surprised even Isaboe. Using that bit of self-assuredness, she spoke a bit louder and a bit bolder, feeling a fresh determination to complete this task, even as her heart was beating wildly. "I have been chosen to deliver an alternate prophecy, one that was magically placed in an amulet before being implanted within me." She touched the warm spot on her chest as she spoke. "I am here to have this amulet removed and the alternate prophecy revealed so that Lorien, the Queen of Euphoria, may be dethroned and removed from power." Isaboe was jittery with nerves as she waited for a response.

"My, that is a very hefty request," said Oak.

"May I ask who placed this amulet within you?" inquired Elm.

"And who instructed you to seek our help?" asked Ash.

"It was the Keeper of the Knowledge, the Mundahli, who both placed the amulet within me and instructed me to come here. She told me I could only have it removed at the Grove of Raghii and that doing so would reveal the prophecy. That is why we are here. Please, can you help us? *Will* you help us?"

The silence that followed left Isaboe wondering if she had said something wrong. As the trees stared down at her, she glanced nervously between their scrutinizing faces.

"The Grove of Raghii?" Elm questioned. "Is that what we are called by the fey?"

"I believe Raghii was the name of that fey visitor we had all those many years ago," said the ash tree.

"Yes, it was," confirmed Oak. "And I find it amusing, if not a bit arrogant, that he should name us after himself." The giant tree's canopy began to shake, as if a great wind had whipped it to life, and Isaboe realized that he was laughing. His massive branches fluttered with his amusement, causing a few leaves to float slowly to the ground.

"I am interested to know more about you," said Ash. "Tell us; how have you come to be the Chosen One? Why would a mortal be chosen to deliver a fey prophecy?"

"My grandmother, Alaina—a mortal woman—married Nicholi, the previous Fey King of Euphoria. They conceived a child, but before the child could be born, Lorien, Nicholi's sister, uncovered a prophecy. It forewarned that a leader born of mixed fey and mortal blood would rise up as a powerful ruler in the realm of the Underlings, and her reign would bring death and destruction to both worlds. When Lorien brought this to the attention of the council, my grandfather was forced to send my grandmother back into the mortal world before my mother could be born. That was when Lorien took the throne.

"However, in her lust for power, the queen realized that if she could take possession of the prophesied child, she could raise her as an heir and be empowered by the fulfillment of the prophecy. Though she tried, Lorien failed to take control of my mother, but now she is trying again with our daughter. Some years ago, I was brought to Euphoria against my will, and Lorien used me to create a special child—our daughter, Kaitlyn." Isaboe paused and gestured toward her husband. "Connor and I conceived Kaitlyn in this world, and Lorien manipulated the conception. Though we are both mortal, I carry the blood of my fey ancestors, and as a result, our daughter was born with fey magic.

"Even before Kaitlyn was born, Lorien did everything she could to take possession of her. So far, we have been able to prevent that. However, she kidnapped a human baby from my family, an innocent little boy named Gabriel. The queen was convinced that we would exchange Kaitlyn for him, but she was wrong. We found a way to come into this world to rescue Gabriel. Shortly after arriving here, I was told of an alternate prophecy, one which Lorien has kept hidden away for over twenty years. With help from Petrina, a brave young fey, I was able to open the vault and discovered not only the alternate prophecy but also the Keeper of the Knowledge, who had been locked away along with the prophecy. It was then that the Mundahli placed the prophecy into the amulet and embedded it into my body. She told me that I am the vessel now and instructed me to come here." Her mouth dry, Isaboe finally took a breath, and realized how unbelievable her story sounded, just how complicated the history of her family was. Now, she could only hope that the trees would offer a solution that would lead to the end of this long journey.

"It appears you really are the Chosen One," acknowledged Ash. "In more ways than one, it would seem."

"What became of the Mundahli?" asked Elm.

"I—I don't know. After embedding the amulet into my chest and instructing me to come here, she just vanished."

"I thought we hadn't seen her for some time," mused Oak. "So, she was being held prisoner and has sent her liberator to us."

"You know the Keeper of the Knowledge?"

The giant oak tree chuckled. "Where do you think she acquires the knowledge that she keeps?"

"From you?" Isaboe guessed.

"Correct, child," replied Ash. "That is why the Mundahli sent you to us. Combined, we hold the wisdom of our ancestors deep within our roots. From the seedlings that manage to sprout, surviving from sapling into full maturity, and producing yet another generation of seeds, we preserve the ancient memories of the trees embedded in our rings. Our ancestors have seen and experienced the beginnings of life, and only the strongest of us have managed to journey all the way here to live out our lives in this garden paradise."

"Then, will you please remove this amulet and reveal the prophecy?"

"Of course," answered Oak. "You have done very well in making it all this way, Isaboe. Your trials have been great, yet you met them bravely. You have earned the right to our knowledge." The mighty oak tree regarded Isaboe and Connor for a moment. "Are you ready?"

"Will it hurt?" she asked timidly. Just asking the question made her feel weak, especially after the oak tree had just praised her for her strength. But Oak only smiled, and his chuckle, which made him sound like a comforting old grandfather, helped to ease her nerves.

"Relax, my child," crooned Ash as one of her branches bent down and gently pushed Connor aside so she could wrap her limb around Isaboe.

Startled by Ash's grasp around her waist, Isaboe didn't see the other branches reaching down from Elm and Oak, but soon she felt them all wrapping their leafy limbs around her. In the next moment, Isaboe was being lifted up, suspended above the ground by the gentle cradle of their branches.

"Isaboe, are ye alright?" Connor called from below.

"Yes. I'm fine." Her words were not just empty platitudes. At that moment, Isaboe felt no fear. On the contrary, she felt protected within the branches of these gentle giants, and she looked up toward their faces with awe and wonder. But as the trees lifted her up to increasingly higher branches, her momentary sense of comfort quickly began to wane. Ever so close to the top of the mountain, Isaboe's heart was now racing as she looked up at the sky and realized just how far above the ground she was. However, it was the direction the branches were moving toward that sent a bolt of fear through her.

Gliding through the air on a bed of twigs and leaves, the branches came to a stop directly in front of the ledge where the enormous gray dragon was sitting. Up close, Isaboe could see that it was indeed a giant among its peers, a truly impressive beast whose head was far larger than her entire body. Its clawed paws were folded one over the other, reminding Isaboe of a cat in repose. A thick boney ridge ran from the tip of the dragon's nose all the way to the top of its skull, where it joined with two striking horns jutting out from the back of its head. Being so close to its snout turned Isaboe's fear into outright panic, and her heartbeat escalated as the mighty dragon examined her closely, its amber eyes glittering with curiosity. Isaboe felt as if her measure was being taken, but she soon realized that it was not this reptile's intent to do her harm.

When the dragon finally spoke, she heard his words in her mind, but his mouth did not move. *"My grandson tells me that the Fey Queen has put you and your family through a terrible ordeal."* His voice was deep and full of authority—the voice of a king.

Startled into silence, Isaboe locked eyes with the immense reptile. She had no idea how to address this unique being. The dragon's words had come to her through her mind. Was she to respond the same?

"Speak, child. Do not fear me. You have requested our assistance, and my grandson would not have brought you here unless he believed in your cause. I trust his judgement. It is not every day that a mortal has the opportunity to visit our sanctuary, or to receive assistance from the Patriarch of the Sardonian Dragons. I encourage you to take advantage of this unique opportunity."

"Uh…yes. Thank you," Isaboe mumbled. "Please forgive my discourtesy, but I am unfamiliar with the proper way to greet such a magnificent creature as yourself, Your Lordship." Leaning again on the good manners beaten into her at finishing school, she was certain that she was in the presence of a great authority, so Isaboe was sure that some sort of title was appropriate.

Apparently pleased with her reply, he spoke again. *"Show me the location of the amulet."* The tip of his long tail swished around and into Isaboe's line of sight, hovering before her like one long lethal finger.

Fighting to maintain at least the outward appearance of calm, Isaboe tore her focus from the tip of the dragon's tail to look back into his eyes. Meeting his stare, she touched the spot on her chest.

Isaboe thought the Dragon King almost seemed to smile, the corners of his mouth curling up in a hint of amusement. *"Of course, the Mundahli would bury it next to your heart. How very wise."*

Before she could prepare, the dragon's tail swooped toward her, and Isaboe automatically flinched back to escape the scaley appendage. Staring wide-eyed as the tip came ever closer, the tree branches held her still, refusing to let her back away from the very purpose of her visit.

The moment the dragon's tail touched Isaboe's skin, a bolt of energy shot through her, bringing a sensation like nothing she had ever experienced before. She felt the tingling burn of the dragon's magic spreading throughout her body, first rushing into her center, then dancing all the way down to her fingers and toes, before finally condensing around the amulet and exploding out of her chest.

When she opened her eyes, Isaboe found herself looking at the blue amulet dangling above her from the tip of the dragon's tail. Watching it swinging freely, she took a few deep cleansing breaths. It was over. Though it only lasted a few seconds, the magic was still crawling over her skin, a bit like the remnants of scrambling ants. But otherwise, Isaboe felt no ill effects from the incredible event she'd just experienced.

"Now would be a good time to say thank you," chimed Ash.

"Yes. Of course." Isaboe felt dazed, coming down from a great shock. "Thank you, Your Lordship. I truly appreciate your help."

The dragon did not bother to respond, but instead flipped his tail, sending the amulet flying into Elm's branches, where it was caught on his reaching limbs. In the next moment, the branches that were still wrapped around her waist began to slowly lower her back down to the ground and into Connor's waiting arms. *"Breagha,* are ye alright?" he asked, after finally drawing back from a frenzied embrace.

"Yes, I…I think so." Still in a state of shock, Isaboe glanced up to see what had become of the amulet, but she couldn't see it through the tree's branches. She was exhausted, and yet she knew this wasn't over. They still needed to hear the prophecy, and Isaboe braced herself for more.

"Isaboe—yer chest!" As Connor gently stroked the soft skin between her collarbone and dress, Isaboe tried to follow his touch with her eyes, but she couldn't see what Connor was seeing. When she walked down to the lake and leaned over the still water, her mouth fell open at the sight of her own reflection. Where the amulet had once been buried under her skin, a white starburst marked the spot, and in its center were three intertwined circles. Standing upright, she pulled back the sleeve on her right arm and saw that the starburst birthmark on the inside of her elbow, the one she shared with her mother and daughters, was now gone.

Connor lifted Isaboe's hair to look at the back of her neck. "This one's gone too," he confirmed, referencing the mark on the back of her neck that he himself had given her with the Ring of Odin on the night in which Kaitlyn was conceived. The marks had somehow merged in the center of her chest, where the amulet had been. Turning, she locked gazes with her wide-eyed husband.

"The mark of a dragon," Connor mumbled in amazement as his fingers again gently touched the spot. When she brushed it with her own fingertips, Isaboe could feel the slightly raised mark on her chest, and it felt warm and tingling.

"The prophecy!" she gasped. Isaboe had allowed herself to become distracted, but this wasn't over yet. When she had last seen the amulet, it was swinging casually from the tip of one of Oak's branches.

"Please," she pled with the tree spirits. "Will you please tell us the alternate prophecy that Lorien has kept hidden from the council all these years? Please, we must know."

"You already know what it is, Isaboe," answered Oak as he dropped the amulet down to a lower branch, then flipped it over to Ash.

Isaboe felt a new wave of concern as the amulet flew freely through the air before Ash snagged it on her own branch. "*What?* No. I have no idea what is in the prophecy!"

"Are you certain?" teased Ash as she swung the blue stone from the tip of one of her lower branches. "You did say that *you* are the Chosen One. And in the Mundahli's own words, 'you are the vessel now.' Isn't that what she said?"

"Well, yes, but that doesn't…"

"Stop and think, child," Oak interrupted her. "Everything you've learned, all that you have experienced in your life, has been to prepare you for what lies ahead."

"Why? What lies ahead?" Isaboe had wanted to believe that after the prophecy was revealed, all of this madness would finally be behind them, but the trees' words were destroying her hope.

Before addressing Isaboe's question, Elm took the amulet from Ash's branch. "Your task is not yet complete, Isaboe." When the giant elm flicked the amulet from the tip of its branch, Isaboe watched as the blue stone spun through the air before it dropped onto Oak's leafy limb and disappeared among his green and gold leaves.

"What? No! The Mundahli was locked away for twenty years because of this prophecy. I released the Mundahli from the vault and have now delivered the prophecy to you. I *have* completed my task!" With her anxiety again starting to spike, Isaboe searched the branches for the blue amulet, but still could not see it through the tree's foliage. "Please, tell me; what is the alternate prophecy that will dethrone Lorien? I must know!"

"You are the alternate prophecy, Isaboe," Oak replied. "You created it when Lorien brought you into this realm years ago."

Stunned by his words, Isaboe felt her jaw go slack. "What?" She turned toward Connor and saw the same mystified look that must have been on her face. The more she learned in this realm, the more questions arose. Would the curiosities never end?

CHAPTER 30

A PROPHECY, A POET, AND DRAGON'S FIRE

"I don't understand," Isaboe said, trying and failing to keep the shock from her voice. "How am *I* the alternate prophecy?"

"The voice of the Oracle demands to be heard," Elm announced. "And the king stag waits in the Avalon Forest for the next High Priestess."

"Impatience will not serve the Interpreter, and a shapeshifter can shift more than just her shape," added Ash.

"I've had enough of riddles! We came to you for answers!" Isaboe's voice rose with her frustration. "None of what you are saying makes any sense!"

"Hear me now, Isaboe," Ash's voice thundered, "Your daughter will be ruler of this realm. When she is no longer a child but not yet a woman. Kaitlyn will be called to take up her crown. The prophecy will come to pass."

The words, filled with solemn foreboding, pierced into Isaboe's heart like a burning rod of failure. Had her struggles all been for nothing? Did everything that Isaboe and her family had suffered mean nothing? Would Petrina's death mean nothing? Would Lorien still win? "My daughter cannot grow up to be a tyrant!" she shouted up into the trees.

"Whether your daughter dethrones Lorien or joins her is up to you," said Oak. "And never forget that the real foe is beyond fey or mortal; it is ignorance, selfishness, and hatred. Knowing this, you can yet change the outcome of this prophecy." When the giant tree spoke, Isaboe watched the lines in the bark above his eyes furrow with serious intent. "But be prepared; your enemies wield black magic and deception as their weapons. Lorien continues to prove her resilience. Can you?"

As Connor's face swam into view before her, he took her hand in his callused fingers and forced her to look into his eyes. The love and faith she saw gave Isaboe a small flicker of strength. Connor had never stopped believing in her. As long as they were both alive and together, there was still hope. She would never stop fighting.

"I swear that Kaitlyn will not be a ruler of death and destruction!" Isaboe declared. "We will not allow that to happen!" She squeezed Connor's hand tightly as she spoke her oath before the Trees of Knowledge.

"And it is that conviction, in your fighting spirit, which will mold your daughter into a wise and empathetic ruler," said Elm. "Queen Lorien's machinations will turn against her, as she has failed to take into account your stubborn mortal determination to protect your family."

"Connor, instruct your daughter in the ways of the blade, so that she is capable of defending herself and those in her care," Ash instructed. "For Kaitlyn will face many difficult battles to come. Prepare her for both death and victory in her future."

"Ye can count on me," Connor said with confidence. As Isaboe looked at her husband, she was comforted to know Kaitlyn had the perfect teacher.

"There is much that Kaitlyn will need to learn, but she will not be alone. She will receive assistance and wisdom from the old ones," the oak tree said as he produced the blue amulet. Oak reached out with one great branch to present the amulet to the dragon king, still perched on his platform high above. "And it starts with the protection of dragon fire."

The dragon king reached with his tail to accept the amulet's green cord from Oak. As the patriarch opened his maw, a burst of red and gold flames erupted from his belly and consumed the amulet. When the dragon's jaw closed, the amulet was white-hot from dragon fire, but otherwise unscathed. After the dragon king returned the steaming object to Oak, the tree's branch descended toward the emerald pond, and dipped it into the still waters. The waters hissed and seethed as the amulet cooled. When it was lifted from the pond's depths, the stone shed a rainbow of sparkling droplets dancing through the air.

"This amulet is a gift from the old ones," Oak declared, as he slipped it delicately over Isaboe's neck. "And now it also carries in it a gift from the king of the Sardonian Dragons. When it is time for Kaitlyn to fulfil her destiny, the wisdom of the ancients will guide her." Isaboe felt the gentle brush of his leaves against her cheek as the branch swept back up toward the canopy. As the cool blue amulet rested against her chest, she felt a spark of energy dancing between the stone and the mark on her skin created by the dragon.

"Raise her to be a wise and strong ruler, and she will be honored and respected," Elm said. "Prepare her for all that lies ahead. Raising a child who will one day lead is a heavy task, Isaboe."

"That is why it is so important that Lorien not be the vessel who raises Kaitlyn," Oak confirmed. "If that were to happen, your daughter would turn sour." The giant tree chuckled, making his massive trunk sway slightly and causing a few loose leaves to float gracefully down onto the grassy meadow. Though she didn't know what was so humorous, the sound of his baritone laugh felt like velvet to Isaboe's ears, and she watched with curiosity as the lines embedded into the bark of his face cracked and deepened.

As Ash's musical laughter drew Isaboe from her reverie, she watched the smile lines cracking on the majestic female's bark as well. "You went deep into your rings for that one, my friend. A mortal wrote that more than a thousand years ago. I believe it was a Roman poet. What was his name?" "Horace," answered Oak, before clearing his throat to recite the line. "Unless the vessel is clean, whatever you pour into it turns sour," the magnificent tree quoted. "Lorien's vessel is very unclean."

Isaboe's mind was swimming with all this new information. There was a sort of ironic humor in knowing that her struggle to save her daughter from this very destiny had only fostered a new path to the inevitable. Her daughter would be a ruler in this bizarre and dangerous world. "So, Kaitlyn will be queen regardless of our actions," Isaboe spoke her thoughts aloud. "But we have the ability to prevent the old prophecy from coming to pass, based purely on how we raise her? It can't be that simple!"

"Sometimes the answers to our greatest challenges arrive in the most simple and obvious ways," answered Oak. "But that does not mean the fulfilment will be easy."

"And it was no accident that you and Connor were chosen to be her parents," Ash went on. "It is up to you to instill in Kaitlyn the morals and values that will serve her as a queen. For her reign is coming."

"And the best way to defeat the evil Queen of Euphoria," added Elm, "is to raise Kaitlyn with all that Lorien scorns: morality, compassion, empathy, and love. Those human attributes that make you mortals vulnerable to the evils of your world are the strengths that will make your daughter a great leader."

Isaboe was speechless. When she looked at Connor, she saw the same daunted expression on his face before she finally said, "So, what do we do now?"

"I'd say we go home and raise our daughter to prepare for her future," he replied, torn somewhere between shock and amusement. But Isaboe also saw that determination on his face she had always loved and admired.

Nodding, she smiled. "Yes. Let's go home." Isaboe felt a new sense of purpose, as if they were finally taking control of their own fates. Their time of running from one fight to the next seemed to be over, for now at least.

But then she looked at the dragon on whose back they had arrived, as well as the tunnel engulfed in a ring of fire at the base of the mountain. Remembering the putrid air that waited for them on the other side, along with the deadly jagged spears covering the land, she knew going home would be much easier said than done.

"If you'd rather, there is another way out." The ash tree seemed to sense Isaboe's concern. "You could go out through the top of the mountain and avoid both the fire and the rancid air."

"There's no way the dragon's wings will fit through that opening," Connor said aloud what Isaboe was thinking.

"I didn't say the dragon could go out through the top," confirmed Ash. "I said *you* could."

"More riddles," Isaboe muttered. But in the next moment, apparently having listened to their conversation, Norvik lifted from the ground with the carriage strapped to his back. Flying back out the way they had entered, he disappeared into the tunnel of fire. "Wait!" Isaboe cried after him. "He's our way home!"

Suddenly, the branches of Elm, Ash, and Oak began to lift both Isaboe and Connor up off the ground, gently passing them up to higher branches and closer to the opening of the cavern. "Not to worry, Isaboe," said Ash. "Your ride home starts with one simple step."

Isaboe and Connor clung tightly to each other as they were smoothly transferred from one leafy branch onto the next. Even though the span of the cavern was wide enough for them to fit, the ragged edges were terribly intimidating as they grew closer.

"We are pleased that our first encounter with mortals was you, Isaboe, and your brave soldier," Ash said sweetly. The tree's face was close, so close that Isaboe could see the wisdom in her ancient eyes.

"We wish you good luck, mortals," spoke the elm as his branches lifted them higher, now only feet away from the opening. "Remember what we have shared with you this day."

"Oh, believe me, this meeting is something we shall never forget! Thank you for everything." Isaboe's words came out shaky but sincere, and she felt deeply honored that they were the first mortals to meet with the Trees of Knowledge.

Looking up through the ragged hole in the mountaintop, Isaboe saw the dragon circling overhead. "How will he pick us up?" she groaned, already aware that her worries would fall on deaf ears.

Now close enough to feel a breeze sweeping into the opening, Isaboe realized it was wider than she had first thought. Slowing their progress, the branches stopped when the mortals reached the top, and she was relieved to see that the trees had delivered them to a rough set of stairs which had been carved into the stone, leading up toward the top of the mountain.

"This is your exit," said Ash. "Step carefully."

Taking her hand, Connor assisted Isaboe off the leafy branches and onto the first rocky step. The path opened out onto a wide plateau. Standing on the top of the Mountain of Ancestors, in the middle of the Harrow Mountain range, the wind gently tossed their hair and clothes as they took in the panoramic view of the world.

"Ye can see the whole realm from up here!" Connor exclaimed as he pointed toward the castle spires shimmering above the treetops. "That must be Sashtonia."

Scanning the land below, Isaboe saw a thin line of blue smoke far off in the distance. She stopped and stared. "Euphoria is still burning."

"Aye. Consumed by dragon fire," Connor agreed. As if mentioning the dragon had summoned him, Norvik circled out over the mountaintop, looking for a suitable landing spot near the mortals.

Isaboe turned her attention back to her husband and took his hand. It was near impossible for her to believe what she herself had accomplished these last few days, and at the moment, she felt pretty damn proud. "We did that. We did what no fey has been able to. We not only rescued Gabriel, we destroyed Lorien's stronghold."

Smiling down at her, Connor squeezed his wife's hand. "You did that, *Breagha*. It was yer damn stubbornness that put this whole thing into motion."

"Was that a compliment or an insult?" she teased. But when he draped an arm around her shoulder, she felt the comfort of his warm laugh, bringing a smile to her own face. However, her next thought instantly subsumed her feelings of success. "We both know that this isn't over yet. Rosalyn still has a mission to complete."

Turning to face her, Connor took both of her hands in his and forced her to meet his eyes. "I have no doubt that Rosalyn and Brighid will be successful as well, my love. Yer mother is just 'bout as stubborn as ye are. She'll not give up without a fight, and she has a pissed-off royal rebel at her side. I'm not too worried."

Feeding off the confidence she heard in his statement, Isaboe felt her anxiety slip away. If the trees were right, she and Connor were destined to raise Kaitlyn, not Lorien. Taking in a breath of fresh mountain air, Isaboe felt a new sense of purpose suffuse her being. For the first time in a long time, she no longer felt afraid of her future. Her path was clear.

But when the dragon touched down and extended his wing, Isaboe still had not shed her fear of flying. Although she felt her body tense up, there was only one way home.

"Come on, *Breagha*," Connor said, a slight smirk on his face at seeing the change in Isaboe's demeanor. "Ye made it here in one piece. Ye'll be fine on the way back too. I promise." Brushing back a lock of hair that the wind had twisted free, he held his hand to her cheek and stared into her eyes. "We've been assigned a task, my love, and the first step toward home is up that dragon's wing."

When she saw the smile spreading across her husband's face, it gave Isaboe a new sense of confidence. "I know, and I'm not afraid," she said assertively as she lifted her chin. "The time for fear is over. Let's go home. We have a ruler to raise." Taking the first step, she led Connor toward the dragon's wing, and back toward the challenging task of raising the next Queen of Euphoria.

CHAPTER 31

TWILIGHT BATTLE OF THE FEY

Back in the mortal world the sun was now low in the sky. Anna had pushed the horse hard during her full-day's ride as she tried to reach Glochmoor before nightfall. Though she had been forced to stop more than once to feed Kaitlyn, herself, and the horse, she kept the breaks short. She knew Jared and the others would have discovered her absence not long after her departure that morning, and logic told her that riders traveling on fast-moving horses could certainly outpace the slower moving buggy. But knowing that didn't stop Anna, and she ignored her guilt as she pushed on toward her destination; the Standing Stones.

For most of the ride, Kaitlyn had sat up or slept in her basket, but there were a few occasions when she became restless and cried for attention. After Anna had fed and changed her sister's soiled under garment for the third time, she placed her back into the basket before slapping the reins, moving the horse into motion. Although Kaitlyn whined and attempted to climb out, Anna forced her little sister to stay in her assigned seat. When Kaitlyn's lower lip dropped in a pitiful pout and tears began to roll down her small face, Anna hardened her heart against her cries. During the short time Anna had known her sister, a bond had formed between them, and the little girl had become very fond of her. Now Anna was preparing to do the unthinkable and hand this innocent child over to the evil Fey Queen. But she had no choice; Gabriel must be saved, so the kindest thing she could do was to break the bond now.

Not used to such hard riding, Anna's exhaustion joined her guilt, silently nipping at her heels as they drew ever closer to their destination. If she could just hold her son again, Anna promised herself all would be well. Rescuing Gabriel was worth the pain, and she would have to deal with the remorse afterward. Right now, getting Gabriel back had to be her only focus, and tonight was the night she had to make the trade. It was now or never.

As darkness swallowed the last traces of daylight, they finally arrived, and Anna could see the standing stones looming darkly against the twilit sky. Kaitlyn had fallen asleep and was laying contently in her basket, completely unaware that on this night her life would change forever.

Fighting back her tears, Anna directed the horse and buggy behind a thicket of brush and climbed down, leaving Kaitlyn asleep in her basket as she walked toward the circle. Ancient and mysterious, the monolithic stones cast long shadows in the moonlight, standing like silent guards protecting this sacred space.

A shiver went down Anna's spine, and she wanted to run. Though this is what she had come for, riding all through the day to arrive at this spot, she now wondered if she could really go through with it. But if her son would be here this night, then it would all be worth it just to hold him again.

The night air was cool, and Anna hugged herself as she cautiously continued forward. Glancing around, the area appeared void of life, and the night sky full of stars seemed more ominous than usual.

"Hello, Anna."

Startled at the sound of a woman's voice behind her, she spun around. *"Isaboe?"* Shocked at seeing the windblown red hair and the big emotional eyes, it was certainly her mother. "What…what are you doing here?" Anna heard the panic in her words. She had been caught, and while she had known she would eventually have to atone for her actions, she hadn't considered that Isaboe would be the one catching her in the act.

"I might ask you the same thing," Isaboe said, and the tone in her reply made Anna shudder. "But I already know, my dear." With a soft smile, Isaboe reached out for her, but Anna drew back. "It's alright, Anna. I understand why you are doing this, and I'm not angry. I wanted to be the one to meet you."

"How did you know I would be here?"

"You want your son back. I understand, and I expected this."

Although Isaboe's words were kind, her eyes darted about, anxious and distracted.

"Where's Gabriel?" Anna demanded, taking a step back. "Where are Rosalyn and Connor?" Something, Anna quickly realized, wasn't right. "I thought you were returning through the portal back at Rosalyn's home. Why are you here instead?"

"I already told you: I knew you were on your way here to trade Kaitlyn for Gabriel. I understand your pain, Anna," she said, as her wandering gaze fell on the buggy, which was not as well-hidden as Anna had hoped, and she watched as a satisfied expression crossed Isaboe's face.

"Where is Gabriel?!" Anna shouted, stepping between Isaboe and the buggy. But with greater strength than Anna thought her mother should possess, Isaboe easily pushed her aside. Panic began to bubble in Anna's stomach. This wasn't right. Everything was wrong. Running on pure instinct, Anna rushed up behind Isaboe and spun her around.

"Get your hands off me!" The strange woman spat into her face, and Anna flinched away from the venom she saw there. This woman was not Isaboe. Although she wore Isaboe's face, everything else about her—her movements, her demeanor, even the way she spoke—proved she was an imposter.

"Who are you?" Anna trembled as she began to realize the scope of her mistake.

"She is not Isaboe, and she doesn't have Gabriel," Margaret's voice called across the moor.

Anna spun around to see Margaret holding Kaitlyn safely in her arms. Will, Margaret's husband, stood protectively at their side. When her eyes found Jared, he was rushing toward her with intensity written on his face. Seeing that her husband and the others had in fact caught up to her no longer mattered to Anna. Gabriel wasn't here.

Now grateful for Jared's arrival, Anna ran into his arms just before the Isaboe imposter cursed violently and vanished. She didn't even have time to be relieved, for in the next second, the sound of a snarling beast drew all their attention. From between the standing stones, a massive lupine creature emerged. Its yellow eyes glowing, the beast bared its fangs and snarled. Frozen with fear, Anna couldn't move. But Jared could, and with a protective arm around his wife, he urged her into movement. They began to back toward the carriage while the incredible creature stalked toward them.

In her wildest nightmares, Anna had never imagined that she would have to face such a creature. For her folly, not only would she never see her son again, but she had also led them all to a grisly death. Her eyes filling with tears, Anna turned her fearful gaze to her husband. "What have I done?" she gasped, "I am so sorry!"

Before he had time to respond, Jared's voice was cut off by a crack of lightning overhead. Even their fearsome foe looked up, momentarily distracted as the thunder rolled so close it shook the ground beneath their feet.

Rosalyn's vision took several seconds to clear from the bright white lightning. When it did, she found herself standing only yards from the standing stones, Gabriel still in her arms with Brighid at her side. Then the scene before her fully registered—a beast preparing to strike as Jared and Anna backed away in horror.

Wasting no time, Rosalyn quickly ushered them back to the buggy while Queen Brighid faced the creature alone. When they reached Margaret and Will, she saw an equal amount of fear written in their wide-eyed faces. Catching her granddaughter's attention, Rosalyn presented the bundle that Anna had come all this way for—her son. As she placed Gabriel into Anna's arms, Rosalyn only had a moment to watch their tearful reunion.

"Thank you," Anna and Jared whispered repeatedly through tears of joy, but Rosalyn had no time for pleasantries.

"Take Kaitlyn and Gabriel and leave!" Rosalyn ordered them all. "I don't know what will happen here this night, but I want the children a safe distance away."

"Wait!" shouted Margaret. "Where are Isaboe and Connor?" she asked, clearly fearful of the answer.

"They are fine, and they'll be home soon! Now, go!" Rosalyn shouted as a battle erupted behind her. She turned just in time to watch as a bolt of energy shot out from Brighid's hands, sending the hideous creature tumbling backward. But the Fey Queen's attempt only temporarily halted the monster's progress. "Go now!" Rosalyn shouted again, finally jolting all four adults into action.

Both women scrambled into the carriage, and Margaret put Kaitlyn back in the basket before grabbing the reins. With Gabriel cradled safely in Anna's arms, Jared and Will quickly jumped onto their horses. Though the animals had been pushed hard all day, and the travelers were exhausted, Margaret wasted no time. Quickly snapping the reins, she had the pony jolting into a hard run back toward Rosalyn's home.

Returning to Brighid's side, Rosalyn stared at the lumbering creature as it moved in their direction. Snarling at them with its yellow eyes glowing and razor-sharp teeth bared, it stalked them with careful deliberate steps, ready to strike at any moment. Just as dangerous herself, Brighid did not wait for the beast's attack, but aimed another of her spells. This time, a long white rope of energy snapped around the beast's neck like a whip. As Brighid pulled the line taut, Rosalyn almost imagined it could really be that easy. But in the next moment, the beast vanished, and Brighid's whip dissipated into vapor along with it.

Spinning in a circle, Rosalyn felt the fey energy tingling on her skin, but she could neither see nor hear anything. "That beast was Lilabeth, yes?"

"Yes. And she's still here," Brighid confirmed, staring wide-eyed into the darkness. Taking a couple of cautious steps forward, the Fey Queen scanned the stones' perimeter. "Show yourself!" she demanded, sparkling with tense, blue energy just waiting to be unleashed. "Or are you too much of a coward to face me fey-to-fey!"

Brighid's insult hit home, and her words had not finished echoing off the stones when the shapeshifter reappeared. This time she was not in the form of a hideous beast, but as her twisted evil self.

"You think I fear you?" the dark muse taunted. Sleek and seductive in black leather, Lilabeth was just as Rosalyn remembered her from Gabriel's nursery: a viper poised to strike. "You think too highly of yourself, Brighid!" she snarled. Crouching low, like a cat backed into a corner, the shapeshifter sprang up and again transformed. This time she became a giant two-headed eagle with talons as long and sharp as a warrior's blade. Screeching with fury, the creature flapped its huge black wings and took to the sky before turning to dive at them. The queen put herself between Rosalyn and the vicious bird of prey, throwing her hands up and casting a glittering shield around them. Lilabeth could only scratch and claw at the shield, but Rosalyn saw death in the sharp grasp of her talons.

Holding back Lilabeth's onslaught was no easy task, and Brighid's foot suddenly slipped, but Rosalyn drew forth her own power and threw it up to reinforce the queen's. With the magical strength of both feymora and Fey Queen, Rosalyn and Brighid were able to hold the creature at bay. But this was not sustainable. As Rosalyn felt their strength against the great eagle waning, the queen apparently came to the same conclusion. "Hold her!" she shouted. That was all the warning Rosalyn received before the queen withdrew her power from the shield. The intensity of Lilabeth's attack remained full force, and yet the shield held as Rosalyn struggled against the assault. But then she felt the fine hairs along her arms and the back of her neck begin to rise as Brighid gathered her power and then released it in an explosion that lit up the sky, blasting Lilabeth back into the darkness.

Brighid's release of power sent out a shockwave of energy, creating a blast of wind that rushed over the mound. After it settled, Rosalyn looked around them, trying to relocate Lilabeth, but her vision was blinded by another crack of lightning that shook the very ground on which they stood. After that, it was easy to locate Lilabeth, who stood not far from their position, but she was no longer alone. A fey woman stood by her side, her blonde hair wild and stark against the night sky.

"I was wondering if you would have the courage to face me, Lorien," Brighid taunted. "Or if you intended to let Lilabeth have all the fun."

"Oh, I wouldn't have missed this, Brighid," Lorien hissed. Then, her bitter gaze found Rosalyn. "This is something I've wanted to do for a very long time."

Without warning, Lorien threw her own attack at Rosalyn, who reacted too slowly to dodge. When the magic hit her, Rosalyn was tossed like a ragdoll across the stone circle. Landing hard, the breath was knocked from her lungs and her vision was spinning. She was still shaking off the pain when Lorien took flight. At the same moment, the hideous two-headed eagle joined her mistress in the sky.

Scrambling to her feet, Rosalyn returned to Brighid's side. Without taking her eyes off their foes, she asked, "How do we fight that?"

"With a little help," Brighid responded cryptically. She waved her arm over the ground, and from the dirt a number of small rocks rose up into her hand. When the queen murmured a soft incantation, the stones began to glow. "Take these." Brighid placed some of the shimmering rocks into Rosalyn's palm. "Toss one at that beast when she comes too close. That should incapacitate her for a while." She cast Rosalyn a cheeky grin. "And, obviously, you have your own magic as well, my dear. Think more like a fey and less like a mortal."

As Brighid turned to resume the attack, Rosalyn realized who her target was. "No, I want Lorien," she said confidently. The fey had pulled generations of their family into her petty war for power. It was time for their family to fight back, and Rosalyn could feel the flame of righteous anger burning in her chest, spurring her on.

With an approving smile lighting up her face, Brighid switched her focus to Lilabeth as the giant bird screeched a war cry and dove toward them. In response, Brighid's own wings unfurled, and she took to the air to intercept it, launching balls of energy toward the creature, only some of which found their target. Seeing that the ferocious bird was more agile than she had realized, Rosalyn tore her attention from the battle unfolding above to face her own adversary.

Now on the ground, the Fey Queen sauntered forward menacingly. "So, Rosalyn," she sneered, "we finally meet, face-to-face." The vicious fey seemed thrilled at the prospect of a confrontation.

"And this is a meeting I've been looking forward to for a very long time, *auntie*," Rosalyn mocked as she threw the first of her glowing stones at Lorien. The blast caught the queen unaware, and she used her wings to bring more distance between them. Gathering her power, Lorien hurled spears of hot energy toward the ground where Rosalyn stood. Reenforcing her own throws with fey magic, Rosalyn hurled the stones at Lorien's missiles, hoping to redirect them. The blast from the small rocks managed to divert the spears' course, and they dissolved when they did not find their target.

But Lorien's next attack was already underway, hurtling lethal fey power so furiously that Rosalyn was barely able to dodge, much less send up her own power to block them. When a spear sliced through her flesh, she felt a hot shooting pain in her upper arm. Rosalyn grasped at the wound as red blood oozed out between her fingers. Realizing that Lorien was more powerful than she had thought, the sorceress quietly wondered at Isaboe's ability to confront the fey again and again and survive. In raw power alone, Rosalyn knew she was completely outmatched. As if to confirm that conclusion, the sorceress felt Lorien's toxic magic wrapping around her throat, just like Brighid's whip. It began to squeeze, and it was all Rosalyn could do to keep the energy from crushing her throat. Her knees began to buckle, and her vision began to spot. Lorien's black magic was doing its best to take Rosalyn's life.

"You should have stayed in your own world, *mortal,*" Lorien hissed, coming close again when she had Rosalyn at her mercy. "You and your daughter thought you were clever enough to sneak into my world and undermine my plans. But once again, you mortals have underestimated me, and I will not let you destroy my plans for the future of Euphoria!" the Fey Queen shouted, throwing all her strength into the magic around Rosalyn's throat. As the magic whip tightened, the sorceress felt her body convulsing out of control as her vision began to fade. An abstract sort of calm filled her as she closed her eyes and let the darkness take her. Is this what dying feels like?

However, only seconds later, Rosalyn's momentary lapse into darkness was brought to a sudden and jarring end. She gasped in a breath of burning air as she came to with a painful start. With the constriction released from around her throat, life-giving breath now rushed back into her lungs, telling Rosalyn that she wasn't dead. If she were dead, she mused sarcastically, it couldn't hurt this much. She forced several long deep breaths down her bruised throat before finally opening her eyes. Still lying on the ground, she saw only bright white light, and for a terrifying moment had to rethink her conclusion about being alive. When a roll of thunder shook the ground, Rosalyn knew it was a sign, and with mingled hope and resignation, she looked up to see who had joined the battle.

It was a wizard. Demetrick now stood only yards away as she struggled to her feet, still coughing, weak, and bleeding. The space above the stones was lit up as bright as daylight, and Rosalyn watched gratefully as Demetrick sent forth blasts of energy, energy so powerful that the two-headed eagle went tumbling backward with a pained screech. Another movement caught her eye, and Rosalyn looked up to see Nicholi soaring overhead. He and Lorien were locked in a lethal dance of magic in the night sky that sent a rain of sparks down onto those below. Now it was Lorien and Lilabeth who were outmatched, and Rosalyn watched in awe as Demetrick launched a glowing star-shaped disc at the giant bird. Though the beast dodged, the weapon had locked onto its target and redirected its course to attack the shapeshifter. Barely missing her chest, the disc sliced off the tip of her left wing. Free-falling to the earth, the bird morphed back into Lilabeth, who screamed pitifully all the way to the ground.

"When we learned that Lorien had fled Euphoria, we suspected she might be here, and thought you would appreciate a little help," Demetrick said as he wrapped a gentle arm around Rosalyn's waist for support. "Are you alright, my dear?" he asked, glancing at her wounded arm.

"Yes, thanks to you." Though her throat felt tight, and it hurt to speak, Rosalyn managed to give Demetrick a grateful smile. "But what took you so long?"

The wizard chuckled softly but did not answer. Instead, he redirected them both to watch the battle unfolding overhead as brother and sister were doing their very best to destroy each other. But even Lorien couldn't withstand the power of both Brighid and Nicholi assaulting her at the same time. Breaking away from the battle, she fled back to the ground where her wounded comrade lay.

When Lorien helped Lilabeth to her feet, Rosalyn saw that the shapeshifter hadn't survived the battle unscathed: she was missing a hand. Dark blood dripped from the stump at the end of her arm as Lilabeth hung onto Lorien. The once fearsome shapeshifter now looked spent and powerless.

In the next moment, Nicholi and Brighid landed so that they flanked Rosalyn and Demetrick. The four faced down what was left of Lorien and Lilabeth.

"It's over, Lorien," Nicholi chided. "You've lost. Your castle has been burned and your people have all fled. Your kingdom has fallen."

"Oh, that's where you're wrong, Brother!" Lorien shouted. "It is not over until I say it's over. And I will never stop until I have what I want!"

"You had the throne, Lorien. You had the control you've always desired, and you used it to kill and mutilate your own people!"

"I cut off those ungrateful peasants' wings because they didn't give me the respect I deserve," she hissed.

"You don't deserve respect, Lorien. You have become a monster," Nicholi spat as he stepped forward, and Rosalyn heard the anger in his voice, saw it on his face. "Haven't you destroyed enough lives already? What more do you want?"

"I want the respect from the council that I deserve!" Lorien screamed, but then her face softened, twisting into something that resembled regret. "I just wanted my people to love me." Her voice held a trace of sadness, but when her gaze found Rosalyn, her face morphed into something frightening, something that looked like vengeance, and she held up an accusing finger and pointed. "As they loved her *mother!*"

Rosalyn exchanged a glance with Nicholi, and in that moment, she suddenly understood the reason for Lorien's hatred. It was almost pitiful.

"The people loved Alaina because she was everything you're not. She was good and kind, and she cared about them," Nicholi pronounced. "Her love made her more powerful than you will ever be."

"*She was a mortal!*" Lorien screamed. "You not only broke your vow to me that you would never marry, but you put a mortal woman on *my* throne!"

"I was a fool to make that promise. It was made as a child, but more importantly, I could never have imagined that you would grow up to be as foul and hateful as you have become. Alaina was fit to rule. You are not." Nicholi's voice was even and emotionless as he addressed his sister. "The council has already agreed and has given me their approval. I am taking back the throne of Euphoria. I never should have relinquished it to you in the first place." Nicholi paused for a moment and then turned toward Rosalyn. When he spoke again, his voice was softer. "I have always regretted sending Alaina away. And though I don't deserve your forgiveness, I hope somehow to make amends for my mistakes."

"Oh, isn't this sweet?" Lorien taunted. "The pathetic reunion of a father and his long-lost daughter. Well, you may have won this battle, Nicholi, but the war isn't over. I will make sure you pay for this." Sneering at her brother, Lorien roughly righted Lilabeth. "Go ahead, rebuild Euphoria for me. It'll be just that much sweeter when I take it away from you again, Brother!" Lorien shouted, throwing down a burst of light that temporarily blinded everyone's vision. When they could finally see again, the Fey Queen and the dark muse had vanished.

CHAPTER 32

MISSION COMPLETED

Sashtonia's crystalline castle was a looming shadow in the predawn light, and the landing platform was vacant as the dragon touched down and lowered his wing for the humans to dismount. But as they slid down the webbed appendage, both Connor and Isaboe were solemn and quiet. Although they had successfully achieved their goal, the greater success of their mission still hung in the balance. Rescuing Gabriel and returning him to his mother was only half the job. She still needed to keep her daughter out of the hands of the depraved Fey Queen. The fact that Rosalyn was not here waiting for them meant that she and Queen Brighid were still in Scotland, fighting to save Kaitlyn.

As they ran toward the large castle doors, they were met by Demetrick, who looked almost at ease. "Oh, good. You're back!" the wizard announced, obviously pleased. His perceptive gaze swept over Isaboe. "And you appear whole and undamaged. Excellent! How did you find the experience, my dear?"

"It was," Isaboe hesitated over her words, "most enlightening, but right now, I need to know if you have heard from Rosalyn. Are the children safe?"

"Yes, Rosalyn has returned," Demetrick reassured them. "She, too, was successful. Your daughter and Gabriel are both safe and in the care of your family back home."

The relief that washed over Isaboe almost brought her to her knees, and she found a similar expression of joy and accomplishment on her husband's face. "We did it, Connor. We pulled off the impossible!"

"No. You did it, *Breagha.* I was only doing my job—protecting ye."

Throwing her arms around Connor's neck, Isaboe hugged him tight and rejoiced in the feeling of his arms wrapped securely around her waist. "And that you have done perfectly well, my love," she whispered. "Please, don't ever let me go."

"Never," he whispered in return, squeezing her a little tighter.

"Well, this is a sight that makes my heart sing!"

Isaboe unwound herself from Connor's embrace to find that her mother had joined them. She was holding a tall staff crowned with a glittering red jewel which Isaboe had never seen before. "Rosalyn!" she cried, running to wrap her arms around her mother. When she felt the sorceress flinch from her touch, Isaboe drew back and gave her a concerned look. "Are you injured?"

"Let's just say I finally got to meet Aunt Lorien, and it wasn't a pleasant introduction." Isaboe gasped when Rosalyn showed her the injury on her upper arm and pulled down the scarf that was loosely wrapped around her neck, revealing the deep red lines that were burned into her skin. "But thanks to Demetrick, as well as Brighid and Nicholi, we were victorious. Kaitlyn and Gabriel are safe in the mortal world." Rosalyn couldn't restrain her grin as she placed her free hand on the wizard's arm and glanced past Isaboe to where the dragon, despite his best attempts to make himself unobtrusive, still took up most of the rooftop landing. "And what of your mission to the Grove of Raghii? Were you successful?"

Pulling back the fabric of her dress, Isaboe exposed the new mark gracing her chest.

"By all the gods!" Rosalyn gasped. She reached out to gently touch the white lines now etched permanently into her daughter's skin, but then shot a quick glance toward the landing platform. "I want to hear every detail about your experience, my love, but I need to do something first. Then you will have my full attention." She gave her daughter a quick smile and then walked past her. Stopping at a nearby bench, Rosalyn gathered up a large dark-gray cloak, as well as a pair of boots and pants before proceeding toward the dragon.

Isaboe watched curiously as her mother exchanged a few quiet words with the great beast, appearing completely unafraid. The reptile's mouth pulled up into what looked like a smile as he chuffed out a puff of smoke. When he lowered his mighty head, Rosalyn reached up and ran her fingers over his scaly snout, almost affectionately. Drawing back, she laid the bejeweled staff along with the clothing and shoes out before him like an offering, then returned to her daughter's side, utterly unaffected by her proximity to the dragon.

Wrapping her arm around Isaboe's shoulder, Rosalyn then turned their little group away from the platform as they strolled into the foyer. "Now tell me everything. How did you receive that scar?"

Confused at what she had just witnessed, Isaboe finally stuttered, "Uh…it was from another dragon, a very large dragon."

"Another dragon?"

"Yes! And I think he was the King of Dragons!"

"Aye, not only is the Grove of Raghii a magnificent garden paradise with three giant trees who speak, it's also a dragon's lair!" Connor exclaimed, keen to tell his version of their exploits.

"After we'd been welcomed by the talking trees," Isaboe continued excitedly, "I came face-to-face with this giant and magnificent dragon, and, well, it was he who removed the amulet with his tail and his magic. The experience was incredible, and it left me with this." As Isaboe touched the mark on her chest, they were all startled by the sound of a muffled explosion and saw a small cloud of smoke billowing from the platform. When a handsome dark-skinned stranger walked out of the gray mist to join them, he was holding the bejeweled staff and wearing the clothes and cloak that Rosalyn had laid out before the dragon. The landing platform was now empty, and the dragon was gone, although they hadn't heard it fly away.

As Lord Ruz-Zambia joined them, Rosalyn greeted him with a warm smile and a soft touch. "Norvik, I can't thank you enough for all you have done. And I just learned that there was a dragon king, and a dragon's lair in the Grove of Raghii."

"Yes. It was my grandfather who saw to her personally," said the impressive looking man, and the words that flowed from his mouth were rich and smooth.

"Isaboe, Connor, I would like to formally introduce Lord Ruz-Zambia,"

Rosalyn said to them, although her smile was entirely for the newcomer. "It was Norvik and his brothers who led the charge on Euphoria. They burned the spell that Lorien had placed on her borders."

Lord Ruz-Zambia was the most striking man Isaboe had ever seen. His swirling blue-green eyes were captivating, and Isaboe felt she hadn't been so star-struck since she was a girl at finishing school. She didn't realize how badly she was gawking until Connor spoke up.

"Uh, I mean no disrespect, but we met Lord Ruz, and he was a dragon."

"Yes, Connor," Rosalyn said with mock patience. "You are correct. Lord Ruz-Zambia *is* a dragon."

"Huh?" Connor sounded as stunned as Isaboe felt, but then it all fell into place.

"You are the dragon that carried us to the mountain!" Isaboe realized aloud.

When Lord Ruz-Zambia only nodded, Connor's confused look melted into a pleasant realization. "And the dragon who led the attack on Euphoria." Again, the dragon-lord only offered a slight head nod. "Well, be ye dragon or be ye fey, I can't thank ye enough, m'lord. Yer efforts saved our family." Connor offered his hand for a shake.

For a moment, Lord Ruz-Zambia looked down at Connor's hand, as if unsure what to do with it before he spoke. "I have been told that you are a rebel in your world: known to cause trouble."

Connor dropped his hand, and Isaboe watched a curious look shift across her husband's face, as if he were suddenly guarded by the dragon-lord's statement. "Aye, I've been told that a time or two."

Nodding, the dragon-lord quietly studied Connor before he spoke again, "Apparently, the fey needed a rebellious troublemaker from the mortal world to start a rebellion," Ruz-Zambia announced, almost humorously as he blew a puff of smoke into his hand. Reaching out, he took Connor's hand, and when they clasped forearms, the light grey smoke encircled both men's arms like the ghost of a serpent until it dissipated into the air. "From one rebel to another, I see you." Ruz-Zambia then bowed his head in a gesture of respect.

Isaboe watched Connor go speechless as Ruz-Zambia dropped his hand and turned away from her tongue-tied husband. Giving Rosalyn his full attention, the dragon-lord softened. "And of course, this mission needed a beautiful leader with a heart full of passion."

"I'm no leader, but I, too, cannot thank you enough, Norvik. What you and your brothers did for my family, I will never be able to repay."

"Your appreciation is sufficient," the lord replied. "My brothers and I haven't flown together for many years, and I had almost forgotten how exhilarating it is to soar freely." Despite his enthusiastic words, his voice remained stoic. "And though a part of me thought to retain my original form," Ruz-Zambia said, fixing the full force of his attention on Isaboe's mother, "I had something to return for." Brandishing the staff, he shifted closer to the sorceress, "Thank you for taking such good care of my heart."

"Of course. I'm just pleased that you returned for it."

Watching the interaction between her mother and Lord Ruz-Zambia, Isaboe didn't quite know what to make of it. Shooting a side-ways glance at Connor, she saw the same puzzling look on her husband's face.

When Lord Ruz-Zambia spoke again, he only addressed Rosalyn. "And I am pleased to have been of service to you. But now, this body requires nourishment. Would you care to join me in the dining hall?"

"Thank you, but no. My daughter and I have some catching up to do," Rosalyn replied with a soft smile. "Perhaps I'll see you later."

"If it's all the same, I'd like to join you," Demetrick said with a wily grin, as if fully aware that he was a poor substitute in the dragon-lord's eyes. "It's been a night of excitement, and I've worked up an appetite."

Ruz-Zambia only nodded, never removing his focus from Rosalyn. He took her hand, brought it to his lips, and kissed it lightly. "Until later," he promised. They stared into each other's eyes for several seconds, as if unable to look away, until Demetrick, still smiling, cleared his throat, bringing them both to their senses. The dragon-lord finally took his leave with only one more longing look cast over his shoulder at Isaboe's mother, before they turned the corner and disappeared out of sight.

When Rosalyn finally tore her gaze from the two men walking side-by-side down the foyer, Isaboe couldn't help but notice her mother's warm lingering smile. Based on Rosalyn's following reaction, she must have seen the suspicion written across her daughter's face. "What?" she finally asked.

"Oh my God, Rosalyn!" Isaboe exclaimed. "That man is completely smitten with you! No, wait—he is a *dragon*, a dragon who is in love with you!"

"What? No, don't be silly." Her mother shrugged off her comment, but Isaboe could see the blush tinting her cheeks. "Now, please, tell me what you learned of the alternate prophecy," Rosalyn said, quickly changing the subject.

Despite her own curiosity, Rosalyn was correct. The story behind Lord Ruz-Zambia could wait until later. So Isaboe said simply, "There is no alternate prophecy."

"What? But why else would Lorien go through all the trouble of locking away the Keeper of the Knowledge if not to keep the alternate prophecy from being revealed? You told me that the Mundahli placed the prophecy in the blue amulet before she buried it under your skin. After going to the Mountain of Ancestors and speaking with the talking trees, you then had an interaction with the king of dragons!" Rosalyn glanced anxiously from Isaboe to Connor. "How could there be no alternate prophecy?"

Rosalyn's reaction was the same as Isaboe's initially had been, and she exchanged an amused little smile with her husband. "Well, Mother," she said, linking arms with Rosalyn and leading her down the hall with Connor by their side, "it is a bit more complicated than that. Let's go have a bite to eat and we'll fill you in on what we've learned from three very wise trees, and from your new beau's amazing grandfather," she added with a teasing grin.

Despite their great desire to return to Scotland, Isaboe, Connor, and Rosalyn stayed through the night; they were exhausted from their adventures. The following morning, after washing up and changing her clothes, Isaboe silently packed her bag. It did not take long as neither she nor Connor had brought more than necessities. Plus, she was short one dress that a nasty little creature had stolen while she was bathing. Isaboe was still annoyed by the encounter, but she was going home now, and that dress, along with everything else they had experienced here, would soon be only a memory. Doing one more check to make sure nothing was left behind, she found Connor's tunic and pants, the ones he'd been wearing when he jumped into the fight against the trolls, covered in blood and stink. Immediately writing them off as a lost cause, Isaboe left the soiled clothing on the floor.

Although they had only been in the Realm of the Underlings for a few days, their initial arrival into an unexpected war zone now seemed so long ago. Thinking back, she could barely recognize the person she had been on that day, as this entire experience had changed her dramatically. When they had arrived, she had been frightened and scared, even with Connor at her side, but now, the feeling of panic that had always seemed to exist just below the surface of her controlled poise was gone. In its place she now felt a calm confidence. She had faced hurdle after hurdle and come out alive. However, simmering just under that confidence, there still remained a nagging question. When the day does arrive and Kaitlyn is called to take up her role, would Isaboe be strong enough to let her daughter go?

"Ye've been rather quiet this morning, *Breagha*." Connor stepped up behind his wife and placed his hands on her shoulders, planting a kiss on her cheek.

Isaboe turned and smiled, wrapping her arms around Connor's waist. "I just have a few things on my mind."

"Like going home?"

"Yes, and I'm so ready. When we were discussing it over dinner last night, I wanted to tell Rosalyn to open that portal right then and there! Connor, I can't wait to wrap my arms around my daughter, around both of my daughters!"

"What are ye gonna say when ye see Anna?"

Isaboe drew out of his embrace and picked up her brush, combing it through her hair. "I don't know yet," she said wearily. "I need to make it clear that I'm not angry or upset with her. I'm certain she already feels guilty enough for her actions."

Connor only nodded. "And how 'bout you? I ken ye learned a few things from being here that ye never expected. How are ye holding up?"

"I admit I didn't expect to learn that our daughter is destined to be a queen." Dropping the brush into her bag, she searched Connor's eyes for support. "It's just so hard to wrap my mind around the idea of raising royalty—royalty who will someday be Queen of Euphoria in this magical world of the fey!"

Connor gave her a reassuring grin as he placed a loving hand on her cheek. "But we were chosen for this task, my love. With a mother as smart, stubborn, and loving as Kaitlyn has, I am sure she will make an amazing leader."

"And don't forget, her father is the bravest of all warriors, and he will teach her how to be a strong fighter, true to her word. She will know how to protect those in her charge."

"Well, then it sounds as if we've nothin' to worry 'bout," Connor said with a crooked grin.

Though Isaboe knew he was only placating her, it felt good to hear such confidence from her husband. It allowed her to focus on the present and how she only wanted to hold Kaitlyn in her arms and let her child be a child for as long as she could.

"We're gonna do our best to have that normal, simple life, *Breagha,* for as long as we can. I promise." It seemed Connor had been reading her mind as she let her eyes dance with his. This was just one of the reasons why she loved him so much.

Hearing his stomach rumble, Isaboe tapped him on his middle. "Let's go have some breakfast before we leave. Maybe we'll run into Rosalyn in the dining hall. She left here so early this morning she must have eaten by now." Isaboe started for the door when Connor stopped her.

"Wait." He pulled her back into his embrace. "These last few days have been a whirlwind, and we haven't had much time alone."

"Really, Connor? Now's not the time," Isaboe scowled, trying to pull from his arms, but he held her fast.

"That's not where I was goin', but if yer interested, we do have a few minutes." Planting small kisses on her neck, Isaboe feigned annoyance, but he soon had her giggling.

"Alright, that's enough." Isaboe drew back, but only to get a better angle to kiss him. "What *did* you mean, then?"

"I only wanted to say that I'm very proud of ye. Proud and amazed at what ye've done, and not only here in this crazy place, but back in our own world as well." Connor held her gaze, and Isaboe saw the love in his eyes. "Ye are the most incredible, amazing, and beautiful woman I've ever met, and I'm honored to be the man who gets to spend the rest of his life with ye."

Isaboe was almost speechless as she stared into his emotion-filled blue eyes, but her heart knew exactly what to say. "I love you, too."

TRUTH, VICTORY, AND SORROW

Rosalyn and Demetrick strolled arm-in-arm through the atrium, quietly reviewing the previous night's events. In this place, filled with plant life, birdsong and sunlight, the battle seemed now so very distant. "Where do you think Lorien fled to?" Rosalyn asked as they passed beneath a canopy of green foliage.

"It's hard to say. Except for Lilabeth, she doesn't have many allies, and as you saw, the dark muse was badly injured during our encounter," Demetrick answered casually. "We have reason to believe they may have taken refuge in Nacmorid, which borders the south side of the Black Horn Forest. A mysterious fey by the name of Tyrone de Chaveroun rules that land. He and Lorien have history, or so I've been told." The wizard paused and gave Rosalyn a concerned look. "And you, my dear? How do you fare this morning?"

Cringing as she turned to look at him, Rosalyn couldn't hide the stab of pain she felt. "I hurt," she replied bluntly. This was rather an understatement; searing pain shot through her neck whenever she turned her head too quickly, and the gash on her arm had required stitches. "But considering that my aunt tried to kill me yesterday, I feel rather fortunate to be alive this morning."

The wizard chuckled. "Yes. Few mortals are able to survive a fey's battle, my dear. This defeat has surely undermined Lorien's confidence."

"Thanks to you." Rosalyn paused, and her thoughts took her in another direction. "I am a bit shocked knowing that my granddaughter will be a queen in this land someday, at least, that is according to some very intelligent talking trees." A realization suddenly struck her, and she turned gingerly to face him, taking a moment to study the wizard. "Demetrick, that story you told us the other day about Boggle Raghii and the Trees of Knowledge was missing a few details, wasn't it?"

"Whatever could you mean?"

"I've been wondering where you acquired the knowledge to create a portal between realms. Not that I ever doubted your brilliance or your skills, but how is it that a *mortal* wizard had that information?" she asked, staring into his wise eyes. "Whatever became of Boggle Raghii?"

A slow smile made its way across the wizard's wise and elderly face. "Ah, you noticed my omission. It appears the student has become as wise as the teacher." Demetrick seemed genuinely pleased before he continued. "Boggle Raghii felt he had learned all this realm could teach him, and so, using the vision he received from the Trees of Knowledge, he built a portal to the mortal world."

"Where he became known as the wizard Demetrick," Rosalyn finished his confession. "You are fey." When her companion only nodded, Rosalyn saw pride on the wizard's face at her announcement. "Were you really dying? Is that what brought you back here?"

"In the mortal world, my body was aging more rapidly. Had I stayed, yes. I most likely would have been dead by now. Even fey don't live forever," he smirked.

As the reality of his words settled over her, Rosalyn suddenly felt a bit annoyed. "You've kept a lot of secrets from me, Demetrick." She wrestled with a surprising sense of distrust, and it pressed at her tongue. "Why did you hide from me that you were fey? More importantly, why not tell me my father was a Fey King?"

The mirth in Demetrick's eyes dried instantly. "Do you remember the day we met?"

"Remember?" Rosalyn scoffed. "How could I forget? They were preparing to set me on fire! That experience is permanently *burned* into my memory."

Demetrick chuckled. "Yes, precisely." Then he sobered. "The church had put you through such horrors as a young girl. You had so much healing and growing yet to do. At the time, I felt that telling you everything about your fey family would only burden you. But that is why I gave you those manuals, so that when you felt you were ready to find out who you really are, you would be armed with the information you needed to do so." He stopped and turned to look at her. "I am ever so impressed by the choices you have made."

"All this time, you knew the story of my mother's exile," Rosalyn mused. "When you learned of Lorien's plan to take possession of Isaboe, you took it upon yourself to intercede. But why Connor? Why would Lorien have allowed a mortal to be Kaitlyn's father? I have been wondering why she didn't use another fey."

"And give access to the throne to another line of fey? Not likely. Lorien had to keep the lineage pure, as the blood of fey royalty carries much stronger magical powers than that of a common faerie. I simply provided the mortal man Lorien needed, and since Isaboe and Connor are of the same species, a conception was far more likely." Demetrick cast Rosalyn a curious glance. "It is extremely rare for beings of two different worlds to conceive an offspring. You are an anomaly, my dear." When the wizard paused, Rosalyn studied the wonder on his face. "You really shouldn't exist."

Rosalyn was surprised she had never considered that basic fact before. Her mother, Alaina, had been a mortal woman and her father a fey. They were from two different worlds; of this she was aware. But when Demetrick presented the facts to her in this way, it made sense. She should never have been born. The thought baffled her, leaving her with an odd sensation in her chest. "How old are you?" she asked to distract herself.

As the lines around his mouth deepened and his eyes twinkled, the wizard offered her only a mischievous little smile. "Old enough to see life change time and time again, only to have it come back around and realize that nothing has really changed at all. Unfortunately, for both humans and fey, if we fail to learn from our past mistakes, we are destined to repeat them."

While filling their stomachs with a hearty breakfast, Isaboe couldn't help but notice the way her fellow diners eyed her and Connor. As some fey offered respectful nods and others gave hopeful smiles, she could feel the weight of gratitude in their gestures. It was a far cry from the cold reception they had received when they first arrived.

"I wonder where Rosalyn's gone off to," Isaboe mused aloud, sipping a warm beverage her server had called Dremaloo. It tasted vaguely similar to coffee, but there was a subtle hint of mint that lingered on her tongue, and she had grown rather fond of it.

"She probably just wants to spend some time with Demetrick and Norvik before we leave," Connor replied.

"Oh, well, that makes sense." Isaboe had never seen her mother so engaged as she was with the wizard and the dragon-lord. As if discussing the wizard made him materialize, Demetrick appeared at the wide door of the dining hall and headed toward their table. "Good morning," he said upon taking a seat.

"Good morning," Isaboe and Connor greeted in unison.

"I trust you slept well," the wizard said, continuing his polite conversation, "and it appears you've had your breakfast. Are you two ready to head home today?"

"Oh, yes! We are very ready," Isaboe answered for them both. "Have you seen Rosalyn this morning?"

"Yes. We have taken the liberty of moving your bags to the rooftop where Rosalyn will summon the portal for your trip home. I hope you don't mind."

"That's wonderful! Thank you. And Rosalyn is waiting for us there?"

"Correct. So, whenever you're ready," the wizard gestured as he stood to leave. Following his lead, Connor and Isaboe made their way out of the hall. As they went, Isaboe noticed more gestures of respect and gratitude from the fey. One elderly woman even bowed and politely wished them safe travels.

When they arrived on the castle's rooftop landing, Isaboe was surprised to see that a small congregation had gathered with Rosalyn, and their bags sat in the center of the landing platform. Slowly making their way toward the gathering, Isaboe immediately noticed Klute, Nyia, and King Enoch standing among them. Queen Brighid and Amaroth were also there, along with other faces she remembered seeing at the Council of Elders. The lumbering giant, Lord Mordackian, stood out toward the back, and she could see the smile lines on his bark, reminding her of the faces on the Trees of Knowledge. She wondered what relation this tree-man might have with the giants she interacted with at the Grove of Raghii. Standing at his side was the sassy red-haired Princess Reania, and next to her stood the scholarly man with goat horns. The Lady of the Lake—the one who shimmered in the light when she moved—was also there. Seeing the approving smiles on their faces. Isaboe wondered if they were there just to make sure the mortals actually left.

"I'm surprised to see all these people here," Isaboe said quietly when she reached her mother's side and glanced around at the assembled fey.

"They're all here to see you off. I believe someone very special has something to say to you," was Rosalyn's cryptic answer.

Queen Brighid stepped forward from the group of royal oddities and stopped in front of Isaboe, drawing herself up with great dignity before she spoke. "The League of Jarcadian warriors was commissioned when your kind was last in our realm, when human soldiers waged a war to steal the land of Silverleaf from the elves. After that experience, a law was instituted which banned all mortals from this realm forever. That was centuries ago, and the council has come to realize that many things have changed since that time. It was one of our own who first broke this law." When the queen paused, Isaboe watched her glance at a well-dressed fey man she did not recognize. The stranger's face gave nothing away.

"A revolution is long overdue," the queen continued. "You and your brave warrior have shown us how our antiquated ways have been used to manipulate us. I believe we have the opportunity to begin an age of enlightenment for both of our worlds. I speak for all of us here when I say: thank you. We are very pleased that you brought about this reunion, Isaboe Grant of the mortal world, and I am honored to have played a part in this historic moment." A subtle smile lifted Brighid's face, and she chuckled lightly. "I was wrong about you, child. You're not such a hopeless mortal after all."

Brighid's bright smile was the only warning Isaboe had before the queen pulled her into an embrace. Startled by the unexpected show of affection, Isaboe wasn't sure how to properly respond, so she simply murmured, "Uh…thank you?"

Brighid finally drew back, ending the awkward moment. Made speechless by the queen's words and intimacy, Isaboe glanced at Connor and saw the same humbled awe reflected on his face that she felt on her own. "Well, it's time to go, and we best not overstay our welcome." Glancing down at the bags around their feet, Isaboe noticed that Rosalyn's bag and cloak were missing. "Rosalyn, you seem to have forgotten your own things," she chuckled. "Shall I send Connor for them?"

Rosalyn didn't respond right away, but her smile turned a bit sad. "I didn't forget them, Isaboe."

"What?" Instantly, Isaboe understood, but at the same time she didn't. "No. No, Rosalyn. You're coming back with us!"

Rosalyn grasped her daughter's hand. "No, Isaboe. I'm not."

"But why?" Isaboe felt her anxiety spike. "You can't stay here. This is not your home. This isn't where your family is!"

"Isaboe, please, just listen to me." Rosalyn's voice was calm and motherly, but Isaboe would hear none of it.

"No! We just found each other!" she blurted, casting Rosalyn's hand away. "You can't stay here!" Her voice rose with intensity. "All my life I've wanted a relationship with a mother who loves me. Now that I finally have it, you're leaving me?" Isaboe knew she sounded like a spoiled child, but at that moment, the frightened little girl inside her was crying, desperate not to be abandoned. "Why? Why are you doing this, Mother?" Isaboe could feel the tears burning to break free. She knew that if Rosalyn stayed in the realm of the Underlings, there was a very good chance she would never see her again in this lifetime.

"My darling," Rosalyn's voice was soft, and her eyes pleaded for her daughter's understanding. "The mortal world has never felt like home to me. I have never belonged there. You know that I am considered an oddity in that world. I've been ridiculed, banished, and almost killed because of my differences. I'm not a witch or the child of a demon." Rosalyn's gaze drifted to the same well-dressed fey that Brighid had acknowledged. It was Isaboe's first opportunity to look at him properly, and she suddenly knew who the stranger was. "I'm not ready to forgive him yet," Rosalyn confessed quietly to Isaboe alone, "but Nicholi is not a demon. He is a fey, and I am his half-fey daughter. Here, in this land, for the first time in my life, I feel like I belong. There's so much for me to learn from these people—my people."

"But, I'm your people, Rosalyn. So are Connor and Kaitlyn! Do you really want Kaitlyn to grow up without her only grandmother?"

"Isaboe, for the first time in my life I have an identity. You found your mother and discovered who your father was. Please, understand that I need the same. My past and my future are both here."

The sound of a steady tap preceded the entrance of Lord Ruz-Zambia, coming from the castle to join the gathering on the rooftop platform, and he carried the staff Rosalyn had been holding yesterday. Isaboe turned her fearful eyes back to her mother and saw the growing hint of a smile when she made eye contact with the dragon-lord.

"It's him, isn't it? He's the reason you're staying!" Isaboe didn't try to hide how upset this turn of events had made her. "Are you really prepared to leave your world and your family behind—*for him?*"

Isaboe was startled when Rosalyn grabbed her by the arm and escorted her a few steps away from the others before responding. "Did you not leave your world, and your daughter, to follow *your* heart?" Rosalyn hissed, her eyes flashing intensely.

"What?" Isaboe shot a quick glance at Connor, who was doing his best to stay out of their very public argument. "That was different," she said assertively, before locking stares with her mother. "Are you telling me that... that you're in love *with him?*"

"No...maybe. I don't know. But if I leave here, I will never get to find out."

"But..."

"Isaboe," Rosalyn cut her off again. "I've never felt so alive as I do here. There is so much I can learn about who I am that I can't discover back in the mortal world. Please understand."

"But...but what about Leo and Turock? They need you too!" Isaboe spewed out, desperate to change her mother's mind.

"Not that I won't miss them, but they don't need me. They will be fine."

Sensing that he was needed, Connor stepped next to his wife and placed a supportive hand on her shoulder, although it did not ease the pain of separation. "But I may never see you again," she protested one last time. The tears she had been holding back finally broke free when she realized that she had to let her mother go.

"I'm sure that's not true," Rosalyn said compassionately. "Before Kaitlyn comes to take her place as the next ruler of Euphoria, I'll be here preparing the way." Taking a step closer, she once again took Isaboe's hand. "My love, this last year that I have spent with you and your family has been one of the greatest gifts of my life." Isaboe could see the tears welling in her mother's eyes as well. "I never expected to have the opportunity to know you in this life, much less be blessed with having such a strong brave young woman as my daughter. I'm honored to have had this time with you, my darling, even if it was for only a short while." When she hesitated, Isaboe noticed a shift in Rosalyn's voice, as well as her demeanor as she released her daughter's hand. "But my place is here, to prepare for my granddaughter's arrival, and for her role as the next ruler of Euphoria. From here, I can also keep better track of Lorien's plans."

The decision had already been made, and there would be no swaying her mother. Swallowing her tears, Isaboe wiped her face and squared her shoulders. Queen Brighid, who had just commended her, was now watching her crying like a child. This must not be the last impression these fey have of her.

"Your mother is right, my dear," Demetrick said, joining their little group. "The kingdom requires restoration before Kaitlyn takes up her role."

"Euphoria was in ruins," Rosalyn agreed, "even before the dragons burned down Lorien's castle." Isaboe watched her mother once again glance almost nervously at her own father. "But I'm hoping that when we rebuild it, I will not do so alone."

A complicated series of emotions flashed across Nicholi's face, both humility and pride, and something else that Isaboe didn't recognize. The Fey King wavered a moment before he stepped forward to join them. "I would be honored to have you at my side, daughter."

Rosalyn paused, studying the fey for a moment before she spoke again. "Isaboe, this is Nicholi; your grandfather."

Staring at him, Isaboe's mind was suddenly flooded with questions and curiosities, but now was not the time. Nicholi's face then grew serious. "My sister may have run off to lick her wounds, but as long as she lives, she will never give up her desire for control. She will be back, and we need to be ready when she does."

Trying to sound braver than she felt, Isaboe gave Rosalyn her full attention. "So, it seems we each have our own tasks to carry out." Pausing, she swallowed hard. "And yours is here."

"And yours is back in the mortal world, raising Kaitlyn to be the best ruler she can be," Rosalyn replied.

"And that, my dear, may not be an easy road," Demetrick warned her. "Kaitlyn's conception was dusted with Lorien's essence. The young heir may challenge you in ways you do not expect."

"But if you take the advice you received from the Grove of Raghii," Rosalyn interjected, flashing a nod toward Demetrick, "I'm sure the two of you will raise our future queen to be brave, true to her word, and, most of all, stubborn in her convictions." Rosalyn smiled softly as her gaze fell upon her daughter. "You are the Chosen One, my dear, and I could not be more proud of the woman you have become."

Left speechless, Isaboe could only throw her arms around Rosalyn and hug her tightly. "I love you, Mother," she whispered.

As Rosalyn returned the hug, Isaboe heard the hint of tears in her mother's voice when she said, "I love you, too, my beautiful daughter." After a moment, she drew back and addressed Connor. "The only thing that makes this any easier is knowing that they have you. Please, watch over and keep them safe."

"Ye ken I will," Connor said before flashing a confident smile at Demetrick. "That's my job."

"And it's good to know that I chose wisely for this mission." The wizard returned Connor's smile. "I must say, Braden," he placed a hand on Connor's shoulder, "you have exceeded my expectations in every way. I'm quite pleased with how my experiment turned out."

Braden MacPherson was put in the grave when the Jacobite Rebel was thought to have died in a British war prison, but he had been given his freedom and a new identity through the efforts of the great wizard Demetrick. "I was an experiment?"

"Well, yes, in a way. I'd never sent another soul through a portal. I'd only crossed over myself, and I really had no idea how you'd take to the challenge I had assigned you. You might say I was testing the cooperation of the universe, and the outcome turned out most favorable."

The smile that lit up both Rosalyn and Connor's face had to match what Isaboe felt on her own. What a strange set of circumstances that had led them all together, and she could only be baffled and grateful. "Thank you, Sir Demetrick," she said, "for choosing such a man for me. If it weren't for Connor, I wouldn't be alive today." She cast an approving smile to her husband. "And there's no man alive who could love me more."

Returning her smile, Connor gave Isaboe's hand a little squeeze. "That part's easy. It's keepin' ye alive that's been challenging."

"Well, hopefully that's all in the past now. We could both use a little normalcy in our lives, at least for a while."

"Rosalyn, since ye're staying, why dinnae ye keep Sonas around as yer ride? He's a good smart horse. It'd be nice to ken that he won't be turned back to the wild and end up a troll's dinner."

Rosalyn chuckled. "Yes, Connor, I'll be happy to watch over Sonas. It will be nice to have my own transportation."

"Oh, and one more thing." Connor turned serious as he nodded toward Lord Ruz-Zambia, who stood quietly, observing from a distance. "Regarding this dragon-fella; make sure ye go into this with yer eyes wide open. I wouldna want ye to get *burned* in this relationship." The seriousness left his face, and Connor grinned, big and cheesy. Isaboe only rolled her eyes, and Rosalyn had no response to his attempt at humor. "But on the other hand," he added with a smirk, "I'm sure it could get *fiery* in the bedroom!" This time, Connor laughed out loud.

"Will you please take him home?" Rosalyn said to her daughter.

With the end now in sight, they broke to say their final goodbyes. Connor led Isaboe over to where Klute and Nyia had been quietly observing the mortals and extended his hand. "Thank ye, Klute and Nyia, for everything ye did for us."

At first, the stoic lion-man only stared back, and Isaboe wondered if he would take Connor's hand. The Jarcadian warrior had made it clear more than once that he didn't care to be touched. Finally breaking the uncomfortable moment, Klute grasped Connor's hand and shook it heartily. "Well, I could not let you run loose across the realm. You would have created more havoc than the trolls," he said before dropping his grip. "Someone had to stop you foolish mortals from getting yourselves killed."

Connor nodded with a grin. "Aye, and for that, we are very grateful." Turning toward Nyia, he repeated the gesture, but then dropped his hand when she only scowled at him. "Nyia, riding on the back o' yer bird with yer wicked tail slappin' me in the face is an experience I'll never forget. And taking down Kaegron with ye was a real honor." Connor put his hand across his chest in the Jarcadian warriors' pose of respect. "Ye're one hell of a warrior, and I'm truly grateful to ye and Loca for saving me from that velaripper."

Though Nyia's expression didn't change, she gave Connor a slight nod. "Goodbye, mortal," she finally said. "I hope to never see you again."

Nodding, Connor snickered, "Likewise." He then turned to address King Enoch, offering a formal gesture of respect. "And thank you, too, Sire. We couldna done this without yer support. I speak for my entire family when I say we are in yer debt and grateful for yer actions."

"Yes," Rosalyn added, "Your intervention will benefit the entire realm, Your Highness."

King Enoch remained stoic at the mortal's gesture of gratitude. "Though I was initially against this campaign, somehow you were able to recruit the Sardonian dragons. I'm still baffled by how you managed that, but fortunately you did, and this time the attack on Euphoria was victorious. You have successfully retrieved what you came for, and Nicholi is back on the throne of Euphoria. Hopefully, we will now have peace in the realm again and between our two worlds. However, since we do not know what became of Lorien, I suspect that won't be the last we hear from her."

When Isaboe heard the king's words, it rekindled the anxiety she hoped had been put to rest. Lorien may have been dethroned, but she had not been taken out. As long as the Fey Queen was still alive, it was very likely that they hadn't seen the last of her.

Dismissing himself from the king's attention, Connor readdressed

Klute. "And since Rosalyn is staying, I'd also be grateful if ye could continue to watch over her."

"You can rest assured no harm will befall her. I promise you that." Klute then reached down and touched the wrist strap holding Connor's communication stone. "And leave these here. I do not want to have to come into your world to retrieve them."

After removing their wrist straps and returning them to the lion-man, Isaboe gave Rosalyn one more longing look, knowing that it would be a while before they saw each other again. "Please, Mother, be careful. As you know, this world can be quite dangerous and unpredictable."

"I'll be fine. You just take care of yourself and Kaitlyn. And I know Connor will watch over you both." When Rosalyn turned her attention to Connor, Isaboe could see her mother was struggling with her own emotions. Swallowing back her tears, Rosalyn busied herself with preparing the portal. When she cast her arm out to the side, the portal shot out from the ring on her hand and instantly sprang open. "Demetrick has repositioned the portal so you'll be returning back to the ridgetop." In the vortex, Isaboe could see the familiar whirling images and broken forms which would accompany them on their way home.

This was it. As much as she wanted to return to her own world and hold her baby, leaving her mother was breaking her heart. Throwing her arms around Rosalyn one more time, Isaboe hugged her tightly. "Thank you for everything," she whispered in Rosalyn's ear. "Especially for loving me."

"Oh, my darling, loving you came easy," Rosalyn replied, still held in her daughter's embrace.

Drawing back, Isaboe wiped her face and gave Rosalyn a forced smile before looking over to Connor. "Are you ready?" she asked, still sniffling.

"No time like the present." Connor placed an arm around Isaboe's shoulder. "Let's go home, my love."

Giving her mother one more tear-filled glance and a sad smile, Isaboe joined Connor and stepped through the whirling confusion that would take them home—back to the mortal world and back to the enormous task of raising the next ruler of Euphoria.

home

When they stepped out of the portal and onto the soil of their own world, dusk had painted the sky in hues of rose and orange, casting a warm glow over Rosalyn's ridgetop abode. To Isaboe, this familiar sight was more beautiful than any of the fey realm's magnificent castles. Behind them, a sucking, popping sound preceded the portal's disappearance. Rosalyn had closed the passage from the other side. There was no way to cross back over now. For a few moments, Isaboe and Connor stood on the ridgeline and waited for the dizziness of transit to pass. When they were stable enough to walk confidently, the travelers made their way toward the cave.

When Isaboe heard voices rising up to join the whistling wind, she and Connor soon saw the entire family lingering outside in the garden. Watching from a distance, Isaboe could see that Margaret was holding Kaitlyn as she pointed out which vegetables were ripe for picking, while Will strolled obediently behind her with a basket nearly full of harvest. Jared and Anna stood off to one side of the garden, and their focus was on their son who was bundled in Anna's arms. For the first time since they had been reunited, Isaboe saw joy on Anna's face. It made her heart swell to know that she had been able to keep her promise to her daughter.

Coming back into Anna's life had almost destroyed the hope of having a relationship with her, but Isaboe had pulled off a miracle and made it right. Witnessing this simple moment of pleasure made all the pain of Euphoria worth the struggle. Though Lorien had attempted to destroy her family, Isaboe hadn't allowed it. Now, perhaps, she and Anna would finally have that joyous reunion Isaboe had hoped for.

Connor wrapped an arm around his wife as they stood quietly and observed the peaceful scene. "That's our family, *Breagha*," he whispered.

"We haven't lost any time," she said with a smile that she felt all the way to her toes. Although Rosalyn had promised that time would keep pace between the two worlds during their adventure, until Isaboe actually saw her family with her own eyes, she'd had her doubts. When she had been unwillingly transported to the world of the Underlings as a young mother, twenty years had passed her by before she returned, and her family had been stolen from her. But looking upon the faces of those who she loved the most, she knew that fear could now be put to rest.

Connor scoffed when Hamish stepped out from behind the vine-covered wall and joined the family in the garden. "I see the wise-ass scholar's still hangin' round."

"We have a great deal to thank Hamish for, my love," Isaboe reprimanded him with a gentle tone. "We couldn't have pulled off our miracle without his help on the portal."

"Yeah, well, the pompous little twit best keep his mouth shut," Connor grumbled. Then he glanced down at Isaboe. "And he needs to remember that ye're a married woman, or that reminder may just come from the end of my boot."

Isaboe chuckled at Connor's fierce scowl. "After battling trolls, don't you think harassing Hamish is a bit beneath you?"

"D'ye see any trolls around here?" he asked sarcastically. "Cause I don't. Gotta pick my fights where I can find 'em."

Isaboe stared at him for a moment as she shook her head. Connor would never turn down a confrontation. He was a warrior, and Isaboe knew that those instincts would not disappear just because the battle had ended. His dark angry side would always be a bit of a mystery to her, but she loved this hot-headed rebel, despite all of his flaws. Connor was her hero, and she wouldn't want him any other way.

Kaitlyn's squeal of delight split the peaceful evening, and Isaboe's heart gave a jump as she realized that the child had spotted them. As the other adults followed Kaitlyn's excitement and turned in their direction, a huge smile lit up Margaret's face. "Isaboe and Connor!" she squealed, almost matching Kaitlyn's pitch as she began to run in their direction. "You're back!"

Dropping her bag, Isaboe ran to meet them. Fueled by the joy of being back with her family, the smile she felt spreading across her face radiated from her heart. "Margaret! Kaitlyn!" Isaboe hoisted her dress into her arms so she could race the last few yards to hold her daughter. She almost knocked them over as she embraced them both in hugs of joy. Little Kaitlyn wrapped her arms around her momma's neck, pulling out of Margaret's hold to cling to her mother.

"Is it really you this time?" Margaret stood back, giving Isaboe a curious stare.

The baby removed any doubt as she returned her mother's loving embrace with happy squeals and baby kisses. Thrilled and happy to be home, Isaboe began to chuckle. "Of course it's me, Margaret!"

Weighed down by his weapons and both Isaboe's bag and his own, Connor finally reached them. Margaret almost jumped into his arms giving him a bear hug. "I can't believe you did it! You saved the baby, *and* you made it back!"

"Ye had yer doubts?" Connor said with a smirk.

"I sure as hell did!" said a laughing Will as he joined the reunion. He extended a hand to his fellow warrior in greeting. "Ye son of a bitch, ye pulled it off. And ye came back in one piece. Amazing!"

Clasping his friend's hand, Connor returned the smile. "Aye, but it was no easy task. Trolls dinnae fight like redcoats."

"Trolls?" Hamish asked incredulously. "You fought trolls? What else did you see?" he asked, his wide-eyed gaze jumping between Connor and Isaboe. "What did you do there? Did you see faeries and elves? You must tell me everything!"

"We'll tell you all about it later," Isaboe interrupted, waving away his questions when she saw Jared heading in their direction with Anna slowly trudging behind, looking incredibly anxious.

"How's Anna doing?" Isaboe asked Margaret quietly as she handed Kaitlyn to her husband. The baby went easily, smiling affectionately as she patted her father's face. When he kissed her pudgy little fingers, she giggled with delight.

"Well, if you can't tell by the look on her face," Margaret answered, "she's been beating herself up pretty bad. She's been worried about seeing you again."

Jared greeted Connor and Isaboe with the same enthusiasm as his companions, but he too was obviously nervous about the reunion as he glanced back at Anna. Slowly making her way with Gabriel in her arms, Anna looked as if she were headed for the gallows. All at once, everyone's attention was on her, and when Anna stopped several feet away, Isaboe could feel her anguish. Stepping away from the others, she saw that tears were already running down her daughter's face.

"Isaboe, I'm so sorry," Anna gasped, fighting back sobs. "Can you ever forgive me?" As Anna began to cry in earnest, Jared silently slipped Gabriel out of her arms. The torment she saw on her daughter's face moved Isaboe, and she reached out to pull Anna into her embrace. Though initially she seemed stunned, Anna eagerly returned the hug as she sobbed into Isaboe's shoulder. For several long moments, they stood like that, wrapped tightly in each other's arms.

Finally drawing back, Isaboe wiped the tears from her daughter's cheeks and offered her a comforting smile. "No apologies are necessary, my dear. Before we left, I told you that when you held Gabriel again, we would start over. I meant that." Isaboe stood back and cleared her throat. "Hello, Anna. My name is Isaboe, and I'm your mother."

Wiping away the last of her tears, a smile pulled up the corners of Anna's lips. "Hello, Isaboe. I'm so happy to finally meet you," she replied, her face lighting up as she returned her mother's greeting.

Isaboe felt joy all the way to her toes as she squeezed Anna's hands. This was the reunion she had longed for with her oldest daughter—a reunion that was over twenty years in the making. Isaboe felt a warm happiness spreading across her skin as they linked arms and headed back to join the others. But Anna stopped and glanced around. "Where's Rosalyn?"

Instantly, Isaboe felt the pain of separation from her own mother, but she swallowed hard and tried not to let it show. "Rosalyn decided to stay in the realm of the Underlings."

"What?" Anna asked, astonished.

Why?" demanded Margaret with the same surprise.

"Because Rosalyn is half-fey, and she wants to learn more about that side of her." Isaboe thought about all that they had experienced, all the strange and interesting beings she had met, her family's remarkable history, and, perhaps most importantly, what she herself had accomplished. Isaboe was not sure she would ever look at the world the same way again. Her experiences in the realm of the Underlings had left her forever changed. "Let's go in," she suggested. "It looks as if you have a good start on gathering vegetables. What's for dinner?"

"Will has cleaned a pheasant," Margaret said, noticeably happy as she linked arms with Isaboe. Arm-in-arm, the three women strolled easily back toward Rosalyn's comfortable cave. Glancing over her shoulder, Isaboe saw the man she loved holding their daughter. The look on Connor's face was one of complete contentment as he fell in behind them with an easy cadence, chatting amicably with the other two men as Hamish tagged along.

Isaboe felt another pulse of joy flowing through her. There was nothing more wonderful than simply being in the company of the people she loved so much, and she couldn't stop smiling. For a brief moment, she wondered if she deserved this much happiness, but a flutter in her chest told her that she did. She had fought long and hard for it, had earned it, and she would gladly take it.

The End

acknowledgements

When I started this journey to share the tale of Isaboe and Connor, I did so as a storyteller and had to learn the craft of writing. In the words of Ernest Hemmingway: "It's none of their business that you have to learn how to write. Let them think you were born that way."

When I think about the process of writing this story, a story that has turned into a five-book series and taken over twenty years of my life, I am both amazed and grateful.

First of all, I'm amazed that I didn't quit. But thanks to all the profound characters who came to life and would not leave me alone until the story was finished, I was able to stay focused.

Needless to say this story would not be out in the world without my fabulous editors: Sara Kraft and John Thompson. These two professionals have taken me under their wings, shared their wisdom, and helped me fine-tune and polish my words to make this the fascinating story it was meant to be.

I'm also very grateful for my book designer, Erik Jacobson. Erik shared my vision of fantasy, romance and mystery—all the elements that surround the *Mark of the Faerie* series—leading to the creation of this beautiful piece of art.

A big thanks goes out for all the wonderful knowledge and support I have received from my fellow writers in the Confluence Writers group, as well as the Women Fiction Writers Association (WFWA) Facebook group. Thank you also to my ARC proofreaders. What you do for me is priceless.

I am sincerely grateful to Melissa and Riley Housden for the information they shared with me on how to break a horse as we sat at their kitchen table on a cold winter's day.

Much love and gratitude to my husband for his continued support, to my family for their belief in me, and to all the people who have crossed my path during this journey to offer bits of wisdom and sound advice.

Lastly, and most importantly, I am honored and humbled by the readers who love this story, who have shared their great reviews and are asking for the next books in my fantasy adventure. This story was not given to me to keep to myself. I am simply the vessel from which it poured.

ABOUT THE AUTHOR

As far back as I can remember, I've been enchanted by the magic of the fey and fascinated by anything Scottish. My love for literary fantasy and storytelling began at an early age, and I knew I was destined to share this incredible tale with the world someday. I just hadn't expected "someday" to take so long. But as life will do, it threw some obstacles in my path as an author.

Being a career-oriented woman, I've owned and operated two successful businesses, raised two wonderful sons, and have managed to stay happily married to my best friend for over forty years. But my desire to share this story—a story that has been twenty years in the making—has always remained my golden ring.